COUNTERPART

MIKE JOHNSON

First Published by HarperCollins 2001

this edition Published by 99% Press, 2023
an imprint of Lasavia Publishing Ltd.
Auckland, New Zealand
www.lasaviapublishing.com

ISBN: 978-1-99-118988-2

PREFACE TO THE 2023 EDITION

Counterpart was first published in 2001 by HarperCollins under their Voyager imprint. Released before the attacks of 9-11, Counterpart belongs culturally to the 'long nineties.' Like other stories of that era it grapples with the themes of suburban malaise and corporate maleficence to which the capitalist triumphalism of the nineties seemed to offer no alternative. Yet Counterpart was also the result of a long-standing love affair with speculative fiction, in particular the alternate world stories of Phillip K Dick, grandfather of the genre.

What fascinated me was the idea that in another world one might find a morally compromised other-self, a shadow-self, like oneself and yet unlike. The question, to the serious writer of speculative fiction, was how to convincingly cross from one world to the other. My solution was to use Victor Shauberger's notion of negative friction to create a field that would enable the 'jump.' John Bigelow, then professor of Philosophy at Monash University, commented that this was the best fictional explanation he had read of how such a thing might be possible.

Since writing the novel, the idea of many worlds has moved from fiction into mathematics with the mainstream acceptance of M-Theory, which by positing the existence of infinite worlds, allow mathematicians and physicists to make sense of their equations. I resisted the impulse to revise the novel in the light of M Theory, and the subsequent scientific controversy attending the idea of multiple worlds. I decided to leave the novel as it was, knowing that any changes would lead to the possibility that the novel might morph into something else. There was no need to spoil an original work that, I am happy to say, is still exciting, powerful and thought provoking.

Shortly after the novel was released, an author friend of mine, with connections in the film industry, informed me that a TV show of the same name, and with the same premise, was being put into development. At the time I felt rather outraged and wondered if I might have grounds for claiming copyright infringement, but I heard nothing more about the project for many years. It was not until 2017 that a TV series called Counterpart was released. The series was based on a near identical premise, and contained a similar social critique to the novel, though it did take the story in a different direction. Perhaps there is a utopian alternate world in which the novel is acknowledged as the inspiration for the series and the author, my doppelganger, receives a cheque.

Mike Johnson, March 2023, Waiheke Island

ACKNOWLEDGMENTS

The author gratefully acknowledges the support of Creative New Zealand during the writing of this novel, and to Zoe Frazer for her support. Also Chris Else of Total Fiction Services for bringing it up to scratch. And my family, Leila who encouraged me at every step and my children Rowan and Sophia for living with it on a daily basis. For the material relating to Victor Schauberger, I am indebted to Callum Coates Living Energies (Gateway Books) 1996. Special thanks goes to Alison Hunt for patiently retyping the novel from the HarperCollin's edition for this Lasavia Publishing edition.

I entered an alternative time line and thereby avoided the death that would have been certain in the normal course of events.

Jean Houstin, *A Mythic Life*

1

I arrived home after work one summer evening to find a woman I'd never seen before standing by our back door smiling at me.

I smiled back.

There was often a gaggle of women around the place, a fraternity of Playcentre mothers cooing at babies and gossiping. Evonne was never one for an empty house.

With a toss of her long, fair hair, the woman disappeared, and as I arrived at the door looking for Evonne I saw a little boy playing with Lego on the floor inside. I thought it was Timmy. My Timmy. The same bent back and chin resting on an upraised knee, the same degree of Lego absorption. But it was not Timmy. I'd never seen this boy before. It was Timmy's Lego, though; I'd know the Black Knight's castle anywhere, it cost me enough.

'Where's Evonne?' I shrugged my shoulders out of my jacket, shedding my work skin, smiling politely at the little boy who looked up at me without surprise and said nothing.

'What's that, honey?' the woman said from the kitchen. Her voice was soft but clear above the clattering of plates, her movements gentle and sure. There was a head of garlic clasped in her fingers like a white flower.

The jacket still dangling from my hand like a dead man, my

tie only half loosened, I took a good look around the room. At first I thought there'd been a working bee, a spring-cleaning. The Playcentre mothers again. That was all right by me. I liked the place to be spruce and looked after. To see those little signs of care. But this was not just a spring-cleaning; the whole room had been redone.

Here was something very different from the unholy mess Evonne liked to live in. The floor was vacuumed spotless, no magazines were strewn open anywhere, the table was cleared, wiped down and innocent of any dried crud from the last meal, the sofa was not heaped up with clothes, toys were not scattered from Easter to Christmas. There were other, more subtle, differences too, familiar things in unfamiliar places; the cover on the sofa was of a burgundy velvet rather than Evonne's homespun lemon calico, and the smells coming from the kitchen were not those of an Evonne meal. Too spicy, almost exotic, and not enough frying oil.

On the wall hung a strange and disturbing oil painting of a demented clown's face, while in one corner, reclining languidly on a Victorian antique cabinet, was a buddha lying on his side, head propped up on one arm and an insouciant smile on his face.

I might as well have walked into the wrong house.

Except for one minor detail. A small Chinese vase given to Evonne by her mother, containing a delicate spray of forget-me-nots, sitting on a shelf above the telephone, just where she put it.

Still holding my jacket, I approached our kitchen where the woman was putting together a meal with admirable efficiency. She had light, certain hands that knew just where to go amongst the reorganised packets and jars. Her fingers were long and slim, like those of a pianist.

'What did you say?' I said.

The woman came over, kissed me on the cheek and gave my arm a friendly squeeze. 'How was your day, honey? Make heaps of boodle for the multinationals?' She shrugged her hair back over her shoulders.

It looked as if she was making a big effort to be nice.

The jacket I was holding went very still. I had to say something. 'I guess so.' Whatever the game turned out to be, I'd started playing along with it.

The kitchen was a treat. The chaos of packets and jars had been straightened into orderly rows and everything was properly labelled. Evonne could never have functioned in this any more than she could have cooked a meal, as this woman had done, without turning the bench and every available surface into a garbage heap.

'Pour me a scotch, will you honey?' she said, her voice light and sweet, if a shade deliberately so. The garlic vanished into neat slices.

At this juncture it's important to understand what kind of person I am, to understand in particular that I am not given to panic or sudden, precipitous actions. As a senior executive in the Australasian section of an international oil company, I know how to handle myself, how to keep my head when those about me are losing theirs, and how to pour a decent scotch. But I am not a Philistine; I have a certain culture. I can recognise a David Hockney painting or a Frances Bacon; I know the difference between Mozart and Schubert, the Beatles and Brahms; I had a youthful acquaintance with the world of books. I was once thought of as an idealist. What I came to value was routine – and careful planning. I believe in the steady, dependable, thoughtful approach and I'm only a bastard when I have to be. Most of the time I'm just sensible.

Neither am I given to doubting my sanity. I'm too busy to go mad; my mortgage keeps me sane if not always rational.

So this had to be a joke. A cunning and elaborate jape thought up by some of Evonne's devious friends. Maybe half the Playcentre mothers in creation were behind the door of the bedroom, going red in the face from not giggling. A lone male returning home.

Fair game.

The scotch was sitting on a coffee table by the sofa, untouched, and it presented me with some problems. Did she take it on the rocks, neat, or with a squirt of soda the way I liked it?

Or would she take it any way I dished it up and pretend I got it right just to keep the game rolling?

Then I saw the antique soda squirter I'd picked up for ten dollars. It had a burnished silver handle and filigree silver cap. Taking the risk, I poured her a shot and gave it a quick squirt of soda for luck.

When I returned to the kitchen with the glass held at the ready, her back was to me, and she was scrubbing something in the sink. I put the glass down quietly, suddenly intensely shy, as if I really was in someone else's house. I didn't know what to say to that graceful back.

As I retreated, trying to cover my confusion, I saw the little boy at the door looking my way. As soon as I caught his eye he looked down.

Could the boy be in on the joke too?

I went to the only place I knew I couldn't be disturbed, sat on the bowl with my jacket across my knees, stared at the familiar walls for five minutes and didn't feel like laughing once.

Mostly familiar walls. All the scratches and marks were in the right places on the bland, anonymous light blue surfaces, but stuck right in the middle of all this, blazing with colour, was a naked man coming out of a shell of light. I looked closer and saw it was called *Glad Day*, and was painted by William Blake. The naked man held out his arms, palms bent back, in a gesture of surrender; yellow and red flame flared out from his shoulders like angel wings, and he was standing on what looked like a garbage heap of flowers. This arty touch was not Evonne's style at all. I much preferred the old Clint Eastwood poster we had; Clint's flinty look was easier to bear than this stark transcendence.

Sitting there gave me the idea to have a crap anyway. A crap is a very commonplace and reassuring thing.

Having used up plausible crapping time, and growing uncomfortable with the fleshy glory of *Glad Day*, I left the lavatory and headed for the sofa, deciding to have a Scotch myself. Tit for tat, an eye for an eye and a Scotch for a Scotch. I made it the way I liked it and sat back to take stock, watching the boy fitting together the last bricks into the Black Knight's castle.

The sofa wasn't exactly uncomfortable.

On the small table beside me, which was a still life of reading lamp, phone and Scotch, I discovered a book I'd never seen before. It gave me an eerie feeling, seeing a book which clearly belonged to someone else sitting right at my hand, where I would have left the occasional magazine or file. I picked up the book and looked at it, puzzlement growing. It was *The Philosophic Works of Descartes, Volume 1*. The picture on the cover showed a man with very long black hair, a wide white collar, and dark, arched eyebrows. I flicked open the book and read a couple of sentences.

Good Sense is of all things in the world the most equally distributed, for everybody thinks himself so abundantly provided with it... The power of forming a good judgement and of distinguishing the true from the false, which is properly called Good Sense or Reason, is by nature equal in all men.

I put the book down and closed it, thinking the argument very dubious, naïve in fact. Good Sense, as far as I could make out, was a pretty rare thing, and just because people thought they had it in abundance didn't mean they did. It could just mean they were a lot more stupid than they realised.

The boy had finished the Black Knight's castle, the last bricks had gone in. It was a sinister place with towers and dungeons, arched windows where bowmen stood and a portcullis with a real pulley mechanism.

Her was squirming around, somehow refusing to look at me.

'That looks great!' I said. 'Great and creepy too.'

The boy grabbed his castle and rushed off towards his room, Timmy's room.

Then, in the name of Good Sense or Reason, I took a few deep breaths (without which there can be no Sense, Good or otherwise, and therefore no Reason), closed my eyes and decided that when I opened them Evonne would be there, humming a piece of Beethoven, engrossed in her own wonderful clatter of cooking. I could feel her, just a step away, her presence. Almost close enough for me to hear her breathe. The deep, diving breaths she took between staves. Deciding that when I opened my eyes this stranger with the neat fingers would have vanished, even before I had a chance to properly notice how beautiful she was.

That didn't happen. When I opened my eyes she was still there, turning the making of a meal into an exotic dance, and I did have time to properly notice how beautiful she was.

I refreshed my Scotch with a pinch of soda, feeling more uncomfortable with every passing moment. Evonne had to be around somewhere. She would never have surrendered her territory to a woman like this. The joke was going too far.

I had to go into the bedroom to check it out, feeling like a fool. Somehow I thought Evonne would be there, squirming with embarrassment. Someone else had put her up to it. The chief hoaxer. The one who could make butterflies appear from top hats.

The bedroom was empty, the bed made, the top sheet folded back, which certainly wasn't Evonne's work.

The sight of those fresh, sprung sheets embarrassed me. Somebody else had tended the bed where Evonne and I slept, somebody else's hands had smoothed over the intimate hollows made by our bodies and tucked back the sheet. Maybe the woman in the kitchen. Those deft, efficient hands. I'd seen hotel beds made like that, and felt violated – couldn't Evonne have done this bit for herself, for Christ's sake?

I opened the wardrobe and finally got rid of my jacket. This was the inner sanctum for my shirts, suits and ties, and I noted with satisfaction that everything was in place, the suits hung quietly as suits should, dark and impervious as armour. On impulse I plunged my hand into the pocket of a jacket I rarely used. It contained a two-dollar coin and a receipt from Sea View Motels on the southeast coast.

A clever touch this, a little mystery, like a paper chase clue. Drawing me in.

I searched through the rest of the pockets and found a blue sheet of closely printed paper. Across the top of three columns a single headline read 'Practise Random Kindness and Acts of Senseless Beauty.' I read the first few lines. It told the story of somebody who gave something away, quite randomly, like a hundred dollars into some unknown letter box just for the kick of selfless giving.

Maybe this was a clue too, somebody trying to do me a favour. Dish me up a tidy new life, a tidy new wife – and all the rest of it. Maybe I'm mortgage-free here, I thought. On the pig's back. Random acts of kindness. Senseless beauty.

Refolding the sheet, I tucked it away in my pocket for future reference. Then I opened Evonne's side of the wardrobe and saw nothing I recognised. The dresses, the blouses, the shoes placed together toes pointing snugly inward as if someone were still standing in them – none of these were Evonne's. The colours were all wrong. The shapes, the neatness. This was a worryingly clever hoax.

How far had they gone?

Could this have been done in one day? Perhaps. Like a military operation. Clean out the house and decorate; manufacture a buddha here, a *Glad Day* there; a sofa that might have been a shade more comfortable than my own, a random pamphlet in my pocket.

Closing the wardrobe doors more quietly than I might otherwise, I crossed the room to Evonne's dresser and pulled open the top drawer, feeling like a thief in my own home. And a pervert too, given the underwear I found. The black bra with a little frivolous lace across the top. The knickers with the sexy straps. Evonne, who'd been my wife fifteen years and who was dark and short, a little bulky too since Timmy, comfortably round in the belly, wouldn't be seen dead in gear like this. Her face was roundish also, with a small mouth and mellow brown eyes. I suddenly remembered.

The hoax theory was developing a wobble. And the wobble was in my walk. I took a last look around the bedroom, desperately trying not to feel like an interloper. Surely this was somebody else's life I'd walked into. Some other Harry Blackman.

Back in the lounge, I chugged a Scotch, stuck my elbow on top of Descartes and positioned myself where I could study the woman in the kitchen. She was tall and long-waisted, with fair hair that came halfway down her back and slid this way and that as she turned. Her face was narrow with an elegantly shaped nose. Her eyes were a light, refined blue. She had a polish that Evonne envied in women.

Very classy. Very corporate. The kind of wife my colleague Cranner would like, if he could get his hands on one at all.

She turned to me and smiled. Her teeth were somewhat rough, giving me a glimpse of the fifteen-year-old tomboy she must have once been. This homely touch somehow added to her beauty. She held out her glass. 'Just a touch more.' There was an edge in the light, refined voice.

As I obliged, I noticed my hand trembling. This conversation was suddenly harder than any business negotiation, where the rules are known. This was walking the plank with every sentence.

She wandered over, took the glass from my hands and sat down by me on the sofa. 'You haven't put enough soda in,' she said, her voice like her smile; both airy and restrained. 'I can't drink rocket fuel.'

I offered her the soda, feeling as if I were on a first date.

'When's dinner?' I asked automatically, just as I asked Evonne every night, to which she would invariably reply, 'Ten minutes.'

'When it comes,' the woman said with a touch of exasperation. Apparently she was losing some inner struggle to be nice to me.

Sometimes it is sensible to be afraid. 'You can be afraid when you realise that somebody is not acting, that they believe everything they say, and what they're saying puts an end to all that is familiar, all that is trusted and known. Fear stopped up my tongue. Stopped me from asking about Evonne. About Timmy. The Black Knight's castle. About anything I'd ever done since God knows when.

'It smells delicious.' Which seemed like a safe, unthreatening thing to say.

'Thank you.' She studied me. 'You're very preoccupied tonight, Harry. Had a hard day at work? Is Lexon putting up their crude price? Shipping problems?'

This reference to the company's competitor, and an apparently accurate reference to work-related matters, threw me into red alert; I never talked to Evonne about work and she, quite sensibly, never asked.

'Maybe. There are just some days nothing seems to work out. Maybe it's the humidity. This hurricane weather. Everybody's tired and on edge.'

This vague statement, which would easily have pacified Evonne, evidently puzzled this stranger, who now regarded me critically over her drink. Lightly plucked eyebrows and a subtle trace of eyeliner. Her fingers were long and slim around the glass. 'Do I take that to mean you let Big Bill outstare you?'

'We were on the phone.' I clutched automatically for my laptop computer before remembering that I'd left it at the office, and felt a vague, uneasy sense of loss. I always had it by me. It was a security blanket of sorts; why should I have forgotten to bring it today?

She turned her face away. 'He could still outstare you.' There was a touch of pique in her voice, a twinge of disappointment, a hint of bitterness that bespoke something long-standing in our relationship, some evident failing of mine. Her lips were in a pressed line.

By now the joke hypothesis was a dead duck, or at least, on its last quack. She knew things about my work I hadn't told anybody, not my boss, not Evonne, not some old school friend or confidant; she could only know these things because I had told her. Or somebody equally in the know.

And what of the things it could be dangerous for her to know?

'What would you have done?'

'You've never asked me that before.' Her eyes, blue and very lucid, were fixed on me. 'You're usually keen to tell me how wrong I am.'

'I'm happy I can still surprise you.' The line tripped off my tongue as if it had been coined for me. With every line I was being pulled deeper in.

She wiggled the Scotch around in her glass, getting the soda to fizz.

'If I was your boss, I'd make a deal with Maritime behind Big Bill's back. Behind the whole cartel's back. A secret deal. The cartel gets screwed and the company makes a profit.'

'Pepsi would never do that," I said, a little shocked. I thought of my amiable boss. His commitment to the cartel would preclude any secret deals with shipping companies. Besides, we already had a shipping contract with Poseidon.

She looked at me sideways. The cartel! Somehow she knew of the illegal existence of the cartel.

'Nothing ventured, nothing gained.' She finished her Scotch and went back into the kitchen.

Her suggestion might work, but it would wreck the delicate structure of self-interest that ruled the cartel, and you don't step on Big Bill's toes as easily as you throw back a slug of Scotch. That was the hole in her argument. I was getting down to the icy, weak slush at the bottom of the glass, reflecting that perhaps I was wrong about how much inside knowledge she had. A few names and a few shrewd guesses might give her enough to carry off a conversation like this. Might. I wouldn't want to bet my neck on it.

I tried to line up her brisk, efficient movements in the kitchen with the bra in the drawer. The image was fractured. Would she carry on this farce right up to the bedroom scene, happily fuck me and go to sleep?

Would I?

On the coffee table beside the book, the phone began to ring.

'Hello Harry,' a strange voice said, 'it's Tess here. Is Evelyn there?'

'Evelyn,' I said, loud enough for the woman in the kitchen to hear. She wiped her hands on her tea towel and came to the phone.

'Next Sunday. Right. I hope so. I know, I know. I'm the world's worst.'

'What's happening Sunday?' I asked when she put down the phone.

'Playcentre trip. Of course parents should be there and I never am. Thing is,' she gestured to the child. 'Goldilocks has just about grown out of it. In fact he has grown out of it.'

'Yes,' I said, thinking of the castle. 'Kids grow up fast.'

Too restless to sit, even with the Scotch glass as prop and comfort, I escaped casually out onto the deck as if to catch the last of the mild if humid day. There were evenings like that that made the cramped drive across the bridge worth it, drought, flood or hurricane. The property was worth it too, except for all the work it made. Driveways, gardens, retaining walls, drainage, you name it, I'd thrown money at it.

From the wide, spacious deck there was a view down a valley to a narrow road, which wound down to a small shingle beach, marked at one end by a hug Pohutukawa tree. Evonne and I had diligently planted the whole lot out in flax, tree fern, red pine and several large palms along the bottom edge. I could single out the trees we'd struggled to put in and remembered how we laughed and joked together as we dug and got covered in earth.

Everything I saw belonged to the familiar world except for a small green creature with a brown spiral tattoo on its face, which made me think of camouflage, squatting in a tree fern.

It wasn't doing anything, just crouching there very still on top of the plant, in the hollow where the fronds sprouted. I stared at it for a long moment, becoming as still and quiet as it was. Warm, damp air, restless from Hurricane Hildegard to the north of the country, caressed my face, and the world went still and quiet. I was seeing something I wasn't supposed to see, that I wouldn't normally see. The creature was conscious of me, although not looking in my direction; we were held in a bond of awareness as if we were the only sentient creatures on the planet.

At that moment the child Goldilocks came running out onto the deck. My eyes were drawn away momentarily and when I looked back the tree fern was empty. A trick of the light. A trick of the Scotch.

Then it occurred to me that I'd been wasting my time with the woman who might be acting or pretending anything. This boy was four and a half years old, and at this age he couldn't act, couldn't lie, could he? I bent down to pick him up and he drew away from me. Both of us hesitated, me half bent over holding my arms out, him dead still, just looking at me. I had the feeling he suddenly didn't know me, that he recognised me as a stranger.

I squatted so that I was level with him.

'Where's Mummy?' I said playfully.

The boy pointed to the kitchen.

'And what's my name?' I said, as if starting a naming game.

'Daddy,' he said, after a brief hesitation.

'And what's your name?'

'Timmy.'

'And what's Mummy's name?'

'Mummy.'

So there were two Timmys and I was father to both of them. The woman in the kitchen was this Timmy's mother. And her name was not Evonne but Evelyn. That's the way the world was and had been, apparently, for a long time. I had no theory left, just a strange child by my side and an ache of loneliness. I smiled at the new Timmy, went back inside and into the bathroom, properly frightened this time. Where were Evonne and the real Timmy? Were they somewhere now, waiting for me, expecting me home?

I sat on the bath and stared at the packed of contraceptive pills lying on the glass shelf above the wash basin. Not Evonne's. Evonne refused to take them. Said they gave women thrombosis and varicose veins. She once told of how the women of Mexico had been used as guinea pigs to test the pill. I could hear her voice in my ear and knew again she was right next to me, a single breath away, if only I knew which way to turn. She was telling me something about the natural world and how we were all guinea pigs for some horrible, new kind of world.

The back of the door showed a lighter square where Evonne's *Universal Declaration of Human Rights* had once been. I never got past the first few sentences. Someone had removed it. The house had been doctored.

A giggle bubbled up and was burped out with the taste of whisky.

I made it through dinner and almost through putting Timmy to bed. It was the one-eyed teddy that got to me in the end. Teddies have a powerful aura of pathos, and this Timmy's teddy was the same as my Timmy's teddy except its missing eye was on the left, not the right.

It was a fanciful notion, the way it came to me, that this was a different universe, and while it might look like the old one in most respects, it was not quite the same. In this universe, Teddy winked at me from the other side of its face, just to remind me. Spirits squatted in tree ferns. Witch wives stirred pots.

'Good night, Daddy.' Perhaps I just imagined that his voice echoed the same sense of loss I was feeling.

I put the teddy down on the pillow beside the boy. It stared back at me with its wrong-sided eye.

I leaned close to the child to kiss him. He flinched. 'Where's Evonne? Do you know Evonne?'

'I don't know,' the child said. He took hold of the teddy and randomly twisted its remaining eye.

I was already in bed when Evelyn came in from kissing Timmy good night and nonchalantly got undressed. I tried not to stare at her slim nakedness as she slipped into bed, apparently preoccupied with something else. She sat up with the pillows propped behind her and busied herself writing on some letter-writing paper, using a hard-covered book to press on. From where I was lying I could see the smooth curve of her shoulder and the gentle split of her underarm.

In my early twenties, a fantasy of picking up a strange woman and taking her to a motel had dominated by masturbatory life. It was the anonymity of the motel and the woman that had somehow excited me. I associate this fantasy with an unpleasant short story by Milan Kundera in which a married couple play a titillating game. They go out for a drive, stop at a service station and while he's getting petrol she walks up the road alone. He drives on and, pretending to be complete strangers, she hitches a ride with him. He takes her to a motel and they keep the game going, pushing each other further and further. The situation is too fraught to be really erotic, but I was able to strip it of its art, that is to say its angst, into something far more pungent and useful. It took two years for that fantasy to wear out, during which time I concluded that literature was dangerous and not to be tampered with. These writers know how to play on people's weaknesses.

Now, however, with a woman about whom I knew nothing other than her name sitting up in bed beside me, the fantasy returned with all its old power, as if it had never worn out at all, just gone into hiding. I wanted to reach out and gently stroke that smooth shoulder, kiss that secret underarm. At this moment of reckoning, however, I suffered a serious loss of nerve. A childish fear that this situation might be the whole point of the exercise. A setup. Framed. In a moment the door would burst open and cameras would click wildly. Furious Playcentre mothers would beat me over the head with plastic toys for being unfaithful to Evonne. Maybe Evonne herself would come through the door, weeping, accusing, lawyers following behind. And a Lexon spy with a lapel camera.

Then the fantasy, and the joke, died, leaving me lying beside a beautiful stranger feeling as lost as any shipwrecked sailor. Everything around me was huge, as if I'd shrunk to the size of an ant. Even that sleek, tantalising shoulder rose up on my right like a massive cliff. A gulf lay between me and this world I had been stranded in. Where was Evonne? Familiar, loving, comfortable Evonne. I was like the teddy, staring out at the world through the wrong eye.

'Why are you looking at me like that?' Evelyn said, turning my way. A small, neat breast bobbed into view.

'Like what?' I said, not knowing what to say or where to look. Hopelessly shy.

She considered me for a moment without warmth, then turned back to her writing. 'You're an evasive bastard,' she said in a conversational tone, not looking up from her page.

I thought I'd let that one pass. I didn't have any answer to it. The longer this went on the fewer answers I'd have. But I am a cautious man, and this whole situation screamed for caution. Years of corporate negotiations had taught me never to make a move out of ignorance, to refrain from action until gaining a proper grip on the situation.

With the words 'evasive bastard' still ringing in my ears, it occurred to me to ask myself who the hell she thought she was speaking to. Who this evasive bastard was. Somebody called Harry Blackman, a person she believed to be me. And since it was not me, then who was it?

Another Harry Blackman. There were two of us. One honest and upright and one an evasive bastard, if the testimony of his wife could be believed. I remembered the left-eyed and right-eyed universes of the teddy, and my fancy as I bent over the strange Timmy's bed, that I was in another universe, a universe that looked to be mostly the same as mine. If that were the case, and there were two teddies, there could well be another me, my antiparticle, my counterpart. Husband of Evelyn, father of the left-eyed teddy. The other Harry Blackman.

You, by courtesy of symmetry.

This notion was not as funny as it had seemed before when I'd looked at that misplaced eye. By default, *you* were assuming a shadowy, hypothetical form. And now that I had imagined you, named you, I seemed to sense you nearly, in the house somewhere, in the next room maybe.

'You're very thoughtful,' she said.

'I've got a lot to think about,' I said.

'What are you thinking about?'

'Work.'

'You might as well be there, if you're going to lie there thinking about it.' Her voice was small, clipped short with resentment.

I was tempted to simply tell her, to announce that I was new here, just come down in the last shower of rain, just dropped in from another universe; but Evelyn struck me as a shrewd, practical person, too shrewd and too practical to believe the truth, or at least my wild double-universe theory. She would read some kind of cop-out into it, or simply conclude that I was insane. That was her best option, her most promising hypothesis. Poor Harry had gone off the deep end. Making up the craziest stories and expecting her to believe them. The boys in the white coats would be her tidiest, most hygienic solution. Concerned, friendly doctors questioning me about Evonne and the other Timmy. Quite a meal they would make of it. Of me.

The best thing to do would be to turn over and go to sleep, I decided. Everything looks different in the morning light, a voice within told me. I didn't believe it.

'Actually,' she went on in a somewhat softer tone, 'I'm rather surprised that you're home tonight.'

'Oh?' I didn't see any surprise in it.

'But you told me this morning.' She put her pen and pad away and moved the big book off her knees. 'A meeting you said. The Canada trip.' There was a faint, sceptical emphasis on the word Canada. 'Have you forgotten?'

'No, I flagged the meeting.' It was my first outright lie; the Canada trip was coming up for sure, but there had been no meeting set down for tonight that I knew of.

She looked at me curiously. 'Why?'

'Tonight was all about logistics.' I waved an airy hand. 'Delany and Cranmer can take care of that stuff.' I was close to the truth. A logistics meeting was scheduled for later in the week.

She looked as if she were about to say something, then bit it back. Instead she rearranged her pillows and lay beside me, facing my way but not touching me. Her neck was a long, sweeping curve, and her hair, tossed behind her, fanned out on the pillow in shining strands.

'It's good to have you home, Harry,' she said , as if making some far-reaching concession. 'It's just that … I haven't felt close to you lately. I was starting to make a joke of it, you know, my husband the stranger, and I get to see the dentist more often than I see my husband.' She gave a short laugh. 'You know the sort of jokes company wives make. And even when you were here it felt like you were really somewhere else.'

I didn't have a ready answer for that and, as the moments dragged by, she realised it. I was like an actor, thrust into a role I'd never played with no idea how to play it, forced to ad-lib desperately as I went along.

'Then I'm going to have to get to know you all over again, aren't I?' I said at last, and with great care. This was true in any event, if this strange situation were to continue.

She looked at me when I said that, apparently not quite sure how to take it. Her eyes were very blue and direct. She wanted to look right inside me to see what the truth was. I opened up to her. Let her see the truth if she could. The sudden, intimate intensity of it made me aware of my body and hers. Something arose between us and vanished. It was like catching a glimpse of a submerged creature that rises just close enough to the surface to tantalise you with its form before disappearing back into the fragmented depths, unidentified.

Evelyn registered it with the flicker of my eyes over her body. A faint flush appeared in the hollow of her throat and her eyes widened with surprise. Then with a slight, inconsequential movement of her fingers, she drew the sheet above her nipples. I looked around for something to look at, feeling like a virginal teenager in bed with an experienced woman.

'Good night, Harry,' she said, not unkindly, and leaned forward and kissed me on the cheek before turning over.

'Good night, Evelyn,' I said.

Of course there was no sleep for me. With my eyes wired open, I lay back and stared at the ceiling. The darkness put a soft, fuzzy edge to things, like a narcotic, and I could almost believe that nothing had changed, that the world was still the same and the woman lying beside me was not some sinuous, long-haired stranger but my own Evonne.

Somewhere, at some time during the day, I'd crossed over, switched lanes, passed through an unseen checkpoint to join this world. Evelyn's world.

And *you*, you evasive bastard, where were you now? The logic of symmetry, the very logic that invented you, now suggested that you were in my world. And what were you doing there? Lying in bed like me, staring at the ceiling trying to make sense of it all? Making love to Evonne? This was not going to unhinge me, I decided, not this Harry Blackman. It was all only speculation after all. A working hypothesis.

As I lay there, for hours it seemed, stewing in this cauldron of speculation, the bedroom grew deeper and darker, its edges softened with darkness, its depth fuzzy, opaque. The brief feeling I'd known earlier, that there was some other presence in the house, returned, and grew stronger.

Then I saw Evonne, my own Evonne, standing by the window looking back at the bed. It gave me a shiver to see her standing here, staring at me, unseeing. I sat up to make sure I wasn't asleep, certain that this wasn't a dream or a memory. Suddenly my laptop appeared, floating through the air. As I stared at it, it began to change; its keyboard unfolded, its screen rolled up and turned into a tube. My laptop turned into a rifle, pointing at me. Behind it, Evonne approached, heading for the bed.

'You'll make a mess of it,' I heard my father say. It sounded like him, although I'd never heard him use quite that tone of voice.

Evonne and the laptop vanished, the overwhelming sense of someone else in the room receded.

The air assumed the graininess that precedes dawn. Objects in the room groped for their original shape.

I thought of my father, who had the strange, strong name of Vernon. After Mum died, Vernon was made redundant, abandoning the Big Smoke for his native Nelson in the south. The move was something of a retreat. 'It's a human-sized community down there,' he said, but I thought he was just repeating something he'd heard on the radio. He wanted to return to Nelson because Nelson was the past, and the past had become a big hole in his life he wanted to fill with real images. Since his move I hadn't seen him much; a few letters, a couple of whirlwind visits, a brief Christmas.

I'd lost touch with him. He withdrew and I didn't stop him, didn't even try to stop him. I just took his bags out of the airport, that's all I did. Shook his hand and hugged him before he got on the plane. I didn't see the look of defeat on his face, or if I saw it I didn't take any notice. I didn't care or was too busy. Too busy to care. So why think of him now? The answer was there, written in the counterfeit dark.

I'll take a few days, I'll run home to Dad.

2

I got up next morning, made myself a quick cup of coffee and slipped out the door with the rest of the house barely stirring.

I often enjoy these early getaways, taking a moment to fuss with the car in the dawn stillness before taking on the day – another day, another dollar. This car, a Ghia Serenissima, was ridiculously rare and should have been closeted away protectively in a garage somewhere rather than driven on the Northern Motorway, but I couldn't resist the style of it. The Ghia was my one indulgence, my single permitted eccentricity and I looked after it with scrupulous care.

But this morning I received an unpleasant shock. What I saw was a gash along one side, across both doors. Chipped paint, dust, dirt and neglect. This was not my car. My Ghia. Staring at it, I was confronted with the first direct evidence of *your* existence, proof that I hadn't just made you up out of the contingency of the moment. This was *your* car. I wondered how you'd feel when you slipped in behind the wheel of my impeccable Ghia?

I counted myself lucky that everything seemed to be working.

At the top of the drive two neighbours stood together, pointing and talking animatedly.

The taller of the two, Sam Walsh, a very rich and very retired man, approached the car with his loose, dignified steps. He must be as old as my father. It was a sultry, hurricane season morning and the chopping wind tugged at Sam's grey hair.

'Look at this,' he said in a deep, rounded accent that spoke of English public schools. 'someone has planted flowers all along this verge here, on your side. Did you do it?' There was a touch of antagonism in his voice.

'No.'

But they were there. Three neat rows in freshly dug earth where the grass had been removed and flowers planted.

'Who put them in?' I asked. 'The council?'

'Not on your nelly. These weren't here yesterday. They've been put in overnight. I don't know of any council that works at night.'

'It's hard to catch them at it by day.' This was Paterson, a commuter with a bald head and thick, hairy hands, snickering at his own cheap shot.

'You're right there,' Sam Walsh said. 'But that doesn't put us much further ahead.'

The council will probably come along and pull them up, Paterson said. 'There'll be an ordinance against them.'

'They'd better not.' Sam Walsh looked horticulturally stern. 'Those flowers will brighten up this corner. You wait until the spring.'

Paterson said, 'We've got all winter to do that.'

'Won't bother the flowers. Unless of course it doesn't rain.' Sam Walsh looked sombre. 'I wonder if our mystery Johnny Appleseed will come back to water them?'

It'll rain when the hurricane arrives,' Paterson said complacently. 'It's the drips in council you've got to watch.' He gave a broad, satisfied grin.

'I hope you get to the bottom of it,' I said, waving and pulling out on to the road. Walsh lifted his arm stiffly, an odd, incomplete gesture.

Sam Walsh I could stand, but Paterson I could only take in small doses.

On my way to work, zooming in along the Northern Motorway with all the other commuters, I tuned into National Radio for an update on the current scene.

Everything sounded reassuringly familiar. My family situation may have changed but my country and the world sounded the same. My time and place. Despite slipping stock markets, business confidence had picked up, the radio told me. You could hear the determined snapping of briefcases, the tickling sound laptops make when they're booting up, the repressed buzz of cellphones. I listened carefully for signs of change, something that would indicate the larger world had also slipped a cog, and found nothing. All the bits were there.

Our dollar was still down, exports were up, Japanese banks were tottering, hard-nosed bankers were talking of soft landings, war was flaring again in central Africa, the Middle East was once more on the edge of the edge, mass chunks of ice were cracking off the Antarctic continent, frogs were dying globally, the police had made an arrest in a serial rapist case, new varieties of Aids were being discovered, the male sperm count was dropping, there was an oil spill in Japan, someone had invented a computer virus which emailed itself to other computers. UFOs were popping up over South America, an alien abductee had scars to prove it, a large pod of whales was passing through our own Cook Strait heading for a beaching on Farewell Spit, the health service was falling to pieces, the teachers were getting ready to strike, New Zealand films were making it big abroad, rabbits were eating up the pasture, possums eating up the forests, foreign investors eating up the land, babies were getting thrown into concrete mixers in the former Yugoslavia, Americans and Russians were docking spacecraft in orbit, there were bush fires in Australia and hurricanes in the Pacific, a plane had gone down, a treaty had been signed, criminal hackers were cruising the internet like sharks, looking for virtual deals.

There was something satisfying in the particularity of real time, real place; a mess of interrelated detail threading me to the world.

I had no wish to remove myself from the jumbled mishmash of my time and place; this was my time, my hour, my universe, my nexus. For better or worse. My familiar world. Someone makes a bungee jump and cracks his ankle, I can read about it in the newspaper. The precisely historical world of Harry Blackman, forty-three and keeping his eye on the road as he headed towards the Harbour Bridge along with thousands of others just like him. It was these particularities that bolted me in time and place, anchored me; I knew just where I stood in relation to them. If I could trust this background, the macropicture, if I could bluff it out with Evelyn…if I could make it with the new Timmy…if I could close my eyes and still see the corners…

With typical bad manners, a car pulled in front of me, hemming me in. Already cars were juggling for position before the Harbour Bridge crossing; the daily, centipede rite of passage for the North Shore commuter. It swung close enough for me to read the sticker on the back window.

'Twas brillig, and the slithy toves
Did gyre and gimble in the wabe…

My mother liked to quote this when something nobody understood came up; she had a deep, spooky voice reserved for those lines.

Remembering her voice, the same shiver went up my spine.

It was the same universe, just a few anomalies, that's all they were. Anomalies. A teddy. A wife.

The car in front waggled its rear end at me dangerously, warning me against trying to pass, forcing me to slow down. I tailgated the bastard all the way over the bridge and on into downtown.

The layout at work, too, was comfortingly familiar. Sophie still sat between Cranner's office and mine, fielding our calls in a polite voice. Her carefully made-up face, a mask as thorough as any TV presenter's, was as bland and neutral as ever. By being utterly invisible. Sophie achieved that necessary impression of efficiency. Pepsi Rigold, the boss, still lorded it from down the corridor where he could often be heard, talking and chuckling, and Mary Delany still strode about with a confident look on her face. Lesser mortals came and went.

My arrival was so unremarkable no one seemed to notice it except Sophie, who never forgot to smile.

I kept a watchful eye out for differences and anomalies. It was necessary, at every moment, to test the world for authenticity. I found nothing out of place. It seemed the changes were restricted to house and family. A localised effect. It was a reassuring notion.

As reassuring as the sight of my laptop, sitting pertly on my desk.

Except it wasn't my laptop, not quite. The same make and model, but the keys were worn in different places, and when I booted it up, I found the desktop arranged somewhat differently. Not only that but *you'd* upgraded the power of the computer – something I had been intending to do – and had added some new features. I resolved to have a look at those later and did a quick search of your files to see if there was any variation from mine, and found nothing amiss, no missing documents or mysterious folders.

What I did find, however, were three words scrawled on the blotter beside the laptop. *The Kober Project*, it said, and there was a circle around it. I did a search through *your* desk drawers and found no file under that title. A search failed to show up anything on the laptop.

When I got a break I looked *you* up in the phone book, just out of curiosity and there you were, H and E Blackman. I promptly rang and a woman's voice answered.

'Is Evonne there?' I asked in a thick, disguised voice.

'I'm sorry, you must have the wrong number.'

'Who am I speaking to please?'

'Evelyn Blackman, and who am I speaking to please?'

I hung up.

My next job was to hunt out our marriage certificate and check it with the registrar. But what would it matter which universe the marriage certificate was in, or whose name was on it? What I was really seeking was Evonne. Some proof of her existence. Did she exist at all in this universe?

All I had to do was ring her mother.

Which I did.

I'd always got on well with Evonne's mother, who had the same sense of humour as her daughter, the same flash in her eye. The feisty old woman had even flirted with me a couple of times. The phone rang without being answered, bleeding its sound out into some deserted space. I suspected that no one would ever answer it, and was just about to hang up when Evonne's mother came on the line. I'd know her voice anywhere; she had a special way of saying yes that made it sound like no.

'Is Evonne there please?'

'I'm sorry, no. Who's speaking please?'

'Harry.'

'Could I take a message? This is not her home, you know.

You could always ring her there.' A cautious note had entered her voice. She didn't know me.

'Thank you very much,' I said.

The boss called me into his office.

Bob Rigold, or Pepsi as he was known, after his habit of drinking the stuff all the time, was, for all his bluff heartiness, a careful, thoughtful man who valued those same qualities in others. Rarely did he approach a situation without some solution already in mind, and he was skilled at arriving at a consensus reflecting that solution. To achieve this he had what he called his 'thinking along' sessions, a term inherited from some course he'd been on. Now, sitting at his desk, a freshly opened Pepsi in his hand, he was biting his lower lip and thinking along with me.

We were thinking along together.

'Sometimes I think it would be better if the OECD could settle on a common price,' he said with apparent candour, although his mild blasphemy was a common observation; with the producers making deals behind each others' backs, it was hard for the big oil companies not to do the same. All this made illegal price-fixing a delicate and difficult business. The cartel was an impossible creature, for this was an open, competitive market. They almost didn't have to be illegal, for dog must eventually eat dog and treachery could achieve what anti-monopoly laws could seldom touch.

'And shipping costs too? You'd like those companies to stick to their cartel?' I thought of Maritime's special offer and Evelyn's callous assessment.

Rigold didn't even grin. 'I'd say the trend there was downward anyway. Now they've broken the Aussie wharfies.'

I was pleased to find Rigold already looking forward to a time when the prices Maritime was talking now, as an under-the-table offer, might become general par for the course, with the whole cartel benefiting. Shafting Big Bill and putting the noses of the other cartel leaders out of joint for a quick one-up didn't sound like Pepsi's style to me. I said, 'The whisper is that Maritime is cutting corners to cut costs. There are safety and environmental issues.'

Pepsi waved his bottle in a dismissive gesture. 'We're insured. There are always safety issues. Environmental issues. Those two areas alone keep us understaffed in PR. Cutting corners is not the point.'

'What is the point?'

Pepsi shifted in his chair; at the same time changing tack. 'This guy McBride, of Maritime, this deal is his baby. Is there anything in it for him, personally, I mean, other than for Maritime?'

'If he can get us to break the cartel it will enhance his reputation in Maritime, that's for sure.'

'That's not what I meant, Harry.'

'He's never fished me for a payoff.' It went without saying that I had not offered one. Again the line of thought prickled me. There were strict rules in the company with regard to bribes, and the question never normally arose.

Rigold nodded. 'The young will do it for glory,' He observed.

I had nothing but commonplaces to offer to that.

'Tate wants to meet you here tomorrow. The K project,' he said, as if still speaking about the same thing.

'OK.'

Pepsi shifted in his chair. 'I hate these undercover jobs. I really do. I can't see why you and Tate have to meet here.' He held up his hand as if for silence. 'I don't know,' he said with sudden heat, 'if the company's interests are being served by this meeting.'

I covered up with an embarrassed silence. It was the best I could manage with a sharp old bastard like Rigold. He covered up the silence with swigs of soft drink. We had consensus.

I could feel his gaze eating into my back as I left the office.

Back at my desk I did another search for anything I could find on Kober or Project K. Any hint, any clue. There was nothing but the single blotter note, a trigger to open a mental file, but that mental file was in your head, not mine.

I made sure, this time, that I had the laptop firmly in hand when I left the office.

At the lift on the way out I met Cranner, who was working late. Cranner always worked late. It was part of his strategy. The strategy of thin, pasty-faced young men. When I stood back to let him out of the lift, he gave me a smile. Just a grimace of the teeth. An expression I'd never seen before. On Cranner's face or any other.

'Going down,' the lift intoned.

Returning along the Northern Motorway, I allowed myself to be lulled into the activity of driving, immersed in function like an automaton. It was a way of not thinking. Once across the steel arc of the Harbour Bridge, the car chewed up the kilometres all by itself. The radio babble was full of talk of dollar flight and inflation. There was no sign that we would suffer the soaring temperatures experienced in Melbourne, but authorities were on the alert. Temperatures worldwide kept pointing towards global warming, a result of all that oil we were burning. That was my cure to congratulate myself for having installed a rainwater tank. Forty thousand litres. Like having money in the bank when reservoirs run low.

Hurricane Hildegard was hovering a few hundred kilometres north of the country.

For a moment the double row of steel girders holding up the outer lanes of the Harbour Bridge, crisscrossing with the speed of movement, created the impression that there were two bridges, a multiplicity of girders.

Then I saw my car, or what I thought was my car. It was in a lane to the left of me, and about a hundred metres further up, affording me tantalising glimpses. The model was unmistakable, of course; I thought I had the only one in the country.

I sped up and sought to move into one of the other lanes in order to get a better view and catch a glimpse of the driver, but my quarry moved in front of a lumbering old Bedford and vanished.

Of course it wouldn't be *you* driving my car. My whole theory was built on the notion that there were two universes. You'd be heading home along another motorway somehow parallel to this one, to another house where Evonne and Timmy would be waiting, unless this innocuous, boring piece of motorway were some link between the two worlds, a bridge that arced across realities; maybe we both had to be on the motorway at the same time, heading for different exit ramps in different worlds.

What would I find when I got home?

A house, clean and tidy and empty; it hardly seemed lived in at all. The kitchen had a remote, sparkling look like a window display and no homely smells came from it. The lounge was a smooth, tasteful surface with no lumps or bumps to show human occupation. The rooms fitted together as if they had been culled from the best modern magazines. The feel was of a house waiting for new occupants to arrive, to fill out the space and humanise it. Set it in motion.

It did not wait humbly, however, but with an aggressive and studiously expensive pride. Alone here for the first time I began to notice some lavish touches Evonne would have eschewed; a cappuccino machine many a café would have envied; chair and sofa coverings of a rich, velvet textile; a

French dinner set with plates thin enough to breath through; a stove that came out of *Star Wars*; crystal wine glasses so pure they went on ringing for half an hour after you tapped them with a silver spoon, itself part of a cutlery set positioned, in terms of fancy handle work, way above its station.

I had time to examine things I hadn't taken in properly. The demented clown I'd noticed was not a reproduction but a canvas by someone called Fomison, doubtless some modern artist priced far in excess of his value. A speculative hedge. And the reclining buddha, with the rounded, feminine hips and the ironical smile was not from a mould but an original bronze casting, the metal convincingly aged with green rust in the Enlightened One's profoundly human curves and cavities. That must have cost. What I'd taken for an old coat hanging on the deck wall turned out to be made of lead and looked like a piece of armour with pockets; there was a deceptive crudity in it which suggested expense.

Conceptual art is hard on the pocket.

There was more in this vein, from feather duvets to silk and hemp dust covers, and a rare corkscrew with what looked like a 24-carat-gold death's head for the grip and arms of filigreed angel's wings that rose as you screwed the head down, and fell as the cork came up. Very funny and clever and extravagant. A nice touch. A credit card touch.

I strolled about like a visitor to a gallery.

The only casual touch was Descartes, sitting askew where I'd left it under the reading lamp. I picked it up and had a better look; it had been purchased from a second-hand book store for $3.50, which was scribbled in pencil on the inside cover.

I went from room to room, and in Evelyn's absence the puzzle merely deepened. I knew from my call to her mother that there probably was an Evonne out there somewhere, but that was no comfort. I wanted my Evonne, with her old Royal Doulton china, her trusty Shacklock stove.

It was as if she had been expunged from the world, had never existed. Wherever I looked I encountered the shiny, impervious surface of Evelyn's tidiness. A tidiness that had come back to mock me. It wasn't fair. Other people were not subjected to this sort of treatment. They lived their ordinary, orderly lives in good faith, just as I had. They worked and loved and economised.

My strolling patrol of the rooms became a resentful prowl. I wanted nothing more than to pull everything down and smash everything up. To uproot the feature-page kitchen, to overturn the *Home & Entertaining* living room, to rip up the *House & Garden* bedroom, the *Vogue* bathroom. To tear at the *Metro* walls with my bare fingers.

While I was working myself up like this, I kept roaming about the house like a burglar; poking into every corner, resenting everything I saw that was out of place, alien, belonging to the woman Evelyn and the little imposter Timmy.

I wanted my world back.

I slowed down and tried to get a bit of order into my thoughts.

At the cold-blooded level I was searching for clues that might give me some insight into the life of my double; letters, photographs, anything. I found very little, and lots missing. Holes through which my life had disappeared. A box of photographs Evonne and I had taken in Europe no longer existed. Some letters I'd written to her had been replaced by postcards with brief messages in my own hand to Evelyn. *You* had no taste in postcards.

Finally I found a wedding photograph and there he was, I was, *you* were, smiling out at the camera, looking damned pleased with yourself in fact, arm in arm with Evelyn who looked cool and poised. By your side stood Vernon, tall, already a little stooped, with a stern look, while standing by Evelyn was a woman I didn't recognise who was flashing a professional, camera-ready smile. A bridesmaid stood in the background holding flowers. I didn't recognise her.

The photograph couldn't tell me anything. This grinning groom was not Harry Blackman but a stranger dressed in the flesh of him. I wanted to rip it up, slowly, into very tiny pieces. I held it firmly in my thumbs, ready for the tearing. And did nothing. I had to play it very carefully with Evelyn; ripping up wedding photos was not a good way to start. Nor was smashing up the house. If I allowed impotence to turn to rage I was a goner. Everything depended on staying in equilibrium.

And what if she'd walked out already? I had no idea what had happened between you and her; God knows what you might have done to forfeit her love. And you were well away from it all in my secure world in perfect disguise; that's where you had to be. With Evonne.

I headed for the scotch and tried to distract myself by thinking about work. The bottle made nervous, unsteady sounds against the rim of the glass. Work was at least familiar ground, but the X factor of the Kober Project immediately leapt into mind. I kept telling myself that work was the same – but it was not. It had the Kober Project. The sudden eruption of the Maritime deal, if I could count that. And maybe there was something out there I didn't know about yet. Something hidden in the jumble of the world. Some nasty surprise lying in wait.

'Christ, what a day I've had,' Evelyn said as she came through the door at nine o'clock. Timmy in tow. She swept on into the kitchen and looked around in disgust.

'You didn't cook anything, you bastard.' She scrutinised

me briefly, noting the scotch glass which had gone warm in my hand. 'You just got stewed, made a sandwich for yourself and left a mess all over the bench. What am I going to give Timmy?'

I was sitting in the lounge like a passenger at an international airport terminal whose plane is forever delayed and fear is starting to set in. The sound of my own voice startled me. 'Where the hell have you been?'

Actually, I was foolishly glad to see her, and would never have admitted that I was growing frightened.

'Don't give me any of that shit,' she said, throwing down her bags. 'Help me get Timmy to bed, he's tired and hungry. I'm tired and pissed off.'

'You're late,' I said. My voice sounded resentful, like I'd been stood up for a date. That's exactly how I felt, in fact.

She gave me a harder look. There was no love in it. 'You've been drinking. I never argue with drunks.'

'Drunks! Three scotches and I'm a drunk!' I'd had four but the principle was the same.

'Then why didn't you cook for us, swine?' There was no special, or particular malice in her voice. She called me 'swine' the way some people call each other darling. 'You knew we'd come in tired and hungry.'

'No, I didn't,' I said, immediately regretting it. Perhaps I shouldn't have had the fourth Scotch.

'What?' She swung around and gave me a toxic look.

'I thought you must've already had dinner.'

'Why would you think that?'

I shrugged. It was the best I could do in the situation. Shoulders can hide lots of tension in the back.

Evelyn saw its insufficiency. 'I see. Come on Timmy, I'll make you a cheese toasty.'

'I like cheese toasties,' Timmy said.

So did I but I didn't say so.

Evelyn slammed and clattered in the kitchen while I affected a wounded dignity, feeling like a child who's decided, when darkness falls, he can't stay overnight at a friend's house after all. For me, this was our first row. With Evonne I'd been able to defuse rows by making certain key concessions and acknowledgements, because Evonne's grounds were never without justice; somehow this hadn't happened with Evelyn.

'At least,' Evelyn said, cutting the bread with swift, brittle strokes, 'you usually manage to think of someone other than yourself and get up and help when I come home.'

Being unfavourably compared to *you* got me on my feet. Her voice was so even. The phrase 'other than yourself' was delivered as a choice irony against which I had no comeback. Evonne would have shouted back at me. We'd have had a good row. One thing about Evonne, she never played the Ice Queen, but was always warm towards me. Even when we argued, it was from heat. Never from cold. I didn't know how to deal with cold. Cold was nowhere to go but to contempt or hatred. I had nowhere to go but to feel stupid, and surely that couldn't last.

I went into the kitchen and sliced some cheese and tomato, the basis of a cheese toasty whichever world you're in.

Evelyn ignored me, which she was very good at, so good that in the end I didn't even claim a cheese toasty for myself.

While Timmy ate, I sat in the chair and pretended to read Descartes. Running my eye over the print, I noticed that someone had underlined certain passages. I chose one at random, a single sentence, and read it.

It is prudent not to trust entirely anything that has once deceived us.

That at least was sensible.

It was a painful thing for me to kiss that strange little face under the baleful stare of the false-eyed teddy. He turned his face away and I had to kiss him on the cheek. I didn't blame him.

The truth was, I couldn't remember my other, real Timmy's face right now; struggle as I might I could not bring it to mind. All I remembered was him crying himself to sleep at night, Evonne sighing and cursing if she had to get up to him, and all I succeeded in seeing was the ubiquitous teddy clutched by a pair of boyish hands. How much time did I ever spend with my Timmy? How much effort did I make to get to know my own son? It terrified me to think that my Timmy had been as much a stranger to me as this little boy was now.

I went into the kitchen for a restorative drink of water with no stomach for the battle I'd set up with Evelyn.

She came in behind me. 'Now, Harry, what the hell was all that about before?' She was so classy, so cool, so swish. No wonder *you* fell for her.

'I just got lonely,' I said, trying to stick to as much simple truth as I could. 'Where were you anyway?' There was a note of whining complaint she was not slow in picking up.

'What is this?' The Inquisition? For Christ's sake, don't pull any patriarchal shit on me, Harry. I'm long past that.'

Evonne didn't swear; funny how I'd never noticed.

'I'd still like to know.' I tried to sound reasonable, conciliatory even, without backing down. How do you wave the white flag and act tough at the same time? I was beginning to appreciate the skill of Evonne's mutual face-saving devices.

Evelyn, with no interest in allowing any face-saving, slammed the fridge door.

'Why this sudden interest? After years of not caring, now suddenly His Majesty wants to know? Are you jealous or something? Suspect me of what you, yourself, have been up to?'

'Not that.'

'Of course not.' She snapped her fingers as if she'd just seen the light. 'Now I see. Hubby gets home and dutiful wifey is not there with dutiful meal ready on the table. Hubby has a tantrum. Tosses a few down. Oh dear, oh dear. What a pretty little mess you are. What a can of worms.'

'Well you could've called,' I said. It seemed like a good fallback position. But it all rang false again; was this how *you* used to sound – full of rear-guard action petulance? The last thing I wanted was to fall into *your* behaviour patterns.

Evelyn was onto it like a shot. 'Called?' That's what my mother used to say when I was sixteen. What's got into you, Harry? One minute you're pissed and aggressive, the next you look like you're about to burst into tears. Any minute now I think I'm going to get the Great Speech about how you work so hard to pull in all the money. Please sober up in time to spare me that.'

She turned on her heel and walked out of the kitchen.

I wanted to clap. But I felt sick, as if I were on a pitching ship.

A moment later she returned. 'Talking about ringing. I had a nutter call today for someone called Evonne. You don't know any Evonne do you?'

'I don't.'

'Are you sure?'

'I'm sure.'

She was still wearing her smart, outdoor clothes, and she was a snappy dresser; tasteful and urbane. Taking a second look, I saw at least fifteen hundred dollars from hairdo to shoes. In my world I'd seen these smart tarts, these elegant, corporate giraffes, and wondered what it would be like, and how much it would cost, to have one of my own.

Apparently you took the plunge and found out.

Evonne, too, had her breaking points. Once she'd lost her mind and screamed at me just because I ran my finger along the windowsill to see how much dust had collected there. I was made to feel a real wanker over that one. I had to beware the temptation to idolise Evonne and see our relationship through rose-tinted spectacles. She was earthy, her ambitions within bounds, but life with her had been very frustrating at times; I'd made adjustments and compromises there too, and the Harry Blackman from this universe, *you,* husband of Evelyn, might very well wonder at the kind of things your counterpart had put up with from Evonne. There were vulnerabilities all round.

Since we were just wandering about getting nowhere, we drifted into the bedroom. Evelyn started casually peeling off her blouse. I turned my back on her and fiddled around at the wardrobe, suddenly reluctant to get undressed. There were vulnerabilities in that direction too. Even so, I couldn't help a quick look behind me as I was slowly pulling off my shirt. Evelyn had taken off her blouse and bra and was wriggling out of her skirt. Her knickers were cream coloured and lightly laced around the hems and the seams.

I got undressed quickly and made my way to bed with my dignity relatively intact. Evelyn, oblivious to all of this, still with her knickers on, had one leg up on the bed and was rubbing some scented ointment on her feet with brisk, firm movements, making sure she got some between each toe. I sat up, the blankets around my waist and watched her. Her legs were long and sleek and her feet, although narrow, were slender and bony, like those of a boy.

'Getting a good eyeful?' she said, not looking up.

'I am,' I said calmly. 'You are a very beautiful woman,' I added sincerely.

She said nothing but wrinkled her nose a little. Then she

pulled off her knickers and swung into bed. The hair between her legs was blonde.

'Do you remember,' she said as she slipped into bed beside me but emphatically on the other side, pert breasts bobbing, 'what you said to me when we met?'

'You're going to remind me.'

'Too right I am. You said that one of the things you loved about me was my sense of independence and adventure. Remember? You complained about these stay-at-home puddings who just sit around looking after the kids, watching soaps or Oprah Winfrey on the box, drinking too much coffee and getting fat.'

'OK.'

'OK he says. All right. So why go wobbly on me because I'm late? Shit. I can think of a time when my being late was an opportunity for you to show your love by cooking me up a wonderful meal, with a bottle of wine and candles.' There was a sharp, wry grin. 'So why go wobbly?'

I couldn't think of any good reason, except fear and helplessness and wobbly things I couldn't talk about.

'Just sheer bloody-mindedness I suppose,' she went on, speculating. 'Or is it a case of taking out your frustrations at work on the wife and kids? You read about that. Men who are wimps at work and monsters at home.'

She'd started the conversation with her back half to me, tossing her remarks over her shoulder in the manner witches are said to toss their breasts. Now she had turned right around and was facing me, forgetful of her nakedness. Her breasts, still small and smooth enough to suggest she had never breast-fed her Timmy, started at me with squinting, accusative nipples.

The only intimate connection I had in this world was with this woman, and I wanted nothing more than to crawl up onto her breast like some Palaeolithic crustacean crawling up a beach, and lie secure in the warm, mother-scented heat.

'No you don't, Jacko,' she said pushing me away as my infant head lolled towards her chest. 'I don't feel a bit like that right now, to tell you the truth. Anyway, you stink of scotch.'

I'm in a state of shock, I thought. Deep shock. Whatever else happens I must try to remember that. I am not in a position to trust every passing whim of feeling.

'You have to feel close to a person to want to make love to them, and I don't feel close to you at all right now. I told you last night. You know, when I came home tonight and saw you slumped in that chair glowering at me over your scotch you looked like a complete stranger. It was just like I'd never known you at all. You'd become something else, not the man I fell in love with. The man I fell in love with loved me and respected me. He didn't ignore me to death on one hand and act the jealous monster on the other. The man I'm talking about had some sense of integrity. He had values and people were important to him.'

This came close enough to the truth to convince me further, if I needed further convincing, that if I told this smart, brittle, sceptical woman what had happened to me I'd end up in the hands of the white coats very quickly indeed. Then I'd lose the lot; house, wife, job, car, child, everything. The economic power I'd wielded so easily over Evonne could be turned against me by Evelyn if she decided to leave me, I mean *you*. Could be fleeced in a matter of weeks, I'd seen it happen to colleagues at work who became involved in nasty divorces. Quicker than you can say 'liable parent' they were down the tubes.

She sat up in bed facing me, the bedclothes pulled loosely around her waist, her torso flushed pink from anger, her long fair hair smooth as a river down her shoulders, her eyes very blue and hard.

'And why didn't you cook something, you slob? You might've known I'd be delayed at Timmy's music lesson. Then I called in to see Tess. I haven't seen her for a month, you know. It's ridiculous. And I stopped in at the Colemans' to see Keith.'

Tess I hadn't met, and it took me a moment to recall Keith Coleman, an old school friend who'd never really been a friend and who had become some sort of bohemian architect – a poncy prick. The point about Coleman was that in my universe, the universe with Evonne in it, Coleman was somebody I only read about occasionally in the papers. He didn't figure in our lives at all.

'I wanted to see how the plans were coming along, of course.'

'Of course. And how are they coming along?'

She said nothing. Just stared at me for a long moment. 'Sometimes I don't understand you at all,' she said.

With deliberate motions, Evelyn rolled over and presented me with her back. She signed with the weary air of one who has grown bored with the conversation. 'Anyway, there's no bloody excuse for dumping on me as soon as I come through the door. Don't pull that one on me again Harry, or I'll turn around and walk right out again.'

'Agreed,' I said. 'And I apologise. My attitude was all wrong. I was tired and hungry. I didn't sleep last night.'

She turned over and looked at me, frowning a little. Apparently I was wasn't acting in character – did *you* never have the grace to apologise for anything? With a tiny, negative gesture she turned over again. The sheet formed a diagonal from her top shoulder to her lower hip showing the graceful curve of her back while hiding all but the soft outline of her buttocks. I wanted to gently lift the sheet aside, run my fingers down her back and cup her buttocks with both hands.

Instead I contented myself with a tiny, contrite kiss on the back of her neck.

There was a lot of ground to make up.

Eventually Evelyn went to sleep. I lay in the same posture as the night before and stared at the same ceiling. Patches of sexual heat floated around my body as if a powerful light were being passed back and forth over me, raising the hair on my limbs and bringing a sweat out under my arms. If I closed my eyes I would see Evelyn in various postures of desire and abandon. To combat this I concentrated on Evonne, trying to evoke her, see her face and hear her voice, but I kept on seeing Evelyn, bare shouldered, blue-eyed and eager for love.

I tried to evoke my Timmy, too, but kept seeing a one-eyed boy, with the eye changing from one side of his face to the other.

I got up, drank some water and went back to bed and nothing had changed. I got up again and padded around the house like a restless ghost; at least that way the sexual heat was left behind in the bed with the sleeping Evelyn. My circuit took me into Timmy's room where the other Timmy lay sleeping. As with all children, there was an angelic aspect to his sleeping face, as if butter wouldn't melt in his mouth as my mother would say. A saying that always puzzled me as a child.

I thought of my own father, Vernon, who had taken me out in the evenings to pop rabbits with a spotlight and a .22. We'd drive along the border between the pine plantations and the paddocks looking for eyes that shone in the light and we'd shoot them and their eyes would pop out of existence. Vernon let me use the .22 when I can only have been about ten; I still had the gun around the house somewhere. Vernon had done his best for me. I had done my best for my Timmy, and this Timmy had done no harm to me.

He was just a little boy. Children at that age are warmth-seeking creatures. They need emotional heat to grow. How was I going to achieve that among all the other things I had to do here?

In the softening dark, memory and reality blurred. I could look at familiar walls and softened shapes and believe I knew them, close my eyes and believe I breathed the same air I had always known. Maybe there's a gateway, I thought. A door somewhere. All I have to do is walk through and I'm home. And there have to be clues, for there's no such thing as a perfect crime. The criminal always leaves a sign. That this joke on me was a crime I had no doubt. Someone had pulled a fast one on Henry Blackman.

Real events have rough edges, leave traces, grow mould and hair. Footprints are left beneath the window. If I looked, I'd find it, whatever it was, the anomaly, the footprint; the little something somebody left behind in their haste to overturn my life, the bastards.

Then a crazy idea occurred. I was a secret agent from another dimension with a mission unknown even to myself. I had something to do here, some work, something to discover – whatever it was, I would have to work quickly. There was something in the air, a vibration, a quiver, a sense of quantum uncertainty that suggested this whole strange configuration wouldn't last forever, that it would break down eventually.

If only I had something simple to deal with, like memory loss. It would be a relief to find great gaps in my memory, but no, there was an unbroken line from spotlighting rabbits to my first date with Evonne to the birth of Timmy and all the rest of it. Everything exactly where it should be. Seamless.

I was moving from Timmy's room into the doorway of the living room when I saw a figure standing by the easy chair, bent over, one arm outstretched. At first I thought the intruder was reaching for the Descartes, perhaps the scotch, but then I saw it.

The laptop!

I'd left it down by the side of the chair, where I always put it when I come home.

Then a voice came through the house, calling my name. It was a distant voice, as if from very far away, and it sounded like Evonne.

The form by the chair stiffened, then rose and turned towards me. It was *you*; even though it was a crosshatch of shadows, it was still you. I was starting to recognise it now; a frailty in the air, a sudden nostalgia, a graininess to the look of things.

I walked straight towards you but you weren't there. You dissolved into the night textures of the room.

The far-off voice of Evonne faded.

It might have all been an illusion – a product of night and sleeplessness. But I took the laptop with me when I returned to the bedroom in search of sleep.

Getting back between the sheets next to Evelyn was like slipping into a warm current, bringing me again into a state of useless sexual readiness. As morning approached I slipped into an uneasy half-life in which, while retaining consciousness, I became sodden with body images and drunk with body smells. I pushed up against Evelyn, who still had her back to me, the way I'd push against the pliant walls of a dream. There were two of me, and we were making love to Evelyn from both the front and the back, sharing each others' sensations.

A moment later I was jerked into full wakefulness by fingers raking my face and Evelyn screaming in my ear, 'No you fucking don't you arsehole. Fuck me while I was asleep! What a filthy fucking trick!'

Actually I wasn't in the bed at all, I was on the floor looking up into a face puffy with sleep and scorn and rage.

Heedlessly beautiful too.

'I dreamed we were making love,' I said.

'Well we fucking weren't!'

'Well I dreamed it.'

'I don't fucking believe it.'

The face vanished.

I went and lay down in the spare room. The sheets of this unused bed were cool and damp. Sometimes I'd taken Evonne like that, half asleep, and there'd been a certain slothful, somnambulant eroticism in it for both of us.

I pushed my legs out, looking for further cool places.

3

Sam Walsh was at the top of the drive again that morning. He was patrolling the roadside like a colonel who had lost his troops. He saw me coming and turned his head the other way, perhaps to give me a chance to drive on by. I pulled up and slid my window down.

He approached, walking stiffly as if from an old war wound.

'Any news of the phantom flower plotters?' I called jovially, hoping to put the old man at ease.

'They've been at it again,' he said importantly. 'It's been planted out below the dairy at Crocker's corner. That must have happened last night.' His jaw was stern but the loose skin beneath it was all wobble.

I couldn't think of anything to say, yet I felt like I should hand him something, a passport to stamp, perhaps, or a visa to check over.

'I rang the council and they don't know any more about it than I do. I'm thinking of staying up at night and trying to catch them at it. Especially if they're locals.'

'Like the shoemaker and the elves.'

'Ha ha. Yes.'

His manner stiffened and he drew back, as if at the touch of a private grief.

'You've been watering the flowers,' I said, observing the

flourishing plants in their wet beds.

'Yes.' He was on the defensive, as if I were going to scorn him for it.

'You've done a good job,' I said.

'Thank you,' and after a moment's hesitation. 'Flowers need plenty of water after transplanting.'

'Of course.'

'And I still have my own garden.' He shuffled awkwardly. 'There's enough work at home to keep me going, believe you me.'

He looked dolefully down at the flowerbed as if it were some orphan who had been thrust upon him.

'I also rang the police. Can you believe that what they've done isn't actually legal? I mean someone's broken a law to do this!'

I laughed. 'What would they be charged with, beautifying public property?'

'Damned if I know,' the old man said, in the tones of one for whom the world is too big a mystery to fathom.

There was a break in the traffic and I gunned into it. Up ahead the Harbour Bridge beckoned, spanning the city, a silken web in the early light.

Between times that day I made further discreet inquiries into my business affairs, starting with a close look at your previous daily schedules. Like me, you kept a meticulous computer record. There was my lawyer's name, Peter Coveny, but I hesitated to ring him. It might be too easy to reveal my ignorance to a sharp man like Peter Coveny.

Coleman's name was there too. Keith Coleman. Architect. What was he building? What were these plans Evelyn was checking out?'

There was only one way to find out. I picked up the phone.

'How are the plans coming along?' I said when he answered.

Coleman was as falsely jovial as I remembered him, and talked too much. It seemed that he and *you* had a long-standing relationship, but I couldn't work out why you had cultivated an association with this devious, greedy man.

You and Evonne apparently owned an expensive piece of property with a view overlooking the harbour, and planned to put an even more expensive house on it. As Coleman kept talking, I slowly realised that you were in, that is, I was in, for a round million, maybe more, and was so amazed I checked out your bank statements as soon as I'd finished talking to him to see if you were earning twice as much as me. I wanted to know where you'd got the money to buy that harbour property in the first place.

Further shocks awaited me. Not only were you not earning any more, but you were already spending to the hilt, wiping out a nest-egg fund I'd put aside for retirement. Where was the money going? From which pocket was I bleeding? The answer was in front of me. Evelyn. That long-waisted harpy had been spending up large all over town. Stuff for the new house. Stuff for herself. Stuff for Timmy. I was haemorrhaging money from every account and you could have built a small house in the country with the money I already owed Keith Coleman. The disappearance of my retirement fund was a mystery in itself, the account being identical to mine in every respect except one – all the money had been drawn out three weeks before, but there was no record of what you had done with it; there were no corresponding sums credited either to Coleman or anyone else. What the hell were you up to? Looked a bit like someone getting ready to do a runner.

I'd have to ring my lawyer, Peter Coveny, after all. I'd have to talk to Evelyn. Get in control here. Put the brakes on. A good start would be to pay off that bloodsucker Coleman, throw the plans away, sell the property, the ownership of which was the one bright if mysterious spot in this whole mess, clean up your debts and get our affairs back in order. In other words, do everything I could to halt the slide to financial ruin.

With Evonne I had a housekeeping account into which I paid a sum each week based on the morning newspaper's calculations of the cost of living. What could be fairer than that? I put into the account what the newspaper said a family of three could live on, and if Evonne didn't make it last there were no cornflakes on the table on Sunday for Timmy. With Evelyn the whole thing had got out of hand, for not only had she swallowed up *your* generous housekeeping allowances – more generous than prudent – to little effect, but she had decimated the cheque account as well, where you'd kept money for bills, car expenses and the like, just the way I did. Similarly the credit cards were stretched to their maximum.

In fact I was broke. Living on overdrafts and credit cards. Mortgaging the future.

It was inconceivable that Harry Blackman would, in any universe, allow this to happen.

I had the accounts spread out on my desk when Cranner walked in but I refused to be embarrassed. I was too shocked. Without moving to put anything away, I gestured to the chair opposite.

'How are you doing, Ken?' I said in a friendly voice. I really had nothing to bitch about as far as Cranner was concerned, except that he was a weasel.

Cranner shrugged, ignoring the chair. 'The daily round, the common task.'

Cranner was fond of quoting the Bible or the prayer book or whatever it was he was currently reading. A font of facile homilies. I didn't know him well enough to judge him; perhaps he was a Christian. People who pray a lot can get thin around the mouth.

'Getting ready for Canada?' Cranner had a slender, intense face, pale and lined from overwork. The overgrown, diligent schoolboy. He's tenacious, I thought. He'll scrabble away at the pile until he gets to the top, or at least as near the top as he's going to get. While others are sleeping he'll be scrabbling.

'He hasn't confirmed it yet,' I said easily, leaning back in my chair, hoping that was as true here as back in my world. 'Vancouver in autumn. The central park will be red with maples.'

'And white with frost.'

We both laughed.

'You don't have to go, you know.'

I leaned further back in the chair. 'How do you mean?'

'I mean you can say no.'

'But why would I want to?'

To hand the job over to a younger man, perhaps? If that was Cranner's play, I was disappointed in him.

Instead of answering, Cranner got up, looking angry at himself. He walked around the office and stared out the same piece of window I like to stare out. I get a view of the harbour. A large ocean liner was pulling in – the *Oriana* on its post-millennial southern tour.

'How's Evelyn, Harry?' It was intended to be a polite inquiry but it didn't come out that way. It came from a throat that was all strangled up. I felt I'd missed the point of the entire conversation.

'She's just fine.'

'Still playing tennis?' Cranner was trying to peer around the lump of Devonport to the distant hump of Rangitoto Island.

'Whenever she can.'

He smiled. It was the same strained rictus I'd seen the day before in the lift. The man seemed to be riding under a tremendous amount of tension.

He stood in the doorway. 'By the way, I notice Southern Oil has risen a couple of points.'

'Yeah,' I said politely. I didn't know Cranner was into shares. It was not something we talked about.

'Someone's been buying in quite heavily.' He grinned as if that should mean something to me.

'Oh yeah?'

It was awkward. Company executives were discouraged from stock market gambling, especially in ethically dubious stocks like Southern Oil, because they were too close to our own inside knowledge. It wouldn't look good for people in our position to be involved.

When he had gone, I went back to my desk and stared at your accounts. Now my accounts. None of it made sense: Evelyn, the accounts, Coleman, Cranner. Especially Cranner. Running the recent encounter through in my mind I decided that it made no sense at all. It looked as if he was trying to lever me out, but maybe he was warning me, or trying to warn me, about something.

I might have been wrong to imagine that it would get easier as time went by, that I might slip into life in this world with hardly a ripple. Now I was not so sure. It got harder, not easier, as if further little fissures were opening, anomalies cropping up, discrepancies widening. Fissures that turned into great crevices. People used the same words here, it was true, and had ostensibly the same conversations, but it seemed they were using these words to say different things, the same conversations to reach different conclusions. As if the words themselves had lost their anchors in reality.

Still, I had work to do and settled for more coffee. And yet behind the busy work of problem solving lay a new knowledge. If it all fell over now I'd be totally wiped out.

Bankrupt. Fucking bankrupt.

That was sure to mean the same thing in both universes.

Halfway through the morning, Sophie put a call through from McBride of Maritime. Handling overseas calls, she always sounded like a professional telephone operator, her voice as unruffled as her hair.

The unmistakable Aussie twang came down the line. I found it hard to take the Aussie accent completely seriously, as if they were sending themselves up when they spoke.

'Between droughts and floods and bushfires, Harry, there's not much left of New South Wales, and Melbourne keeps going by faith alone.'

'Over here, of course, we put our trust in good works.'

'Ha ha. Won any yacht races recently? Got that America's Cup nailed down?'

'They'll never take it back. We've got our secret weapon – the winning yacht.'

'Don't understand it myself, you know. I mean, those yachts would go a lot faster if they put engines in them.'

'That would defeat the whole purpose.'

'Get away. So how's the Canadian deal?'

'Shaping up.' I assumed he was talking about the oil purchases we would make in Canada, oil which, he hoped, would be carried in Maritime's ships. What I didn't know was what you had told him. I wanted the deal to go to our regular shippers, Poseidon. In my universe I'd told McBride to take his secret deals elsewhere.

'Good.' McBride sounded cheerful. 'And I've done my legwork on this side. Everything's sweet here.'

'That's great,' I said, not knowing what 'legwork' he might be referring to. In fact, I was not quite sure why McBride had rung at all. Just as I didn't have a clue why Cranner had come sleazing into my office earlier.

'We'll be crewing with Russians, Slavs.'

'Fine.' I didn't ask what they would be paid but I could guess. By alluding to lower costs, he was fishing for an answer to the secret deal offer. Or assuming one.

'Fax when you have a firm date for Sydney, Harry. I'll show you the sights. We've got to have something to put on the old expense account.'

'We don't have expense accounts any more this side of the Tasman. We're leaner and meaner and much more competitive now, remember?'

'Good Lord! I hope we don't start doing that here. I only want to do one man's job, thanks, not three. See you in Sin City.'

I was about to come back with some crack or other when my call waiting signalled.

'By the way,' I thought I heard McBride say, 'I see Southern Oil's heading north.'

I signed off McBride and switched lines, wondering what I'd missed, just how ignorant of the real situation I was.

It was Pepsi on the line. It was time to face the Kober Project.

Pepsi wasn't in his office, just one empty soft-drink bottle sitting on his desk. His absence made the other man's presence there eerie. He was sitting to one side leafing through a magazine. As soon as I came in he stood up. I knew right away he was not in the oil business. The wrong look. I picked the motor industry. Detroit maybe. Young.

'I'm glad you could see me,' he said. His voice was mild and pleasant, almost inflectionless but certainly American. Transatlantic.

'The boss is always free with my time,' I said, hoping that

Rigold had the place bugged and was listening in. Somehow it just didn't fit; Rigold letting something take place in his office over which he had no knowledge or control. This guy must carry weight.

And I wasn't sure if I was supposed to know him or not.

He smiled and the effect was pleasant if not charming. Everything about him was light and pleasant and comfortably thirtyish. His skin was smooth and fair, his eyes a mild grey, his hair sandy and well minted. He was the top graduate from the best business school. He would have faded to nothing in a crowd, for there was nothing distinctive about him. Even his name. Jerry Tate. Inoffensive and nondescript.

He waited until I sat down before resuming his seat.

'Harry, we've got to know what Kober is doing. He got out of hospital six days ago. He's been getting deliveries of computer gear. We assumed the accident destroyed his device, but we don't know for sure. Nor has the good professor resumed his prior agreement with us. What's your assessment?'

I shrugged. I seemed to be doing a lot of shrugging. 'It's really up to you.'

He looked interested. 'Why do you say that?'

'There's no way I can second-guess a mad professor.'

'Mad? Do you really think he's mad?'

'It's hard to tell sometimes,' I paused and took a punt, 'but my guess is he doesn't want anything to do with us.'

He looked out through the glass. 'This is a beautiful harbour. It's good to see it again.'

'The City of Sails, it's called.'

He smiled as if I'd made a joke, and said, 'I don't like this secretiveness of Kober's. Maybe he's taken the development of this machine to a new stage.'

'In such a short time?'

'We value your technical background, of course,' he said.

I inclined my head in acknowledgement. I had the feeling he didn't give a shit about my technical background.

I said, 'There's any number of reasons why Kober could've put us on hold. If he lost all his records in the accident, he's probably trying to rebuild his database.'

He leaned back in his chair and rubbed his knee. It looked like a reflexive, spontaneous gesture. Whoever he was, Jerry Tate was studying me furiously. I got the feeling he knew I was only feeding back to him what he'd given me in the first place.

'Or he has some other source of funding,' Tate said, half to himself it seemed. He came to a decision. 'I think it's time for another approach, Harry. You'll continue to play your old role as an investor, but,' he moved his hands gently through his hair, as if sifting sand, 'your real job is to assess the stage Kober has reached. I assumed he would be months away from building a new model, but now I'm not so sure.'

'Is he still at the same address?'

'40/1b Fort Street,' Tate said, as if his mind moved more easily in details than in generalities. I nodded, wondering at the ease with which he had given me the address. I found it hard to believe Mr Jerry Tate; everything he did was completely calculated, right down to the movement of his hands across his clean-cut trousers, hands that were as bland and anonymous as hands can be.

The sweat came out from under my armpits. Why did I feel suddenly, that I was fighting for my life? I needed a real backhander and couldn't think of one.

'Have you any evidence,' I said, as if just emerging from some heavy analysis, 'that Kober has made technical advances with his device? Maybe at the conceptual level?'

Tate looked started, but only for a moment. I was taking a hell of a risk, but there it was; I badly needed more background.

All this was Special Branch stuff, I'd never been involved in that side of the company.

'No. We have nothing. But any rebuilding he's undertaking is going to cost money. He may well be open, therefore, to another approach from his previous benefactor.'

Is this information I should've known, I wondered. Was that why he'd looked startled?

'That's true,' I said, trying to put it all together, wanting to know a lot more about the role you had played as 'investor' and 'benefactor'. For a moment I recalled Rigold's face when he said how much he hated the undercover stuff. He'd tried to turn his face away to cover up his feelings. The Rigold from my world did not have to deal with this; there was no Tate where I came from. No taint of espionage. I remembered my fear, in those first few hours, that Evelyn was part of some kind of undercover plot.

'Offer him whatever it takes. Ten or fifteen million, the same open terms. A lot depends on how far he's got with the device.'

I nodded, as if I understood.

'And if we can't buy him off?'

'I get back on the plane a disappointed man.'

Somehow I couldn't see that happening.

When I walked through the door, Timmy was on the floor with his Lego and Evelyn was in the kitchen with beautiful cooking smells all around her. I might have been doing this all my life.

Evelyn kissed me brightly, if a little briskly on the lips, 'Let's have a good meal, darling. Look, I bought your favourite sauvignon, picked it up from the supermarket for only twenty-four dollars. That shark at Wine Supplies was charging us thirty-five.'

She handed me a glass.

'Don't look at me like that, silly. You know I don't hold things over. At least, I try not to. So you were a shit and we had a row, then you were a shit again and I threw you out of bed.' She gave a practical shrug. 'Only twice in one day. How are you?'

'I'll live.'

'You're Mr Cryptic these days.'

That didn't need any answer but a raised eyebrow. I grabbed a quick quote from Descartes, just to keep me on the philosophical alert' I couldn't afford to miss any clues. I found one you, I assumed it was you, had heavily underlined.

At the same time we must confess that all things which are represented to us in sleep are like painted representations which can only have been formed as a counterpart of something real and true...

As I read this, I wondered if Evelyn and I would make love that night. I was ready for it. Somewhere along the way I'd made up my mind. Thinking about it almost banished all thoughts of Kober and his 'device'.

The meal was excellent and the wine matched it. A thirty-five-dollar wine tastes as nice at twenty-four. Timmy smiled at me. Evelyn was making a visible effort to save her marriage, which suited me fine. Evidently you were worth one more turn of the domestic wheel, or was it something in me she was responding to?

Reprieved for the first time since I'd arrived, I felt like one of the family. Cautiously I let myself relax. After dinner I read Timmy a story and got involved in it, deciding, as much out of torpor as cowardice, to put off the confrontation over the money situation until the following night. After all, it had gone on for this long, it could go on for one more night. One more twenty-four or thirty-five-dollar of wine. *C'est la vie.*

The story was about a boy on a magic horse, one that spoke

to him, giving him necessary advice. He had to pass through dangers and temptations, overcoming various obstacles, to get to where he wanted to go, because he was really a prince although he'd been brought up a peasant. Timmy enjoyed himself too, nodding with approval as the story unfolded, identifying heavily with acts of virtuous heroism.

I tucked him into bed like an old hand, making sure that Teddy was snuggled up close. As I kissed him goodnight I wondered, with a twinge of guilt, why I hadn't done more of this with my own Timmy.

Reluctant to let the glow of dinner fade, Evelyn and I sat on the couch and had an after-dinner sherry.

Evelyn was at her best. Alert, graceful, full of good humour. That long, fair hair that fell down her back, clinging to her shoulders, shone with a magical light. We laughed and joked and had a second sherry. I was courting her and she knew it, while at the same time, I did a tolerable job of becoming someone she had known for years. With nothing older than two days at hand to talk about it was a temptation to tell her about Jerry Tate and the Kober device. It was such a temptation I gave into it after the first taste of sherry; I knew she'd like it and she did. At the mention of Kober's device, which I told her I couldn't tell her about – true enough since I hadn't a clue myself – she put her finger up to my lips. I stopped talking to inhale the scent coming off her hand.

''You've done this before, haven't you, this kind of work?'

'I can neither confirm nor deny…' It suited me, this whiff of mystery.

'Naturally.'

'But this is a straightforward negotiation. I'm empowered to offer some crank inventor a most remarkable deal.'

'Which he's sure to turn down because he'll turn out to be

a paranoid who believes an international conspiracy is out to suppress his invention. He'll look to the faceless men behind you…'

'… and find Jerry Tate.'

'Exactly. CIA or SIS if ever there was one. Special agent from hell.' She was having a great time.

'You're frightening me,' I said. 'And I don't even know what SIS stands for.'

'I'm frightening myself,' she said, putting down her glass. 'I don't like the sound of this Tate.' She slipped off her shoes and absently scratched her ankle. I indulged myself in a moment's admiration for that slender foot. Perhaps you and her often did what we were doing, which was to take evasive action and divert an explosive domestic row into the machinations of the oil industry. Maybe this was how she'd built up her knowledge.

'You see, I shouldn't have told you. I should have stuck by the manual.'

'A person like that could be very dangerous.'

'Nah,' I said, remembering the young hero in Timmy's book. Then again, he'd had a talking horse to guide him. I didn't have a horse of any kind. 'I'm just the errand boy. Pick a local. It adds a touch of verisimilitude.'

'Vera who?'

'Vera Similitude. She looks exactly like the real thing.

'What does she look like, Harry?'

'She's got long black hair as lustrous as a raven's wing. And she's got hairy nipples too. Which I like to suck.'

'Christ, you're crude.'

I chuckled crudely and tweaked her wriggling toes, just to prove her point.

'You're not supposed to tell me about this,' she said, delighted, removing her foot from range. 'This guy Tate would not be happy to know that I knew.' She kicked off the other shoe, got up quickly and walked around, which was something, I was learning, she liked to do when she was thinking hard. 'You are breaching security like crazy. I wonder why.'

'That kind of secrecy goes against my marriage vows,' I said lightly.

'What? What are you saying?'

'To be of one mind, one heart. One being.

'Am I to believe what I'm hearing?'

'In other words, Lady Beautiful, I don't want to lose my marriage.

When I said this she was standing by the ranch sliders that opened out onto the deck, looking lithe and sexy. She turned and gave me a piercing yet coquettish look, then went out onto the deck. I followed her. The atmosphere was sluggish. Although the air looked clear enough, the humidity was still high and the sky ached to rain. A tricky wind was pulling here and there, whisking back and forth as if it was unsure of which way to turn. A few freckly stars were out.

Quietly, she said, 'Do you know what you just called me?'

'What?'

'Lady Beautiful.'

'Oh.'

'How long has it been?'

I tried to give her a complicated look, as if I didn't want to remember.

'Are you now saying that this Kober business is what you've been hiding from me?'

'I didn't say I'd been hiding anything.'

She stood with her hands on the railing, peering out. She appeared to be silently interrogating herself on some profound inner question. I was moved by the honesty of it. You had yourself an amazing woman here, you fool, why did you fuck it up?

And where was I in this? Busy falling in love with her? Emotionally, too, I had to stay solvent.

She moved closer to me and took my arm. 'And am I Lady Beautiful?' she said.

'You are Lady Beautiful,' I agreed, my body trembling as if I were taking marriage vows, repeating the litany.

'And this is living happily ever after? This is what it feels like?'

'This is what it feels like,' I said, glancing around at the world, 'to live happily ever after.'

Gently, she took my hand off her shoulder. 'Not yet, Harry,' she said. 'We've a little way to go.'

The first kiss had been sweet. The second, I knew, would be sweeter. Her fingers lingered on my arm. 'I know you're trying hard, darling. I appreciate it.' She stroked my arm lightly enough to bring the hairs up.

We were lying in bed face to face talking in the low, intense voices lovers use.

'Of course,' I said, shifting back a little. There was no way I could push this, no way of forcing the issue. I had to take this at her pace entirely.

She clung to me for an instant, turned over and snuggled down to sleep.

I resigned myself to another tour of the ceiling.

Later I came to with the sensation of a hand pushing down on my chest and images of Evonne and my life with her flashing through my mind so fast I could not dwell on them or derive any comfort from them. No foothold upon these sliding images. I could reach out and put my hand right through them, and I wondered who could confidently divide memory from dream. It was like casting the first stone.

My previous life was a wheel of enfolded images spinning like a cog uncoupled. I was the one who had to change gear, and was unready. Not a prince born a peasant, I was a company man, reincarnated; and now that I was confronted with the ultimate duality of life I didn't believe it. I secretly believed I was mad. It was the only way to make it all commonplace.

Madness might be a letdown, but it would also be a wonderful excuse. It would domesticate the truth, socialise it satisfactorily.

I pushed against the invisible hand that was pushing against me, fighting for breath like a man having a heart attack, and had some made thoughts. Perhaps I can't sleep in this universe. That's the one big hitch. I can live here but I can't sleep. If I go to sleep I stop breathing. When I stop breathing I have a panic attack. The third night now. A person who can't sleep is like a drowning man who can't come up for air.

Every time he opens his mouth the sky disappears.

I made myself sit up, open my eyes and steady my breathing. The world stabilised but did not completely settle into its old, familiar configuration. There was a grainy effect to everything, as if matter had become faintly attenuated. The bed, the door, the hanging mirror, the gently sleeping woman by my side, all were there, in place, but at one remove, as if I were seeing everything through a very fine gauze.

Then I really saw Evonne, not just a hectic, sliding image but a steady series of frames. She was walking from the door towards the bed and she was crying. This was no memory, I was sure of that. It was really happening. What the hell had you been doing to her?

When Evonne reached the bed she stared down at me. Then she started to say something but before any words made it to the air she had dissolved into the darkness.

It seemed possible then to get up and simply step through

the fabric of this world and into my own. The feeling was so strong I got up and tried it. As I moved through the room, however, the fabric of the world retreated from me. I was only a step away.

Always only a step away.

4

Heading for the Harbour Bridge the next morning, I scanned the lanes for a glimpse of the Ghia I had seen two days ago. There was nothing. Perhaps I'd been mistaken. The shape of the bonnet, the glint of a grill. Endless curved metal. The circular logic of exits and roundabouts infiltrated my thinking. I had always assumed that it was the bits at either end of the motorway, home at one end and work at the other, which were important – but what if it were the other way around, what if home and work were mere appendages and it was this endless stretch of road which was central, the only constant reality?

There were idle speculations. What my mind was really dwelling on was Evelyn's kiss, the promise of its sweetness, and of Evonne walking across the bedroom, tears running down her face.

Mary Delany came sweeping into my office as if it were hers. I liked the big, forthright Irishwoman. Everybody liked her, especially the boss, for she could work like a draught horse. The image was her own. 'My ancestors were peasants,' she said once. 'They knew how to work. They worked like draught horses. In fact they kept working even when the horses fell over.'

Everybody liked her and that's how she'd got to where few women get – upper-level management. She exuded a warmth and big-heartedness that carried everybody along with it, especially clients, right up to the dotted line. She'd sealed more deals than Pepsi could shake a stick at.

'I've been talking to the boss about Canada,' she said warmly, giving me the straight eye-to-eye as she always did. There was no bullshit about Mary Delany, her stare informed you. Here was a straight shooter.

'You too?' First Cranner yesterday, to soften me up, now Delany, to make it official. By the time I met Rigold tomorrow there'd be nothing much more to do than shake hands, and Rigold was good at that, good at working through other people – something Harry Blackman had never quite mastered, which was why I was Harry and Rigold was the boss.

'You look tired, Harry. You've got bags under your eyes like drift nets. Pupils like flasks of plutonium.'

'Thanks. I need all the support I can get.'

'Been working too hard?' she clucked sympathetically. I thought you were a five-o'clock-out-the-door man.'

There was welcome refuge in this genial, workaholic banter. Everybody boasting about how hard their nose was to the grindstone compared to everybody else's. How wasted they were from working. Workaholics are different from other addicts in one crucial respect, they are inordinately proud of their addiction. There is no Workaholics Anonymous because everybody is too busy getting on with it.

'Well, I've got a heap of loose ends to tie up here before I can think of going anywhere.'

She nodded. 'The transtasman order, for one.'

We grinned at each other. We both loved to hate the quarterly transtasman order.

'So what's the burden on the Aussie deal this time?' I gave

a martyred sigh.

'Do you want my apology in triplicate, Harry, with a copy for the boss? He's got a pin in me over this, but Domestic's in a mess. Nobody knows if the Australian drought will drive consumption up or down. Martin is doing a night class in chaos theory and keeps blabbing about the sensitivity of initial conditions and its effect on the data outcome. Change one tiny variable at the beginning and end up with a massive outcome change at the end. It's called the butterfly effect, have you heard of it? A butterfly flapping its wings in South America causes a hurricane in the Pacific. There's Hildegard for you, waiting to strike. Data curves shoot off in all directions. Now Martin's got me going cross-eyed over spreadsheets. Which set of data would you like? Choose your own initial conditions. Aristotle's out; the price of oil is going to go both up and down. Demand is going to both increase and decrease.'

She spoke at full volume, flapping her hands around turning butterflies into hurricanes.

I played quiet to her loud. 'Then we'll just order what we usually order, and beef up some of the specials.'

'Good old steady as she goes. When you can't see anything fly blind.' Mary Delany shook her head in despair. 'The boss'll start to wonder what he's paying me for.'

No he won't, I thought. Pepsi knows exactly what the company's getting for its money; right on the interface between the stats-and-data crowd and management, Delany could pull common sense out of the most obtuse data gubble. Talk about being abundantly endowed with good sense. Most of the time, she liked to complain, to be one of the boys. Hide her brains behind Irish bluff.

'I tell him I'm spying for the IRA but he won't believe me. I don't think he knows who the IRA is. I think he thinks it's the tax department or something.'

We both had a laugh at Rigold's expense. I thought that if I had to tell someone of my predicament, she would be the one I'd choose. But I quickly changed my mind, almost before the thought was tabled. Whatever she may seem, Mary Delany was the company's creature, just as Harry Blackman was. The fact that I was tempted to tell her, to trust her, showed how beguilingly dangerous she was. Mary Delany was one of those people who could make you feel at home, making you think they were interested in you for your sake only.

'And how's that beautiful wife of yours, Harry?'

'Beautiful as ever.'

'I bet she is.' Her smile was all warmth. It made me feel like someone special. 'I don't know how she does it.'

'Are you going to ask me if she still plays tennis?'

'I didn't know she played. Why?'

'Cranner asked.'

Mary grinned. Suddenly she looked tired too. We were all tired; cheerfully killing ourselves with work under the grinning tutelage of Pepsi Rigold. 'Don't let them get to you, Harry.' Her voice was heartfelt.

'I won't.'

'Maybe Evelyn would like to go to Canada with you.'

'I'm sure she would. But she's had her trip this year.' I hoped that was true; Evonne had had a trip in my universe.

Mary waved away the detail. It was a gesture full of largesse she'd learned from the boss. It spoke of inner knowledge and imperial dispensations. Not a problem. Anything for you, Harry.

We left it there, and sorted out the details of the transtasman deal. Working through this sort of nuts and bolts, logistical stuff, she revealed a mind as organised as a beehive; it's a pleasure to work with someone like that.

She's carried out her orders, I decided, whatever they

were, and she was too clever to allow me to see that. Besides, I hadn't fooled her for one minute – she knew; not consciously (she might not have been able to put it into words), but she knew nevertheless. She hadn't got to where she was by letting people fool her; she always knew who she was dealing with. Her judgements were swift and accurate. My face was an open spreadsheet to her.

When she left, bright and breezy as ever, I slumped in relief.

Worse than Cranner, a million times worse than Cranner.

The obsessive, vainglorious strains of Ravel's *Bolero* came pumping down the narrow, pink stairway, mixing with the hoarse, guttural sounds from the porn parlour below; the effect of a symphony in a slaughterhouse. I pushed on upstairs, deeper into the music, looking for nonexistent door numbers, humming along with the familiar theme.

I hammered on the door several times before the music faded. The door opened and I looked into a pair of deep-set eyes and the tangle of a thick beard.

'Professor Kober.' I tried not to make it sound like a question, assuring myself that the professor could hardly be more difficult to deal with than Evelyn, who must have known a lot more about *you* than Kober did.

Kober looked annoyed. 'I do not have any girls here,' he said, his voice heavy with German inflections.

'Professor, it's Harry Blackman.' I took a deep breath. 'We have spoken before.'

'I do not remember,' he said firmly, shutting the door in my face.

More likely doesn't want to remember, I thought, knocking on the door again. 'Professor Kober,' I called against the rising tide of lust and music behind me, 'I am here to offer you some money.'

The door opened a little. Kober didn't smile. He looked like a man who had over the years learned, painfully, the cost of trusting people. He poked a finger into his beard. 'Are you from the motor industry?'

'Not quite.' I gestured to the dingy pink hallway. 'Can we talk inside?'

Kober might have said no; he almost did. When I got inside I found an office and foyer space filled with computer gear, some of it half unpacked, and other gadgetry. There was a faint smell in the air, like charred timber.

'The oil industry. You must be from them.'

'Professor, I work for an independent research unit in what we now call the energy industry. Yes, I am attached to an oil company, but our interests extend far beyond oil.' He grunted and sat down on the end of a packing case, looking dejected. 'Even here,' he said gesturing to his meagre office, 'they catch up with me.' He spoke a correct, if lugubrious, English.

Although it wasn't an issue I wanted to push too hard, I said, 'Professor, we have met, before the accident ...' I left it hanging, hoping he'd fill in a few gaps for me.

'I'm sorry, Mr...'

'Blackman. Harry.'

'Some things I forget after the accident. But it doesn't matter. I cannot accept your money.'

'My offer will be open and unconditional.'

Kober looked at me with a scepticism bordering on loathing. He pushed himself off the edge of the crate and pointed to a sheet of paper on the wall. His voice was tired as he read the typewritten text.

'I must furnish those who would protect or save life with an energy source which produces energy so cheaply that nuclear fission will not only be uneconomical but ridiculous. This is the task I have set myself in what little life I have left.

'These words were written by the great Austrian scientist, Viktor Schauberger, in 1946, when he was approaching the end of hope, as I am now.' Kober spoke with great reverence and melancholy, addressing the words on the wall, rather than me.

'Did he find the energy source?'

'He had already found it, Mr Blackman. He found it by observing the movement of water.' He lapsed into silence. 'It was there for everyone to see.'

'And what is the principle behind it?'

Kober produced his first smile, the smile of a teacher who is about to pull a trick on a credulous student. He raised a finger. 'Schauberger said, "Nature is not served by rigid laws but by rhythmical, reciprocal processes."'

I wandered to the window and looked down at the seedy daytime aspect of the red-light district where Kober had doubtless rented the cheapest rooms he could find. Faintly, from below, came the seesawing sounds of another kind of rhythmical, reciprocal process. When I turned around, Kober had gone back to his work, taking no notice of me.

'Every natural force has its counterpart,' he said.

'How do you apply the principle?'

Kober picked up a circuit board and looked at it bleakly, its soldered landscape apparently an anathema to him. 'Surely your people have briefed you. And you say you have spoken with me before?' He looked up at me with sudden curiosity.

'I like to hear it from the horse's mouth,' I said.

'The horse's mouth,' he repeated, and I wondered if he knew the idiom or if he was laboriously trying to derive a literal meaning for it. Again the ghost of a smile, recalling a long lost sense of humour. 'And I am the horse, yes?' He picked up another widget and inspected it. It was a piece of pipe with some intricate grooving on the inside. 'Then the horse will put it like this. There is a reciprocal process to gravity that our science knows little of, although it is the reason why trees can grow to great heights, above the reach of capillary action, and why springs can appear at the tops of mountains, gushing with great force...' He lost himself, and his sentence, as he contemplated these wonders. 'Schauberger knew all these things,' he assured me as I doubted it, his finger back in his beard again. He handed me the widget.

'What is this counterforce to gravity?' I took the widget and weighed it in my palm; the grooves on the inside made spirals. It looked like a tricky piece of engineering.

'Our science has no name for it; it is a levitational force.'

'Anti-gravity,' I murmured – another old sawhorse from the nutter brigade. I looked up from the widget to find Kober watching me as if he knew exactly what was running through my mind.

'My generator,' he said proudly, 'is a modified anti-gravity device, an implosion motor which works by setting up as oscillation between gravity and this levitational force.' He pulled another package from the rubble. I thought he turned away from me to keep me from seeing the passion in his face.

Now I understood why somebody like Tate was interested in Kober.

'Professor, have you a working model?'

Kober looked at me then as if I'd just come into the room and he'd never seen me before. He gestured to the mess around him. 'I have another day's work, Mr Blackman, before I am ready for the first test.' He sounded resentful, as if this were my fault. 'Much work.'

A test of a new model after six days? I wished I knew more about this damned accident.

Pulled to one side of the window and tied with a ribbon was

a lace curtain which had been there for so long it looked as if it might fall to dust if breathed on hard enough. 'I'm sorry to interrupt you, Professor, but I am here to offer you help, if I can.'

Kober started working with the martyred stubbornness of one who had heard such offers before. 'I wonder how long it will take you to destroy me,' he said.

I didn't finish with Kober until five-thirty and, having no need to return to the office, slipped into the Vulcan Lane bar I'd noticed the day before to ring Jerry Tate on my cellphone in a quiet corner.

'He hasn't turned me down flat,' I said. It's taking time to gain his trust.'

'Does he have a machine?'

'He does. Don't ask me how he's managed to get it together so fast. He's running the first test tomorrow. He's going to let me watch. That's a big step forward.'

There was silence at the other end. Finally he said, 'Did you see the device?'

'No.'

'And Kober himself?'

'I don't pick him as a hoaxer.'

'Neither do I. Please continue with your approach.'

Struck with sudden curiosity, I said, 'What do you think of this reciprocal process he talks about, generating power by using levitational energies?'

There was utter silence at the other end.

'I mean, he's contravening the Law of the Conservation of Energy, surely.'

'Harry, what does Kober claim the machine does?

'Generate electricity. No more, no less.'

'How?'

'By utilising rhythmical, reciprocal processes. You have to read your Schauberger.'

Surely, I thought, Tate must know all this, and much more, otherwise why come here to offer him all that money? Was Kober throwing me a fast one on the nature of the device?

After making my report I went up to the bar. The barman raised an eyebrow at me. 'The usual?' He shuffled me a brandy-laced coffee. My counterpart's done this, I thought as I handed the money over. This is one of his haunts I've discovered. If I wait around long enough I'll meet his buddies. Jesus. The other Harry must have sat here, fretting, probably over the accounts, making resolutions, trying to peer into the future. Trying to juggle Evelyn in one hand and money in the other. Doing dirty work for people like Jerry Tate.

Your life. Superficially like mine, yet so different.

Despite the leavening effects of the sugar, brandy and cream, the coffee was still acrid, poisonous to the taste. I put the cup down and worked the taste out of my mouth. Instead of going so hard at keeping up appearances in this world, I could abdicate from it. Strictly speaking, it wasn't my world, my wife or my debts. They were yours. I didn't owe any loyalty to Evelyn, not personally. Or her Timmy. A few days ago I didn't know of their existence, so by what imperative was I now required to carry the can for them? No imperative. No moral bonds could hold me since the principle of free choice, the basis of moral obligation, had been violated; I didn't ask to come here. Care of Evelyn and the child was *your* joy and obligation, not mine. It was someone else's life. Someone else's car. Somebody else's home.

These arguments had a flaw, and the flaw was that Evelyn wouldn't see it that way. Nor would the boss. Nor the banks. Nor history. No one would doubt that this was my can to carry.

The law would see it that way too.

The coffee was down to a few oily dregs. Around me, with its architectural hints of Europe, Vulcan Lane also pretended to be somewhere else. At that moment I saw Cranner walking up High Street earnestly talking to someone, a man dressed in a dark, executive suit. Taller than Cranner, he was inclining his head and listening intently. They vanished before I could identify him, but I was sure I knew the figure.

I was still puzzling over it when I found a folded piece of paper in my pocket and opened it.

...Join the Guerillas of Goodness, the underground movement of senseless acts of beauty...

I went on to read that a man in Portland, Oregon, puts a coin in somebody's expired meter. A woman pays a tollbooth fee for half a dozen cars behind. Somebody else slips money into a proud old lady's purse. A bunch of people descend and clean up an old couple's house.

... let us transform the world in a deluge of random kindness and senseless acts of beauty!

Returning on the Northern Motorway, tuning into the latest on Hurricane Hildegard, which was finally making up its mind to swing our way, I saw the Ghia again, the one that looked like mine. This time it was peeling off an exit ramp and I had a clear view of the car but not the driver. It was the same, well kept, almost immaculate. Almost, because there was already a film of dust over the vehicle, taking the sheen off the paintwork.

There is a subtle degradation or coarsening of effect in Evelyn's world, I thought as I crept with all the other snails up the clogged lanes of the Harbour Bridge. Like the wilful neglect of the Ghia Serenissima. Like the state of Harry Blackman's accounts. Even the approaching sunset had a garish aspect, a ruddiness I'd never seen before. I knew this was due to massive winds in drought-hit New South Wales ripping off topsoil and hurling it into the air, swirling it our way courtesy of the approaching hurricane from the north – but this rational knowledge didn't help. This universe was starting to feel different. It had a different shape, with different corners, an inner light that made space go hollow. It wasn't just Evelyn; it was Cranner, Delany, the boss, Tate, Kober with his weird and wonderful machine – everybody.

Fuck them all, I thought, zooming down the other side on an arc of lights, and derived great comfort from it.

After putting Timmy to bed I sat with the chequebooks, the account books and all the relevant bills and talked to Evelyn. We were on the couch together, sitting side by side. She faced me, her feet tucked cosily up under her.

I had decided to be very quiet and reasonable, not to raise my voice, not to get angry, but simply to point out the facts. There is a terrific, brutal force in facts. She was a practical woman, she would see that. And after our wonderful dinner the night before, I was sure we had the basis to reach agreement.

In a quiet, reasonable tone, I pointed out the weaknesses of our finances. 'We have to look a little more closely at our expenditure,' I said.

'Like what?'

'Well, I don't know. Let's go through the chequebook and see what all these sums are for.'

I pointed to the bank statement to show the sums in question.

'Is this the Inquisition again? Is the court in sitting?'

Placidly, I said, 'It's just standard budgeting practice. It keeps us in touch.'

'If it's so standard, how come we don't do it every month?'

'We should, and we have to start.'

'Why? What's different?' She picked up the chequebook and thumbed through it like a book in a second-hand book store, putting it down again as if deciding not to buy.

'Because I think we're in over our heads.'

She shook her head sadly. 'Harry, what the fuck are you laying on me now? You know that we've both been through and approved every item relating to the new house. We made out a list with the prices, remember? We agreed to every step. The bank put up the money. You knew how deep in we were getting. Why didn't you say something at the time?'

But I had anticipated this, and had devised the perfect answer, one she would find hard to refute. 'Because I was an idiot.'

She was not impressed. 'What the hell does that mean?'

'It means I didn't see the total picture. I didn't realise how big it was all going to be.'

In one swift movement Evelyn was off the couch and pacing, slapping the chequebook up against one hand. I had to admire her lithe movements, the predatory sleekness of her body. 'Listen, Jacko, we went through all that. The prices, how they would escalate. We did worst-case scenarios. We did bail-out scenarios. You went through it all with Peter Coveny. We couldn't lose, you said. When it's finished, the house will be worth at least one and a half, you said. Even if we have to turn around and sell it immediately, you said, we'd still make a cool half.' She shook the chequebook as if some clue might fall out of it, some large cheque perhaps. So what's changed?'

'I want to bail out.'

'That's no answer. What's changed? Has the company knocked your bonus or something? Have the company shares fallen?'

'No, no, nothing like that.'

She walked over to the table and picked something up. It was a drawing Timmy had done showing a house with Lego walls. There were two adults inside, so big their heads were cramped up against the ceiling. 'Then what is it?'

'There's nothing new. It's just all come together in my mind, that's all.' I wondered at how defensive I sounded, and how quickly I'd lost the initiative in this conversation, undermined again by my ignorance of your past actions. 'Look. Whatever we said yesterday, it's the reality of the current situation we have to deal with. I'm the guy who gets the bills. Let's check the accounts. Do a review.'

How is it that it was difficult to do with the efficient Evelyn what Evonne and I would have done in five minutes?

She said, 'Sure, sure, we'll look at the accounts, but I just want to know one thing before we start.' She put the chequebook down on the table.

'OK.'

'What's bugging you? I mean, is there any particular item?' She looked to the reclining buddha, as if he might have the answer, and ran a casual hand over his serene shoulder.

'Well for a start, Coleman's bill is astronomical.'

'Keith? How come he's Coleman all of a sudden? Keith, as you know, is in no hurry for his money.' Her voice became very chilly. Coleman was a raw nerve. Why?

'Everyone is in a hurry for their money, sweetheart.'

'Don't patronise me, Harry, or I'll break something expensive over your head. Like that vase with those flowers.' She stood in the middle of the room, her hands straight down by her sides.

'Forget-me-nots.'

'Don't kid yourself.'

I made sure my voice was quiet and reasonable. 'OK, so let's go through the chequebook.'

Somehow we got into this thing, her and I. It was like a game lying in wait for us as soon as we opened our mouths; a bitchy, flip, backbiting, wound-scratching, point-scoring, lose/lose dialogue that we slipped into, some old familiar groove *you* and her must have built up over years of neglect and carelessness. You must have found, as I was finding, that it is much easier to slide into this mode of relating than it is to get out of it.

Still, when all was said and done, I had a point to make.

Going through it item by item was a painful process for both of us. Virtually every item was met with the same refrain. You agreed that one. You saw that one. You picked that one out yourself in preference to the cheaper model. We took Keith's advice on that one. You told me to buy the light fittings when the specials came up.

Finally we came to an item which was *yours*, fifty-five dollars marked 'entertainment' on the cheque stub. 'What's this? Evelyn said, pointing to the stub. 'Beers with the boys? A cocktail or two with your girlfriend?'

'There isn't a girlfriend.' It was hard to keep a touch of impatience out of my voice. Somehow, because we needed to go through this simple, rational exercise, I was losing all the ground I'd gained the night before. She was acting as if nothing had happened the night before, no sweet kiss, no brief clinging. We were miles away from that now.

'I do know what an accomplished liar you are. And I'm not sure what the hell's got into you or why I'm sitting here going over items we already know are there. Christ, we could tick them off the statement in five minutes without grinding through this routine.'

I saw that from her point of view this was perfectly correct. I was the one learning things here, and what I learned appalled me. This monstrous buying spree was all part of an overall design, each purchase relating to that conception and therefore indispensable. It was a meticulous profligacy, and it galled me to see *your* hand in the very fastidiousness of some of the details. It was as if you had set out to block the very chiselling exercise I was now trying to carry out. All the angles were covered, and the whole setup was heading straight for bankruptcy. You had, with characteristic precision, set the controls for financial suicide. Why? Was some huge windfall on its way?

'What do you want to do, Harry? Stop Timmy's music lessons? They are very expensive. Shall I stop buying feta at seven bucks a throw? Are you telling me you're not going to have any more scotch or sauvignon? Or blow fifty bucks on your girlfriend? Fifty-five, sorry.'

I put the chequebook aside, got up, wandered across to the mantelpiece and stared at the vase with the now drying forget-me-nots, perceiving their delicacy and remoteness; even in death they were like tiny stars with white cores. They were a living metaphor, a tangible manifestation of Evonne's reality. A reminder of the days we had spent when we first met, how serene and high we'd been, making love all over the place, on beaches and lonely roads, in the back of cars and people's bathrooms, and how she would leave a spray of wild flowers by our bed every morning.

'Harry, look, you've got a face like a funeral. Let's invite Keith around for dinner on the weekend and we'll talk it over, review the whole plan like you say.'

'Now who's patronising?' I said. This woman was a stranger to me, she only thought she knew me, yet here she was talking the way a mother talks when she's buying a child off with sweets.

I wanted nothing more than to go home.

"You're so touchy, Harry. I'm only making a suggestion

and Keith's been in on this from the very beginning.'

'I know. I've got the bills to prove it.' I picked up the vase and turned it around. It was certainly Evonne's. 'Did you put these in here?'

'Who else? And they didn't cost a thing.' She clapped her hands together and rubbed them. 'Chris, you make me want to smoke. And forget-me-nots are my favourite flowers, if you've not forgotten.'

My skin jumped. They were Evonne's favourites too. It was the only tangible link between the two women.

'Where did you get the vase?'

She glanced at it with indifference. 'I forget.'

We went to bed soon after that, but there was no wonderful bedroom scene in the offing; the chequebook had seen to that. We were thoughtfully abstracted from one another. I wanted to tell her about going to Nelson to see Vernon, but decided to put it off for a more propitious moment when the question of money didn't hang between us like the sword of Damocles.

Evelyn fell straight into an exhausted sleep, which is what I should have done. Instead I saw a ghost. It was Timmy, my real Timmy, walking across the room from the door towards me in his striped pyjamas, standing by the bed and looking down, not so much sad as puzzled, as if he did not know his own father. I wanted to call the boy's name but my throat was frozen up. Timmy turned his head slowly to look at Evelyn. It's all right, I called out in my mind. It's only a dream, you can go back to bed.

Solemnly, as if he'd heard, the boy turned his back and walked across the room, vanishing somewhere near the door. Silently, so as not to wake Evelyn, I cried. In my weeping I began opening doors. The doors looked bulbous due to the tears, and the rooms were all empty except for a door closing just ahead. I was a child and my feet wouldn't carry me fast enough. The person just ahead must be Vernon who would surely stop and turn around and come back to me, gather me in his arms and hold me as close as the world.

There was no sleep, so I got up and sat in my chair and read Descartes. Again I was drawn to remarks you, I presume it was you, had underlined, and the mystery of the Descartes volume struck home to me. It didn't fit. It wasn't you. It was a different order of anomaly because it didn't fit in with the picture that was emerging of you as a man, estranged from your wife and your finances, adroitly manoeuvred by others at work. A guy on skids.

I shall then suppose not that God who is supremely good and the fountain of truth, but some evil genius not less powerful than deceitful, has employed his whole energies in deceiving me; I shall consider that the heavens, the earth, colours, figures, sound and all other external things are naught but the illusions and dreams...

The sentence had not finished but I had run out of concentration span. Of course, Descartes didn't have to believe in his evil genius, he was just presuming one for the sake of argument. To prove a point.

I wished I had that luxury.

I got up from my chair and took a walk outside.

The night was restless and muggy when I hit the street. It was all blue and black, but there was, faintly visible, an undercoat of red from the city lights. There was a niggardly, dissatisfied feel to the wind as it flipped the leaves around and scuttled some paper along the dry gutters. Tiny flecks of rain raced about me searching for somewhere to land, and I could hear the air dragging heavily through the pines on the peninsula.

I turned downhill towards Crocker's Store to have a look at the new flowerbed. Sure enough, there it was, exactly as Sam Walsh had described it, built into a crappy part of the verge. The flowers were pansies; pretty, tame and domestic. And thoroughly inoffensive. Only the most bloody-minded local council or police officers would rip these up and put the grass back.

As I looked, a few raggy clouds pulled away from the moon and the scene was set in silver. Feeling the moon on me, like a spotlight, I sensed I was being observed. Someone in the shadows. I knelt and ran the moony earth through my fingers. It was light and friable, perfect for flowers, not the heavy clay that belonged to the district. It'd been brought in bags, in a truck.

The plot had been freshly watered.

I walked slowly, casually, back towards my own house, stopped under a tall red pine by the upper flower plot and looked around at the hanging darkness of the houses, trying to spot my observer.

'I know you're there,' I said aloud, feeling foolish.

'Good Lord, is that you Harry?' A figure detached itself from the shade of a fence across the road and walked over to me. It was Sam Walsh. He did not particularly pleased to see me.

'Couldn't sleep,' I said with a little laugh. 'I thought I'd come and have a look at your garden plots.'

He paused, considering this. Gravely he said, 'I'm surprised you want to talk to me.'

'Why wouldn't I want to talk to you?'

'I mean after last time we met at this hour. I may be a lonely old man, as you said, but that doesn't mean to say I have no pride.'

'Of course,' I said placatingly. 'I'm very sorry. Life hasn't been that easy for me, either.'

'After all, Harry, I know very little about you, your financial or domestic situation.

'I was hoping we could let bygones be bygones.'

'We shall. Don't think this is all easy for me. I was a man of action, a doer. I was never one for sitting around talking about things. While others were talking, I was out getting things done. That's why I like this flower-planting business. It has all the hallmarks of a well-executed commando operation, behind enemy lines as it were.'

'That's a curious way to look at it.'

'You need a soldier's eye. Anyway, I was saying, old age has brought no comforts. I had to watch my wife die an agonising death from cancer, then watch my own health begin to slip. I've reached the age at which we lie awake at night and live in our memories, and I don't want that. It's not as if I have a string of glories to look back on.' He gave a short laugh.

'No shame in that.'

'Exactly!' The word came out as a bark of triumph, as if he had just proved a profound line of argument. He held out his hand. 'Apology accepted.'

We stood for a while longer in the dark, talking about the mystery of the flowerbeds. With no stars to guide the night, it was impossible to tell what time it was.

The wind and the night went on and on without end.

5

The light poked in around the mirror-glass towers. Denuded of its brightness by the darkened glass of our own tower, the light looked pale and alien, incapable of warming anything.

I was in Pepsi's office and he was talking to me in a chummy, buddy-buddy way. This was his soft, genial mood, which I knew to be his most dangerous. He had fired people, roasted them or put them on ice, careers had been made and broken with that good-natured smile, that soft, friendly voice.

Cranner was in the room too, and he was not smiling. He was looking out the window which showed nothing but other buildings and the sky. His face was in neutral, conference mode. We're sky people, I thought, sitting hundreds of metres in the air talking of far-off things, our faces as solemn as totems.

Mary Delany followed, fully in her role as the boss's chief whip. She wore a grey business suit with the padded shoulders of the female executive of the eighties. She smiled briefly at me and sat down.

The boss was watching me with friendly, twinkling eyes. 'Tell me about Evelyn, Harry. I haven't seen her since the last staff party.'

'She's doing fine. Running around spending money hand over fist.'

Rigold chuckled and took a sip at the brown, bubbling liquid in front of him. 'That's what wives are for, Harry.'

Cranner smiled to himself. All very well for him, since he didn't have a wife.

Delany snorted with derision. 'You can't let him get away with that one, Harry.'

Rigold went on. 'Well, we've got the Canadian trip coming up. Maybe she'd like to go along and spend your money over there.' The boss, who'd been leaning over his desk, still in greeting mode, now sat back, swung his chair around and appeared to join Cranner looking out the window. He wore his 'we're-just-thinking-along-together' face. In the distance a helicopter circled a high-rise, making a halo above it.

'It's not her turn yet. She had a trip last…'

'It's a freebie. Must be a computer muddle. He winked. 'I'd just take it and ask no more questions.' He took a file casually from his desk and leafed through it, much the way Evelyn had done with the chequebook the night before. 'Anything new from Maritime?' he put the file down again. At the mention of Maritime I saw a swift glance pass between Cranner and Delany.

'McBride rang yesterday.'

'What did he want?'

I hesitated. 'He's talking about crewing with Slavs and Russians. It looks shady to me. I'm glad we're sticking with Poseidon. Going with Maritime would have created big problems for us in Canada.'

The silence spread out through the room like whipped cream over a sponge cake. Pepsi pulled out a sheet of paper and handed it to me. It contained a few brief calculations. The derived profit was underlined. It was in the millions.

'You're going to do it,' I said.

Rigold nodded and took a swig of his Pepsi. I looked around

at the other two.

'You can't argue with a profit like that,' Delany said.

I wondered, desperately, where *you* had stood in all of this. McBride had made it sound as if you and he were great buddies. Had you anticipated this shift, because I hadn't; in my world Maritime was a maverick, outsider outfit, not to be trusted, and I didn't think that had changed.

I glanced down at the file that Pepsi had opened earlier. My Canada brief. I knew immediately what I'd have to do there, now that Pepsi was prepared to double-cross the cartel. Nearby, Cranner shifted uneasily in his chair. Mary Delany had gone very still. The boss motioned him to get some coffee and Cranner hastened to obey.

'You want me to lie to them,' I said, putting the folder down. 'Big Bill, Uncle Tom Cobbly and all.'

Rigold nodded cautiously. Cranner poured the coffee. Standing behind Rigold, he gave me an I tried-to-warn-you look.

'Why me?'

The boss's voice was very soft. 'Because they know you're a man of integrity. They trust you, and they've dealt with you for years. They know you are as good as your word.'

'Not for long, once they find out.'

'Why should they find out? McBride's not about to ring up Big Bill.' He took a sip of Pepsi and sank back into his chair. 'And what if the cartel does find out?'

'If Lexon gets a whisper of this before Canada, Bill'll blow the whistle on us, of course, and we'll be in horseshit up to our necks with the cartel. If he only finds out afterwards…'

'Yes?' said Rigold encouragingly.

'He might keep quiet. Someone might start asking why he didn't think of it first.'

Rigold nodded and smiled. 'That's about what I figured too.'

It sounded as if he had figured a lot more besides. I could see the delicate balance within the price-fixing cartel breaking up into a morass of secret deals between us and shipping companies. But there were dangers in being the first to break ranks; the Pepsi I knew was a more cautious man that this.

Cranner gave me my coffee and I blew across its surface, playing for time. Here was further evidence of a subtle difference between my home universe and this more bloody-minded one. In my universe the crisis within the oil cartel had not quite happened this way, I was sure. Here a different card had fallen on the table and my number was on it.

'It's not going to be easy.' I was thinking of the people I'd have to meet, the hands I'd shake, the spouses I'd smile at, knowing I was lying to them all. Playing the fraud. I knew these people. They were friends; they'd wined and dined me. We'd bonded over beer and blackjack at the casino.

The boss nodded sympathetically. 'You'll have support. Cranner will be along with you, and Evelyn of course.'

Cranner nodded in my direction.

Oh yes, Cranner would be there. There to keep an eye on me and make sure there were no slips, to nod and wink at the right people behind my back because certain people would have to know I was lying, that was all part of it; Cranner would be there at my elbow, the shadow man. And Evelyn would be there at my other elbow to ease me through the unpleasantness as only a woman can, which was why Mary Delany was in the room now, mentally holding my hand; Harry Blackman would be the sacrificial lamb while the boss, and everyone else, scrambled to cover their asses as the cartel fell to bits.

I looked up, realising I'd been staring at my coffee for a shade too long. The boss was looking at me, and he was not smiling. The twinkle had gone from his eyes.

'None of us like it, Harry,' he said.

As we were clearing up the loose ends, I casually mentioned the Nelson trip. Vernon.

The boss was immediately on the alert. He raised an eyebrow as a way of saying – family matters? I met his eye and nodded. He wanted me to signal if this was some kind of code for the Kober Project but I kept a poker face. I could keep Kober up my sleeve.

This interchange was not lost on Mary Delany, who was now watching me closely. She was unerring when it came to this body language stuff; it made me sweat every time I told a lie with her around, and even the truth could give trouble sometimes. I'd found a way of holding my hands so they didn't move. I was sure she knew it.

'It's been a long time since I saw him. He's getting on.' I gave the appearance of not wanting to give too much away.

'I think it's a great idea,' Rigold said, keeping it hearty, keeping the twinkle going. 'Relax before the Canadian trip. Before the staff party.'

'What about me? I'll be carrying his workload,' Mary Delany said. 'Why should he have all the privileges?'

'Because I'm going to be shot at dawn,' I said. 'I get a blindfold if I want one.'

The room was quiet. A look of delight flitted across Cranner's face. A very swift look passed between Rigold and Mary Delany.

Then Rigold laughed a rich, burpy chuckle. 'You're right of course. But it's not quite kamikaze. We'll have you right back in the negotiating field next year, Harry, believe me, we'll front you right back up again. They'll respect you for that. They'll know who they're dealing with. And, you don't have to do this, Harry. Nobody is indispensable. You can pull out now with no blame, no shame. I think I speak for all of us here.'

Mary Delany and Cranner murmured in agreement. A ghoulish litany.

Rigold spoke sincerely, he probably meant what he was saying, but I didn't believe it and nor did anyone else. Except the indispensable part. If I refused this I'd become a lame duck, I'd get passed over for everything, cut out of all the real action. It wouldn't be long before I'd be kicked sideways, downstairs even. Rigold had no time for deadwood. Nobody was indispensable.

Smiling, I said, 'I'll settle for the trip to Nelson.'

Rigold sat back, apparently relieved. He swigged from his glass and beamed around the room.

'We're going to clean up on this deal,' he said.

Professor Malcolm Kober looked like he hadn't slept for a week; there was a grey hue around his eyes. For a moment he didn't recognise me.

'You said you'd be testing your machine today, Professor...'

Along with recognition came resignation. 'Ah, yes, Mr Backmann...'

'Blackman.'

'Quite so. Who sent you?'

'We talked about this yesterday, Professor.'

He looked tempted to pretend not to remember our meeting. 'You are the man from the oil industry,' he said without enthusiasm. So he remembered me from yesterday, but not from *your* previous visits.

'I'd love to see your machine in action.' That thawed him enough to get me in the door. 'There's a new wave of thinking in the energy industry which strongly suggests we align ourselves with the new technologies, I said. 'My interest in your machine is *bona fide*, as is the offer of support.'

'I'm sure it is – how much were you offering?'

I shrugged. 'Five million, ten million, whatever it takes...'

'So simple,' he said sarcastically, leading me across the room, which had not grown any less chaotic, to a side room I'd not noticed the day before. There was a large, black egg supported by a scaffold of steel wire, sitting in the middle of an otherwise empty room.

'How do you generate the levitational forces?' I asked, hoping to sound knowledgeable enough to ask a good question.

Kober stared at his machine with the sullen ecstasy of a mad inventor. 'It circulates water at very high speeds through helical whorl pipes,' he said slowly, as if to a recalcitrant student. 'I followed Schauberger's lead and based my pipes on the shape of a kudu antelope horn, a cycloid-spiral space-curve.' He didn't look at me but spoke to the machine as if telling it what to do, and pulled at loose bits of his beard.

'Water?' I'd heard of motors which separated the hydrogen from the oxygen of water and burned the hydrogen. 'Do you burn the hydrogen?'

'I burn nothing!' Kober snarled, as if we'd been arguing for hours and he had finally lost his patience. 'It's so typical that you think of explosions all the time. Always something must explode! It doesn't work unless it goes bang! This is an *implosion* machine. Have you ever seen a waterspout? Pictures of one? Generating enough power to pick up trucks and whirl them in the air like bits of straw? That is a vortex. This is a vortex machine. His outburst apparently exhausted him for he simply went across to the machine and picked up an ordinary electrical extension cord, plugging one end into the wall socket, holding the other in his hands. In quieter tones he went on, 'I set up a centrifugal-centripetal dynamic, which imparts a double spiral motion to the water. The water becomes supercool and supercondensed, and a vacuum is created. When you add certain colloidal catalysts to the water, magnetic polarities may be converted into bioelectric and electric power by creating dynogens, a result of negative friction.'

'Negative friction?' Now I knew he must be crazy. You couldn't put water through pipes at high speed without running into friction. Negative friction would result in a net gain of energy.

I decided to take the professor on. 'You can't manufacture energy, you can only change it from one form to another. There's no such thing as a free lunch.'

'But of course that's not true.' He looked quite outraged at the idea. 'That's just a stupid thing people say who think they are worldly wise.'

'Why isn't it true?'

'Because the whole universe is a free lunch, Mr Backmann! I mean the Big Bang. The sudden release of unimaginable amounts of energy. A free lunch to end all free lunches. And you know something, Mr Backmann? The Big Bang was not an explosion but an implosion! All those dimensions collapsing in upon themselves. *That* created the universe!'

'I can understand that,' I said a little hastily. 'But how does that relate to your generator?'

'You can do it at high enough speeds, if you direct the flow of the water away from the walls of the pipe towards the centre. Energy is pulled in from the quantum dimension.' He gestured apologetically to the power lead. 'We don't really need a starter motor, Mr Backmann, you can crank it into motion like your old Model T Ford, but I don't feel like cranking.' He threw down the power lead and drew, from underneath the machine, a crank handle such as you might use for a Model T, and flourished it in front of my face. 'Perhaps you would like to try,' he said with heavy mockery, pointing to a small slot in one side of the machine.

'Why not?' I said, surprising myself, and taking the crank handle. I recalled that the Ghia, being based on an old 1960s model, had the same shaped crank-handle hole beneath the radiator. I had always imagined it was just for decorative purposes.

As I approached, instrument in hand, I saw that his device was small enough to fit under the bonnet of a modern motor car – a silent egg, made of black alloy.

I fitted the crank handle into the hole and gave it a couple of exploratory turns, meeting a satisfying resistance. There was something there to turn over. Feeling foolish, I gave it a hard twist, with a wry grin to Kober, letting him know I was aware of the absurdity of supposedly setting in motion a post-modern energy machine with a welded piece of nineteenth century tooling. There was a whine and faint hiss and nothing more. Kober nodded encouragingly. 'Try again,' he said, raising bushy eyebrows into the oddly clear, line-free spaces of his forehead. I gave a couple of hard cranks and there was a higher whine, a slushier hiss – and something caught.

The machine began to vibrate. It became a great humming egg. Suddenly the humming changed, taking on a deeper, more meaningful tone. Ceremonially, I gave the crank handle back to the professor.

'It's on full power now,' he said, throwing the crank onto the floor. The machine continued to hum. He indicated some dials. There was an output gauge showing that the machine was generating eighteen horsepower. He was staring at me now, watching carefully for my reaction. 'All I need is money and complete freedom to work,' he said.

'You have them,' I said. 'No strings attached.'

He shook his head sadly. 'Ah, Mr Backmann, there are always strings attached. You would kill me with your kindness.'

All the time he was speaking he was watching me out of the corner of his eye, trying to gauge my reaction to the still humming egg.

'Call me Harry,' I said, trying to ignore the egg.

'I don't want to,' he snapped irritably. 'I don't want to get on familiar terms with you.'

'You are in a catch-22'.

'What do you mean?; The beard bristled with its own free energy.

'Anyone with the kind of money you need will want something in return.'

He rubbed his chin with a thumb and forefinger up against the grain of his beard. 'Of course you are right,' he said. At the same time he kept looking at me sideways.

Then it hit me. The machine had not stopped humming. In other words, it worked. I put my hand out and touched the surface. There was a faint vibration but no heat. Of course it worked. Tate wouldn't be here if it didn't. That damned humming unnerved me as he knew it would. It was the sound of the death of the oil industry.

'There is water inside, travelling at four times the speed of sound through graduated vortexes,' he said softly. 'It produces ten times more power than it uses.' He waited for this to sink in. 'That's a ninefold gain.'

He knew I believed him, he could see it on my face. 'Who sent you?' he said. 'Was it one of the Specials?'

'Who are the Speciais?'

'You know them when you see them, Mr Backmann. They are after the patents for every energy device ever conceived. They blink their eyes at regular intervals. About every thirty seconds.'

It was time to laugh. He laughed too.

'Now get the hell out of here,' Kober said with infinite

weariness.

His wondrous black egg went on churning out power.

Without asking, the barman at the Vulcan Lane pub handed me over my special coffee. At least I had something to thank *you* for.

My eyes loitered across the shop fronts and doorways. I'd lived in this city for nearly twenty years and these streets were built upon familiar patterns of thought as much as on solid ground. Buildings changed, businesses opened and closed down but the underlying pattern remained the same, or changed only very slowly. Now, however, the familiar scene of the streets filling up after work as the office towers and shops emptied was no longer reassuring, and behind the constant bark and honk of the city there was an unpleasant grinding noise, like metal scraping along concrete.

My insight that this universe was a coarser version of my own, even though it might look the same, had been vindicated. This everyday appearance, Rigold slapping me on the back, Mary Delany making Irish jokes, cars going back and forth, Kober laying a black egg, was a charade, a pretence at authenticity; and behind the pretence was a malignancy of purpose, some unholy laughter, if I were not mistaken. With no doubt that the joke was on me. Surely my own universe had not contained little green creatures in tree ferns or bizarre conspiracies in the energy industry; it was these little garish touches that gave the game away, whatever the game was. For lack of a proper explanation, I'd conceived of two universes, and had invented a counterpart who'd lived in this universe and was now, for symmetry's sake, probably in the other universe, but these were just assumptions.

And, as Descartes says, we have nothing else to go on but our senses.

Maybe there was no other universe. Maybe Evonne and Timmy just disappeared to nowhere land, into the quantum foam, to be replaced by Evelyn and her Timmy. Some random fluctuation in the void. Some roll of the dice. This sort of thing might happen to people all the time and they never talk about it for the same reason I never talked about it. Too busy covering their tracks. Staying on red alert.

I plucked out my cellphone and called the number Jerry Tate had given me. His cool, rational voice answered.

'No dice,' I said. 'He's not biting. Not yet. But I think he likes me. I got him to laugh. Well, once.'

'Did you see the device?'

'Yes.'

'And what is your assessment?'

'It makes a nice humming noise.'

'Is that your assessment?'

'Yes. You'd have to take it apart with tweezers to really know. My impression is that it works.'

'And what does it do?'

'Nothing. It just sits there and hums, and according to the meters, turns out eighteen horse.'

'And the science?'

'You'll have to get his maths, and we both need to read our Schauberger. But as to negative friction, I can't buy it. Sounds like he's got a flying saucer in a bottle.'

'What is negative friction?'

Again I had to tell him what he already should have known. 'Yes, water,' I said as I finished up. 'At four times the speed of sound.'

'What does the machine look like?'

'A black egg the size of a small car engine.'

'Just hand him a cheque.'

'You mean…just give it to him, no contract, no nothing.'

'That's right.' His voice was impersonal, as if he had no particular stake in the outcome.

'For how much?'

'Let's say fifteen million. I'll have it made out for you.' How cool can a cucumber be? Fifteen mil!

'Would you like a receipt?'

This touch of sarcasm was lost on Tate. 'That's not necessary,' he said, 'but leave it for a day or two. Let him settle. He's got expenses to face.'

'I'm sure he has.'

Tate put the phone down and I did the same.

The coffee tasted like a cocktail of toxins. I walked out into the endless street. Home, I thought, I'm just one step away from home.

At home, we all played it so quiet you could have heard a pin drop. Everybody was being extremely polite, even Timmy. I sat on the floor and played Lego with him while Evelyn sat quietly under the benevolent eye of the reclining buddha, reading a book. Timmy had put together some remarkable looking Lego creatures to inhabit the Black Knight's castle and I immersed myself in these, remembering how as a child I would make paper creatures to inhabit strange places and colour them in laboriously with crayons. It was an ancient memory. Each creature had created its own place.

At first the boy was quiet and self-absorbed, slowly becoming more talkative when I did not go away and ended up explaining everything. 'This is where this one eats,' he said, pointing. 'And it has legs to walk on.' I tried to set it upright and walking but one leg was too short. I pointed this out to him.

'I know that, Dad,' he said, placing it carefully in a spiral staircase in the castle where, as a stair climber, the short leg fitted perfectly.

Teddy gave me a friendly wink when I put Timmy to bed. You're coming along fine, it seemed to be saying.

As we sat up in bed that night, I told Evelyn about the Canadian trip, the Maritime decision, and the lying I would have to do.

''They're getting you to pass the dummy,' she said, brushing her hair in long, steady strokes, 'while the real ball gets passed somewhere else. What do you think happened in Jakarta last year?' Her voice, still tinged by the chequebook aftermath, was faintly contemptuous, as if she was only reluctantly talking to me at all. Her hair flowed down over her smooth, still untouchable shoulders.

'Jakarta was completely different, Eve-, Evelyn.'

'What were you going to call me?'

'Nothing. A word play. Look, in Jakarta everybody was watching everybody else, for Christ's sake; the big deals hadn't gone down yet, you know that. Big Bill had spies behind every pot plant.'

I said nothing. There was thin ice everywhere and, it seemed, the longer I was in this universe the thinner it became. Sooner or later I'd make a mistake I wouldn't be able to cover for, and fall right through. I'd say something and there'd be a silence and that silence would never end.

She finished brushing her hair and leaned back against the bunched pillows, took my arm and stroked it. 'I asked Keith to come around tomorrow, if that's all right,' she said. 'Do you still want to bail out of the house deal?'

'Yes, but I've got an open mind.' I hated giving myself an out but prudence dictated it. Everybody needs an escape clause. Besides, if I wasn't going to return, ever, to my universe, if my exile here was permanent, I had to make my peace with things as I found them. It was a depressing thought. At the back of my mind I had imagined that I'd see Evonne again, now I was not so sure.

'Good,' she put her arm around me. The tip of her breast touched my chest. 'Are you sad?'

'I don't spend enough time with Timmy.' I tried to put Evonne out of my mind.

She looked at me in amazement. 'You're telling me that? All you company men are the same. Sixty hours a week and buggered.'

'Fifty-five.' A weak joke was in order. The last thing I wanted now was a row. I was too lonely to fight. 'It's for you and Timmy that I do it.'

I'd had similar conversations with Evonne, which usually ended at this point, particularly when Evonne reflected that she was the major beneficiary of all these hours of work, but Evelyn pressed on; she knew a good argument when she saw one.

'Are you sure about that, have you thought about it?'

'No.' This was true. I had taken my motivation as self-evident and had never questioned it, nor imagined that anyone else would. Least of all my own wife.

'I think you're happy that Timmy and I benefit from your work,' she said carefully,'but I wouldn't say that's why you do it.'

'What would you say is the reason?'

'Habit. Obsession.'

'Obsession? Fuck...'

'You've been with the company for over fifteen years, Harry. You're a company man, and you'd be lost without it, as you well know.'

The words rang in my ears from my afternoon talk with the boss. A Company Man. The honour and the shame. The invisibility. Like a bug getting squashed. I gush out of myself; my pathetic bit of surface hardness and adaptability, protection and defence, crunched in the process. A Company Man. His heart drives him out of himself and he can't get back in.

'Oh I know there are corporate women like Mary and secretaries and so on but let's face it, it's a man's world you go to out there. It's men making their deals, pissing on their boundary lines. You love it, and you're good at it.' She hugged my arm. 'Remember how we met, all the to-ing and fro-ing around the boardrooms. Keith finding us in the bathroom. Quick fucks in the lift.'

I nodded, apparently with appreciation, and put my head on her lap as she stroked my hair, just as Evonne might have. If I closed my eyes I could imagine that it was Evonne. A warmth came up off her body, and a smell like kitchen spices.

I lay awake the whole night holding her sleeping hand.

Keith Coleman was a small, bouncy man tending towards the portly, with a fringe of hair around a balding dome and sporting a ridiculous looking goatee on the end of a wagging chin. He wore brown corduroys and a polo-neck sweater that might have been trendy with left-wing intellectuals in the 1950s, and his conversation was peppered with dated literary references. Under his arm he was toting the predictable bottle of French wine.

He was, all in all, the kind of person I detested, and had to wonder how you could have got yourself in so deep with him.

'It's the ennui that links Sartre and Camus,' he was saying to Evonne as he popped the cork on the red. 'The dissipation of the left and the right wing. Their common accord in despair.'

Didn't he realise this was a new century, people didn't talk about Sartre and ennui any more; they talked bout Chronic Fatigue Syndrome and homeopathics, or they danced until they dropped. They didn't talk about despair or grief but about depression and Prozac. Or they didn't talk at all, because they hadn't formed the right neural pathways. Coleman's line of conversation must have been old when he was young.

I noticed, too, that he seemed quite familiar with the layout of the kitchen and found the wine glasses without any fuss. 'That wonderful sense of fatigue. *Fa-ti-gue*', he said slowly, giving the French its proper pronunciation. 'I'd quite forgotten it. Current writers just can't match it. They're much too frenetic.'

Evelyn smiled. It looked as if she had heard this speech, or something very much like it, before. I saw the fatigue around her own mouth, the sudden sense of weight in her body. She's not finding this any easier than I am, I realised.

I tousled Timmy's hair and he went off to bed. 'Goodnight, Dad,' he said, giving me a sideways look as he went through the door. I'm building up some sort of relationship with him, I thought. A bridge made of Lego pieces. The Black Knight's castle.

Evelyn put Timmy to bed and Keith and I were left alone in the lounge over the French red, which was being allowed to breathe.

'He's a fine boy,' he said. 'You have every reason to be proud of him.'

I acknowledged the remark with a smile, noting that now Evelyn had left the room the trendy architect had become uneasy, rubbing his chubby hands together and smiling too much. Suddenly he said, 'Evelyn says you've been having some doubts about the house.' He fiddled with his empty glass.

'Have one of our reds as a warm-up,' I said. 'We've got an Australian claret here that does justice to Oz.' I poured the wine. 'Not the house itself,' I said, realising that I was going to have to cover for an awful lot of ignorance on that score.

'I've no quarrel with the plans. I think Evelyn might have got you here tonight on false pretences, Keith. It's not the design or the concept. It's the money. I'm rethinking the whole commitment.'

Keith Coleman nodded. 'Of course, you must do that. Everything else on course, I trust?' He'd dropped his literary flourishes and now spoke in the brief, practical language I understood, and I was forced to appreciate that this ridiculous man was an astute and wealthy businessman with more than a casual interest in half the building projects in the city.

'It's the long-term financial commitment and the depletion of our reserve,' I said, annoyed at having to explain myself at all and wondering just exactly what he meant by 'everything else' being 'on course.' I was reminded of McBride's reference to legwork.

The architect sipped appreciatively at the wine and smacked his lips in an absurd fashion. 'Thank you.' He put the glass down and grew serious again, even expansive. 'It doesn't have to be a long-term commitment, Harry. In three months that place will be completed. There'll be nothing like it in Australasia. I've got clients flying in from Sydney who'd look at a proposition like that. I mean if everything else fails...' He paused to look at me keenly but I put on a poker face. I was starting to get good at this. He meant something specific by 'everything else.' It was a signal of some kind, and he was probing for a response. 'Everybody's looking for a little slice of paradise,' he finished up when I said nothing. Was there not, perhaps a touch of ennui in his voice? 'Property's still booming. At least the top end of the market.'

'I appreciate that, Keith.' With a sinking heart I realised how much in the grip of this man *you* had been. It was not going to be easy to shake him loose; after all, he had a stake in this too, a stake in my money. All the beard wagging and red wine in the world couldn't hide that.

'I want to live in it for six months before we sell it,' Evelyn said, coming back into the room. Just looking at her you could see her in *House & Garden* magazine, gracing the swimming pool, flirting with the mobile stove unit in a sparkling kitchen or draped across a suite in the lounge. Keith Coleman gave a Latinate shrug of helplessness. His manner changed completely; his beard jutted out in an absurd fashion and he was once more the intellectual phoney, stuck around 1962. Or was it '52? Perhaps Evelyn had that kind of effect on him. He turned to me and quoted. 'All women born are so perverse no man need boast their love possessing.'

'You always were a misogynist, Keith,' she said dryly. 'Now let's pour the good red.'

We were halfway through the meal when it all fell into place for me. The red had proved unexpectedly good, a result no doubt of the price Coleman had paid for it. A wry little red, I thought after the second glass. Then the penny dropped. I saw what I should have seen a lot earlier, and nearly spilled a glass of the precious red all over the lily-white tablecloth.

Keith Coleman was Evelyn's ex-husband.

6

The following Monday, on my way out to find some lunch, I saw Evonne.

There was no possibility of a mistake. She was coming out of Deka with that distinctive sloping walk she had when she was in a hurry, and pushed right by me without recognition. Her hair was being dragged at by the toughening wind. I followed her to the bus stop and, after a moment of waiting, got onto the same bus. I hadn't been on a bus for years and it made me feel like a child going off to school. I remembered sitting at the back, watching the girls get on, not saying anything, just watching.

I didn't sit near her but further down the back, and numbly watched the city roll by. Then I saw Cranner waiting on the curb by the traffic lights, talking to a dark-haired woman who glanced up idly as the bus went past, a moody, withdrawn look on her face. Behind her a newspaper headline read 'The North Battens Down.'

I got off when Evonne did and wandered towards a shopping centre close behind her, glad there were a few others around to help mask my clumsy trailing. She turned into a driveway right near the shopping centre. I lingered for a while then approached the ordinary, somewhat ill-kept house. It had the look about it houses get when the owner is struggling to pay the mortgage.

She answered the door. It was her all right. I could see the clothes strewn down the hall behind her. I knew an Evonne mess when I saw one.

'I'm very sorry to disturb you. The land agents gave me this address.'

'Which land agents?'

I gave her a name.

Evonne looked puzzled. Behind her a little boy of four or five appeared. 'I don't think Alec's put it on the market,' she said with a little giggle, happy to reveal possible ignorance of her husband's plans. The little boy stood back and considered me gravely. Like our Timmy, he had Evonne's eyes.

'Well, it's not a bad house,' I said.

'You were on the bus, weren't you?' As it always had, her light, friendly voice put me at my ease. Evonne was remarkable in that she did not judge people. Her face was frank and open; she always approached people in a receptive, sensitive mode, which was what she was doing now to me, a stranger.

'Yes, the agents sent me from town.' I didn't have to pretend to be embarrassed. My voice was trembling.

She laughed then and held her brown hair back off her forehead. She was Evonne in every respect except one; she did not know me. I wanted to throw my arms around her and hug her tight and scream with relief. I wanted to swing her round and dance and laugh and shout. Above all, I wanted to pretend that this terrible nightmare was over and that this was Evonne and I, somehow, just as we had always been.

A young, female voice called from inside. 'Who is it, Mum?'

'A man who thinks the house is for sale.'

'I'm Harry.'

She smiled. 'I'm Evonne,' she said.

There was a movement from inside and an astonishingly

pretty young girl appeared. She was what Evonne might have been like at fifteen, only taller and more solemn, with dark gentle eyes and a wide, full mouth.

She looked at me dispassionately. 'Come inside, Timmy,' she said to the little boy.

I said 'I'm sorry to have bothered you.'

Evonne smiled, full of sympathy. 'That's all right. Would you like to leave your phone number? I can ask Alec when he comes in tonight to give you a ring.'

I hesitated. I had a picture of Evelyn picking up the phone and talking to 'Alec.'

'Dad's not selling the house, Mum,' the gird said reprovingly, not looking at me. 'No way.'

Evonne was looking at me with compassion. I remembered that there had been lots of lame-duck characters to feel sorry for, and now I had joined their ranks. 'I do think the real estate people have got it wrong,' she said, sounding as if she would sell the house to make me more comfortable if she could. 'I'm sorry you had a wasted trip.'

As I turned away, the girl gave me a hostile look. 'Get a life,' she said.

It was a long wait at the bus stop. Long enough to remember how, when we met fifteen years ago, Evonne had got pregnant. There was no question of us having a child at that point and Evonne had the pregnancy terminated. Afterwards she cried every night for two months, almost the exact length of time the pregnancy lasted, as if she'd had to mourn every day in reverse.

Now I had seen just who she had been mourning.

Cranner gave me a brief, curious look when I walked into the office an hour late. I winked at him. Let him wonder.

There was a pile of stuff on Sophie's desk relating to the

Canadian trip, including tickets, insurance forms and the like which I shuffled through without enthusiasm. Among them was a plain envelope with my name on it. I peeked inside and found a cheque made out to Professor Kober for fifteen million dollars.

'Call for you today,' Sophie said. 'Mason from Lexon.' Her voice was as cool as an iced shandy.

I stood by Sophie's desk, not moving. It finally struck me that I couldn't come into Evonne's life, not in this shit-faced universe. No way. No way forward or back. No way to finally obliterate the bubble of isolation in which I had been trapped since my first moment here. All I could do was breathe. Just stand by Sophie's desk and breathe.

I did that until Sophie grew restless, then went into my office to ring Mason at Lexon. This call could be the beginning of a play by Big Bill, Mason's boss. I could hear my heart in my chest; that necessary double thump. No way, it kept saying, no way.

'Busy preparing for Canada?' Mason said, coming onto the line.

'Who are you guys sending?' I said, knowing full well. I picked up a pen and tapped it idly against my notepad, wrote down a series of random numbers and put a circle around them.

Mason's flat, harsh voice came down the line. Haven't your spies told you? I'll be going.' He would be there, in the back rooms where the price-fixing deals would take place, illegal deals, since they contravened the anti-monopoly laws in most countries. And I would be there, double-dealing behind his back with Maritime to undercut the very prices he was in process of fixing. I would have to lie to Mason's face at these meetings and I was not looking forward to it. Mason had Big Bill's ear and was very keen to justify the privilege.

'Great. We can sit and get bored in one of those tinsel nightclubs Hamish will take us to.'

'Yes, and pretend we're enjoying each others' company.'

'I'll look forward to it.'

'Harry, have you heard anything about low crew wages? Like as little as two or three dollars a day?'

'Where? Give me their phone number.'

'This is no joke, apparently. Some of our union boys are all steamed up about it.'

'I've heard rumours.'

'I'm sure you already know this, Harry, and I assume you've worked out what it means.'

'The shipping companies are getting greedy.'

'Maybe they're prepared to lower their prices to us.

'Then maybe we'd better approach them.'

'After Canada. A united front.'

I began to sweat. Canada be damned, I was lying to Mason right now, making a deal I'd already broken.

'After Canada,' I confirmed.

'See you at the strip show,' Mason said.

A bump and grind routine from hell was coming up from under the pink stairway to Kober's room; a bunch of harpies being sodomised by creatures with leathery wings. My fingers tightened around the cheque.

I banged on Kober's door, trying to shut out the moaning of infernal pleasures. It sounded louder today, carried perhaps by changing internal draughts in this condemned old brick monstrosity of a building.

The door opened a crack and a slice of Kober's face appeared. A nose, an eye and a half.

'What do you want?' His German accent sounded a lot thicker today, as if he's forgotten English.

'Professor Kober, this is my last visit, and I have something for you..."

'I don't want anything from you, Herr Backmann,' the beard said. 'I know what is coming. I can feel this hurricane in the air. It is as Viktor Schauberger predicted, increasing volatility of veather patterns as a result of global varming.' The door opened a fraction further, and more face came into view. More words came out too, quotes from something he was reading from behind the door. 'Schauberger said, "In nature all life is a question of the minutest, but precisely graduated differences in the particular thermal motion within every single body, which continually changes in rhythm with the processes of pulsation. The slightest disturbance of this harmony can lead to the most disastrous consequences for the major life forms. It is vital that the characteristic inner temperature of each of the millions of microorganisms contained in the macroorganism be maintained.'"

I pulled fifteen million dollars out of my pocket and handed it to him through the crack in the door, noting that he looked a lot worse than when I'd last seen him. The grey had spread from around his eyes to cover his whole face; his lips were bloodless, his beard, a lifeless scramble of dull wires.

He gave the envelope a jaundiced, sceptical look. 'Ah, now comes the money. How much I wonder?' he opened the envelope and studied the cheque. A myriad of infinitely satisfying organisms floated up behind me.

'They are starting to panic, Mr Backmann. I know you are just their tool; you don't even know the masters you are serving. They know that they are losing control. They are growing desperate. Human control over natural processes, is the great illusion of fascism.'

So saying, he tore the fifteen million dollars into tiny, useless little bits of paper not worth their space in the garbage bag. A noble gesture or a petulant one – take your pick.

Annoyed, I said, 'What makes you think you are so right about everything?' The professor seemed to need a humbling dose of Cartesian doubt; I was sick of standing in this dreary hallway talking through a crack in a door.

'For a person who lives a hundred years in the future, the present is no surprise, he said.

And shut the door.

After work I didn't go to the Vulcan Lane pub but to the London Bar further uptown. Like Vulcan Lane, the London Bar was also pretending to be somewhere else, but that suited me fine. So was I. In the anonymity of the place I could imagine myself back in my old world. I could forget about Kober and all the rest of the nonsense.

It hit me, with the first tart shot of scotch and soda, that seeing a real, live, flesh-and-blood Evonne earlier today was altering my memory of her and my Timmy. Laid over this memory was an image of the new Evonne, who lived in an unkempt house with the beautiful daughter she and I aborted and a boy named Timmy. Yet another Timmy. Three Timmys. Two Evonnes. One Alex.

Seeing her had placed me at one remove from the memory of her. In some way my retreat had been cut off. I downed a second drink and was heading for the door when a short, busty woman caught me by the arm. She was pertly dressed, a little florid in the face, which was rounded and full, and had a thickish, prominent nose. She looked as if she worked in one of the offices nearby.

'Hello stranger. You been hiding out?' her manner was mildly flirtatious and she had a way of looking straight at me that made her seem taller. Her throaty voice had a North American tinge and her eyes were big and limpid.

'Hello stranger yourself.' I glanced towards the door.

'You're not running off, are you Harry? Come and I'll shout you one of those horrible scotches of yours.' She waved a vague see-you-later to a group of people at a table.

As we sat down the woman gave me a faintly roughish grin. Her eyes were dark brown and prettied with long black lashes. Her gaze was direct. 'Come on Harry, don't stare at me like that. Have I grown antennae?' She laughed a little too hard and I saw she was somewhat drunker than she seemed. Her hands moved nervously on the table top and her foot jiggled in sympathy.

'Evelyn might be jealous,' I said. 'Me drinking in bars with strange women.'

Her face flushed. 'Thanks, Harry. The earth moved for me too. A little bit.' Her voice had a dusty, smoky quality.

I was suddenly gripped by the urge to tell this woman, with whom you appeared to have some sort of casual friendship, the whole story. I was possessed by the sudden notion that if I told someone in this universe what had happened, I would change it. Like uttering a spell. A counterspell. Send this phoney reality back to where it came from. It was something to do with the truth, which has the quality of a magical utterance, capable of banishing hobgoblins, foul fiends and false universes.

So, risks and all, I told her. I recapped evens from the moment I returned home to find a strange woman there who said 'What's that, honey?' from the kitchen, only missing out the bits relating to my week. When I had finished there was a long silence as she toyed with her glass.

'Does this mean that you don't know who I am?'

'That's right. I've never seen you before.'

'You don't even know my name?'

'That's right.'

'And you're telling me all this shit.'

'That's right.'

'Well fuck you then,' she croaked, getting up and walking away from the table. Her brown hair, cut to just above the shoulders, swung firmly around her neck like a curtain between her and my face. 'Good one, Harry. Thanks a lot.'

'Wait a minute,' I caught her by the arm. 'How do you explain it?'

'That's easy.' She didn't sit down. 'How much booze do you put away, Harry?'

'Not much at all,' I said automatically.

'That's a matter of opinion,' she said, shaking my hand off her arm. 'You've been blacking out. Losing weeks apparently.'

'That wouldn't replace one family with another.'

'How would I know, you're the expert.' She gave me a bitter, disappointed look. It wasn't the best expression for that ripe, plmp mouth. 'I bet you haven't forgotten your deal with that guy, what's his name. Dorf or something.'

I looked at her blankly.

'Even in a blackout you wouldn't forget a cool half million, would you Harry? It would pay the bills. Always an eye for the dollar. You probably don't remember pumping me for info on the Telex deal while trying to seduce me at the same time.'

'No I don't.'

'Then you're riding for one hell of a fall. I don't want to be around when the pieces start coming down.' She started to leave again.

I leaned forward earnestly. 'Please, you're the only one who knows. With everyone else I'm faking it through. Tell me who you are and what sort of relationship we had. I mean, you had with the other Harry. Tell me everything you can remember about my counterpart – his life, his business, everything.'

She lowered her body to the edge of her seat. Suddenly

she laughed. 'Your counterpart? This is a hell of a con, Harry. Suddenly I'm supposed to believe you're Harry's twin brother from another dimension. Where's the punch line?'

'It's no con. Right now you're the only person in the world I have a straight-up relationship with.'

'Christ! Then you're in trouble.'

'I know it. Come on, I've trusted you.' I motioned to her half-full glass.

'All right. This is going to sound silly. My name is Julie Horton, I work for Image, and supply the computer network for your company. You and I had one of those flirty, hurty, almost on-but-never-quite-happened relationships, you know, we heard voices for a while. You were married. You wanted inside info from Image. I wanted everything. I was the younger woman and you were the mature man. That was before I became mature and you became more mature.' She laughed and looked beautiful. 'Wasn't I in this other universe of yours?'

'No.'

'Why's that then?'

'Who knows? Evelyn wasn't in it either.'

We talked on but Julie, it seemed, was getting bored with the subject. The game. She'd got sick of Harry's games years ago, apparently. This one had proved but a minor distraction. Her eyes kept roving across the tables and the doors and several times she greeted people with evident enthusiasm. She didn't know anything more about the Dorf deal and nothing about my home life. You had been uncharacteristically discreet with this woman. What should have opened up into an evening of confidences and revelations died its own death in half an hour. I was disappointed. The truth had done nothing but rapidly lose its novelty; the spell had not been banished; the enchantment, if that's what it was, had not lifted. It was not that easy to lever a universe out of its course, difficult moving a fish from its accustomed depth. It takes more than just a story.

She took out a packet of tobacco and rolled herself a cigarette with edgy motions. Then I remembered her. I remembered her rolling a cigarette with those same half-clumsy movements. In my universe, Julie Horton had joined Image eight years before, very much a junior in the office. I had spoken to her once or twice and had a drink with her and some others from Image. A year later she drowned in the rough surf on the West Coast and her body was found washed up on the black sands.

'Harry,' she said, getting up again when her glass was empty and the cigarette was alight, 'there's Crystal and Sue. I've got to run. Why don't you tell Evelyn about this? If you can tell me, you can tell your wife.' This sounded like a line she'd used before, with other men.

'If you can get me to believe it, she'll believe it. Wives want to believe their husbands.'

'And do you believe it?'

'No, of course not. Bye.' She gave me a quick peck on the cheek.

I finished my drink and left. She gave me a little wave from a crowded table as I went through the door.

Evelyn stroked her leg reflectively as she listened to my plans for visiting Nelson. I tried not to let that distract me from what I was saying.

I said, 'I want to see Vernon. Touch base with him.'

Evelyn looked at me with deep puzzlement; her fingers came to rest on her knee. She thought for a long moment.

'I think that's a very good idea,' she said at last in a quiet voice.

We were sitting on the couch in what was becoming our

regular after-dinner chat; sushi rolls and salad, superbly her style, were settling in nicely. Evelyn was dressed in a short dark skirt and simple white top, looking beautiful enough to make my heart ache with what felt like an old pain. Where does that pain come from? I wondered. And did I really want to run off to Nelson now, leaving matters with Evelyn unresolved?

'A break before the Canadian trip will do you the world of good,' she said brightly, lifting one knee up close to her chest and absently rubbing her inner thigh. 'And you're right. It is time you caught up with Vernon…' She was about to say something else but stopped herself.

'What were you going to say?' I said, suddenly curious.

She hesitated. 'It's just that…'

'Yes?'

'Well, you haven't shown a lot of interest in your father for a long time … why now?'

'Because now's the right time.'

She thought about that one too. 'You should go.'

I gave an inner sigh of relief; I'd expected pointed questions as to where the money was coming from, but that particular blow never fell. I thought of Rigold and his guarded support.

They were humouring me, I realised, and maybe that was a good sign. I needed humouring and good signs. I was bloody lucky my father was still alive and well and living in Nelson when, in this capricious universe, he might easily have keeled over from a heart attack years ago or some other horrible fate. Good old Dad. The rock in any age, any universe.

I played Lego on the floor again with Timmy who wanted to build a house, and found myself absorbed in it. It was such a simple universe, the Lego universe; it all fitted together and it all came apart. Everything was shiny and congruent; Timmy's house took shape to the dictates of a steady, binding logic, and there was a pleasing predictability of result. A pleasing neatness. It was a smooth universe with no chaotic, infinity-dogged edges. There was the Black Knight's Castle itself, with its clever drawbridge, which was the centrepiece of the action. There was a pirate den and a pirate ship and a cannon and lots of little men with Lego feet carrying swords and crossbows, halberds and banners. And there was the house Timmy was trying to build, one long wall shaping up in white. It was an ambitious project and Timmy was excited to have my help. He knew that Dad was really playing and not just doing time. At one point, when we'd calculated how many white bricks we'd need to get to the end of the wall, I glanced up to find Evelyn watching me curiously. I said nothing. Timmy was feverishly searching for white pieces, prepared even to dismantle the pirate den to find some for Dad. A moment later Evelyn vanished from the doorway.

The evening's story was about a peasant who had a very foolish brother. One day the peasant found a bag of gold and wondered how he could prevent his foolish brother from telling everyone. So he set up in advance a series of impossible situations, a fish in a rabbit trap, jam tarts hanging like fruit from a tree, and other such crazy things, the climax of which was the discovery of the gold. When his foolish brother, who took everything at face value, blabbed the story out before an inquisitive and rapacious noble, no one believed him. Who could take such a fool seriously? I liked the story and thought the peasant very smart. Timmy thought so too. He pointed out, however, that the smart peasant took a risk, for if the foolish brother had seen through the trick, and given the game away, the noble would surely have killed the smart brother for trying to pull a fast one.

'But that couldn't happen,' I said, amazed that a four year old could come up with such advanced literary criticism.

Timmy clutched his pillow and put it on his head. 'Why

not?'

'Because he's too foolish. He's the foolish brother. He's very silly, so silly he can't see through his brother's trick.'

'No one's that silly, Timmy said with deep scepticism.

I tended to agree.

Evelyn was still quiet when I came to bed. A book lay open on her lap, pen and paper beside her. 'I've never seen you like this with Timmy before,' she said as I stood by the wardrobe and took off my shirt. It was an ongoing embarrassment, this undressing in front of her, especially when I knew she was watching me, as she was now.

'I told you I don't spend enough time with him,' I dawdled over removing my shirt.

'You were like a child yourself in there, playing with him.

'The pirates were going to attack the castle, and, oh well…' I shrugged, and slipped off my trousers – oh so casual.

'Don't be embarrassed. It was beautiful. I'd given up on the idea of Timmy having a father. I mean, a father like that. Who would get down on the floor and play with him.'

I was shocked, but how much time had I spent with my own Timmy, in my universe? How often was I down on the floor with the Lego? Was I any different from *you* in that respect?

Naked now, I had no choice but to turn around, face her, and walk ever so naturally to the bed. My body is no mystery to this woman's eyes, I told myself. Fortified by this thought, I strode manfully to the bed and slipped boldly between the covers.

'There are absent fathers who still live at home, Harry. Neglect. Sons without fathers. Sometimes now without mothers. The sibling society, Tess calls it. You know, there's never any time to be with the kids.'

'Vernon was like that.' I propped myself up on one elbow, facing her impeccable shoulder which I could touch now, lightly, gently enough to get the silky feel of her skin.

'Too busy.'

'That's right, too busy to stop.'

'And when he did…'

'I was already gone.'

'There you go.'

I laughed. 'We've got it all wrapped up,' I said.

She laughed. 'Timmy's even building a house. Just like us.'

'I hadn't seen that! You're right. But I don't think he's got enough collateral in white bricks to get the end of the wall.' I stroked the arm nearest to me.

She grabbed hold of my hair and pulled it, pulled my head onto her chest, half crying with relief. 'God, Harry,' she said, 'I thought I'd lost you.'

'I've had a few full-on days.'

'I don't mean a few days, I mean years. Sure you kept coming home, but that's all. I mean, you were no father to Timmy and…'

' no husband to you.'

'Christ, Harry, where have you been, the man I fell in love with and who one day stopped seeing me? You know, really seeing me. And turned into a man who would fuck me without kissing me and walk right past his son.'

I kissed her collarbone. I was starting to cry myself, which might have been a good sign too. Somehow I was involved in this, in her feelings, as if I really had been with her for many years and had just rediscovered her after a long estrangement, an exile worse than banishment. I felt absurdly grateful to be holding her like this, smelling her skin and kissing her collarbone. I felt as grateful and as humble as all hell, for when we are loved we know, deep in ourselves, that it is not of our deserving but by the perversity of grace.

'Do you know something, Harry?'

'What?' My voice was muffled against her skin.

'It's been a long time since you've told me you loved me.'
There was a catch she could not keep out of her voice. 'I mean
really told me.'

I pulled back onto my elbow and looked at her. 'I love you,'
I said.

Deeper and deeper in.

As she went off to sleep, Evelyn cuddled into me from behind.
Her breasts rested against my back, and I could feel her body
all the way to the back of my knees. The light tickle of her
pubic hair against my buttocks. I lay awake with my eyes open
and my erection in my hand.

A faint crackle went through the air, like a touch of static
electricity. I thought I saw it, a wave that went through the
fabric of things.

There's someone in the house, I thought, slipping out of
bed. I stood for a moment, listening to the house breathe,
trying to discern the difference, then drifted to the door.

The passageway was empty.

But when I looked back to the bed I didn't see the peacefully
sleeping Evelyn. It took me a moment to understand what
I was seeing, because I couldn't hear anything. It was you,
fucking Evonne. It didn't look like lovemaking. She was
holding her knees up, close to her chest and you were leaning
back, slamming into her below.

This was no memory for I'd never done it like that, never
wanted to do it like that. I approached the bed on tiptoes, as if
they might hear me. There was such a triumph, fury even, in
the way you were pushing into her, that I sensed that this was
the first time. Surely Evonne would have sensed the change.,
maybe held you at a distance for a while.

Standing by the bed, I saw that Evonne had buried her face

in her knees and was rocking backwards to ease your access. You were staring down at her, dominant, grinning, in control, but she was not meeting your gaze. Her eyes were tightly closed, lips drawn in a tight rictus.

Suddenly you saw me, and threw back your head victoriously. You wanted me to watch, you wanted me to see what you were doing to her, it added to your pleasure.

I returned my gaze to Evonne. I reached out to touch her face but my hand passed right through her.

A single tear rolled down one check. I couldn't catch it.

'I've seen them,' Sam Walsh announced as we stood under the red pine at top of the drive, our backs to the wind. A thin moon fought against the clouds.

'Are you sure?' I was trying to forget what I'd seen on the bed. This vision, if that's what it was, hadn't faded until you had come; in fact it faded as your orgasm faded, leaving me standing by the bed, staring down at the sleeping Evelyn.

'They drive an old green Bedford. Can you believe that? Nothing wrong with the Bedford of course. We won the war against Hitler driving Bedfords.' He gave a short laugh.

'What happened?' Good old Sam and his dramas; he was a comfort to me tonight.

He tapped his head to signify a working brain. 'I realised I'd never catch them by hanging around these old plots. They weren't coming back to do any watering.'

'They probably keep well away from their old plots.'

He nodded vigorously. 'They may well do. Anyway, I went walking and got as far as Cavendish Street, which is about as far as I'd want to walk, when I saw this old green Bedford parked by the side of the road...' He stopped, pulled out a voluminous handkerchief and honked into it. 'I knew straightaway something was going on. There were maybe eight or nine of them. I thought at first they were breaking into a nearby house. Then I stood in the shadows and watched them. They were just packing up, throwing spades and bags into the back of the truck.'

'Sounds exciting.' I could see him peering through a bush at the phantom gardeners the way one might peer at lovers, dry mouthed and expectant.

'It was. And do you know something, Harry?' He looked at me, shyly at first.

'Tell me.'

Sudden hope flared in his eyes, like a man who's been offered a vision of angels. Everything except youth was in his face. Fiercely, he said, 'I wanted to go with them. They were doing things. They were having an adventure. I wanted to climb into the back of the truck and go with them to the next site. The next adventure. Instead...'

I looked down the sleeping street. Some stray headlights from somewhere momentarily lit the trees above us.

'Instead what?'

'I was just an old man watching from the shadows.'

'It sounds very self-pitying, Sam, when you say it like that.'

'Does it?' His voice was filled with grief. 'It doesn't matter which way you say it, it still looks the same. I've never envied anyone anything, but last night I envied those young people and their mischievous joy. I never realised what a horrible feeling envy is.'

'It's like jealousy.'

'You're telling me. I could hardly walk away when they left. My knees were so wobbly. When they drove away it seemed like they took the best of me with them.'

He walked around the flowerbed, and pointed down at the damp earth of the plot. 'Flowers! Nothing but silly little flowers. But I've got a thing or two up my sleeve.' He gave the appearance of great cunning, like a child, with a master plan. Cloud shadows from the moon raced across the ground around him.

'Come on, confess. You're dying to tell me.'

He tapped his top coat pocket, a man in possession of a secret. 'I've got the licence number. I'm going to ring them. Arrange to meet them. Then I'm going to offer them some encouragement.'

'How?'

'The usual way, with money.'

We paused as a car swished by, as if the glass and metal beast had ears. We both stood back a little into the shadows so no one in the car would notice us. I wanted to leave, but old man Walsh had me in thrall.

'What do you mean?'

'I don't have any family, Harry. I've outlived my family as you well know. I want to find these people and give them a decent sum of money. Get them set up properly.'

'How much?'

He hesitated. 'Fifty thousand dollars. A good modern truck will cost twenty-five.'

I thought about that.

'It's a wonder that old Bedford is still on the road,' he said, full of awkwardness again.

'Have you spoken to your lawyer?'

'My lawyer,' he said with dignity, 'is a dimwit.' The old man knelt awkwardly at the edge of the flowerbed as if to pray, and sifted the earth through his fingers, as if he could not believe the evidence of his own hands.

The moon was suddenly covered and his hands went dark, like gnarled wood.

'When will you ring them?' It occurred to me that he'd already had the licence number for a day.

He waved his hand vaguely. 'I need to think it all out first, step by step.'

'That sounds like a good idea.'

'No sense in rushing into things.'

'No sense at all.'

He looked at me critically. 'You know, Harry, I've never liked you that much. You never had the time of day for me, really, but you're different now.'

'In what way?'

'I feel like you're a friend.'

'Thanks,' I said.

'It's good to have a friend,' he said in a lonely voice.

7

Come Friday, I rang my father, getting up early enough to discreetly look up the number to make sure it was as I remembered.

It was a relief to hear his voice on the phone. The old hearty tones. I am Harry Blackman, son of Vernon Blackman, son of Walter Blackman all the way back to when Adam was a Blackman and there is only one of me.

'Harry! What are you doing up there? How's Evelyn and Timmy?'

'They're all fine. Would you like to say hello to them?'

'What? Are they up this early?'

'No. Actually Timmy's still asleep. Evelyn's not up.'

'And you still get to work at seven a.m?'

'Sometimes. I've got a Canadian trip coming up.'

'Listen Harry, if it's the money you've rung about, don't worry about it. I'm refinancing the house anyway, over a longer term.'

I heard the grey strain in my father's voice. Christ! I hadn't seen any reference among your things of a loan to your father, and I hadn't made one in my universe. 'I didn't ring about money. I rang because I want to come down and see you.'

There was silence at the other end.

'Come to check out the assets, huh?'

I was shocked to hear the bitterness and suspicion in the voice; it had never crossed my mind that I wouldn't be welcome. I tried to imagine what my father, your father's face would look like saying something like that, how his lips would move. I kept my voice light and easy. 'More like a holiday is what I'm after, Dad.'

'I didn't think you ever took holidays. I've never seen you have a holiday yet.'

'Come on, of course you have.'

'You spend all your holidays working around the house. Driveways and water tanks.'

'Go on! I bet you do the same. How's the garden?' The garden's a sure bet with Vernon. I thought of his love for me, and his wonderful, clumsy attempts to comfort me after my mother died. Vernon's world too, I saw, had fallen to pieces in the space of two years, first losing his wife then his job. My father, tired and washed out, thrown up like a piece of driftwood on the front porch, eyes bony from overwork. My father, weeping at my mother's funeral. Too many years suddenly rushing out from under everybody's feet. My father looking lost in the eyes, wandering around the city with his redundancy in his pocket.

'I'm not ready for the old folks' home yet.'

'I'm glad to hear it.' I was aiming for the bantering tone I knew Vernon liked; it was the way the guys used to go on in the army. 'You never will be, Dad; the Blackmans die with their boots on.'

Dad took the bait. 'You bet your boots they do.' There was a little of the old crackle in his voice, but only a little. I made the arrangements and rang off.

The phone call had not been a particularly good sign. Vernon was too querulous, too suspicious. The whole trip could be a disaster. I'd lost the sense now of why I was going at all. Running home to Dad seemed like a very silly idea in the cool light of dawn. As ever, the Dad I wanted would not be home. A familiar stranger would meet me off the plane. Our closest, best moments would be our first.

It was not until I was on the Northern Motorway that I figured out why I wanted to go to Nelson. I wanted more images from the cutting-room floor. I wanted memories, and plenty of them; those that would secure a past. I wanted memories I could trust. I wanted verification of my childhood. I wanted Vernon to be *my* Dad and not *yours*. I wanted to find out if there was a point at which this universe had peeled off from mine, if that's what had happened. I wanted to trace back time to a point where there was only one Harry Blackman, one universe, one life.

I'd never give up. That was the truth of it. I would track you down. Get you before it was too late. Get my hands around your neck and ask you what the hell you had done with my life.

And I tried not to think about what I'd seen you doing with Evonne. That was sleeplessness, that's all it was, I told myself. Sleeplessness and stimulation.

The traffic was sluggish and the weather was heavy. The clouds were low, humidity way up. It was dirty, pre-hurricane weather; the outer skirts of Hildegard, it could go on for several days depending on what Hildegard did.

Even the traffic was affected. We all ground slowly up the steel girders of the Harbour Bridge, which were the same grey colour as the sky, and down the clogged arteries into the city. There were civil defence guys talking on the radio. Stay at home. Hold onto the roof. Ahead of me, on a back window, I read these ominous words:

Beware the Jabberwock, my son!
The jaws that bite, the claws that catch!

Beware the Jubjub bird, and shun
The frumious Bandersnatch!

Suddenly the other Ghia Serenissima passed me before I could get a look at the driver, travelling too fast. Could that be you, I wondered, driving like a madman? Using my credit card to pay your speed-camera fines.

Despite it being Friday, and the last day of work before the Nelson trip, I found time to pry further into your affairs, trying to discover some record of a loan to Vernon, or to see if you had been involved in any shady financial dealing, but turned up nothing except the missing retirement fund. No unusual investments. No man named Dorf that Julie Horton had talked about; no cool half a million. Or, at least, no record of them.

I did a thorough search of the laptop files, too, checking the contents of all my documents, frustrated at the thought that I might be missing something. It was time to go and see Peter Coveny. Lawyers always know what is going on.

The rest of the time I spent with Cranner and Delany sorting out the details of the approaching Canadian trip, at every step giving thanks that not too much had changed in the work world. At the back of my mind, however, I couldn't shake the fear that I might run into another mismatch, like Julie Horton, and make some mistake I couldn't cover up. Some gap in the Lego no piece could fit.

They didn't refer to the lie I was going to tell, except in the most pragmatic way, and I did the same. It was almost as if it were someone else going to Canada. A creation of faxes, files and visas. A certain Mr Harry Blackman who might at any moment walk in. Meanwhile Pepsi came and went, keeping a check on progress, chatting to me between times. Hail fellow well met. I wondered how vast was his contempt for *you*.

It went on like that until Pepsi arrived with a grumpy look on his face. He took me aside to tell me that Tate was in his office waiting for me. He seemed on the verge of saying something but held himself back.

Mary Delany looked busy, as if she had no idea what was going on.

'He ripped up the cheque?' A cool and well-groomed Jerry Tate appraised me from his chair. We were both sitting in the 'guest area', which faced Pepsi's empty desk from the back of the room. Two steaming cups of coffee sat on the low table in front of us.

'Into tiny little pieces.'

We both thought about this for a while. Tate lifted the coffee cup out of its saucer and held it over his lap.

'Which means he'll never get the money from anyone. He'll piddle around in the margins,' I said.

'Not necessarily,' Jerry Tate said. He blew coolly across the surface of the coffee. 'He may have some source of funds already. We made our last payment to him just before the accident. Maybe his first model was not destroyed in the accident, only damaged.'

How come you don't know more, I wanted to ask, but what if *you* had been the one to inspect Kober's place after this accident, what if *you* had reported the device destroyed?

'We don't know it's a working model. We only have his word for that.' There must be plans, I thought, schematics, diagrams, graphics. If Tate was so cool and in control of this, why didn't he already have these in his hot little hands? Kober's office wasn't exactly a high security zone.

'What was his attitude towards you?'

'Hostile, world-weary. At first he pretended not to know me.'

'Maybe he's the absent-minded type.' He lifted his coffee to his lips but I didn't get the impression he was drinking it.

'Maybe. He just didn't want to talk to me. Then he lectured me about Schauberger.'

'Ah yes, the German inventor. Now tell me about this machine.'

I went over it all with him in detail. He seemed equally interested in every aspect. The argument about free lunches and implosions. He wanted to know everything as if he's never heard it before. I had to describe the egg and the crank handle all over again.

With regard to the last visit, and the ripped up cheque, he seemed quite indifferent. His imperturbable veneer rankled; nobody can be that unfazed by life; we are all, finally, perturbable, if there is such a word – I mean open to disturbance.

Nobody can be that impervious.

'Jerry Kober has a pretty big persecution complex, if that's what it is. He is frightened by people he calls the Specials. These Specials, who work for some secret organisation, go around soaking up patents for alternative energy devices, making sure they never see the light of day. That's the impression he gave me.'

I waited for a moment.

'People like Kober seldom live in the real world,' Tate said. The coffee cup made another trip to his lips. 'If he changes his mind, please let me know.' He brought the full cup to a perfect landing in its saucer.

'I'm very sorry this hasn't worked out.'

'It was a long shot.' He got up and left the room. I checked his cup to see if I was right. He hadn't drunk any.

By the afternoon I realised I'd be working late and rang

Evelyn, who promised to keep some dinner for me. It was reassuring to hear her voice. Then I asked to speak to Timmy.

'You can carry on and finish that white wall,' I said, 'if you can find the pieces. There'll probably be enough.'

'All right, Dad,' Timmy said importantly. 'I can finish that wall with yellow ones. I've got plenty of yellow ones.'

'That's a good idea. I'll look in on it when I come home.'

'I'll be asleep by then, probably.' He sounded very serious, very adult.

'It doesn't matter. I can creep in and have a look at it anyway.'

I went out to get some sandwiches and saw Evonne again, walking up Queen Street. I slipped into a shop doorway so she would not see me, but got a good look at her as she went past. She was walking in the dogged, determined way she did when she was tired or in a hurry. There were strain lines around her face, her coat was old and her shoes worn down on the sides. Her face was different because her life had grown into it in a different way. She looked dowdy and unremarkable. Clearly she'd made a poor marriage. Whoever this Alec was, he had not made her either happy or rich, but Evonne is loyal to the core. She wouldn't jump ship. Evonne never complicated love.

And she wouldn't fall in love with me in this world no matter what I did. Because things like that, like falling in love, had to happen at the right time and the right place for people. In love, timing is everything, seizing the day and running with it is the name of the game. There are a lot of people dashing around hoping to catch boats that have already left, waiting at train stations that have closed down years ago. And there are people who have given up and find all sorts of reasons why it is so good to live alone. Nothing when I get home but dead flies on the windowsill, a friend sighed ecstatically after his wife left him.

Maybe the flies died of boredom.

I shadowed her far enough to see her get on the same bus. She looked bowed but determined. Here, in this world, there was nothing I could do for her.

Back at the office I got into work mode and enjoyed myself, when I wasn't being haunted by images of a bent, round-shouldered Evonne getting onto a bus.

The business world is a little like Lego, only much more complicated and the pieces don't always want to fit. I enjoyed working at night when the telephones stopped ringing and the office emptied of voices. I found that the Harry-you-are had allowed quite a lot of work to pile up, more than the meticulous Harry-I-am would permit.

Little neglects, odd loose ends. Signs of strain, bro. A bit of a worry. It was naïve to think that Pepsi hadn't noticed it. You were slipping, just a little. Just enough.

Then I found a piece of paper with a phone number on it, a small piece torn from a larger sheet. Several tight circles had been drawn around the number. On impulse I picked up the phone.

'Hello.' A woman's voice, a soft contralto.

Had the voice belonged to someone I recognised I'd have bluffed it out, pretended to have had a message to ring them. Say hello for old times' sake.

Anything.

'Hello? Is someone there?'

No. Nobody. I couldn't answer. After all, I was not *you,* and I couldn't take the risk. I was learning the hard way to keep in the shadows.

'Hello, hello?' A trace of anxiety in the voice.

I'd have to take some risks sooner or later, I thought, hanging up. I wouldn't be kept back from the answers for ever.

Cranner wandered in and sauntered over to my desk. I slid

a piece of paper over the phone number. I'd forgotten he was still around.

'I'm off,' he said, fiddling with his jacket. He looked even more tired than usual, something of a haunting around the eyes. 'Ah…' The young exec lost direction, as if he'd forgotten where he was and what he was doing. He opened his mouth and there were no words. Then there were words all in a rush. 'I wanted to tell you, the boss is planning a little surprise party for us all when you get back from Nelson. A pre-Canada party.'

'Are you supposed to tip me off?'

He grinned awkwardly. 'I don't think I am. Mary's handling the details. I'm probably not supposed to know myself.'

'Thanks for telling me, anyway. I don't like surprise parties.'

'Neither do I. I don't like having things sprung on me at all.'

He was like a cat on hot bricks. He didn't know where to put his feet down next. He wanted to say something. He brought himself to the brink of it and pulled back.

Finally he left and I watched him walk to the lift. There was a defensive hunch in his shoulders. He waved self-consciously as he stepped through the door. I pulled the phone number out again and tried to forget Cranner. Looking closer at the number, I saw that it was not written in my handwriting. Someone had jotted it down and given it to you. I committed it to memory and screwed the piece of paper up, feeling like a criminal. Just as I was chucking it away I noticed the series of random numbers I'd jotted while talking to Mason the day before. It was the same number. Without knowing, I'd jotted down a phone number.

With everybody now gone, I made some coffee and strolled about the halls and offices, vaguely taking possession of the territory. The sense of power this gave me made me realise how hemmed in I was becoming, herded even. I was being pushed towards something I couldn't see. Whenever I stepped out of line, a little jolt brought me back. A hand reached out and slapped me. One day I'd see them. They'd have little piggy eyes and talons for hands. The claws that catch!

Powerless, that's what I was, caught between office and home, home and office. On the bounce. Off balance. A surprise party. Mary Delany plotting with Rigold; the manipulators, their tongues slithering down the phones to each other. Plots hatched for the good of Harry. To make sure Harry – who's been showing some signs of stress lately – has a good time before being led to the slaughter in Canada. Keep him on the move. Keep him laughing. Keep him mystified, sleepless. Maybe that's what was bothering Cranner. Guilt. Cranner was getting squeamish; no matter how hard he worked, his own head might one day be in the same vice, for that was the nature of the beast.

And whatever it was, it would come in some unknown, incomprehensible way. I might get only seconds of warning. Split seconds. One moment you have a sky. The next moment you have nothing.

Timmy's Lego house was on my mind as I pulled into my drive that evening. I didn't even glance at the flowers in their mysterious beds.

Evelyn was cooking a late dinner and Timmy was still up, doggedly working on the Lego house. I could see the dark, heavily bedded sky through the kitchen window behind Evelyn, lit orange-red by the city.

'I'll be with you in a moment,' I said, remembering the curl of her body against mine the night before. Could I stop it now, even if I wanted to?

The Lego wall was not quite finished. All the whites had been used up and the yellows called into service. There was a gap at the top for half a dozen more pieces. Already a Lego man had taken up residence inside, a soldier with a crossbow sitting in one corner on a custom-made stool. He had a curly moustache. I picked up a yellow piece and fitted it into the gap.

Timmy turned around, seeing me for the first time.

'It looks fantastic!' I said and grinned from ear to ear.

'He left that gap just for you. So you and he could finish it together,' Evelyn said from behind us. Her voice should have been warm but it was not; there was not a trace of warmth in it. She was delivering her lines as if someone was holding a gun at her head.

Slowly I turned to look at her, afraid of what I might see, but she had already turned away.

'I'm going on a Playcentre outing with him on Sunday,' she said. 'Everybody's going to the park for a picnic.'

'I want to go,' I said. Following her, taking off my coat. Evelyn, who'd been walking across the room, paused and went very still. Her hands were frozen in midair like two people greeting each other. Her head turned slowly in my direction.

'What did you say?'

'I said I'll go.'

'Do you know why you're saying that?'

'We went through this before. Last night, in fact.' In fact I wanted to finish the Lego house before I went to Nelson. The outer walls at least; I didn't know what plans Timmy had for the inside.

'You'd better pour me a scotch,' she said. It didn't sound like she needed any ice in it.

I hastened to oblige. Still she hadn't looked at me. She kept finding things to do in the kitchen. I left the drink for her on the bench where she was working, threw a quick one back myself and went into the lavatory where I sat looking at *Glad Day*. Rise up! Blake's universal man was saying, rise up and shed your earthly skin. Surrender, and by surrendering, transcend. Spread back the palms of your hands and come to life with wings of glad light. A new being; half man, half angel.

Back in the lounge I poured myself a second, careful scotch. Evelyn came over for a refill. There was a frozen smile on her face and her eyes were like glass. I poured her one without talking, feeling that a single word might, like a pistol shot, smash every fragile thing in the house. I noticed that the forget-me-nots had vanished from the vase. I thought of their tiny, white, cosmic centres.

Evelyn stood waxen, still as a shop mannequin. 'You're not just *saying* that you want to go on the Playcentre outing?' her voice was dry and powdery, the way a mannequin would talk if it had a voice.

'What for? Why would I say it?'

'To win me over. To use his affection for you to soften me up. To con me into thinking you're a good person.'

'And why would I do that?'

'Out of guilt. A cover-up. I'm surprised you haven't brought me flowers. That's the usual pattern.'

'What do you mean?'

She opened her hand and on it appeared, as if by courtesy of some malicious genie, the motel stub I found in my spare jacket that first day.

'I noticed that the other day, what about it?' I said carelessly.

'Take a good look at it. What do you see?'

'Nothing special. A receipt.'

'The date. That was the weekend you had to go to Wellington for the conference. I thought, I was told, you'd put in four nights down there. Well one was put in here.' She stabbed a finger at the ticket.

I was silent.

'Now take a closer look.'

'What is it?'

'It's a double ticket. A room for two. And you paid for two people. Who did you sleep with? Pepsi?'

'Nobody, I haven't been to the motel at all.'

'Then how come this is in your pocket?'

'I don't know.' I cursed you. I cursed you for the fool you were.

'You don't know? You don't know? Jesus, that's pretty lame.' Her fist clenched around the offending ticket.

'I don't know anything. Someone stuck it there. God only knows. It's not made out to anyone.'

'You're a monstrosity. I won't even get into bed with you. It's unclean. It's unholy. It's tainted. I'll sleep in the spare room tonight. Better still, you sleep in the spare room.'

I spaced the words out. 'I have not been to that motel. I have never heard of it.'

'You want me to believe that this somehow appeared in your pocket, your inside pocket, by some sort of magic.'

'There may be harder things in the world to believe.'

'Like what? What kind of lie have you prepared for this eventuality?'

'I'm not telling a lie. Everything I am hangs on that.'

'Sounds dramatic but what does it mean?'

'It means that you have to give me the benefit of the doubt because there's no direct evidence.'

'I'm not a fucking lawyer, Harry. I don't give a shit for direct evidence. Your face is enough evidence for me.'

'Then you condemn me without justice. On one motel stub. There are a thousand scenarios for how that might have got into my pocket.'

'I don't need a thousand. One's enough.'

'Then you make a terrible mistake.'

'I don't think so. It all fits now.'

'No it doesn't Eve-lyn…'

'What did you almost call me?'

'Nothing.'

'I warn you, Harry, don't mock me. Don't give me shit or I'll kill you. Not because of some junket in a motel, but for your contempt for me, for the horror of this great show of love for me and Timmy you're putting up. This great act you're putting on for the world. Playing Lego with Timmy on the floor. Courting me as if we had just met, forcing me to rediscover my love for you, so I'll forgive you, so I'll let it pass, so I'll make amends for something torn and soiled.' Her voice gave out in grief and disgust and she retreated into the kitchen to the comfort of cooking.

I went and played Lego with Timmy.

'Dinner's ready,' Evelyn said in a dreadful imitation of a bright and cheery voice.

The dinner was a set piece, staged for Timmy's sake. It was clear that I was expected to rise to the occasion, and I did, pointedly having a fruit juice instead of another scotch. I was through with scotch anyway. Maybe it was scotch that was destroying my sleep.

'They say that drinking before a meal dilutes the gastric juices,' Evelyn said, serving up a rich spicy soup. Was that a real glint in her eye?

'Well they don't have gastric juices like mine,' I said, tipping Timmy a wink, but Timmy didn't understand.

'I want some,' he said, looking from one parent to the other. 'What's it like?'

We got a laugh out of that one. We laughed at the same time if not together. It's great the way children can hold a marriage together through its rocky patches. Everything here was fine as long as we pivoted around Timmy, feeding off him, feeding to him. Playing to a gallery of one. Eat your veges, Timmy. Eat your carrots and you'll see in the dark. Eat your greens and your hair will curl.

Timmy chatted on, those inconsequential things children say and adults never entirely hear, directing most of his comments to me punctuated by phrases like, 'That's right, isn't it Dad?' and 'Dad says so.' I nodded and murmured agreement.

'Dad can do no wrong, apparently,' Evelyn said to me, not quite making it to the lightness of tone she wanted, falling short just a bit. Just enough. 'Dad's the man of the moment.'

'That's what I like to hear,' I said, beaming at Timmy.

'I'm sure you do,' she said, with just enough tartness for me to get the message.

That's what these situations are like. At any moment anything you say might fall short, any topic, no matter how apparently neutral, might turn out to have hidden snags in it.

Any utterance can blow up in your face.

Evelyn fiddled with her spoon. There was puzzlement in her voice, fragility in her expression. 'You've changed, Harry. Maybe this affair has changed you, I don't know.' For the first time since I had met this direct, decisive woman, I saw her stranded between certainties. In that insecurity there was a deeper hurt, an old pain that showed and revealed her self-confident air to be something she'd worked on, fought for.

I knew then I would have to tell Evelyn the truth no matter what the consequences. It was not so much a matter of if, but when. She deserved to know. How much more did I have to find out about my situation before speaking to her? After Nelson, I told myself. I'd put off everything until after Nelson. I'd learn something in Nelson. I'd bring something back that would help me.

Timmy banged the table with a spoon to bring us back to

him again. Some food flew off. I got up and got a dishcloth to wipe it up.

Back at the table, Evelyn was quietly trying not to cry.

I put Timmy to bed first and that didn't take long. As he lay back on the pillow he looked up at me wistfully.

'Let's do some more on the house tomorrow,' he said.

'Of course we will, we'll finish it off.'

'And we'll build a wall down the middle.'

'OK.

Propping Teddy up by the pillow, I noticed something strange about him; his remaining eye had gone. Now his face was blank.

Teddy was blind.

Tired, I went to bed in the spare room. It was not possible to forfeit sleep tonight; the body must succumb. There had to be a limit to how many nights I could survive without sleeping. Lying awake, fighting the dark.

Evelyn came in and sat on the edge of the bed brushing her hair. I was coming to love the way she did it, the arch of her back, the smooth, luxurious movement of her arm. Slowly, delicately, I was building up a history of connection and association with her. Apparently having decided something during dinner, she turned to me, brush in hand, her face calm and determined.

'Come on, Harry. It's confession time. I'll find out one way or another. I've suspected this for a long time.' She flicked her hair around her shoulders.

'Where is this wondrous mistress? And who could she be? Produce her! Show me the evidence.'

'Sooner or later you'll produce her. Or rather, she'll produce herself. I've got a feeling we won't have to wait too

long. Unless she was a prostitute.' There was a chilling finality
in her voice, that of a woman who had faced the worst.

Weary as hell and defeated, I turned over to sleep, carrying
your humiliation. After all, how was I to know what *you* got
up to? Perhaps Evelyn was right. Maybe you paid for escorts
and took them to motels. I had given up on you, anything
was possible. I fervently hoped it was an escort and not some
lover I was busy jilting right now.

Your damnable motel stub had doomed me. But surely, and
I tried to evoke your face which would be like mine but sitting
differently on the bones, if that stub was really such damning
evidence of wrongdoing, why did you keep it carelessly in your
jacket pocket? I would never have done such a thing. I would
have chucked it out, burned it, anything but taken it home
for a sharp-eyed Evelyn to find it. It was not in character,
or was it? Had you grown so reckless? Or was there another
explanation entirely, a perfectly innocent one? You got drunk
and had to pull over. The motel had no single rooms left.
Something incredibly simple.

'Sweet dreams,' she said as she slipped to the door.

Perhaps I slept, finally. What happened was this; one minute
I was sitting up in the narrow, uncomfortable spare bed
looking at the door Evelyn had just closed on a lot of hopes
and plans; next minute, I found *you* sitting beside me on the
bed, horribly close. At first you were just a scattered fizz of a
human body with the laptop on your knees, then you filled
out as the molecules of your body slowly took substance. I was
paralysed; I could sit and watch you but take no action, not
even to lift up a hand and try to touch you. I was a helpless
witness, just as I had been all along in this affair.

You had papers arranged on the floor in front of you. I
thought you were looking over the stuff for the Canadian deal

until I looked closer and saw all my bank books, chequebooks, shared accounts with Evonne, statements with matching credit cards, property deeds, my whole financial position all laid out in front of your eyes.

Of course it would have been an unpleasant surprise for you to find no Coleman, no big house deal, no crooked McBride, no immediate rip-off deals. But certainly, if you wanted to cash up all my careful savings, you could realise a tidy sum. But what would you do with the money, my money?

For the first time I wondered if there was a Kober in my world too, an energy device that could revolutionise the world sitting in some dingy flat in the red-light district of downtown.

You made notes, fast and furious, on your laptop – *my* laptop. Your fingers whizzed over the calculator, leaving a coating of temporal fur on the keys which slowly faded. You worked with the speed of a thief who must discover the combination to a safe before the owner arrives home.

You were going to clean me out, fleece me, leave Evonne and Timmy with nothing.

Suddenly you got up and went to the door, listened intently and slipped out into the passage, a look of cunning on your face. The further away you got from me, the more clearly I could see you. Moments later you were through the back door and flitting through the shadows across to the garage. I followed you, bobbing along behind in my unlikely role as helpless observer, impotent ghost.

In the garage you fossicked around among some boxes stored under the workbench and found what you were looking for. A slender, innocuous looking thing.

A .22 calibre rifle.

You ran your hands over it and looked towards the door. I didn't have to guess the memories that might be passing through your mind. Rabbit hunting in the twilight on the Canterbury plains; the quivering death of the small creatures. The cool steel of the barrel and its brief utterance. A line of pines, the wind running through them making the same sound as the empty washing line in a rising gale. A dreary, sagging sound. They come out at twilight to feed, Vernon said. They cluster along the tree line. You do the world a favour when you shoot a rabbit.

Vernon was a young man then. He hadn't yet moved so the Big Smoke where all the money was.

Maybe you and I were the same person then.

You put the rifle away, but not before you checked the ammunition supply which I had stored in another box, as suggested by regulations. I noticed how fastidiously you returned the rifle to its hiding place and stacked the ammunition away. Here, in this one regard, you seemed to respect my conscientiousness.

You stole back into the house, your shadow shrinking around you in the doorway.

I didn't know why you would check out my .22 and assert your authority over it, but I thought about it, even as I was being hauled back into my body. I could feel the spare bed, hard on my buttocks; I could see you fading down the corridor towards the lounge; there was a moment in which the two worlds lay in counterpart to each other, like trees reflected in a still lake; the two universes momentarily shared realities, then vanished. And I was back in bed. I lifted up my hand and looked at it. I bit my arm hard enough to taste the salty skin. I rubbed my body with my hands as if I were smoothing down some ruffled surface.

No sooner was I back in my body than I repeated the actions I had just seen. I slipped out of bed and went to the door. I worked my way through the shadows to the garage. I went in under the workbench, pulled out the .22 rifle and slid the bolt into place. I knew the weight of it in my hands, just as you had.

To be sure it had not been recently oiled, as you would have found mine to be, but it was still well kept and in general working condition. The ammo was where it should be. It was heavy and untouched by time. My memories were likewise in place; my mother was still alive; we had a coal range which roared on frosty mornings. Vernon would load the kindling wood onto yesterday's scrunched-up news and put a flame to it. The flame would leap up, brief, eternal.

I put away the rifle as I'd unpacked it, taking care to remove the bolt. The habit of exactitude, my precision matching that of the weapon itself, perhaps in mimicry of it.

I saw then the danger of my position. It was not a stable system; this double universe thing was not at rest. An instability had been created. An asymmetry. This world was closing in around me, squeezing me like an orange pip, threatening to send me spinning out into the alien dark. Or a .22 slug spiralling down a rifle barrel.

Or it could collapse in on itself, from its own contradictions, like Kober's machine, destroying Evelyn, the new Timmy, the Lego house, the bills, motel stubs, Sam Walsh's flowerbeds, Descartes: everything. Down in the flood. I would wake up in my own bed, the world restored, Evonne burning toast in the kitchen, Cranner on his way to Canada in my place, Descartes properly embalmed in history. I would laugh often, get religion and buy my Timmy a new Lego set and never had another scotch and soda in my life.

Evonne and I would live happily ever after.

Sam Walsh was standing close to the shadows of his own property, across the street from ours. His lined face looked stark and cadaver-like under the orange streetlamp. He lifted one arm in his odd, half gesture. The wind tore loose bits of his hair. I stood with my back to the approaching storm, leaning into it, rocking on my heels.

He crossed the street to meet me, his coat flapping. Our own little Insomniacs Anonymous meeting. Only the haunted are still around at two, three and four in the morning; the dead never walk alone.

I gestured to the flowerbed. 'Do you think they'll survive the hurricane?'

He nodded abstractly. 'I hope so. Flowers know how to stay close to the earth.' There was a wistful note in his voice, as if he wanted to join their ordered ranks in the flowerbed. He ran his fingers through the earth. This nightly pilgrimage had become for him a ritual witness-bearing to a miracle. One morning it appeared, where there had been nothing but plain grass. Flowers nodding in the morning sun, sitting in neat beds of freshly turned black earth, and amazement had taken hold of him; at each nightly visit that amazement was briefly reawoken.

Tonight, however, the edge seemed to have worn off the miracle.

'You're very sombre tonight, Sam. I kind of rely on you for my wee small hours entertainment.'

'I guess it beats the radio talkback shows,' he said, visibly failing to lighten up. It was like he was giving a funeral oration.

Don't tell me you've fallen out of love with your orphans here,' I gestured to the flowerbeds.

'I don't know Harry, I just don't know.' He looked at me sharply. 'I can trust you, can't I Harry?'

'We're friends, remember?'

He looked dubious. 'Just because I'm old doesn't mean to say I'm a fool.'

I laughed. 'I'm glad. There's time for me to wise up.'

He looked at me searchingly. 'I'm not about to be had, not by anyone.'

'Is someone trying to take you to the cleaners?'

'I don't know. You see, I finally rang up the flower planters. I spoke to a very nice woman. We agreed to meet, and I ended up going for a ride with them. Having my adventure.' He reached out his hand and closed his fist, as if he could pick up a rag of wind.

'Good for you. Was it fun?'

For a moment his voice glowed. 'It was, by God! We all piled in the back, I insisted on going in the back with the rest instead of a privileged ride up front. I had some sacks to sit on.' He laughed briefly at the quaintness of it all. 'We bounced along in the back of that old Bedford, stopped somewhere and they dug a new bed. Boy, did they move then. Twelve and a half minutes it took them, eight operatives. Brilliantly coordinated. I timed it to the last second.'

'Then what went wrong?'

He took a deep breath. With great dignity, he said, 'I wrote out a cash cheque. For five thousand dollars.'

'I thought you were going to give them fifty.'

'The five were just openers. A test run, if you like. Anyway I put it in an envelope and gave it to the nice woman who had sort of taken me under her wing. She didn't open it. She didn't look at the amount. I imagined them opening it later, how tickled they would be. How impressed. I took a certain satisfaction in that.' The strain of yearning showed on his face, and a deeper, bleaker look I couldn't read.

'Of course.'

'Anyway, we were driving along and suddenly the Bedford stops, the nice woman hands my cheque to someone else who puts it into somebody's letter box. Then the truck takes off. I

asked whose letter box it was, I mean, I naturally expected...'
His eyebrows drew together into a frown, which added lots of
lines to his face.

'And?'

'Nobody knew!'

He stared at me, dumbfounded, the frown working deeper
into his face.

'You mean...'

'Yes, they'd just stopped at any old random letter box.'

I had to laugh. I tried not to, but he was so incensed by it
he certainly couldn't see the funny side.

'They didn't look at the cheque,' Sam said, by way of a
dogmatic answer to my laugh. 'No idea how much it was or
who they were giving it to.' He shook his head. 'Just some
letter box, the same as all the others. It could have been fifty!'

'Did you tell them?'

'You bet I did.'

'And what did they say?'

'They laughed. Thought it was a big joke. The nice woman
said that there was someone in the city who would certainly
have a nice day.'

'She's right there.'

'But imagine if they did that with the fifty thousand! What
I really had in mind, Harry, was to outfit these people a bit
better, you know, a new truck. Some new boots and gardening
stuff. That doesn't come cheap you know. I could have given
a hand with the logistics; I've plenty of experience of that...'

'Maybe they like their old truck.'

He snorted in disbelief. 'I can't trust them, Harry, if they are
going to do something like that. My God, imagine if they put
it in somebody's letter box around here.' He seemed appalled
at the idea that one of his neighbours would end up with the
money. Even a stranger was preferable. 'Imagine if someone

like Mrs Bailey got it! My fifty thousand. God! I couldn't have that.'

'That's true,' I said, kneeling down and looking closer at our patch. The faces of the violets had turned black. They were bobbing around uneasily. Many would be damaged by a real storm, I thought.

'You have no guarantee that somebody like Mrs Bailey won't get it. In fact, if Sod's law operates, Mrs Bailey is just the sort of person who would end up with it. And boast about it at Crocker's on a Sunday morning.'

'Do you know Mrs Bailey?' he said sharply.

'Wouldn't know her from Adam.;

He now considered me with great suspicion, as if by possibly knowing her I'd implicated myself in something unsavoury.

'Then you don't know what a spiteful, miserly person she is.'

'I can imagine.'

We stood there for a moment in the gathering wind, thinking about how spiteful and miserly Mrs Bailey was.

'So you've decided not to give them the fifty grand?'

'Not exactly.' He gave me an agonised look. 'I can't decide. I would have to put conditions on it.'

'It might just be a test,' I said, thinking of Evelyn. Descartes' evil genius putting us through his maze. 'A test of your sincerity.' I thought of Kober and the fifteen million dollars lying in pieces on the floor.

'What do you mean?' He was ready to jump on me.

'I mean, you could've cancelled the cheque when the banks opened. 'Twenty bucks to save five thousand.'

His nostrils tightened. 'That's what she said. The nice one. She said I could cancel the cheque.' The bleakness in his voice told me this was no comfort.

In among the prim rows of pansies there was a different

flower that had grown there at random, tiny and unobtrusive. At first I thought it was a weed. I leaned forward for a closer look. 'Well, did you cancel the cheque?'

'No, I didn't.'

I looked up at him. 'I wonder why?'

The stray flowers were a tiny cluster of forget-me-nots. Blue corona. Yellow star. Late season.

'There's still time,' he said.

Heading back down towards home, I paused where I'd first stood and seen Evelyn, briefly, at the door. The house sat snug and secure, like all the other houses, silent in the dead hours before dawn. There was nothing to distinguish it from the world around it, no special mark of fate or mysterious atmosphere. A house like any other, it made no special claim on things.

All the same, I couldn't enter it. There was no welcome there but a cold bed in the spare room. No intoxicating body to snuggle up to. I went back into the garage and started up the car, glad of the familiar purr beneath my feet.

The Harbour Bridge was deserted as if some catastrophe had hit in the night. The steel girders rode past me, huge and remote, coldly and garishly lit. A lone police car watched as I cruised sedately and very soberly down towards the city.

8

It took two hours to drive out to the Sea View Motels on the southeast coast. The place looked deserted when I arrived. I sat outside in the car for a while surveying it, trying to read some sort of clue into it. The motel was discreet and unremarkable, the location between two beaches strategic. I got out, walked around and tried to get a feel for the place, then drove to one of the beaches and walked along a rocky shore, looking out towards the brooding Coromandel Peninsula where heavy cloud hung, lit hazily by the dawn. The water chugged up over the rocks and around my feet. I took off my shoes and walked gingerly forward, eventually finding a mini beach where I could sit down.

The water changed colour as the light grew from dark to grey; a band of rain swung across the gulf on a hoop of shadow. A moment of tremendous calm steadied me. There is only one world, I thought. Therefore it must be me; I'm the problem. Evelyn is my real wife but somehow I've replaced her in my mind with Evonne; I've fabricated another wife, another past, another son, at least fifteen years of false memories. The immensity of it staggered me. I wasn't capable of it. I couldn't do something like that alone, not without some sort of apparatus, some sort of helmet filled with electrickery. Frankenstein in the basement. Or some

incredible psychotropic drugs to aid the process. One day
I would wake up out of this world and discover I was really
Arnold Schwarzenegger.

A bigger wave came up and splashed over my shoes.
Remember the medieval witch trials? The suspect would be
thrown into deep water and if the water accepted her, and she
sank and drowned, she was innocent in the sight of God; if
the water rejected her and she floated and lived she was guilty
and got burned at the stake. I could put myself to the same
test right now, find out if this world would, once and for all,
accept me, take me to its bosom and embrace me, or reject
me, force me to carry on and go through the fire to come.

I toyed with the idea, and the idea toyed with me. I put my
hand down and let the water toy with that, let it suck at my
fingers as it moved back and forth. I saw myself borne in the
warm, slopping waves, soft as wool. No need for a .22. The
lullaby ocean would do the work. This image was being held
out to me on a watery platter; my death offered up for my
inspection, my approval. A ghastly nod or wink. The grave
mask of the servant. Death with no absolution. This was a
temptation, no more or less, I could outstare it anytime. And
what I could not outstare I could walk away from. Another
idiot wave licked over my shoes.

I'll be back, I promised the ocean as I walked away.

At the motel someone was up and moving about. I walked
to the office and a man came out. He was in a short-sleeved
shirt and looked brisk.

'Can I help you?'

I smiled. 'Actually I'm just after a cup of coffee. I've been
on the road.' The lie came smooth and easy.

The man nodded. 'Too early for breakfast.'

'That's OK. Nice spot you've got here.'

'Been here ten years now.' There was pride in the man's

voice. 'Where have you come from?'

'Down south.'

'Tiring for the eyes.' He was looking at me critically.

'Yeah.'

'That's night driving. I haven't done any night driving for years.' He looked appreciatively at my car. 'That's a rare machine you have there.'

'You wouldn't see too many of those around, I suppose.' I said, trying to play the private eye.

'You wouldn't.' He jerked his head towards the house behind. 'Come and have a coffee. I can't give you any food though.'

He served me strong percolated coffee and we talked of this and that. He gave no indication of knowing me, or my car, or of having ever seen me before. And no hint that he was just being discreet. He pointed out the cabins and I duly admired them. There were more doubles than singles, if that meant anything. I glanced as if idly through the visitors' book, found the date, but didn't see any handwriting I recognised. I didn't expect to. I left a little later without learning a thing.

A brief squall of rain had come and gone, leaving everything looking shiny and expectant before the next roll of clouds. The tarmac gleamed clean and black between the green hills.

I turned the car for home.

When I got home Timmy came running up and threw his arms around me. 'You're my daddy,' he said. I knelt and kissed him back. The kiss of a child is like a blessing. I had to remember who I was.

'Can we finish the house today?'

'Straight after breakfast. We can put that back wall on anyway.'

'What colour do you think I should use?'

'Well, one wall's white…'

'With a bit of yellow.'

'Yes, a bit of yellow. So the other wall could be…'

'Green.'

I nodded as if this were quite logical. 'But do you have enough green?'

'We could use some black ones off the castle.'

'The Black Knight's castle?'

'Yes.'

'Green with some black ones to finish.'

'That's right,' Timmy said.

'That'll make a fantastic house.'

From the kitchen Evelyn said, 'Peter Coveny rang. I said I didn't know where you were.' Her voice was not so cold this morning. More worried than anything.

'I made an appointment to see him,' I said, sitting at the table, and buttering some toast. 'Timmy, why don't you collect up some green bricks?'

Evelyn came and sat down beside me. 'Listen, Harry, tell me, are you in some kind of trouble?'

'What do you mean?'

'Maybe legal trouble. I mean, someone blackmailing you or something? Is it this woman? Is it the Kober thing? Christ, Harry, trust me. Look at me. I'm Evelyn. I can handle the truth. You don't have to try to protect me or any of that patriarchal stuff. You don't have to tiptoe around me as if I were made of eggshells. Just spit it out. I don't care how grubby it is. Grubby is life. Trust me. And I'm not about to divorce you, not straightaway anyway, so come clean.'

She was too smart to fool on a long-term basis. I knew I had to tell her. I owed it to her, if only I could delay that moment until I returned from Nelson, or, better still, until I found out more about what *you'd* been up to.

'You're taking a hell of a long time to answer. I suppose it gets harder and harder to make up lies.'

The bitterness in her voice was becoming habitual, a constant, driving edge.

'All right.' I poured myself some coffee that was still hot in the pot and took a last fortifying suck at it. 'There is something, you are right, but it is nothing along the lines you imagine. Right now, I need to do more research...'

'Is this why you're going to Nelson?'

'In a sense.'

'I thought it was just to get away, you know, to run out when the heat goes on.'

'Thanks.'

'You forget, Harry, I know you. I know how your mind works. I can see the gears and cogs whirring around in your brain. I can see the fear on your face. I know that you lie awake at night without sleeping. I watch you fighting against the third scotch. Or the fourth.'

'OK, you asked for my trust. Now can I ask for yours?'

'What do you mean? You haven't told me a thing yet.'

'I mean, can you trust that I'm not yet ready to share this, but it is not what you think. Does that sound reasonable?'

'Suspiciously bloody reasonable. Don't fob me off, Harry, truly. I couldn't bloody bear it.'

'I'm not fobbing you off.'

'You're asking me for the benefit of the doubt.'

'Why should there be doubt in the first place?'

'That's a dangerous kind of question for you to ask, Harry. It's a very dumbshit question.'

'Forget the question then. Just give me the benefit of the doubt. Any stranger would do it.'

'Give me one good reason why I should?'

I gestured to the other room. 'Timmy.'

'Oh you cunning bastard. You cunning, cunning bastard.'

'It's not that way.'

'Of course not.' She shook her head in disbelief. 'How long do you need to sort out your story, Harry? A week, a month, ten years?'

'I don't know. I want it cleared before I go to Canada.'

'Why not tell me now and save yourself the trouble?'

My cellphone rang. Cursing, I pulled it out of my side pocket.

'Harry,' a male voice said.

'Who is it?'

'Peter Coveny, Harry, I know you're a busy man…'

'Peter, I didn't recognise your voice.' I moved out of the kitchen, away from Evelyn. I was suddenly very glad to hear from my old friend and lawyer; this amiable if somewhat jaundiced character had the status of an old buddy.

'I blame it on the phone lines. Did you know that now it is possible for any telephone conversation anywhere in the country to be tapped? There was a guy busted for cocaine recently and do you know what he'd been doing? Ordering white paint over the sweet, user-friendly telephone. Beep-beep beep-beep. So they've got the computer rigged to throw up certain patterns and code words like "cocaine" and "phone tap" and "white paint." So, if you bastards are listening to me now, you'll know what I'm talking about.'

'This really bothers you.'

'Of course it does. I'm a lawyer. How can I do any kind of business over the telephone knowing what can happen to people. Christ! This threatens the whole race of lawyers.'

I was happy to laugh. 'You're assuming that all lawyers have something to hide.'

'Are all lawyers liars? Of course they are, even the one who's telling you about it is doing so *sub judice,* which sort of puts a legal nicety on the old paradox. This phone-tap stuff will be the death of commerce. Haven't your crowd bribed your way into the nest of sweet bytes yet? I'm surprised Harry, you're not keeping up with the times. There are a few who know the secret of the law, that the law is just a bunch of faggots sitting around in wigs talking to themselves and wanking. The law is starting to look as stupid as Parliament, and that's saying something. Do I have to spell it out for the cocksuckers? The IRD are in on this I'm sure. They'll be tuned into code words like "Cook Islands" and "tax havens" and "laundry powder." Right now, this very innocent conversation is lighting up alarm signals right across the board. Code signs are tripping. Weary SIS men are rubbing sleep out of their eyes and reaching for their earphones. Are you coming to see me this afternoon?'

'Now would be better.'

'Perfect, bring your chequebook.'

'What do you mean?'

'Nothing, I say it to everybody. Just a reflex.'

I didn't like his tone. His undertone. Whatever. I didn't like it. It didn't sound like Peter Coveny.

Evelyn had moved to the table and was sipping her coffee. 'Was that Peter?' I could hear the distaste in her mouth. 'What's he plotting now?'

'It sounded like him.'

'What do you mean?'

'I mean... he's got a nasty laugh.'

'I don't like Peter's little schemes.'

'Why not?'

'Because you lie to me about them.'

'Right now, I don't know of any little schemes like that, cross my heart and swear to die.'

'He'll have an angle, Harry, admit it. I'm worried about you if you don't know that.'

'I know that.' And I was worried about Peter Coveny, too. A lot depended on him. But he didn't sound like the Peter Coveny I knew. He sounded like a cheap, smartarse, small-time big shot. Where was the compassion and humour of the old Peter Coveny? The man who would advise clients for nothing and talk for hours to people who were emotionally on the line, trying to convince them that suicide was not the way out of a nasty divorce settlement or something of that nature. He once told me ninety per cent of his clients were either hyper or depressed. Folks who don't have problems don't need lawyers. Where was the old Peter Coveny with his smile of goodwill and his outrage at the government's attacks upon the poor? 'You're one of my rich bastards,' he once said to me. 'I have to soak people like you to pay for my charity cases.'

'You're going to see him.'

'He wants to see me now.'

'You see, you're lying already. You told *him* you wanted to come now.'

'You're right. So I'd better go.'

'You're making too many mistakes, Harry, for the game you're trying to play.' Her voice was thoughtful. It contained no malice. 'Way too many.'

I couldn't handle any more freewheeling dialogue. There wasn't enough control in it. I'd be better off behind the wheel of the Ghia Serenissima, heading down the Northern Motorway to see Peter Coveny. Get in the car. Drive.

Instead I went and sat down with Timmy and helped him with his house. He had laboriously collected enough green bricks to build a good portion of the second wall, and was studying the house with a frown of deep concentration.

'You know,' he said, 'I think we could build another wall joining the two long ones.'

'About in the middle. About here.' I pointed. Two rooms would be created.

Timmy nodded. 'And we'll have to find something for a roof.'

'What colour would you like for the interconnecting wall? I mean, this new wall?'

'Any colour you like. We could make that wall up with any old colour. You won't be able to see it from the outside.'

'I notice a Lego man has already moved in.' I picked up some pieces and fed them to him as he worked, putting one or two bricks in and leaving most of the fun to him.

'Yes. He's really a pirate but I've taken off his pirate hat.'

'That's a good idea. Pirates don't like it so much inside. Is this his house we're building?'

'I'm not sure. He just sort of came here.'

'We'll have to move him when we build that wall across. He's right in the middle.'

'That's easy, look.' Timmy pulled the man out and held him up. 'He fits in on the bottom of his feet, see, he has little holes in his feet and they fit into the round bumps on the floor. He can go anywhere.'

'That's very clever.'

Timmy smiled proudly.

'You're going on a Playcentre trip tomorrow?' I didn't go to Nelson until tomorrow afternoon. I had the time, just, if I made the time.

'Yes.'

'Can dads come too?'

'Yes,' Timmy said. 'Dads can come too.' He said it with great decisiveness, as if it were a great truth he had just discovered about Playcentre trips.

'I hope the big wind doesn't come and spoil it,' he said.

I said it could hold off for another day or two.

Place photographs of the two Peter Covenys side by side, the one from my universe and one from *yours,* and it would be hard to recognise them as the same human form. It is not the flesh of a face that counts, it is how the flesh has learned to live with the skull beneath, how the muscles have coped being hinged, as they are, to thought.

It was as if Peter Coveny had been scooped out and another mind and personality placed in his body. His manner, his speech, his movements, the cast of his mind, everything. His house had been rejigged too, replacing a modest suburban décor with a bad imitation of big money. Everything shouted money in the crudest voice. I had to look twice at the letter box to reassure myself that this was the right place. The Peter I knew would never live like this. Once he said he didn't want to live inside a wedding cake.

The inside wasn't any better. It had been gutted and refitted in the cheap, junky, nineties style which still managed to cost a hell of a lot of money. He poured a couple of coffees and we sat in two large easy chairs, both of which also belonged to the other Peter but were now covered with something shiny and nasty.

'I hope this living room of yours isn't bugged,' I quipped, sipping the coffee he'd just given me.

'Who the fuck knows, Harry. They've got a big surveillance problem. I mean there's just not enough people to watch everybody otherwise nobody would be doing anything but monitoring someone else. Commerce would grind to a halt.'

'That's rational.'

'Rational! Hell. All I know is that if they have to start monitoring small fish like me and you, then they are in deep shit. I mean very deep shit. Or we are.'

He smiled. An empty imitation of Peter Coveny's smile.

'Right now, if I was them, I'd be more worried about the stock market than small fry like us. In fact I am worried about the stock market. Down go the shares, up go the mortgages. Small investors get fleeced. Honest, hard-working home owners like yourself now have to pay more for the gambling losses of the big boys.'

'You've always got the solid core stuff like Telecom.' Here I was talking shares again and wondering why.

'Straws in the wind, Harry my friend, little straws in a big wind.' Remembering Cranner's comment on Southern Oil, I wondered again if *you* had traded in shares.

'How's Southern Oil going in the Dairy Flat field?' he asked.

I hesitated. These were industry secrets; *you* had no right telling Coveny this. You'd dumped me in it. Again.

'They've got a flow,' I said, keeping it safe.

He laughed as if I'd made a joke. 'We don't want the news to break too soon. A week, that's all we need.'

'It's breaking now. Some supermarket chains are already staking out properties. That's premature thought.' I had no right to tell him this, it was privileged information – but I had to put it out to get it back.

Coveny licked his lips. 'Your retirement dough won't bring enough in, not at the present price.'

And there it was, Harry Blackman's missing retirement nest egg, sitting in a trust fund operated by a caricature of Peter Coveny. Now invested in Southern Oil, whose Dairy Flat flow could go dry tomorrow. Pushing up the stock price to make a killing.

'We've got to get that other money in there.'

Other money? I didn't know how to probe this one out of him, so I changed the subject. 'I'm getting cold feet on the house deal.'

'Buy some warm socks. You're already in over your head.

You're breathing in the shit now, Harry. Orf is all lined up. The bank accounts are waiting with their mouths open. The shares are getting ready to spike. You just have to keep your nerve. A million dollars later you can get the shakes. We'll get them together.'

Again the thin, bloodless smile. The myopic, twinkling eyes had been replaced by hard, brittle pieces of mica and his lips had settled into a contemptuous shape.

I stared at my coffee, watching the froth cling to the side of the cup.

'Before I take the plunge I want to look at the whole thing from top to bottom. I want to review the case before I go into court, as it were.' I spoke quietly and forcefully, as I would with my own Peter Coveny.

For an instant he looked angry, very angry, but suppressed it quickly.

'What do you mean, review it? You know the details already. It's very simple.'

'To coin a phrase.'

'You don't think so?'

'Peter, in your experience, am I a careful person?'

'Ah.' Coveny groped for a cigarette. I watched while he lit up; the cigarette stayed in the corner of his mouth, his lips twisting to one side to hold it. 'Thorough is the word I'd have used.'

'Well, there you go, I want to be thorough. I want you to run the whole deal past me as if I'd never heard it. I want to hear it with fresh ears. See it with fresh eyes. I'm always inside the details. I want to see the larger picture.'

Coveny looked puzzled. 'Harry, you've already taken the plunge, pal. Like I said, the papers are signed and sealed. The hen is about to lay the golden egg. Let's hope you don't lose it all when the stock market opens again on Monday.'

'Christ! Just read it back to me, Peter.'

Coveny signed deeply and dragged at his cigarette. The impeccable lawyer, the fine-brained man who never touched tobacco, now looked like some cheap, crooked lawyer in a Humphrey Bogart movie. 'It's your money, Harry. If you want to pay me to tell you things you already know, be it on your overdraft.'

'We'll face that later.'

With a martyred sigh he went ahead and sketched in the outlines of an ingenious pay-off scheme by which the negotiator for a certain firm, a man named Orf, could obtain tax concessions from the government paid directly into an account run by a company set up for the very purpose of loaning another company a million dollars at ridiculously low interest and payback rates. One of the directors of that company would be Peter Coveny who would take out an investment for almost half a million dollars in Harry Blackman's new dream home. But the money doesn't go to the home. It goes into the stocks of Southern Oil to ride the spike. Then they'd sell when the price was right. That would take care of the house.

Harry gets a house for nothing. Damn near.

This Orf, as Coveny explained, was a very clever man. He swam through tax laws like a fish through water. This was the most elegant bribe he'd had ever run into because it not only bribed the mark, Harry Blackman in this case, but his lawyer at the same time, showing a deft cunning beyond the common garden backhander. Someone seriously into bribery would know that the mark's lawyer would have to be involved. None of this suitcases-full-of-money business, or statues of Ganesh full of cocaine. No, no; Orf was a craftsman. A pleasure to do business with. A gentleman of the old school, so to speak.

After Coveny had finished explaining it all, I saw why I

hadn't found a reference to any Dorf or Orf. Orf was not the man's name but a code name. McBride was Orf and Orf was McBride. Orf was the same Dorf Julie Horton had mentioned.

You'd lined yourself up a kickback for the Maritime deal. You'd dealt behind Pepsi's back; what you had not foreseen was that Pepsi would still send you to Canada.

Ordinary old bankruptcy was nothing compared to what would happen if Rigold or anyone else found out about this payoff and share investment tangle. My balls would be roasted at a corporate cannibal feast. Rigold would find out about this scheme somehow. That's what he was paid for, to sniff out things just like this. He didn't sit behind his desk just to drink Pepsi all day. He did other things, like keep a frothing eye on his staff. No one took kickbacks. Not even a bottle of wine, or perfume for the wife. No one even thought about it.

It was all I could do to keep the coffee steady in the cup.

'But you have to understand that the house deal's gone too far. Pull out now and you lose big. Coleman could sue breach of contract.'

'No escape clause?'

'Not unless you file bankruptcy.'

What made Coveny's voice different, for the vocal chords that produced it were the same, was tone, resonance, the way breath goes over the strings of a harp. My Coveny's light-hearted pessimism had given way to something else. Something that slid and hissed and stank.

Peter Coveny couldn't wait to get his hands on *your* money. My money. Couldn't wait for the money to start flowing from one phoney account to another. He'd pull the plug on me himself if I tried to get out now, he was capable of it.

He'd watch me go down, grinning.

'Sell the Southern Oil shares,' I said, gesturing to his computer.

'For God's sake why? That sucker's about to take off. There's no law against insider trading in this country; she's a wide-open beaver, man. We know they have a commercial flow. The share price can only go north.'

I hesitated. He was right. Another week and I could realise a good profit on those. I could see now how you were trying to play it. You were on the trapeze. You were in midair, between swings, when you vanished and I took your place.

'Don't then,' I said, fully realising how weak I was sounding.

I left shortly after. As I went out into the muggy, shifting air of the afternoon, Peter Coveny called after me, 'Give my best to your dear lady.'

In his mouth it sounded like a curse.

Coveny's mockery was still hanging around me when I stepped into the empty house.

There was a note on the table, and it was very explicit.

Actually I've just about had enough of all this. There have been too many years of mistrust for me to turn around and start taking you at face value just because you are nice to Timmy for a couple of days or because you suddenly want to start fucking me again. I try and talk myself around to give you the benefit of the doubt, to bend over backwards as I have always done, but I don't succeed because I feel as if I'm being abused. I can't talk myself out of feeling that. It's not just a question of another woman, I don't even know if that matters now. It's everything. I don't know you any more. I don't recognise you. I think I lost you years ago. Some moment when you lost yourself. And that's sad. I don't know why you do things. I don't even really know why you are going down to Nelson, and you've always only told me what you wanted me to know.

I'm worn down. I've lost faith. Lost too many nights. I don't know if I can set myself up for another fall all over again. Trust and be shafted, that's the world of Harry Blackman as I know it. And since our marriage must be in such a fragile state for me to be feeling these things, maybe it would be best to halt the house project, although I'm loath to give up something that might offer me a little nest egg in the future. I might need it. Anyway, I'm going to stay with Tess tonight and take Timmy on his outing tomorrow. He'll be disappointed but I can't help that. You've left your run with him too late, I'm afraid.

I know you're hiding something and until I know what that is, we don't have a fool's hope in hell.

Evelyn.

I found the number in the phone list, simply marked Tess, with no address or further clue. The woman who answered it , who had to be Tess, greeted me politely.

'I'm not taking sides in this,' she said.

'I understand.'

'You're welcome to talk to me anytime, Harry. I mean that.'

'Thanks.'

'I'm not sure that Evelyn wants to talk to you right now.'

'I want to talk to Timmy,' I said.

The silence became strained.

'I'll have to get Evelyn,' Tess said.

'It's Timmy I want to speak to,' I said.

'I rang to talk to Timmy,' I said when Evelyn came onto the line.

'What for?'

'To apologise for not taking him on the trip tomorrow.' Silence. 'I promised I'd take him. I asked if dads could come and he said they could.'

'Jesus, Harry.'

'What does that mean?'

'You play mean. You really pitch it as low as you can.'

'I'm not playing. I'm not pitching. I'm not an American. I want to speak to Timmy.'

'You'd use him. You'd go that far. You'd play that card. Jesus.'

'This is not a casino. I have an apology to make to Timmy. Can you stand aside and allow me to make it?

'Stand aside? I've never heard you talk like this. Worming, scunging and lying are your normal methods. Are you trying to say you are sincere?'

'Can I speak to Timmy?'

'Hello?' Timmy's voice came on the line.

'Looks like Mum wants to take you on the trip,' I said. There was a lump in my throat, that was the crazy thing. 'Next time,' I said.

At four years old there is no next time, there is just this time. I put the phone down and turned to the empty house.

Never had it felt less like home.

Usually I would take the opportunity of an empty house to get into the laptop and catch up on some work. Arrange all my personal Canadian files and generally refamiliarize myself with the territory, but I was in no mood to work. I didn't want to stay in the house, even, because that silence could build up and reverberate between the walls like the roar of a far-off throng.

I walked outside and wandered up the drive, hoping that I wouldn't see Sam Walsh. I was lucky, or perhaps it was too early for the old man. I wandered past the mysterious flowerbeds with hardly a second glance and walked the zigzag road down to the waterfront. My first visit to this spot since I'd arrived here. Our waterfront was a little austere and stony but still pleasing with its quiet, enclosed bay, a view of the peninsula capped with pines. At night the pines looked delicate, feathery. The wind made low hard sounds in the branches.

When the house was first built I used to come here often and sit on the rocks beneath the pines and thank my lucky stars I had a good job and a woman who loved me.

An old wrought-iron park bench, much beloved by lovers and loners, would be there, bolted into the roots of a huge Pohutukawa tree, those great coastal oaks of the Pacific. Evonne and I often sat there, before Timmy was born and while we were building the house, and kissed, because it was a wonderful place to kiss.

I headed for it now. Sitting in the privacy of those shadows, a figure couldn't be seen at night.

The bench was gone. Not just gone, there was no sign of it ever having been here. I should have been getting accustomed to these anomalies by now, but still I reached out around me to steady myself in the known world, check prominent landmarks, take my bearings from familiar rooftops.

Walking on, I followed the road as it swung back up the hill leading to my home street. Halfway up this incline there was a flat-roofed house the colour of pink icing, a detached layer of wedding cake. At night it assumed royal purple, the right to look interesting and mysterious. I noticed a cluster of gnomes holding court in the middle of the lawn. I'd never seen them before, but they went with the décor; they too were clothed in royal purple. Their hats were bent like dunces' caps gone lame.

There are some things we never want to see changed.

At the junction, where the seafront loop reconnected with itself a few hundred yards above our place, I had the choice of heading on up to Simon's Point, where there is a lookout over the ocean, or back down to the house. Obeying my feet, I headed for Simon's Point.

There, I could look at the pines on the peninsula from above, and imagine myself as I would have been a few minutes before, strolling along the beach heading for a nonexistent park bench or winding my way up the hill; look down on myself plodding along. Or I could look up , at the wide sky. Looking at the stars helped because although they were very cool and analytical in themselves, snuggled in behind the hurricane winds, their overall clustered distribution suggested some deeper, hidden order,. Theirs was the language of patterns and codes, their passions a monstrous geometry. A living augury. Only from a distance is the crystal clarity of the argument of the stars visible. But what was the augury saying? I would leave for Nelson, deeper in trouble but no further ahead than I had been on that first evening when I'd stood at the top of the drive and seen Evelyn.

I turned into the wind which poured in a moist, unbroken rhythm off the gulf; everything was streaming away from me, part of the night's flowering substance.

A single star may belong to one of many constellations.

I waited forever and nothing happened.

9

We left for Nelson a step ahead of Hildegard, one of the last planes to take off. We bumped and thumped our way into the air then headed south, away from the approaching hurricane. One step ahead of the posse, Vernon used to say, mainly in reference to his tax bill and finances but also as applicable to life, the universe and everything. That saying seemed grimly appropriate now; it sounded as if a million screaming demons were at my back.

I got out a book I'd picked up at the airport, hoping to distract myself from that vision, only to find myself confronting it again from another flank. *Hyperspace*, by Michio Kaku, was an argument in favour of a ten-dimensional universe. Since we only know four of these dimensions – time, plus the three dimensions of space – where have the other six gone? Rolled up into a little ball, says Kaku, so little we can never see them. The Big Bang occurred when the ten-dimensional universe split apart into the four we know and the rolled-up six. And how do we know all this? Because the maths tells us so; the maths is so good it almost has to be true. That maths, however, turns into a Pandora's box of possibilities, among which is Stephen Hawking's parallel universe theory. Hawking's vision is of parallel universes connected by 'wormholes', billions of wormholes, connecting billions upon billions of universes.

These wormholes arise courtesy of a tunnelling effect at the subatomic level; a particle which should be in one place suddenly finds itself somewhere else. This effect, Kaku assures us, takes place only at the subatomic level, and while there is the possibility of something big, like a person, experiencing this quantum tunnelling we would have to wait longer than the lifetime of the universe for such an event… unless there were giant wormholes.

The idea of a person ending up in a parallel world was the kind of scenario that happens in television and the movies, Kaku continues. I was shocked to discover that my very situation had been foreseen, not by some great prophet, but by overstimulated scriptwriters and hacks. Even science-fiction writer John Wyndham had had a go at it, around the middle of last century. Imagine, I said to myself, telling Evelyn the truth and ending up being accused of dishing up a cheap plot I'd seen on TV.

As we came into Nelson in ordinary space, I put the book down and put parallel worlds on hold. Did it really matter how I got here? What help was it?

I saw a tall, stooped man waiting at the barrier, and was relieved to recognise Vernon.

He shook my hand and banged me awkwardly on the shoulder. I took a deep breath, enjoying the crisper, colder air.

'You look dreadful,' Vernon said. 'What have you been doing to yourself?'

'Worrying about money. I'm about to go down the financial tubes.'

'Your own fault, no doubt.'

We walked through the terminal and into the car park, Vernon leading the way with long, determined strides. The sky looked very blue. I wondered if the mountains could change the colour of the sky. 'You're not taking Evelyn and Timmy down with you I hope. There's something in her name? A trust fund or slush fund or whatever you do to cover your family?'

'I've got a couple of backstops,' I lied.

Vernon had pale, watery-blue eyes and a long, craggy face. His hair had not turned grey but rather faded to a bleached, sandy colour.

'Let's get you home,' he said.

The south! There's something about it, about the way the light falls straight and clean. Everything looks sharper. And distances, there's more lateral space somehow, as if you can see further. And the humidity was gone. The muggy, gloomy hand of Hildegard did not extend this far.

We drove around the waterfront with the ocean on our left and steep, rocky cliffs on our right.

'I've forgotten how nice this place is,' I said. 'There's more sky.'

'How do you figure that?' Vernon drove slowly and correctly.

'Not so many tall buildings.'

'Yes.' Vernon knew about tall buildings. Somebody sitting in one of them had put him out of a job before he was ready. Somebody he'd never met. 'I got to hate Auckland in the end,' he said, changing down for a right turn.

'I know.'

'I couldn't breathe. The Big Smoke! They say it's a terrible place for asthmatics.'

'But you're not an asthmatic.'

'In Auckland I was.'

We swung up onto the hill and the car slowed to a crawl. I saw a child walk past swinging a bag. There I go, I thought, off to school or home from school or whatever, scuffing my shoes on the pavement, the air passing in and out of my body without thought.

'How is Evelyn?' Vernon said, holding onto the wheel with both hands as if driving at a high speed. Apparently the car needed his conscious will behind it to get up the hill.

'Actually our marriage is in the shit.' I hadn't meant to say that. I'd meant to say she's fine...

Vernon's face went tight. 'I'm not surprised.' We pulled up outside a familiar front gate. Vernon turned off the engine and got out of the car. 'You've been riding for a fall for some time now,' he said, slamming the door. 'I never understood how a son of mine could be so arrogant, so self-centred.'

I got out of the car and pulled my suitcase and laptop from the back seat. The glitter of the sea got into the back of my eyes. 'That's a pretty horrible thing to say. I hope you've got good reasons for saying it.'

We went through the gate which clicked behind us with a metallic, musical note.

'Look here,' Vernon said, stopping. 'I was a soldier in World War Two, my father was a soldier in World War One, my father's father was a soldier in the Boer War. World War Two was no picnic, believe you me. But we knew who we were and why we were there. We knew evil when it stared us in the face. When we got home we took our money seriously because there wasn't much of it – unless you were a farmer – and we gave our kids an education. We worked our guts out to do that. We didn't play around with our money or our wives, there wasn't time. We buckled down and got to it. We didn't gamble with the food in our kids' mouths. We didn't build casinos to screw more money out of our own pockets. And marriages stayed together, if for no other reason than decency. Yes, decency. A redundant word. People stuck it out because there was a life to be lived and they got on with it and lived it without...'

'Is that what you and Mum did? Just stuck it out?'

'Penny and I loved each other,' Vernon declared. 'We loved each other for forty years. And we didn't stop loving each other, even in the bad times. We didn't turn against each other as people do today. You know, people tear the skin off each other's backs nowadays. Penny and I faced everything together. Do you know why? Because we were grateful. We were grateful just to have each other. We made vows and we believed them. We stuck to them. And if we did make some mistakes along the way, we left them behind us and got on with it.'

'Dad, can we go inside? I'm tired. I need a cup of coffee. I feel like I need to sleep for a week.'

There was a stiff-necked moment of silence before Vernon smiled. It was a big, warm-hearted smile that made the craggy face, with its fierce, sandy eyelashes, ruggedly handsome for a man in his seventies. 'It's the privilege of parents to go on worrying about their children even when they're grown up and are big enough and ugly enough to take care of themselves.' I grinned at the old family joke. 'But I knew you'd ruin it with Evelyn. I knew it. God knows I thought at the time that she was too good for you.'

'Thanks Dad, for the vote of faith.'

This was Vernon, all right, but the bitter, personal edge was new; just as *you* had alienated Evelyn, you had earned this man's contempt. Wherever I went I faced the ruin you had left behind.

We walked up onto a honeysuckle terrace with its view out over Golden Bay. I looked northwards, around the sweep of the bay. 'Farewell Spit,' Vernon said, pointing northwest, 'they say it's the biggest natural whale trap in the world. Whales keep beaching up there and all these Greenies run around pushing them back into the water.'

He spoke as if he's said it all before, which he probably had.

He probably said it to everyone who came up here. I flopped into one of the deck chairs and shaded my eyes against the sunset, hoping I could ignore the anger in his voice.

'There's a pod out there right now, heading for the spit. They'll probably have it on the telly tonight.'

I took the binoculars that were lying beside the chair and looked into a great blue circle in which everything glittered and moved; a ceaseless, merciless play of particles and wormholes. Into it moved a yacht with a yellow sail, and a windsurfer in a black wetsuit leaning out over the glitter. The windsurfer was elegant, controlled, sexy; sliding through the water, his limbs fully stretched, apparently effortlessly at ease in his medium. Sprawled there, watching him, I felt ugly-limbed and clumsy. I felt cluttered. You couldn't be cluttered out there in the wind with a piece of shaped wood and a sail.

I put the binoculars down and Golden Bay sprang into the distance.

Behind the terrace was a modest house. A bedroom, study and lounge-come-kitchen. Vernon had put a spare bed up in the study where there were a few books and a couple of van der Velden prints. One of them showed water racing down between bunched rocks; the water, which was splashing down towards the viewer, was possessed of a dark, potent energy. The other was a sepia-tinged portrait of a Maori with a sad, quizzical look on his face.

I looked around me with a sinking heart. The top bookshelf contained a dozen or so *Reader's Digest* abbreviated novels. The spare bed, which was an old army stretcher, had that starched clinical look of a bed just made up. Five days suddenly seemed like a long time. Maybe three days, I said to the Maori face that stared out at me from the van der Velden print. The face did not appear to be looking at anything very hopeful.

The lounge-kitchen was equally sparse, like a motel or

a rented place; Vernon looked too big and gangly for the neatness and proportions of the room, shoulders hunched over as he made coffee in the kitchen. Only when he was back outside on the terrace did he appear to straighten up.

'I'll have to show you the garden,' he said, suddenly very awkward, as if covering up for having nothing to say. 'That's where I spend most of my time these days.' It was his 'retired' voice and it had a little edge in it. 'And Grey Power. I help them produce their newsletter.' He waited for a moment to see if I would respond. 'If the elderly don't stand up for themselves, nobody else will. It's a dog-eat-dog world they're bringing in out there. The pack will pick off the old and the useless first. Thank God I won't live to see too much of it. You've got no idea, old people are very fearful. They know when the knives are out. But you don't have to worry about putting me in a home. I'm not going to one. I'm going to die, standing up, just like this, spitting tacks. You won't have to asset-test me. You won't have to asset-strip me. You won't have to sell your home to keep me in mineral water and blankets.'

'The way you're going, you'll live longer than me.'

The old man swung around on me, his eyebrows darkened, drawing together as if he were some wizard. 'Has Evelyn left the house?'

'Not quite. Look, Dad, it's not that bad. I just need a rest.'

'You're a bloody fool if you've got on the wrong side of that woman, Harry.'

I wandered restlessly into my makeshift bedroom, wondering what the hell I was doing here and trying to feel the peace and clarity I'd hoped I'd feel. The questions I had to ask Vernon had somehow evaporated; the things I wanted to discover had disappeared down a wormhole to some other dimension.

For something constructive to do, I began poking around

the study and found a box of photographs stacked under a pile of children's encyclopaedias. It was a random collection from the years; Vernon had never cared about photographs that much. There were several of my mother, a couple of wedding photographs and some family shots. Most of them were very boring. There were a couple that were clearly *you* in unknown places with people I'd never met. There was one of you and Evelyn at a table, your faces turned towards each other full of admiration and love, looking like young movie stars.

Then I found one of me, or you, as a teenager, standing outside a house I remembered, an old aunt's house. I stared hard at the photograph, trying to remember the occasion of it, hoping that it was me, not you, I was looking at; my own independent existence would be validated. Or I might find a time when you and I were one person; perhaps we shared a common childhood.

Here was a shot of us as a youth, with a young woman on our arm. Arm-in-arm, but pulling apart, grinning at each other. Bending down to look closer, I saw a resemblance between the two faces, the shape of the nose, the line of the chin…some relative I'd forgotten, perhaps.

I put this photo to one side with a growing sense of unease. I was looking for proof of my own past, but what if I found only yours? Perhaps my past belonged completely in the other universe.

A picture of Mum gave me pause. I remembered her as a haggard, sick woman dying before her time, but there she was in the flush of her youth, standing on a beach talking to her brother, one of my uncles. I recognised the shape of the nose, the line of the chin. He must have just made a joke, for Mum was laughing and joy lit up her face. It occurred to me that this had been taken before she met Vernon. I put the photo softly back on top of the pile.

I looked back through them all with more care now, noting the people I didn't know, finding two more photographs of the young woman. In one she was at a party, talking to one of my uncles on Vernon's side. She looked younger, no more than thirteen or so. Mum was standing in the background holding a glass. That would be sherry. She always allowed herself a sherry or two at a party. The other was a posed group shot; father, mother, older brother Matthew, me, and the young woman. Everybody had a frozen smile. A *say cheese* smile.

I looked at the photograph for a long time. I could not remember the occasion of it because, for me, it had never happened. This was you as a child. I didn't come into it all. The division of the universes had taken place before I was born. Maybe if I did some study I'd find anomalies further back in history. But surely anomalies would accumulate rapidly and change the world, as in Mary Delany's butterfly effect. The fact that this had not happened suggested a more recent splitting.

And what if I was some kind of schizo? But a new kind. A mutant schizo with emergent God-like powers capable of creating real universes in which to house alternative personalities. What a hell of a cosmology that would lead to. What would the maths be like? It seemed a lot more elegant just to assume that I was plain crazy and that I was really *you* having some kind of weird episode. But I'd been down that line of thought before and it didn't lead anywhere but the equal absurdity of having to believe that I'd invented a whole lifetime of memories, years of marriage to someone who didn't even know me.

I took the three photos with the young woman in them into the lounge just as the news was ending. Vernon guiltily clicked off the TV when I appeared, but went on staring at the screen for a while as if watching an invisible picture.

'Can't for the life of me remember the occasion of this one,' I said, showing him the arm-in-arm one. He took the photo and adjusted it a good distance from his face.

'I took this, don't you remember? You were off to the Big Smoke for the first time to make your fortune. Paula and I took you out to the airport.'

'Of course. It seems like a long time ago.'

'That's the airport in the background. See.' He looked sad. 'You'd be a millionaire in five years, you said.'

'The dreams of youth,' I said.

He took the other photos and examined them. 'This is Paula talking to Uncle Bruce. You weren't there that night. I don't know where you were. I think it was Aunty Madge's birthday or something like that.' He looked at the last one, the group photo. 'You can't have forgotten this one. It's a studio shot. You and Paula had been squabbling like a couple of kids. Penny got angry and nearly walked out although the photo was her idea from the beginning. And the whole thing was ridiculously expensive. We could have just taken a snap at home.' He turned it briefly to look at the back. 'I'm surprised we kept a copy of it.'

'I remember it now,' I lied. 'It's strange the things you forget.'

'I guess so.' Vernon got up and put on the coffee. He had the restlessness of someone who really wanted to turn the TV back on. I wanted to ask more about Paula but didn't know how to without giving the game away. Several times Vernon looked at me, apparently biting back something he wanted to say. It reminded me of Evelyn. The seething resentments on the tip of the tongue; this is how *you* affected those closest to you.

'Tell me about my birth, Dad.'

He was pouring the coffee grounds into the plunger for a

new cup. 'That's an odd question.'

'I don't think I've asked it.'

'Not since you were a kid.'

'Then tell me?'

He half laughed. A variety of embarrassment. 'Why do you want to know?'

'Because I'm having a midlife crisis, let's say. I'm trying to piece together who I am.'

He looked at me suspiciously, as if I were pulling his leg, taking the piss out of him. 'Nothing special,' he shrugged. 'It started in the middle of the night. We'd been watching her for days, I mean…' He went into the fridge and brought out some milk and sugar.

'I'll have some of that.'

'What?'

'Milk and sugar.'

He looked startled. 'You don't take milk and sugar.'

'I've changed my habits.'

'Christ.' He poured the milk into the cups.

'Why had you been watching Mum?'

'Because…we knew she was near. Even a bit overdue.'

'OK.'

'There's nothing to tell. We got her to the hospital. You were born hale and hearty.' He tried to smile at the reminiscence, but something went wrong with his mouth. There was something he was not telling me.

'Was it a long labour?'

'Many hours. Child-bearing takes its toll on women, Harry. What she went through…' The water boiled and he poured it into the coffee maker.

'What did she go through? I thought you said it was normal.'

'How many sugars?'

'Two. Was it normal?'

Vernon was breathing really hard, as if he were carrying enough to keep two bodies upright instead of one. He began stirring the coffee.

'Penny was pregnant with twins,' he said. 'You were born first and lived. Your brother was stillborn a few minutes after you. Penny nearly died of blood loss and exhaustion. No wonder she was terrified when it came to Paula.'

'I had a brother with me – in the womb, who never lived?'

'Never drew breath so we never gave him a name.

I turned the story around, looking at it from every angle. At first I couldn't see how it fitted the parallel universe theory; it seemed more like an extraneous fact than a real clue. Then it struck that if the dead twin in this world was me, killed in the womb by your scrambling feet, then in my world the dead twin would be you, and that this was the origin of the split I had been seeking, this was where my world had peeled off from yours. At birth, in the scramble for air and life.

If this were true then you were not just some mirror image of me, courtesy of symmetry, but a person I had known in the uterine ocean, who thought and communicated with me through blood and waves and touch; someone who shared with me the same stem and navel. And being twins, we were still linked, which was why I was now experiencing your life; after all, not everybody had the kind of experience I was having. Being twins made the difference, and not even that invisible membrane between the worlds could sever the connection – a connection strong enough to open a 'wormhole' between us?

But, even if I was right, and was now in possession of a more complete theory than before, it was still only a theory, and gave me no practical help in dealing with this world. In that respect I was no better off than I had been right at the beginning, on that first day, when I walked into a house I didn't know.

'Why didn't somebody tell me?' My voice sounded into the room, forlorn and depressed.

He sighed and went on stirring the coffees. 'Didn't they? I thought Penny... well, nobody wanted to remember, I guess.'

He brought the coffees over. They were lukewarm and stirred to death.

'What the hell is going on?' Vernon said when the conversation ran dry. 'I mean at home.'

I got up to get some more hot water. He crossed to the cupboard for some biscuits. He went in for those thin, odourless, tasteless biscuits. It was a little evasive, domestic dance we did, shuffling around each other.

'It's the house project,' I said, wishing I could skip the explanations. 'We're in over our heads, making a lot of very expensive decisions. Right now we're riding a couple of overdrafts too hard. The first thing you know is you can't use your chequebook. The second thing you know is that they want you to clear your overdraft in seven days.'

'What I mean,' he said, 'is what is going on with Evelyn?'

'Well the house is part of it, Dad. Evelyn wants to plunge on, to keep going.'

'Nothing other than money matters, then?' he said with a great show of patience.

I had to remember that this man never did half the things I remembered him doing, nor said half the things I remembered him saying because Paula would have been there; different things would have been said and done; life would have unfolded differently, the differences compounding as time went on. I had never existed in this universe at all. None of the photos were of my life; they were all of *yours*. My memories didn't belong here, which meant I had to be very careful what I said to Vernon.

'The money's the main thing,' I said.

'It always was with you,' Vernon said.

I sipped my coffee. An infusion of hot water hadn't done it much good.

'So you want me to sell up so that I can pay you back so that you can cover for your own financial mismanagement. Is that what you're saying?'

'That's the last thing I want you to do.'

'Why else are you here? The squeeze is on.'

I drank my coffee, thinking that Vernon probably had some brandy stuck away around here somewhere. *My* father always did. And knew when to bring it out.

Vernon said, 'I know you too well, Harry. You don't fool me.' There was almost a loathing in his voice. 'I knew when you said you were coming there'd be something like this.'

'You were wrong.'

'You mean you've changed your mind? You're not going to throw your poor old dad to the wolves after all? Well, the wolves will get him anyway, eventually. The old are consumed by the young.'

'I came here for a rest, Dad. Just to get away for a while, you know. A refuge. A place of calm where nobody's being consumed.'

But Vernon appeared not to hear. All his deafness was gathered in one ear, and that was the ear nearest to me. It wasn't worth saying anything at all; this man was a stranger to me.

Vernon sighed deeply. 'And there's Paula, another mess. One marriage down and no prospect of another. Take a good look at yourself, Harry. You look sandbagged. Like death warmed up. Like you've been on a bender. And then you tell me you're losing Evelyn, you're blowing your marriage like Paula did. You won't find another one like Evelyn you know, not at your age. Women of that calibre are rare. Penny was like that. One out of the box, you could say. True through and through.'

I got to my feet. My head felt swollen, and a thousand miles from the earth. 'I don't have to listen to this stuff, Dad,' I said. 'Actually, it's the very last thing I need.'

Vernon said nothing. He was sitting on the floor, propped up on one hand, staring down at the carpet where the photographs were spread, his mouth in a thin, grim line. I'd never seen my dad look like that. This was *your* dad, this was his experience of *you*.

'And you don't have to worry. I'm not going to sell you up,' I said, standing there stubbornly, refusing to go to my room just as I had done when I was a child. Being sent off to my room with the feeling that I was irrevocably in the wrong.

Vernon turned on the TV to catch the news and I stood there, too stubborn to sit down, and watched Hurricane Hildegard hit the north of the country. Dramatic photos showed cities lashed by heavy winds and rain. There were roofs flying and desperate struggling campers. Roads were subsiding. A crash on the Southern Motorway tied up traffic for six hours. I thought of old Sam's flower plots, the nodding pansies in their freshly turned beds. I thought of Evelyn and her Timmy huddling in bed listening to the wind, praying that the roof wouldn't fly off. Thinking of Evelyn and Timmy brought me back to the reason I'd come to Nelson. Surely I'd known I would never discover why or how I came to be here, the essential mystery of it. Some key or magic lever that would bring it all tumbling into place like a line of winners on a poker machine.

I hadn't come to Nelson to discover those answers, because I knew underneath that there would be nothing in any boxes of old photographs that would make a shred of difference to me and Evelyn, or to me and the machinations of the oil industry for that matter. No magic levers.

I'd come to get away from Evelyn because I was falling in love with her. Abandoned her and Timmy to the hurricane and got out, one step ahead of the posse, to Nelson where I could watch it all on TV at a safe distance. Detached. But now that I was here, watching it all on TV, I wasn't detached. I felt like a fool with Evelyn and Timmy hundreds of kilometres away in a ferocious storm; no matter that they had sprung from nowhere into my life, usurping my known reality, no matter what shit might have to fly.

If I thought I could win some battle against falling in love with Evelyn then I was equally wrong. That love had a grip on me now, pulling me to the edge of my seat.

Hurricane Hildegard, the presenter assured us, as if somehow he was responsible, was already fading and the north was dragging itself back to normality. But we couldn't relax just yet for a second hurricane had gathered and was hovering almost two thousand kilometres north of the country. Hurricane Luke, already tearing with eager fingers at Fiji. More gravity defying roofs and supplicating palms. Cars knee-deep in rain. Shuddering helicopter shots. Pleas for aid.

The whale story seemed tame in comparison. Blurred shots of deep-sea creatures coming up to breathe. Helicopter shots of vague lumps on an endless beach. As Vernon predicted, the pod had headed straight for the inside curve of the Spit. Heroic efforts were being made to turn the creatures before they reached shore, providing some dramatic TV footage, almost as good as the hurricanes, and while most of the pod was turned, a dozen whales still hit the sand and were left stranded when the tide went out. Covers were erected over them to protect them from the light, and sea water was bucketed over their skin. The rest of the pod were still milling around further out. A scientist who, thanks to Vernon's rather badly tuned TV, had a flaming red face and flickering teeth, was on land to speculate that some environmental factor was affecting their navigation. There'd been an increase in these beachings, he said. Scientists were puzzled.

Suddenly the scene switched back to the Auckland studio. A racey-voiced presenter announced they were cutting live to downtown where there had been a mysterious explosion in the workshop of Professor Malcolm Kober, inventor. There was a quick still of the professor, looking dazed, and one lacklustre shot of smoke pouring out of an upper window, being whipped away in the dying hurricane winds, before the camera returned to the richer eye candy of short skirts and blue uniforms. Professor Kober was being treated for shock. The police were investigating the possibility that the bomb had been intended for the strip joint and porno shop below as part of a gangland battle for territory that had been going on for some months. The wind-blustered, on-the-spot reporter was keen to point out that this had been the second explosion in this building in the last ten days.

This had to be Tate's work. If he couldn't buy Kober off, he'd have to destroy him. But no shit would stick to him, only me. That was the name of the game. Guys like Tate were invisible to the authorities; no Jerry Tate had ever come here, or had ever left. Not even Pepsi would testify to his objective existence, I was sure. If police found fragments of explosive, these would not hold the fingerprints of any Jerry Tate. Specials don't have fingerprints.

You can't outthink a person like Jerry Tate; they are immune to reality.

There was a grumble from Vernon's chair as the camera lingered for a moment on the swaying backside of a prostitute heading away from the scene down Fort Street, the wind bowling the lid of a rubbish tin along the street beside her, before cutting back to the grinning presenter.

Since it was clear that Vernon was going to carry on watching this daily apocalypse, I got up and wandered listlessly around, picking up this and putting down that until I realised that I was unsettling him.

I escaped to my room where I flopped on the bed and idly picked up Descartes, whom I had brought along for some godforsaken reason. There was something in there I couldn't just leave behind. This time, instead of randomly reading a quote, I read a whole section, forcing my brain to concentrate on his proofs for God. They didn't help. It seemed he needed to prove God's existence in order to prove the existence of everything else, except maybe himself, whom he had already thought into existence. After all, he had argued that we couldn't trust our senses because some 'evil genius' might have pulled the wool over our eyes, and I would go along with that – I wondered about that 'evil genius' myself – yet, the proofs for God were lame, one of them pretty much claiming that God must exist as a matter of definition, as if the word itself was its own proof. I wasn't prepared to go along with that. Just as Descartes had thought himself into being, now he was trying to do the same with God.

At the same time the evil genius who was organising my life might just have fucked up. This latest attack on Kober couldn't be pinned on me. I had an alibi – I was in Nelson at the time, sir, watching it all on TV.

Weary, I reached out into Vernon's bookcase and the first book my hands encountered turned out to be volume eleven, WXYZ, of the *Children's Britannica,* published back in 1964, a once proud twelve-volume set which would have represented a considerable family investment at the time. I had no memory of it from my childhood. I casually flicked through it and it fell open at Whales and Whaling. There was a photo of a whale jammed between two whaling vessels. I learned that whales can stay under the sea up to forty-five minutes before having to come up to breathe, and that they may have evolved from creatures who once lived on land, their flippers being hand-like in shape. In other words, they went back. They took one good evolutionary look around at dry land and said, to hell with this, let's go back. Let's go back to the deep where we can move these heavy bodies around properly. In their true element. Get out from under this senseless gravity.

Then I took from my bag a bottle of sleeping tablets I'd discovered among Evelyn's bits and pieces; a final line of defence against sleeplessness. I shook one tablet out onto my palm and held it up. It looked completely innocuous, like a little ball of pastel-coloured sugar. This was it; sleep at any price. It was a step up. A step down into a soundless, viewless room with only locked doors. A step nowhere. Survival. If you can't sleep you can't think and if you can't think you die, I thought, in a variation on an old maxim, tossing back the sugar pill and wondering why I was so desperate to live anyway. I thought of the whales, cast up on the wrong shore, uncertain how to breathe, the weight of a vast sky above, the rasp of air like razors on their skin.

I didn't sleep. I was knocked out as if I had been hit on the head with a sledge-hammer, and came to some hours later with the sound of the hammer still ringing in my ears. I had not slept, I had simply been oblivious, nonexistent, and woke as weary as when I had hit the pillow. I had not dreamed. Nothing had happened at all except the passing of time.

And people functioned on these things. They kept going. The nightly kick in the head was somehow enough. I hauled myself to my feet and waited for feeling to trickle back into my body, the numbness to go from my head.

It was 4 a.m.

I got up, crept into the kitchen, put on the jug, made a quick cup of tea, took the radio, and scurried back to my room. I sat down and snapped on the news. One of the whale rescue organisers was being interviewed. He sounded tired too. 'We need more people,' he said. I sipped at my tea. 'It's not so easy up there, volunteers have to go by truck up the Spit. Because of that, the inaccessibility, we don't get the usual hoards of passersby and casual volunteers.' 'Would you say you are short-staffed?' the interviewer asked inanely. 'Yes,' the rescue organiser said. 'I'd say we are short-staffed. The tide's heading up now but towards the next low tide we'll be needing a line of bucketers to keep the whales wet. We're facing thirty or forty whales being beached here today. The situation will get more desperate for the whales when the sun comes up.'

I turned off the radio and stared up at the ceiling. It was a jiggly dark, with no rhyme or reason to it.

I got up and stood naked in the room, looking at my clothes. My body beneath me stood firm, the breath flowed in and out of my chest. I was there, where my flesh met the air; I stopped at the edge of my skin. I was, indivisibly, Harry Blackman, and I made a decision.

I dressed hurriedly.

'No one's going to understand it,' I said silently to the Maori face as I pulled on my pants. Least of all Vernon, who would take it as some kind of cruel joke.

In the kitchen I found, as I'd hoped, the car keys on top of the fridge. Some things don't change, even across universes.

I found a piece of paper and a pen and wrote, *Dear Dad, going to save some whales,* and crept quietly out of the house.

10

I drove out of Nelson as the sun was coming up, turned on the radio and listened to the finale of Douglas Lilburn's *Second Symphony* on the Concert Programme. The grey, dead place in my mind left by the sleeping pill was slowly broken apart by the rising light and the wide sweeping lines of Lilburn; the grandeur, the discipline, the forward, rhythmical movement. A music of wide landscapes.

I tried not to think of Vernon getting up, going into the kitchen and finding the note. His stooped-over shoulders as he read. Vernon wouldn't be fooled; he'd know a childish gesture when he saw one. He'd recognise a petulant act. Bless him!

It was time for a senseless act of beauty. A random devotion.

I stopped only once for a quick cup of coffee before getting back on the road, possessed by a sense of urgency. I didn't stop at one or two of the places that might have given me pause as I drove around Golden Bay towards the tiny village of Collingwood which lay at the base of the Spit. The early sun made long, stretched shadows of the beaches, and patches of forest in the gullies steamed. Somehow I'd always had at the back of my mind that I'd like to retire around here somewhere, just as Dad had. There are old dreams lying around in places like this.

I tuned into the news to hear what was happening to the whales and heard the latest on Hurricane Hildegard which, having vented its spleen on the north, had now veered east. Hurricane Luke, however, was already gathering strength in the Pacific, causing problems in Fiji. I was glad to be out of it.

Driving felt good, dawn looked clear.

I was lucky to just catch the midmorning truck in a bustling Collingwood with hardly any wait. This quiet, sandy town looked settled and timeless. To the north, the spit curved like a great shark's tooth into the ocean. Since there are no roads on the spit, we were transported by the big, high-wheeled trucks used for tourists. There were about ten others in the back of the truck, only two women. The looked like locals with their gumboots and parkas. No one talked much and a couple smoked. I watched the tussocky sand dunes roll by, trying to envisage where we would be on the sickle-shaped spit. Everything glittered. I felt ridiculously dressed in pressed slacks, tan brown city shoes and a light, decorative windbreaker.

We passed a truck going the other way. The drivers paused and exchanged news. More whales had been washed up although the whole pod had not beached.

As soon as I saw them I felt that something profound was taking place but didn't know what it was. It looked like a tranquil holiday scene; a long, scattered beach camp with clusters of human activity around a dozen or so erected tarpaulins. The beach was a shining expanse. The men could have been children playing some game, the beached whales their playmates, their huge humpty-dumpty bodies rolling on the sand.

As we got off the truck and stretched our limbs, mugs of steaming coffee were put into our hands. A whale-rescuing expert from the Department of Conservation arrived and briefed us. I hardly listened. It was so huge and quiet out here that the man's voice went nowhere.

I was led onto the reflecting sand and shown my whale, a large female I was told, that had beached only half an hour ago and still had no tarpaulin. Her skin would soon dry out and start to burn. I stood helpless, looking at her bulk. Then I took off my shoes and socks. I had a sense of reverence, as if I were undertaking something tremendous, some right of passage. As I approached, the animal looked like a huge, fat garden slug that had been caught in the wrong place; closer, I saw how helpless she was with her long bulk and tiny flippers. A large, naked eye fixed on me as I came up. Two or three other people were already there, digging a trench from the stranded whale to the now retreating tide. One of them, an older man with grey hair and sharp black eyes, came up to me. He didn't bother with introductions.

'She might be pregnant,' he said. 'We're getting a vet in to look at her later. She's strong and very alert at the moment.' He pointed to some buckets lying nearby. 'You'll have to get in beside her and start bucketing water over her back. There's plenty of water around her just now, but as the tide goes out, we'll have to get a chain going.' He looked at me critically. 'You can do that, can you?'

I nodded, rolled up my city slacks and got down beside the whale. The retreating tide had created a channel around her. A thin umbilicus stretching back to the ocean. I found myself a mere head height above her back as she loomed very close and palpable.

I set a steady, mechanical pace with the bucketing, not pushing it, hoping to get into a rhythm. Standing this close, I could not escape the sheer physical presence of the creature, the bulk of her, the quivering sensitivity of her skin. I made sure I didn't touch her or let the bucket scrape her, for I sensed she used her skin to feel and see, and was aware of me through it; each time I released a bucket of water over her back I could feel the cool relief flooding across her surface. That was how she knew me, through this sensation.

After ten minutes I felt I couldn't go on. It was backbreaking work, and I wasn't going to be able to keep it up. I wasn't the least bit prepared for this and decided that if I could push myself through the next ten minutes I'd take a five minute break. After five minutes the tarpaulin team arrived and hurriedly erected a shelter above her, giving me the opportunity to stop. There were more whales beaching right now, a kilometre or two further along the spit, they said. I looked up the beach. The nearest whale was about a hundred metres away.

The tarpaulin team moved on and I resumed work. Another man joined me and we worked on opposite sides of the whale in silence. After ten minutes I still felt I couldn't go on but it didn't matter, I'd go on anyway. I'd stop after an hour and have a decent break. It was only work. It didn't require thought, just faith; the faith of the body. After ten more minutes I sat down. I wasn't going to make an hour. There was sweat on my back and chest, and I took my shirt off to dry out. With the tide receding, the whole beach had turned into a glare of sun and sand. A few seagulls had gathered, moving about with their busybody walk or just standing, watching. Waiting.

There were still only five people tending my whale, and three of them were working on the channel, trying to keep the water flowing up around the animal. I poured myself some water from a jerry can and drank. There was sweat all over me and I stank but it didn't matter. Her eyes were on me, assessing me, patient in the face of my weakness, grateful for my strength and stubborn with the will to live.

I stepped back into my spot and kept working, determined to go for fifteen minutes this time. There is a way of working into this kind of physical labour, even if you haven't done it for a while. You take it slow and steady and you keep going.

Push through a few boundaries. And I did that, pausing only once to watch another truckload of volunteers go past, heading for the new beachings. As I worked, my feet, in turn, worked themselves deeper into the sand until I was sinking right in beside her over my ankles. I got through the fifteen minutes, stopped and drank more water. A lot of water. An acrid smell was coming up off my body, and I wondered, perhaps absurdly, if she could smell it and if she found it offensive. I had no clue about a whale's sense of smell out of the water.

Back at her side, I placed my hand on her for the first time, feeling the texture of the skin, oddly surprised to find her faintly warm. She's a mammal, like me, not a fish, I reminded myself as my palm lay flat on her side. If these were sharks we wouldn't be doing this. Then I glimpsed the cool green deep where a creature can slide fifteen metres forward with the single flick of a powerful tail.

I began to bucket, ready to do another fifteen minutes, but after a few minutes I noticed that the water was getting sandier, the pool at my feet more shallow. I could see the grit on her skin and feel her discomfort. A moment later the man opposite me stopped. I recognised him from the truck. We looked back along the line of her body and saw that the channel diggers had run out of ocean.

'We're near low tide,' the man said. 'The ones that beach now will be the first off.'

I nodded and drank water. My body needed buckets of it. I even turned down coffee in favour of it.

'We've got another six hours with this one,' the man said. 'And we're going to need a bigger channel than this to ease her down.'

A helicopter came through flying low. I looked up and saw cameras at the window.

A couple of men came up and one examined the whale. He took out a stethoscope and put it against her skin. The effect was somehow ludicrous. 'Well I'm only a country vet,' the man said in a Scottish accent, 'and I know nothing of whales, but I'd say this girl was very pregnant.' He pointed. 'There're two hearts beating inside her, and I've never met a beastie yet with two hearts, land nor sea.' The men all grinned. 'She's strong and she's pulling well,' the vet went on, 'but she has to keep both of them going, remember that. She's going to be one hungry mother when she hits that ocean tonight.' The men grinned again.

'We're going to need more men,' I said.

The others looked at me.

'They all need more men,' the man who had come with the vet said.

The five of us devised a bucket chain. We dug a hole about mid-tide level, where it would fill up if kept clear, and set up our chain from that. There weren't enough of us and we had to walk to meet the next bucket. I was at the end of the chain, throwing the water over the whale, and had to walk out past her tail to get the next bucket. Being part of this greater rhythm kept me on my feet. But it wasn't enough water, and she was drying out. Dehydration prickled her like pins and needles.

It was mid afternoon, the day was at its hottest and the tarpaulin didn't protect her from the slanting sun which now covered her lower body. I found myself needing to throw buckets to every place at once, especially on the sunlit side. I stopped and suggested the tarpaulin be shifted and we did it quickly enough, angling it to cover as much of her as possible.

After this I became aware that I now thought of her as *my* whale, my project, and no longer counted the minutes; I was engaged, the way I would be at work, and resented having to take breaks, particularly in this case, since I didn't want to lose precedence in the line, the privilege of being the one to throw the bucket over the gleaming bulk of her back. I was prepared to push myself senseless to stay there.

The vet returned with his stethoscope and looked very sombre. 'She's weakening,' he said to anybody listening, 'and if she starts to go she'll go fast.'

'We need more men,' I said to the man who seemed to go everywhere with the vet. I guessed he was from DOC and in charge of the operation.

'We've had two die already,' the man said.

The work passed into dream. The buckets were filled and then they were empty. I lifted my arms and threw the water over the quivering body, whose life she had drawn far inside herself where it would be used, right up to the moment of death, to feed her young. The water and the sand became an undulation and the undulation became light and the light became ocean over which walked a figure, coming towards me.

It was Rene Descartes, looking rather dapper and with dry feet despite his ocean walk. He came right up to me and I saw he had a grim, rather sardonic face, one deeply marked by the ravages of thought, and the dome of a brow thoroughly jaded by wisdom.

'How do you know you exist?' he asked.

Couldn't he see that I was working and had no time to stop and talk to him? 'Because of this bucket,' I answered, forcing my tired arms to hurl the water as far as I could over her back. 'First it is full then it is empty.' That would fix him. Descartes meets Harry Zen Blackman.

'To err and deceive oneself is a defect,' he said. He looked very regal and aristocratic. 'And how do you know the whale exists?'

'Because of this bucket. First it is full, then it is empty.' I hoped he'd take a hint, but that old intellectual tenacity would not let him go.

'If your knowledge of yourself and the whale rests on such a frail basis, why are you doing this?' I noticed what an arched, sensitive nose he had. To sniff out error no doubt.

'It's the bucket,' I explained. The soul of patience. 'When it is empty it must be filled and when it is full it must be emptied.'

And I kept on doing it, to demonstrate, feeling he wasn't much use unless he could lend a hand. Instead he just looked sad. Somewhere on his face a new line of scepticism was born, but I noticed he kept well clear of the whale, as if the helpless mass of her intimidated him.

'What am I then?' he said, a touch of sarcasm in his voice. 'A thing which thinks. What is a thing which thinks? It is a thing which doubts, understands, conceives, affirms, denies, wills, refuses, which also imagines and feels.'

'It doesn't matter any more,' I said. 'The bucket tells me what I am.' I paused to hold out my raw, scraped and near bleeding hands to him. 'It is my pain that assures me of my existence, *Monsieur*. The rest is nonsense.' I went back to work, hoping it had put an end to him for good, but I'd forgotten that I was dealing with one of the most powerful and persistent minds the world has ever seen. I'd need stronger medicine than this to get him off my back.

'Ah,' he said, after critically watching me do a few turns with the bucket, still keeping himself well back from the whale. 'You are doing this, then, as some kind of penance.' He was getting prepared to look satisfied; penance was something this devout even pious, man understood.

'You sound just like Evelyn,' I said.

'It's not a question of motives,' Descartes said, finally

looking offended. 'It is a question of Cause and Effect, which must flow in an unbroken chain from the first breath of God. The cause must contain at least as much reality as the effect. Look at Newton's laws of motion...'

'I'll show you cause and effect,' I said. I took a full bucket of water and showed him the contents. 'This is the cause,' I said. He glanced into the bucket.

Then I emptied the bucket over his head.

'And this is the effect.'

More volunteers were arriving and a second line of bucketers were forming. Another hole was being dug further out, closer to the low-tide mark. The first line of bucketers were weary and harried. A thousand buckets might not be enough to save her.

When a man appeared with hot coffee in Thermos flasks, I surrendered my place in the line, surrendered proprietorship of the whale; it didn't matter, there would be a place for me somewhere on the line. I'd been working for six hours, the tide was at low ebb, and there was nothing to do but keep bucketing and wait for the ocean to quicken.

It wasn't just the slack water of the ebb, it was everything. Even the sky was drained as the sun headed west over the blonde sand hills. A few seagulls pulled lazily, almost motionless, overhead. The ocean lay idle, flat except for the weak, listless lick of an occasional wave on the bare sand. This was a time of danger for the whale, for the very life force itself seemed to lie, stricken and energyless at low water mark. It was this moment she had to live through, this moment of dead water, and there was nothing I could do about it but eat sandwiches and stare out over the flat ocean. When the tide turned, the tide of life would turn inside her too, I hoped, if she was still alive.

After eating, I wandered down to the water line where the ocean lay quiet. Looking straight up into the west I saw Venus glowing bright as a little sun, visible long before it normally is. At least the heat was going from the day, the warmth from the sand. The emptying light gave the scene on the beach an abstract, fabulous quality; space was made of lines, human activity a dark clutter around the smooth, lumped forms of the whales. Water trickled around my feet. Time eddied. I felt the energy shift as the tide turned; felt the moment of its turning as the reversing of the poles on an invisible magnet. Now life flowed the other way. A wavelet pulled at my foot.

There are such moments, the very fulcrums of existence, but I have rarely allowed myself the privilege of noticing them.

I walked back and took my place anywhere in the line, it didn't matter where. None of us had any proprietorship over the whale for she belonged to the rising tide, to the energy that flowed forward to meet her stranded bulk. It was an energy that would lift her and free her and it could not be carried in buckets.

We worked on, waiting for the tide to take its slow-gathering time. My job was much simplified. All I had to do now was take a full bucket from one set of hands, turn, walk a few paces to the next set of hands, pass on the bucket, take an empty one, and return for the next full one. As each bucket passed out of my hands I imagined it going over her back, staining her with relief.

The vet returned but I didn't break the chain to hear what he said. There was only one thing he could say; she was alive. They were all his whales, in his mind anyway; he didn't want to let any more die.

As the tide crept in, more men were put onto the spades to create as deep a channel as possible, not just to bring the water

closer to her but eventually to float her out. I took time off
the bucket line to go and see the creature I had been serving.
Her eye moved in its socket as I walked by. The bulk of her
was familiar by now, but not the massive sense of presence;
I couldn't get used to that. I put my hand on her again, as if
I were a doctor, and she felt feverish despite the buckets of
water which were now coming thick and fast. Though she was
living deep inside herself, immersed in her own ocean, she
was nevertheless aware of me, a black bipedal shape out there
in the land of hard light.

Around nine that evening she floated in her pool and the
bucket lines were abandoned. I found myself back beside
her again, as I'd been at the beginning, bucketing straight up
onto her back from the water swirling around my feet. A few
hurricane lamps had been brought out and the area around her
was a crisscross of torches. There was a buzz of conversation
but I was too tired to speak. I knew something was up when a
new vet arrived with the man I identified as 'brass', although
he wore the standard Swanddri and gumboots. The new vet
listened to her from several angles and we stopped bucketing
water while he pondered. Eventually he shrugged at the DOC
man who looked more tired than all of us put together.

It's not possible that she's dead, I thought. I hadn't been
pouring water over a corpse.

'We'll try to float her out backwards,' the DOC man shouted.

We all got around her and lifted as best we could and
pushed. She slipped out of our hands, but moved backwards
a fraction.

'Again,' the DOC man said. There was no sound but the
grunting and sighing of the men and the swift, desperate
slock of the spades.

'Again,' the man said, setting up a rhythm. 'Gently now,

no force. Ease her back.' I felt the rush of water in over my knees as the tide strained forward against the backward tug of the moon, which was just now rising to outshine Venus; the DOC man was eagerly watching these surges, watching for the chance to turn her; once she turned, the battle would be half won.

There was already energy going through her as the waves rippled along her body. She knew what we were doing, she was preparing herself. An internal wave that matched the tide, urging her body to movement. I learned that I could apply a little pressure by leaning my body into hers, slightly angled to the direction of her movement. At the same time I had to laugh for this was my own life I was lifting here, and *yours* too, the whole slippery weight; everything. The channel, open to the sea.

'Again,' the man said, and we eased her back into a bigger pool where half a dozen men were making their spades flash in the fitful light. When she floated in this pool there was a shuddering movement through her, along her backbone. I caught a glimpse of the green deep again, and heard her for the first time, a high-pitched screaming, in my head. This was the sound that linked her to the ocean, that drew the ocean back, in ever larger waves, towards her straining body.

'Again,' the man said, and we manoeuvred her to a narrower channel at the back edge of the pool. We'd moved her maybe six metres. A bigger wave swept up around her, seeking to push her back up the beach. She strained against it as best she could, wriggled and flopped.

'Turn her with the backwash,' the DOC man said swiftly, stepping in beside me, 'head to the north.' We swung her around, using the undertow to help us, but the big waves passed too swiftly and retreated too fast. She was stranded on an angle and likely to be battered back around by the next wave.

Wisely, she rested.

'Again,' the DOC man shouted.

Three waves it took us, fighting to keep the gains we made in turning her, but when she finally faced the ocean, with water under her, a bolt of energy went through her. A shudder. A convulsion of memory. An eagerness for the wide, fenceless deep. Her tail was suddenly something full of muscled power and driven purpose. I didn't step back quickly enough and received a whack on my leg, but felt nothing. A cheer went up, but it wasn't over. We had to keep moving her firmly forward with every wave, standing on each side to prevent her from turning.

Then, with a confident surge of power, she was gone, returned to the intimacy of the ocean. We watched her from the shore as she swam out to sea, apparently quite clear in her purpose.

The sky was full of calm stars.

Somebody put a mug of coffee into my hand. The DOC man reeled off down the beach to the next whale. Some of the volunteers went with him to help. I was given a sleeping bag by somebody and lay down in the sand where a few others were resting. I lay back and looked up at the sky with its great palette of stars. I just had time to remember Vernon and his bitter face before a door opened and the sky rushed down on me.

I slept.

And dreamed of Evonne. Evonne was standing at the top of the drive, under the red pine, waiting for me as I drove up. There was something wrong with the car, a horrible grating, screaming noise.

'I can't stay, I'm not really here,' I shouted through the window of the car. 'I'm just visiting you.' There was torment in my words for I was sure that she didn't understand, but her smile was sunny and full of reassurance.

'I know, Harry.'

I looked up through the new transparent body of the Ghia and saw two sets of stars, two sets of constellations. I saw the pot, upside down, emptying its contents over the back of a whale. I said, 'I'm not going to be able to escape, not without a fight. Maybe death.'

Evonne was glowing like a saint. There was a great blazing up around her face. Then I was driving the Ghia over the sand, which was like a vast highway with nobody but me on it. A whale carcass rolled in purple, blue, green, silver and black; black-backed gulls had already taken its eyes. The ocean turned amber. Evonne stood on the sandbank above, hair gleaming like dark wire.

A dumpy woman in her late thirties met me at the door. She looked me up and down, from unkempt face to ruined, salt-encrusted clothes.

'Dad's ill,' she said turning and walking away from me. This had to be Paula, my phantom sister. Her face had changed but the line of her nose was still there.

'What happened?'

'According to the doctor he's been having minor strokes quite often, maybe for three or four weeks.' She went into the kitchen and rattled something.

'He never told me. Where is he now?

She gestured jerkily towards the bedroom. 'He's asleep right now. He's had some pills.'

'Christ.' There was a high ringing in my ears like sounds made under the sea. I flopped down on the chair.

Tension snapped in her voice as she spoke. 'I know I shouldn't be saying this, really, but Dad was worried sick about the house. He was convinced you were going to sell up on him. "Harry wants me out of the way," he said. "I've become a nuisance to him."'

'That's entirely unfair, I said, 'and I told him so.'

'You had a row with him then? I thought you had.' Steam from a boiling jug rose up beside her. Through the steam I could see her eyes looking at me, and they were like Vernon's eyes, suspicious and deep-set.

'Dad's very forthright with his opinions.'

'Sure, and you've never spared anyone yours.'

'Hell, I hardly got a word in.'

'Then stealing his car and going off wacko like that. Where did you go?'

'Farewell Spit.'

'He thought you'd gone off the deep end. He was on the phone to me raving about how sick you looked, and how your marriage was breaking up. Then he was on the phone to Evelyn.' She stopped clattering coffee cups. 'Is your marriage breaking up, Harry?'

'Sort of. I needed to get away.'

'Did you think for a minute before you came down here and dumped it all on Dad that there might be some better way to go?'

'I didn't dump on him. He ferreted it out for himself in the first five minutes.' I kept my tone mild, bland; I was flying blind once more in unknown territory. The high, wild sound in my ears had not gone away. It felt as though I were suffering from jet lag. 'I have to use the bathroom,' I said, getting up.

The mirror told me everything I didn't want to know. I looked worse than a mess. My face was stark and unshaven, eyes wild and staring; my dull, salt-filled hair stood up on end like a punk's. I looked as if I had been washed up on some beach myself, and had a fair-sized bruise on my leg from where the whale had hit me. And, worse still, there was something less easy to define; the fixed, freaked expression, perhaps. Of someone who's aged ten years in a few hours.

I showered, shaved, combed my hair, put on clean clothes and fronted up more plausibly to the mirror. I need to look like *you*. Everything pretty much passed muster except my eyes which stayed the same; there was nothing much I could do about them. There were new lines, a new face struggling out from behind the flesh of given expressions. Muscles tugging different ways.

Back in the lounge-kitchen, I squatted awkwardly on the edge of the sofa and sipped lukewarm coffee.

Paula came up and sat down beside me. Middle age had taken her sideways, filling her out, but her eyes were still youthful, clear and expressive. 'Harry, I don't want to be enemies. So often we've been enemies, especially over Dad. I never wanted you to give him that money. I had to take his side to protect him, especially after Mum died. You know that.'

'Yes.'

'What's happened, Harry? Something big's happened, hasn't it? You've changed.'

'Just an accumulation. Problems at home, problems at work, money problems.'

Paula's mouth grew into a slow smile. 'So what else is new? Come on Harry, at least we could always talk when the chips were down.' She gave me a big warm smile. 'I've been knocked around. Christ. Dad's always held you and Evelyn up as shining examples of marital harmony. Something for me to compare my messes with, if you like.'

She got up, went to the cupboard and pulled out a bottle of brandy. 'Let's have one,' she said.

'Are you on the wagon?'

'Just overdid the scotch a bit.'

'Scotch,' she wrinkled her nose, 'that's vile stuff.' She poured brandy liberally into her half-filled coffee cup and took a couple of mouthfuls before slopping a bit more in. 'I hope Dad's all right,' she said, looking anxious.

'I didn't dump on him, Paula. He was onto me as soon as I got off the plane. I couldn't fool him for one minute.'

'That's funny,' she said.

'What?'

'You calling me Paula. You hardly ever call me that. That's what Dad calls me.' She drank again, her eyes sliding sideways across my face as she did so. She was no idiot, this Paula; I was back on red alert.

'Anyway, he asked me about Evelyn and he wasn't going to believe any lies…'

'And what about Evelyn? Dad said she was cold to him on the phone. She's usually open with him.'

'That's because he dotes on her.'

'Come on Harry, quit stalling.'

'We've had a row over the house project. All of a sudden it's not just the house but the whole relationship that's mortgaged.'

'Fucking money-grubbers,' Paula said with quiet contempt, pouring herself more brandy. Her round face grew bitter, like Vernon's.

I knew the signs; I didn't have to watch. I knew why you and Paula had so often been enemies. I could write out the whole history without even knowing it. It could be summed up in one word: alcohol.

'Whatever you like,' I said. It was not my battle.

She brought her cup to the sofa and sat down beside me again. 'Shit, Harry, let's just bury it. We've got Dad to deal with here, and you piss off and save whales! Did you save any?'

'One. I helped with one. We had to keep her wet.'

'How do you mean?' There were the beginnings of a playful

smile.

'We had to throw buckets of water over her.'

'And that's what you did?'

'Yes.'

'You spent nine hours throwing buckets of water over a bloody whale?'

'Yes.'

'It's not like you, Harry. In fact it's so unlike you that I sort of like it, if you see what I mean.'

'That's a backhander if ever I heard one.' Although I did see what she meant.

She seemed to be drunk almost immediately. There was no crossover point. She waved her glass in the air. 'It's a sort of gesture, if you see what I mean. A statement to the great fucked universe.'

'We had to turn her around.'

She giggled. 'I bet she was one big mamma.'

'She was.' There was pride in my voice, I couldn't keep it out.

'And did you get her back out to sea safely?'

'Yes, but the pod's still out there, trying to find its way past the spit.'

She slurped at her cup. Her smile grew from merriment to roguery. 'And did you have a mystical experience out there?'

It was my turn to crack a grin. 'No. But something happened.'

'What?'

'I had a conversation with Descartes.'

'Who?'

'Descartes. The philosopher.'

She slurped heavily at the brandy. 'I think therefore I am?'

'That's the guy.'

'He can get fucked. Anything else?'

'The sea came back with me. I've brought the sea back in

my head.'

'You're completely crazy,' she said, and she laughed, as if that idea were very funny.

We both laughed and decided that, although enemies, we liked each other. I could see I might enjoy having a sister like this. In another time and place.

'You're not really Harry though, are you?' she said, when she was drunk enough, giving me a meaningful wink. 'You're just pretending to be him.'

I nodded very solemnly and meaningfully, which is one of the best things you can do with drunks. I skulled my tea as if it were brandy.

'Why do dogs look so guilty when they're shitting?' Vernon asked, sitting up in bed, gesturing out the window. The morning was bright and clear and the dog's face looked forlorn as its backside bent towards the turf.

'It's not guilt,' I said. 'It's just the strain of all that concentration.'

Vernon laughed weakly. 'So you're going back north this morning?'

'I have to face the music sooner or later.'

Vernon gripped my arm. His eyes closed as if he were in prayer. He looked very old. 'You hang onto that woman, now. Make it up to her. I know she loves you.'

'Thanks, Dad.' The grip on my arm slackened. The eyes opened.

'Where's Paula?'

'Having a rest.'

'She's got her life to get back to, such as it is,' the old man said. 'I'll be up and around tomorrow.'

A little later, standing at the sink, I saw a cloud of white butterflies dancing around one spot, as if they were trying to make a shape. It was almost impossible to focus on one of them.

Paula, who was lying on the couch, pulled herself up. 'Don't even mention it,' she said, screwing her eyes against the light and falling back again.

I made coffee.

Paula's eyes opened again and she made a weak effort to sit up again. 'Is there anyone else? I mean between you and Evelyn.'

'No.'

'She told Dad she thought there was someone else.'

'No.'

'She must be paranoid then, like I am.' Paula closed her eyes firmly.

Vernon came out, dressed, looking frail and gloomy but on his feet. 'Don't look at me like that, he said to us both, although Paula wasn't looking anywhere.

'That's what I said to Harry,' Paula said, pulling herself off the couch and heading for the bathroom.

The doctor came by and listened to Vernon's heart.

'I'm on my feet,' Vernon said tersely to the doctor.

'Don't overdo it,' the doctor said, and left a prescription.

'I heard on the radio,' the old man said, walking to the door and looking across the balcony to the sea, 'that a new hurricane is on its way.' He made it sound like something that would arrive and never depart.

'Luke.'

'What?'

'It's called Hurricane Luke, Dad.'

'Luke?' He looked vague. 'I always thought they called them women's names.' He sat on the deck chair and looked out towards the north as if he could see the misnamed hurricane.

His look was almost triumphant. See how sick I am, the look said, you can't sell the house on me now.

Paula was groping around the toaster and rattling coffee mugs.

When I left I shook hands with Vernon who biffed me on the shoulder and gave a stiff smile.

'Your house is safe, Dad,' I said to him. 'I didn't come down for that.'

The smile got stiffer.

'I came down to save a whale.'

The smile made a brave attempt.

I gave Paula a hug and she hugged back for so long I thought she'd never let go.

'Your secret is sae,' she said. She gave me a heavy, creaking wink.

It might have been just a muscle spasm.

11

Evelyn's was the last face I expected to see at the airport waiting for me. Yet there she was, standing discreetly to one side of the bulk of the crowd. When she saw me a smile came into her face, a true, involuntary smile, untainted by irony.

She loved me! She was pleased to see me! She'd walked out on me, note and all, and here she was with a gentle kiss on the cheek to welcome me home.

Timmy was there and needed his kiss too.

The remnants of Hurricane Hildegard tore wetly at our clothes as we walked through the car park, as restless and sulky as ever, making conversation impossible. I was grateful for that, for I was suddenly shy of her again, as I had been on the first day. Tongue-tied.

I didn't know her, after all. I'd only met her several weeks ago and somehow she'd already changed; pale but very composed, she seemed to have understood something, reached some certainty, come to some decision.

Inside the car our raincoats came off. I was already more wet from sweating than from rain. Evelyn looked casually devastating in a short dark skirt and a moderately severe white blouse fastened at the neck and wrists. Her hair was swept back off her forehead, showing the intelligent spaces around her eyes. The overall effect was somehow both modest and daring.

She noticed my attention and flashed me a grin as she pulled the keys. It was one of her cheeky, adolescent grins, mysterious almost conspiratorial.

She drove with the same sure calm while Timmy raved about big winds and castles. All the talk was on the storm and how well our place had survived it all.

'I slept in Mummy's bed,' Timmy said with some solemnity.

It was back to happy families once more, but with a subtle difference. Evelyn had changed. At first I thought that she'd done her hair differently or something like that, and she was waiting for me to notice, but it wasn't that. It was even more than the confidence and sense of resolve that radiated from her, but something less definable, a change in the colours of her invisible body.

'I promised to take him to the Parent and Child show,' she said, 'but I thought we'd go to the museum first to fill in an hour or so. How as the ride? As you up to it?'

'I'm up to it.'

'And then we'll leave Timmy with Tess for the night, having given him heaps of parental doting, so we can have some time together.'

'You've got it all planned.'

'Are you up to it?'

'I'm up to it.'

I was up to anything. I could take on this strange world now, take the bull by the horns. I was high, as if still in the air or maybe deep in the ocean.

Whatever it was that had happened to Evelyn, it was making me feel good. I was a survivor. If Vernon was to be trusted, I'd kicked my twin brother's head in to get a lung full of air. I was full of ideas as to how I might handle the diplomacy debacle coming up in Canada. How I could wriggle out of Pepsi's steel trap. But these were just spin-offs; what was really making me high was the thought that I could let down all the barriers, all the memories of probable worlds I might have lived in, and open myself up to this woman and love her the way I knew I could love her. Feeling that, and the excitement it brought, led me to see that something in her had changed, and in so changing, changed me – she had let down her barriers. She was open to me in a way I'd never known but *you* must have known, especially in your early days with her.

When I looked at her to confirm some of these new impressions, she was simply driving. The car was filling up with hot, sticky air.

'We might as well live in Fiji,' Evelyn said lightly. 'that's global warming for you. A hurricane or two, lots of mosquitoes.'

In the oil industry, of course, nobody talked about 'global warming.' The euphemistic 'climate variation' was a big enough stone to swallow.

'And the whales don't know where they're going,' I said.

She said, 'I know, I saw it on TV.'

And she took time off from her driving for another smile. She was close enough to touch, far enough away to ache for.

In the near distance the War Memorial Museum sat on its promontory like a flat birthday cake, complete with curled icing along the edges.

It was a relief to walk into the tall, cool, marbled spaces of the museum after the humid fluster of Hurricane Hildegard's dying breath. Timmy looked around, suitably awe-inspired. Evelyn's heels rapped on the marble floor.

The branching rooms and orderly design bespoke the classical mind with its feel for precision, shape and proportion; a beautiful arrogance in its wide, half-empty hallways and boastful balustrades. Money didn't matter too much in those days, when they built the place. There was still the grandeur of the Empire to consider, if just in image. I would never have approved the building if I'd been on the right committee; it offended the principles of parsimony, the Occam's razor of spending.

Yet these echoing, shadowless, impersonal spaces with their calm exhibits, the tamed jumble of history, were just what I needed. Here, parallel worlds were taken for granted. Gods from different universes gazed at one another across glass and marble spaces. Here, time was vertical. Everything from the Palaeozoic to modern times happened at once inside these spacious halls; who was I to complain about the money it cost?

Holding Timmy's hand, and without much purpose, I wandered into the historical section and we found ourselves inside the Maori meeting house. Timmy reacted immediately to its dimply lit, spooky atmosphere, the hideous carved faces with their tongues lolling out and cheeks tattooed with spirals; each figure was doing its own crazy, bow-legged dance.

The silence was too intense for him.

Evelyn loved it. I caught her poking out her tongue at one of the log demons as we left.

We then walked along the length of the *waka*, the enormous canoe, me telling Timmy of the huge, epic voyages made by Maori ancestors in these long, slender craft while Evelyn wandered loosely beside us, listening in. From one world to another, one myth to another, I recounted how Maui had fished up the North Island with a magic jawbone. Timmy had already heard the story several times at school, but hearing it from me made it real to him. He told me how Maui's brothers had been naughty and carved up the smooth back of the whale while Maui was away, so creating the mountains and valleys. They did that because there were greedy, Timmy said, and I believed him.

A man walked slowly along behind us, giving himself plenty of time to get a good eyeful of Evelyn. I've never been out of the house with Evelyn, I thought, but eyes like those must follow her everywhere she goes. Evelyn ignored the man but he made me uneasy. She was used to this sort of thing but I wasn't. I felt a stab of something like jealousy; this was my woman – but she wasn't, we hadn't made love yet.

It'll happen tonight, I thought with a tingle of expectation. She's set it up to happen tonight. At that moment she bent over to catch something Timmy was saying and both the sauntering peeper and I got a neatly curved eyeful.

I stopped before one of the displays to let the peeper go by. Evelyn stopped too, flicking me a quick, flirtatious look. It was the look of a woman who liked to wear the kind of underclothes I'd found in her drawer the first night. She'd known about the peeper. She'd done it deliberately to provoke me.

We were standing in front of what looked like a modern, stylised sculpture of a naked woman with triangular breasts too small for the sharp, Picasso-like body. The smooth, oval dome of her head. The minimal face. Cracked breadfruit-tree deity.

Evelyn admired it too. With no eyes or ears to speak of, it was possessed of a blind, faceless power. Not a being to be messed with. Evelyn read the inscription in a quiet voice.

This was the Princess Kave De Hine Aligi, of Nukuoro in the Caroline Islands. Kave was a malevolent female spirit who ruled the world in the absence of the divine male.

I got a quick smirk on the strength of that one. 'Seen any divine men lately?' she asked sweetly.

It was a gentle tease but it reminded me of the bitter war between the sexes. Our images of each other were rooted far back, even to our prehistory, our mythological sources in deep time. But I was a modern man, a rational man, happy to work within Cartesian coordinates, more than happy to get along with my wife and raise children – if the goal posts didn't shift too often.

At least, that's what I had always believed about myself – until Nelson and the whale whose cry rang through the ocean.

I looked up at Princess Kave's face but she was giving nothing away. She had a big, world-eating body and minimal features. Evelyn stood close, her fingers lightly on my sleeve. I gently touched the sculpture, feeling the cool intensity of the hardwood trunk.

Timmy pulled me away from Kave to show me a large, ceremonial gong made out of hardwood; two facing slabs resonating into each other. A much more interesting proposition from his point of view.

Evelyn remained in rapt communication with Kave; she wasn't fooled by the male version of the story.

I tried to concentrate on the gong because Timmy wanted to make it sound, but behind and above us, on a tall stand, was a collection of strange ceramic creatures that caught my interest. These were Malanggan figures, spirit beings with birds on their heads, ancestors who return to the village to take away the spirits of the dead while the young were being initiated into manhood.

I didn't like the look of them. They were too sharp-eyed and pale, one having an open midriff with some sort of scaffolding suggesting bones. They were skeletal and demented. I wouldn't like having them come for me to drag me off to death or manhood or whatever. I'd hide, I'd just hide away somewhere, deep in the belly of things, and never be seen again.

At the same time I thought I recognised one of them and

stared harder. This one had a very creature-like appearance, an adze-faced denizen of the forest, bearing a generic resemblance to my little tree-fern being. Here was a cousin of my sharp greenfaced gremlin on show!

I was staring at it, agape, when Evelyn materialised by my side. There were so many ancestors around she had to walk quietly. Evonne would have done the same only more so; she'd have trod as if the marble floor was a lotus flower on the surface of a still pond. I've seen her do it, walk without creating gravity.

'The stuff of dreams,' she said, gesturing to the Malanggan posse.

Timmy had found a way to sound the double gong. He kicked it with baby leather soles.

A soft mellow sound rang through the worlds.

A museum guard looked up and went back to sleep.

At that moment I saw *you*. You were standing in the Pacific Hall, a Bonito canoe house-post with a cheeky hat on one side, a Gilbert Island chief in sennit armour on the other, both sunk in their vat of history.

I couldn't have been mistaken. I knew the clothes straightaway. It was my best suit, looking half-ruined since you'd got hold of it. In about the same condition as your Ghia. I knew the angle of the body, and was suitably shocked by the grey thinning patch at the top of your head. It linked you to me indissolubly with neglected images and the pathos of vanished youth. The unchanging but ever-changing face in the mirror.

I had always thought that I looked much younger than that.

As soon as you stabilised in my view, the museum, with its spacious commons and tall chambers, glass cases and towering larger pieces, became zigzags of shape and colour, a polyphonic mystery; meaning gave way to form, and form gave way to variations of intensity. When Timmy kicked the gong a second time, with greater force, I saw shafts of light cresting like waves coming through the walls. A particle hurricane all of its own. Light was passing through everything. I saw the evil Princess Kave and the demon Malanggan carnival disassemble into standing waves of sound.

Two attuned pieces of wood reverberating into one another could do that.

Abruptly, everything around me seemed to slip like a misplaced cog; like a movie caught between frames, there were two lots of marbled halls, two lots of whispering floors, a multiplicity of Malanggan spirit beings back with a vengeance. A fragmented Evelyn and Timmy, arrested between movements. The museum guard, with nothing better to do, wandered past, a duplicate following him as if he were following a copy of himself.

And you. Standing in front of me, dislocated in the middle as if immersed in water up to your waist. Both here and not here.

Dishevelled, stunned looking, but nevertheless you. Standing on the marbled floor looking at me. You knew who I was, no doubt of that. Then you started to reach for something, something in your universe that I couldn't see. It was beyond the frame of your arms. I saw light pouring in through tall cathedral windows; the peaceful light that hadn't seen the dark windwhirl of Hurricane Hildegard.

You were there at the museum in your universe, tuning into whatever deities you could find to get to me. This was the price I had to pay for my devotion to the whale; while it took me far away from you at the time, the openness it left in me, the openness that even now Evelyn was responding to, also left me open to you.

Wide open. Your arms were swinging back towards me,

throwing something at me, when I took a step to one side. The shock of my movement blew the frames of the dual reality back into one, superimposing them on top of one another so exactly that not a slip showed, not even the blur of a shadow, a shard of misplaced light. Everything was back where it had always been.

You vanished, but not before I'd seen what you were throwing at my head. A heavy greenstone club. You had intended to kill me.

Evelyn was busy trying to stop Timmy from hurtling headlong at the gong for a third and final knockout blow.

I'd lost track of Evelyn and Timmy. Finding myself in another part of the museum altogether, I drifted from one hall to the next, from history to history, the driftwood of artefacts and jumbled time, unmotivated, with no purpose in mind but the next hall, disengaged and in a state of suspension. Lost to the body, I was reminded of how the jet had lifted, had overcome the tyranny of iron and made a miracle for itself in thin air.

Then I saw Evelyn and Timmy coming towards me between rows of glass cases holding pots and ceramics from Eastern cultures. Each pot, like Keats' Grecian urn, told its own story, held its own drama in eternal suspension. Evelyn looked so elegant, a culture all to herself, as slender as an Egyptian goddess, as rooted as the deepest amber.

I was glad to see them. They looked like love to me. I had to stop myself from running towards them, arms racing out from my shoulders, making a great eternal fool of myself by knocking over some exhibits, taking hold of Evelyn and kissing her with heat, solid mammalian heat, and in defiance of all the frozen time around us, copulating in a shower of glass.

She perceived my intention, at least the intensity of it, and she took my hand and held it firm. My hand was as frail as a leaf inside hers. By holding on, she also held my feet to the geometric reality of the marble floor, which was also cool and very dense.

Later, when we were out of the building and back into the humid bluster, Evelyn took my arm in a very old-fashioned gesture. 'You looked all faint back there,' she said. 'Are you all right?'

'I'm all right,' I said, abruptly remembering the promise I'd made to tell Evelyn everything when I got back from Nelson.

'I wanna see Ronald McDonald,' Timmy said.

'I don't want to go to the Parent and Child show,' Evelyn confessed to me as we got into the car.

'Then let's not bother,' I said. 'Life is short.' As short as your skirt, I was going to add, but it wasn't the right thing to say, true as it might have been. When she slid in behind the controls, there was no hiding those satiny legs.

'But we can't take him to Tess just yet,' she said, slipping the car into gear. She glanced professionally at her watch; this was a well-timed operation after all. From airport to bed, I hoped. 'A couple of hours.'

I said, 'It'll probably take us that long to get there.'

I was only half kidding. The roads were jammed.

'Do you think we're going to be in time to see Ronald McDonald?' Timmy asked us both brightly; the traffic didn't bother him. The fumes and the exhaustion hadn't caught up with him yet. He was searching for affirmation, for an assurance that the world really was there for his pleasure and delight and nothing could ever go wrong with it.

'I'm sure he'll wait for you,' I said.

'They've got McDonald's Futureland,' Timmy said as we swung into the Expo grounds, and I had some sort of intimation as to what that future might be like; there would be some plastic thing you could walk up or slide down; the kids would go through the place like a dose of salts in search of junk food.

I didn't want to think about it, as some harassed old man dressed in white, who thought he'd retired years ago, directed us towards the already packed car park.

As we got out of the car I felt the warm, soft air against my face. Lines of people, the bulk of them pushing strollers, were converging on the double doors of the huge Expo building as if it were a great mouth flanked by security guards, buskers and ticket sellers.

As I looked in the direction of the pavilion, towards which we were being drawn, I had the sudden conviction that we shouldn't go in there, that through those jaws of glass something dreadful awaited. Evelyn appeared to feel something of the same thing, or picked it up from me, because she hesitated, stopped as if she had just run into some invisible barrier, some hidden ring-pass-not.

For the moment her cool, calm mask slipped and she stared at me, her eyes stark with fear.

At the same time there was no going back. We were swept along with the rest, fleeced of various dollars, and herded into the huge pavilion packed with stalls and crammed with people and children. Women sprouting toddlers from every hip, a spread of glazed-eyed men trailing behind.

It was the noise that hit me first. A roar, dull yet powerful, abetted by a shrill descant; it consisted of human voices and something more bass and grinding, like vast stones being rubbed together underground. This last sound grew more insistent as we left the doors behind and penetrated down the first aisle.

Evelyn's hand slipped into mine. I liked the feel of it there, damp with sweat, yet light and reassuring. She was looking up, eyes staring wide at a two-metre-long infant clad only in its trusty Trusties, lit by two powerful halogen lamps, floating in a chemically pure azure sky, mouth wide with joy. The great joy of being in the world! The purist of symbols, the Joyful Infant, was enough to rival Blake's *Glad Day*, since the pose of the Joyful Infant mimicked it, chest wide open, arms stretch back, limbs kicking in the free air.

This vast icon floated above its own stall and those around it while beneath, women battling each other with their strollers and pregnant belly give-way signs filled out forms (with their addresses included) and received their free Trusties.

This demigod was served by other acolytes busy taking money for other subsidiary purchases, mostly young women with corporate shoulder pads and black stockings – there were lashings of black stockings, more than you could find in any well-stocked bordello. They all seemed to be trying to look as good as Evelyn really did; sexy and free and in control.

The battling women looked neither pleased nor particularly relieved when they'd finished, since, no sooner had they raised their heads from the Trusties stall than they were distracted by a dozen other sanitary necessities, including the Trusties' great competitors, the Squeakies, who had set up shop just down the way and were giving away Squeakies as fast as their uniformed assistants could stuff them into clean and squeaky plastic bags.

All around us, the cumulative roar of happy families. Evelyn squeezed my hand hard; hold on, her hand said, hold on tight and we can get through anything, even this place. I yearned for the cool marble halls of time. It was seeing *you* that drove us out of there, I thought. I didn't want to face seeing you again.

As if coming here would make any difference to that!

A Parent and Child show was as good a place for a murder as a museum, better even; who would hear the sound of a .22 going off in this cacophony?

You can cross over, I thought, why can't I? Do you stalk me from place to place, waiting for the chance, for that brief, uncertain window to open? Waiting to kill me? That uncanny twins' knowledge of where the other is.

As we progressed deeper down the aisle, deeper into the density of toddlers, strollers and swollen bellies, we found ourselves surrounded by the soft edges of the hard sell into babyland, corporate facades pushing all things clean and polished, needful, tempting and utterly good for baby. I felt as if I had unwittingly been drawn into some great ceremony of sanitary worship, some *geld*-lubricated machine that kept on turning as long as there were people to feed it. Limbs and souls and embryos all mixed up together, one doomed shit-smeared mesh.

I squeezed Evelyn's hand to let her know that I was still there, still feeling her, not entirely lost in the belly of the whale. She squeezed back; there would be time...

Our first properly human landmark was a sad little man with a black suit and bowler hat who was silently demonstrating the three-cups-and-a-pea trick by a stall decorated with all manner of magic charms and tricks displayed. He gave me a lopsided Charlie Chaplin grin as he lifted a cup to demonstrate that the pea was most assuredly not there. And the second cup, the pea wasn't there either. Lo and behold, somehow the pea had changed cups! His smile was one of sad complicity, beguilingly easy to relate to. He seemed about to impart some important secret out of the side of his mouth to me and Evelyn, but Timmy was pulling us on, tugging at our hands, and suddenly Evelyn slipped out of my grasp. Maybe she swerved to avoid an urgent pregnancy, maybe she just saw something and moved towards it, but whatever, she had vanished like one of the peas under the sad little man's devious cup.

Look, no wife!

I turned around, Timmy in one hand, and couldn't see her anywhere in the mass and crush. I had this horrible feeling that *you* had appeared and that she had trustingly taken your hand thinking it was me, only to find herself jerked out of this world into God knows where, what upside-down world.

I can't get away from him, I thought. I'll never know if at any moment he might materialise by my side.

Timmy was pulling me forward, and as we moved on with the flux of the crowd I looked back and saw the sad little man lifting the cups for some other short-term rubberneckers. He gave them the same Charlie Chaplin grin for the same sad reason. Then the noise and the people closed over him.

And Evelyn too, swept away in a tide of swollen pushchairs and children stuffing things into their mouths, and I had no guarantee that I would ever see her again; this universe obeyed its own laws entirely.

I realised that our progress through this garish carnival of baby products had a purpose and direction to it. Timmy had forgotten about Evelyn and was leading me towards the source of the grinding noise which began to resolve into loud thumping music. At the hub of that great vexed grinding was a stage surrounded by munching children and their munching parents, and at the centre of that stage was Ronald McDonald dressed in the colours of the fast-food chain he represented, cavorting on stage and shouting genial abuse at the audience. He was bringing people forward and putting balloons under their clothing so that they looked bloated and shapeless. The audience was laughing and the clown was passing rude remarks about his hapless victims and their body shape. Then he took out a pin and danced around them, popping the balloons as his uncomfortable-looking stooges looked even more uncomfortable and stooge-like.

Timmy laughed when a big matronly breast blew up.

It seemed very important to me that I find Evelyn and get out of there as quickly as possible. I scanned the crowd for her face, for all the stalls led, like roads to Rome, to Ronald McDonald.

Having humiliated some adults for the enjoyment of the children, Ronald now danced and sang:

You put your left foot in, you put your left foot out,
You put your left foot in and you shake it all about,
You do the hokey-tokey and you turn around,
That's what it's all about!

As he sang and performed the actions he substituted for 'hokey-tokey' various menu items from the McDonald's list such Strawberry Sundae and Big Mac. Some of the mums began to clap along. It was a jolly show.

Evelyn was nowhere to be seen.

I quietly took Timmy's hand and edged him away from the stage and closer to the stalls. Maybe I could guide him quietly back towards the entrance while I looked for Evelyn.

Maybe I should just say it to him, let's find Mummy, and give him a new mission in life, but I was afraid, deeply afraid, that Mummy would never be found, ever.

Timmy was reluctant to move, I was towing him backwards when I bumped into one of the stalls. I turned to apologise.

A woman was bent over something with an air of quiet, studious concentration, which was a miraculous achievement itself in that atmosphere. The stall behind her was decorated with bright swirling patterns on fabric and paper. In front of the woman was a tray filled with some clear liquid, beside which were several small jars of different coloured inks with brushes in them. She took a brush from the blue pot, wiped the excess ink off against the side of the jar, and, with a careful tapping motion against her hand with the brush, flicked droplets of the colour onto the surface of the liquid in the tray. As soon as one drop hit the surface there was a little burst of colour as it spread to a circle about the size of a twenty cent piece. More drops of different colours went down, encountering each other, circles jostling against circles, only to be further broken up by more droplets arriving. A pattern began to form on the surface. The more colours that rained down, the brighter the pattern became.

I took another look at Timmy's face and saw that he was absorbed despite the ongoing attention-deficit racket from the stage. I realised I had been so busy missing my true Timmy that I'd never really looked at your child, and further realised he did not have a particularly happy face. This Timmy had a subdued, bewildered air with an edge of anxiety to it, a pinched look that should be no part of childhood.

Obscurely, I felt guilty for this, though you were the one responsible; a feeling I was becoming familiar with in this universe, somehow accepting responsibility for the things *you* had done, barbarities beyond understanding. If feelings had colours, this was a dark purple that spread across the face of my emotions the way these flicked inks distributed themselves across the surface of the liquid in the tray.

Suddenly the woman looked up and smiled at me and I received the tiny shock of recognition that occurs when we meet someone who is strongly reminiscent of a person we already know, for this woman reminded me immediately of Evonne; the same soft plumpness and round face, the same absorbed, abstract air, the same sudden smile with a huge light behind it. Where Evonne was dark, however, this woman was fair; deep blond curls, fair skin, pure, luminous blue eyes and a small lopsided mouth.

'I'm marbling,' she said, in a voice lighter and higher than Evonne's. I could barely hear it over the shrill jangle of Ronald McDonald's routine. It was the silent voice of an unexpected angel. In a sense it was Evonne, come to help me. Still smiling, she picked up a thin stick, like a barbecue skewer, lowered it into the tray and began to move the colours about, cutting through the circles and making leafy patterns.

She met my eye again and laughed, a great giggle which declared everything to be an enormous joke. I suddenly fancied that this woman knew all about me, about Evonne and Evelyn and the triple Timmys. About how I was being stalked by my counterpart from another universe.

Worlds flow together just like colours, she was telling me; there is an infinite blending of universes.

Then she paused, bent over and offered the stick to Timmy, who had drawn closer to the tray, gesturing for him to do it. With a brief look at me, he took the stick and moved it through the colours, dividing and replicating them, a look of pleasure coming over his face. Worlds sprouted.

If only Evelyn had been here to share this moment.

She smiled at me again. She was selling, of course; marbling kits sitting up around her in their gleaming new trays, but it was the softest sell I'd seen in a long time. She was giving Timmy some pleasure and she knew it. Then she picked up an A4 sheet of white paper, deftly dropped it into the tray and a moment later lifted the piece of paper up. The pattern Timmy had created was somehow miraculously transcribed there. All the colours, the angelic blue; the earth red; magenta, bright enough to grace a flamingo's wing; purple, dark as thought – all whirled and whorled in surreal shapes and intensities that suggested rather than imitated form; an acrylic dream in which the colours moved with the nature of their essences within the larger compact of the design.

Timmy looked from the sheet of now brightly patterned paper to me and back to the sheet again with a look of intense happiness.

The fair-haired woman laughed again, looking young and girlish.

Then I noticed a man standing behind her, deeper in the stall, fiddling with some bottles of paint. He was older than her, in his mid to late forties, with a sharp, black and white marbled waistcoat. As I noticed him he noticed me and glanced my way; I had the impression of soft, fair hair, shoulder length, a long bent nose and kind but alert eyes. Alert enough to know, as the woman did, that we arrive here from lots of universes, from a multiplicity of astonishment.

We looked at each other for a moment as people who should know each other. Instinctively he moved back, to give me space to be alone.

There was no time for that, for the gentle woman had taken Timmy's marbled sheet and placed it on some newspaper and proceeded to hand it, with some ceremonial flourish, to Timmy, who looked up at me uncertain, in his yearning, whether or not he should accept it.

'He can have it,' the gentle woman shouted in a high, wild voice over the background thump of Ronald McDonald. It was clear she had understood not just Timmy's enjoyment but something of the feelings this aroused in me, if not in the detail, at least in the essence. It made her laugh and hide her mouth behind her hand just as Evonne would. There was warmth coming from her that formed an invisible protective bubble from the commercial inferno of the show, although it could not cut out Ronald McDonald's harsh, jeering voice.

'Ex-queeze me,' Ronald said, moving through the crowd. 'Please squeeze me.'

Instinctively, I moved closer to the stall and the gentle woman stood aside to welcome me. The man also accommodated me by giving me more space and I was grateful to be able to stand somewhere out of the rush and anxious hubbub of the show, and focus on the quiet patterns of marbling. One large piece of calico was a study in yellows and associated siennas and tawny golds. The whole effect was of a throbbing warmth.

Since I had no cash – I hadn't been intending to spend money – I used my credit card to buy a marbling kit before I left the stall, not quite knowing what my motivation was. I think I was saying thank you to the woman for the moment of unalloyed pleasure she'd given Timmy. The man smiled at me, somewhat roguishly, as I passed the card over.

The woman smiled too. She was grateful for the sale. In the last minute I caught the lines of tiredness spreading from her eyes.

I took the unresisting Timmy by the hand and headed for the main doors, leaving Ronald McDonald behind. Evelyn would meet me outside, she was probably already there. I was just about running, dragging Timmy behind. The man with the magic cups was still at his post. His message was the same as before.

Now you see it, now you don't.

Evelyn wasn't waiting outside.

I hurried Timmy to the car park, pretending that the hurry was all about getting out of the wind.

'Where's Mummy?' Timmy finally asked. 'Mummy's still inside.' He began to drag on my arm.

'Mummy's at the car,' I said, hoping like hell.

'Mummy inside!' He gazed up, suddenly fearless, his eyes blazing.

For a moment we struggled there in the wind. I was glad,

somehow, that he'd grown confident enough of me to defy me, to test me. I knelt down, so that I was at the same level.

'Let's just check the car,' I urged. 'Evonne will be there.' I heard it as soon as it came out of my mouth. How often had I relied on Evonne to be the main caregiver, the backstop, when it came to our Timmy? 'Mummy,' I said, correcting myself. 'I mean Mummy.'

It didn't sound right even to myself, even in the battering wind.

'You're not my daddy anyway,' he said. It just came out of his mouth in a quick, intuitive flash, but it rocked me on my heels. Of course he would know. At some subconscious level.

The blind teddy would know.

'I am now,' I said determinedly.

He looked at the marbling kit under my arm. 'We'll just check the car,' he said solemnly, making a deal with me.

'If she's not there, we'll go back inside.'

He considered this, turning over in his mind whether or not to trust me.

I waited until he nodded. It was horrible having to lie, but I knew deep down that no power on earth would ever get me back inside that pavilion; like a blind whale, I couldn't see the sand bars, but knew the smell of the open sea.

At first I didn't see her. I looked to the driver's side and it was empty.

There she was, slumped on the passenger side with all the windows up, listening to music. Jazz, with a deep base. When I opened the door there was the blast of a trumpet.

Miles Davis.

'What took you so long?' she said with an arched grin. Timmy ran forward and buried his head in her knees.

'You left me in the lurch in there.'

Her grin grew crooked, like someone about to light up a cigarette. 'You can drive,' she said. She held the keys out towards me.

I took the keys. It was the same Evelyn, I told myself, a side of her I'd never seen before. I'd stereotyped her, after all; simplified her character in order to come to grips with her.

'I got a frightful headache in there, I needed some Miles Davis to get me back on track. Sorry about deserting you.' There was a sudden brittleness in the way she folded her arms across her chest.

I turned Miles Davis down to a more gentle vibe.

It wasn't until we got to the harassed old man who thought he'd retired, who had to stop us because the queue had grown too great, that I realised I didn't know which direction to go.

I didn't have a clue where Tess lived.

We were three or four cars from the gateway when I had to choose between the left or the right turning traffic.

I stopped the car and jerked the handbrake on. 'You'll have to drive,' I said, taking hold of Evelyn's hand.

'What's wrong?' There was a flash of sudden, unspoken concern, as if she'd been expecting something.

'A touch of jet lag,' I said. 'I feel like I'm flying a plane instead of a car.'

The sweat I wiped off my brow was real.

Under the overheated gaze of the parking attendant, we quickly changed seats. As she got in I caught a flash of white lace at the top of her stockings.

'Sorry about that.'

'It's OK,' Evelyn said. I got another one of those glances. It was getting harder to read or predict her moods; again I ran up against something, something that had come into being since my going to Nelson. I didn't know if it was in me or her that the change had taken place.

She gunned the car out into the traffic.

'I don't want to stay with Aunty Tess,' Timmy said.

'Beware the Jubjub bird,' I warned him, and Evelyn gave me an even odder look before cracking up into laughter.

12

I still didn't get to meet the mysterious Tess. She was an outline, a figure against the suburban doorway as Evelyn hustled the resisting Timmy towards his babysitting doom.

On Evelyn's advice, I sat in the car. It was much simpler that way, Evelyn said. That probably meant that Tess didn't like me and Evelyn was trying to protect me.

She was back inside the car as quick as you could say I love you, darling.

She breathed deep sighs of relief when she got back into the driver's seat, into the harness. Worlds of tension went out of her body. I've only got it on faith, I thought, that this is the same Evelyn, that I hadn't skipped somewhere along the line to some third universe, one in which Evelyn was different, played a different role, shifted the goal posts in a new direction.

She ran her fingers back through her hair and released the crackling tension that way.

Back home, she flopped down on the sofa and let all the air go out of her body. 'Pour me something long and cold and faintly alcoholic, will you Harry?' She started to laugh. I carefully stowed the laptop on the bookshelf.

'What's the joke?' I poured her a scotch and an orange juice out of the fridge for me, trying to remember how she liked her drink.

'Well, I asked Tess to have Timmy tonight so that you and I could have time together. We've got the staff party tomorrow night and two days after that we leave for Canada...' She sat up and sucked gratefully at the drink I handed her. 'Then I get a lecture from Tess who doesn't think you're worth the trouble, and pointedly lent me a book called *Women who Love Too Much.*'

'Ah, you were setting up for a nice romantic evening?' I popped some ice into my orange drink to make it look good. I could pretend it was alcohol.

She gave me a rueful look. 'Something like that. I had it all planned. First there was that terrible Parent and Child show with all that screaming noise. She tried to tell me that you were manipulating me. Damn it all, I am not a machine. She's supposed to be my backup person in this situation.'

'What situation?'

'Do I have to spell it out, Harry?' She gave me a quizzical look.

'It's not too late,' I said gallantly, sitting on the sofa beside her, suddenly acutely aware of her physical presence; the slender, pale thighs emerging from her short, dark skirt, the intense white of her blouse. The long, sleek river of hair.

I thought I understood. There'd been more phone calls to Nelson, I should have foreseen that. More humouring of Harry was in order. Harry was going off the deep end. News of my whale-saving exploit had doubtless reached her by now, that's why she was acting so differently. Evelyn's plans for the evening amounted to something of a rescue mission; save Harry from himself. That thought made me laugh.

I gestured to her sexy get-up, lightly touching those pale thighs. 'And you were planning a seduction, with the low lights and the wine?'

I couldn't keep the catch out of my voice and I tried hard enough, God knows. But this is what I had come back for – to finish off the job of falling in love with Evelyn.

She gave a throaty laugh. 'Of course. I can prove it, look!' Coquettishly she slid her skirt up to reveal the bouquet of satiny white lace I'd glimpsed earlier.

'Then let's do it,' I declared, rising from the sofa in one fluid, youthful movement, recklessly downing the orange juice. 'The dinner, the romantic evening, the seduction, the words. Why spoil a good evening?'

With a wicked modesty, she pulled her skirt down over the lacy mystery.

There was a flurry of activity, the race of those who have very little time; on came the candles, off went the lights, out came the boutique wine. We found ourselves standing in the kitchen side by side frying snapper with black bean sauce, chopped parsley and squeezed lemon – and we laughed every opportunity we found. A naked carrot caused us childish delight; a parsnip recalled ancient antipathies of taste; we revelled in the fine, frenzied ivory of new potatoes. We plotted the richest sauce we could possibly make.

'Do you know what I thought, for one awful minute, when I saw those lacy knickers,' I said, giving the fish slice a rhetorical flourish.

'What?'

'That you'd been reading a *Cosmopolitan* magazine or *Cleo* on "How to Handle His Midlife Crisis" or "Don't Worry, You're a lot Sexier than She is."'

She sidled close to me so we were touching, shoulder to shoulder, hip to hip. Her face came close to mine, 'I don't read those kinds of magazines,' she breathed. Olive oil and vinegar.

'Why not?'

'Darling, they're much too *morbid.*'

The snapper sizzled and crackled in the pan.

A red candle with a yellow flame. Sparkling white wine with an edge of sunlight. The smell of fish, parsley and new potatoes. A cool and ravishing Evelyn, her skin glowing with the best of Jurlique moisturisers, hair shining with the latest herbal conditioner which smelled both sharp and sweet, like rosemary, lips glazed, eyes sparkling with mischief.

For a moment this world had turned itself into paradise. It was an easy inversion; it took no effort at all. A coin, rolling down a silk thread – which way will it fall?

'I've got a sort of confession to make.' She slid her knife down the backbone of the fish, peeling back a neat furrow of white flesh. She turned towards me, her short skirt riding up her thigh, her knees touching mine.

'What's that?'

'I didn't plan anything.' Her face became serious, her expression suddenly rich with sensual feeling. 'I just hoped, that's all. Nothing but hope.'

The hard, curved legs of our pseudo-Victorian table chairs clashed together as we leaned into one another. Our faces came together. There was heat coming off her body in fragrant waves that smelled of musk; it came up from under the Jurlique – her own scent.

I pulled up her skirt to reveal her thighs hemmed with intricate white foam. It was beautiful, it was sexy, and it was absurd – it was absurd and sexy. I wanted to undo it with my teeth or something equally extravagant.

'Quick Harry, don't fuck around. Do it now.'

'With our clothes on?'

'I don't care. I need to feel you, feel you inside me.'

We made it to our feet but we didn't make it to the sofa.

She just hitched her dress up, milkmaid style, and we did it standing up, facing each other.

'Yaaaa!' she yelled when I entered, flexing her knees to draw me right in and clawing at my shirt. Her upper lip had sprung white beads of sweat. Ringlets of damp, fair hair clung to her cheek.

'Look at me, Harry. Keep looking at me.' She sounded in deadly earnest. I looked.

Her eyes grew huge and serious, opening up into mine, pouring her pleasure into me, filling and swelling me with it. This joy in surrender was a revelation, if a cruel one for me. This is what it was to flower. To fuck. To fuck and to flower all at once, standing up, dipped in the ocean of fucking and flowering. And now I had felt it, I could never unfeel it. It forged new pathways in my body, in my neural system, fired new internal connections; after years of living a shadow life, I was finally coming alive, fully in the flesh.

I'd stepped across a boundary, across a ring-pass-not into a huge expanse of feeling. I wondered why Evonne and I had never stepped over that boundary.

'Look at me, Harry.' Her voice now more breath than tone. Her body began to shudder and I had to support her by the buttocks. 'I love you, Harry. I love you.' Her pleasure poured out of her. The heat made a red blossom of her throat. 'Let me have it, Harry. Now!'

The shudder took her over. Her face folded up, as if the intensity of all that pleasuring had turned into grief. She looked at me with a stark ecstasy, the final letting down, and we both fell over weakly in a tangle of everything.

Afterwards, instead of feeling tired and sleepy, we were both energised and as excited as a pair of teenage lovers who have just triumphantly ended their long virginity. We both knew something had happened, but we didn't want to talk about it, not right away.

We made silly talk about nothing as we prepared a little snack from the ruins of the table to take to bed with us. Then we set off for the bedroom, a delighted little procession of two, me leading with the candle and the wine, Evelyn following behind with a couple of plates of food on a tray.

'I've heard of second honeymoons,' Evelyn said from behind me, 'but this is ridiculous.'

'It's not ridiculous at all,' I said. 'Now let's get decently naked.' I splashed a little wine into her glass.

'What do you mean, decently naked?'

'I mean it's indecent for honeymooners to be clothed.'

She looked a lot more desirable without the lace.

We sat up on the bed with the flame set on a saucer beside us, facing each other with knees touching, staring into each others' eyes and casually eating this and that.

'You see,' she said, 'I saw you on television, out on that big beach, and that changed everything. I was afraid you were having a breakdown...' Her eyes flickered with the candlelight and turned to one side.

'You saw me on TV?' Then everybody would know. Pepsi, Mary Delany, Sam Walsh. Even Jerry Tate, if he were still about. My humiliation was a public one.

'Don't worry.' She touched my knee. 'It was a helicopter shot. No one else would have recognised you. You were half in the shadow of a tarpaulin, looking up, squinting. You had a bucket in your hand. I know you by your posture, as much as anything. I was with Tess when I saw it and she didn't notice a thing.'

'We had to keep the whale wet.'

She took a swig of her glass with one hand, keeping her other hand on my knee and her back straight, breasts forward;

it was a beautiful performance. Candle shadows on the wall leapt to obey. 'And when I saw you there, on the television, all bedraggled like a beachcomber, hair everywhere, I realised how much I loved you. I admired you in a way I've never admired you. I was so proud to see you there. Proud, but scared for you.'

'Proud?'

'Yes. It was such a crazy, off-the-wall thing to do. The sort of thing the Harry I fell in love with twelve years ago would have done. Even if you were having a breakdown to do it, it was worth it!'

'I couldn't hang around the house. I was getting on with Vernon.'

'I rang Nelson. Vernon thought you'd gone completely psycho.'

'Vernon wasn't very easy to deal with,' I said, tenderly touching her face. The delicate, vulnerable skin of the temples where her pulse beat softly.

'Did you save your whale in the end?' she asked. 'It didn't say on TV.'

'We turned her to the open sea. She could smell it. A big shudder went through her and her tail lashed.' I showed her the dark weal on my leg. 'That's her mark.'

'Christ.' Evelyn lightly touched the wound. 'Does it hurt?'

'Like any love bruise.'

'What happened?'

'She swam out. We heard that some of them turned back for the beach. I never found out what happened to her.'

We were both quiet, contemplating the fate of the whale. I thought of the unborn whale floating in the ocean within an ocean.

'I thought I'd lost you for good, before I saw that on TV. Then I knew I hadn't.' There was a catch deep in her throat. No one wants to grow old in a relationship unloved. My love for her was restoring her faith in herself. Love could do that. Its healing properties go deep, just as I wanted to go deep, deep inside her, right up against the door of her womb. And *you*, you had not loved her and that had become a nightmare to you, I thought, the biggest nightmare being Evelyn's reproach, the wearing down of daily alienation. By the time you skipped, you were already living in another world to Evelyn.

Evelyn said, 'Anyway, it made me think about things. That maybe I'd neglected you. Lost touch with you. I saw you with that pregnant whale, and how desperately you were caring for her…' Her fingers stroked the back of my hand lightly, bringing the hairs up along my arm. Her eyes were bright, shining with incipient tears. 'I'd forgotten what you were capable of.'

I had underestimated this woman, this incredible woman, but not as badly as *you*. 'So had I,' I said. 'I'd forgotten who I was.'

'That night I dreamed that you and I were playing in the water. You were a dolphin. You had a deliciously smooth penis that slid out of this special sheath. It was amazing to watch it come out. I climbed on top of you, with my legs on each side and you were able to penetrate me. I had an orgasm. It was so strong it woke me up.'

'It sounds like fun.'

'It was. It was wild.' She stroked my face; her fingers smelled of her body. 'All that warm water, and I was so slippery inside. I've never had a dream like that!'

'It makes me want to make love to you all over again.

She laughed and slipped a black, smooth-skinned olive between my teeth.

'But I would have no legs to wrap around you, no arms to hold you.' I put my arms around her and softly rubbed the back of her neck with my wrist, as if to demonstrate the usefulness of arms.

'That was the exciting part. I was in control. All you could do was offer yourself and hold yourself steady for me while I manoeuvred myself into position. Your body was so broad I just about had to do the splits to straddle you.' She shook her head. 'I had to grow big, like a goddess. I grew these huge breasts and enormous thighs. Fuck! I woke up in love with you all over again. Pregnant with you, that's how I felt. That's when I started thinking about everything that had happened to us.'

I stroked the underside of her breasts with the back of my hand. They were light and silky.

'I wanted to put everything behind us. We'd suffered enough.' She licked at the wine.

'I felt like I was trapped,' I said, choosing my words very carefully, wrapping my arms behind her knees and hugging her legs, stretching my legs out each side of her, 'trapped in a life that was suddenly not my own.'

I wondered if I could substitute the truth I'd promised myself I'd tell for some sort of psychological equivalent, something she could relate to without her innate common sense rebelling. Then I could convince myself that I somehow had told her, and slip between the cracks of the world that way.

'I can understand that,' she said in tones of relief. She took one of my hands, kissed my fingers, then pulled her knees down into a crossed position. 'I've felt the same thing myself sometimes, sitting at Playcentre with the other mothers, thinking back to when I was at art school and wore red and white candy spiral tights.' She giggled. 'And I look around me and I wonder what the hell I'm doing there.'

'That's it, although I never wore tights.'

'But Keith did. He...' she stopped herself abruptly. The

giggle stopped. 'I'm sorry,' she said drawing away from me and composing herself. I drew my legs back. It was a great dance of legs we were doing.

'Why?'

'Because Keith is a part of a few changes I've decided to make. I'm backing you if you can find a way out of the house deal. I'll back you against Keith.' I could hear the resolution in her voice what it cost her to say that. The chubby little architect had gone on exerting power over her long after the marriage had finished; she'd seen it and it had shaken her. Seeing me standing by that great naked whale had shaken her more.

'And I'm backing you against Peter Coveny,' I said. 'I've thought a lot about him too. I'm getting a new lawyer.'

'Do you mean that?'

'He's a slimy little bastard. A twisted little man.'

She laughed triumphantly and upended her glass.

I refilled it for her. 'Between him and Keith, they've just about got us in a nutcracker.'

'Not any longer,' she said decisively. 'Let the dead bury the dead. That's what my father used to say although he could never explain what it meant.' She smiled at the memory. 'He used to say it when he got angry. Now I know what it means.'

I knew what it meant too; the motel ticket was a dead issue. I was off the hook.

If ever there was a time to tell Evelyn the truth it was now; it was the best of times, it was the worst of times. It might in fact be entirely the wrong thing to do. An act of foolish gratuity. If it's working don't try to fix it.

'I have another confession to make,' Evelyn said. 'That night I came back late and we had a row, I was pissed off, remember.'

'Yes.'

'Well I was furious with Keith. I was concerned about the house venture too. I felt responsible. I mean, it was through me Keith got involved. I felt he'd led us on, cost-wise, even though you said you'd have the money. I tried to have it out with him but he came on with his smoothie act because he knows how much I hate it. I even thought he was trying to ruin us. He's never forgiven us, you know, not deep down. He can be a nasty little bugger when it comes to grudges.'

'Why didn't you say something when we went through the chequebook?'

'I got freaked out. I thought you had it all taken care of, you told me you did. I assumed it was one of Coveny's shady side operations you don't tell me about. It made me go cold all over to think the money might not be there. That would put Keith in a position of power over us.'

'You've got it.' What I most wanted to do then was to tell her about the Coveny deals, the McBride kickback and the insider share scam – all the things you had kept her in the dark over. She would be furious at having been shut out of all that. But I told her anyway. As much as I knew, careful to cover for what I didn't know but should have known. She listened in complete silence, keeping her eyes on my face the whole time. Her eyes widened when I mentioned the Southern Oil share deal.

'So it might all be still on? She said.

'Might be. The difference is, I don't want it. It's reckless and it's dangerous.'

'And now you're telling me.'

'You've got to know.'

She studied my face for a much longer time. The colour crept back up into her throat. She leaned across the short gap between us and took my face in her hands, feeling for the shape of it with her fingers. Then she ran her hands down my shoulders and each side of my body.

'I'm just beginning to realise how different you are, Harry. Your eyes are different, your voice is different. You stand differently. You talk differently, you say different things, you look at me differently, your face even feels different...'

We put our arms around each others' shoulders and looked down at our common nakedness, our heads touching. Because of her cross-legged position, her vulva lay open, pink-lined and plump, while my erection swung between us, fully veined and very much alive. She murmured something I didn't catch.

Now was the time to tell her that there was a very good reason for all those differences.

'What did you say, honey?' It sounded strange on my tongue, the very endearment she used with me the first time, her standing in the kitchen, me dumbfounded in the living room.

'You even smell different,' she said, drawing in my scent. 'Christ, it's beautiful.' She leaned back, drawing her hands back along my shoulders and down my arms to the fingertips, which she held. 'And you've stopped using that silly aftershave you thought made you smell sexy.'

'I'm throwing the aftershave out. That's part of the deal.'

'And I haven't seen you with a cigarette for ages.

'Filthy things.'

In the candlelight, the tiny, flat golden hairs on her bare thighs shone like silk threads. I ran my hand lightly enough, just above, but not touching the skin, to feel a gentle tickle against my palm, the prickle of electricity, as the hairs rose to meet me.

She shook her hair around her shoulders. 'Of course I knew you and Coveny were plotting something. You had to be. Christ I've hated that man for a long time. I blamed him for what you were becoming. Thank God you've told me the truth at last.'

'Do you think I should cut all losses and pull out?'

'God, Harry, I don't know…there's too much riding on it.' Which was exactly Coveny's point.

'It doesn't matter. One way or another I'll get rid of Coveny.'

She kissed me, giving me the feel of her tongue. We didn't hug or cuddle, we couldn't because we had knees in the way.

'What about Canada?' she said suddenly. 'I'm hating the thought of it.'

'I don't want to talk about Canada.' The trip seemed far away.

'But how are we going to cope?'

'We'll be great!' I ruffled her hair and tickled her under the arms. 'We'll tell lies all day and make love all night. And we won't care about a damn thing. Pepsi will love it and give us a bonus, Cranner will eat his heart out and everything will be sweet.'

A sly look came into her eyes. 'What about those nightclubs you and your buddies, the ones you'll be lying to, like to visit? Won't I be cramping your style?'

I picked up a wilting piece of fish and inspected it. The snapper had lost its snap.

'Not at all. You can come along.'

'Thanks. I can't wait.'

'You can get up there in your lace underwear. God, you'd have them coming all over their dark suits.'

'Oooo. Don't be horrible. I can't imagine anything worse.'

'I can.'

She grabbed a pillow beside her and began beating me around the head with it. Some slices of white fish dropped onto the bed cover. By the time she'd finished she was crying. There were years of tears to be shed. I wish *you* could have seen them.

'I feel so much better,' she said, trying to laugh thorough the tears. 'It's such a relief.'

This time the urgency was mine. Her body was as slippery as an eel, slippery with tears and sweat.

'I love you, Harry,' she said.

I could have ignored the doorbell, but it didn't go away. It went on and on chiming and chiming while Evelyn and I stared at each other.

Somebody wanted us, somebody who wasn't going away.

The man standing in the doorway had a quiet, respectful air. There was another, just behind him, younger, taller and not as respectful.

'Harry Blackman?' I nodded, after the briefest of hesitations.

Inspector Wildheart was probably used to that.

I did what you have to do when the police come to your door, even if you're wearing a bathrobe. I invited them in and offered them a chair. They came in but did not sit down. Wildheart introduced himself and his sidekick, Detective Sergeant Joe Oggle. Oggle gave me the once-over-slowly treatment. His look let me know that he dealt with scum like me every day. They both noted the suitcase on the living room floor, the chaos on the table.

'Taking a trip, Mr Blackman?' Inspector Wildheart inquired mildly.

'Just returned,' I said. 'From Nelson. A family visit.'

Wildheart said, 'Mr Blackman, we're investigating the bombing of Professor Kober's offices. You visited the professor, didn't you?'

'Yes. Twice. I mean three times.'

'Only three times?'

'I mean recently,' I said. *You* must have visited him too, I realised belatedly. Tate had at least told me that much.

'And before?'

I started to sweat. I wondered if all liars sweated. 'Several times.'

Inspector Wildheart casually drew from his pocket and read off the series of dates. Kober had been in the country at least eight months. You had visited him once a month, roughly, until the time of the 'accident', the first explosion.

'The last occasion was the Monday before his latest bombing of the professor's office.'

'Was it? I've lost track of the days, a bit.'

'What was your business with Kober?'

'To make him an offer. Financial backing to develop his device.'

'An offer on behalf of your company?'

I hesitated a fraction. 'An offer being mediated by the company.'

'What about all these previous visits, what were they about?'

'The same thing. Before the accident, I mean the first explosion, Kober had been receiving some financial assistance from us.'

'And then?'

'I was instructed to offer Kober more money to continue his research.'

While Wildheart asked the questions, Joe Oggle meandered around the room, noticing this and that. If he were impressed by Evelyn's taste, he didn't show it. He gave the reclining buddha a dead-eyed stare.

'And how was your last offer received?'

''I'm sure you know. Kober turned me down flat. Wasn't interested.'

'Why not, do you think?'

'I'm sure you know that too. He was suspicious. He doesn't trust the oil industry. He thought we would bury his device.'

Wildheart stroked his chin and considered me with a steady, not unfriendly gaze. 'Does his device work?' he asked, as if it were a matter of mere academic interest. Behind him Joe Oggle had stopped communing with the buddha and was looking at me over Wildheart's shoulder with something more than academic interest.

I shrugged. 'I never found out. I wasn't briefed that far. You'd have to go up a couple of security clearance levels to get an answer to that one.' Wildheart permitted himself a dry smile but Oggle didn't join him; Sergeant Oggle just continued to look at me as if I'd told him to put a bet each way on a losing horse.

'Could his device explode?'

'I don't know.'

'Did he refuse your money on your first visit after the first explosion?'

'Sort of.'

Evelyn came quietly into the room. She was wearing a floral dressing gown that looked like a kimono, and she looked both ravished and ravishing.

'Then why return for a second or third visit?' Wildheart went on, nodding to Evelyn.

'It's all part of negotiation. He'd had time to think. There was a lot of money offered.'

Wildheart lifted his eyebrows. He looked like a benevolent, retired schoolteacher. 'What did he say?'

'No, plain and simple. He wouldn't open the door for me. Lectured me on Viktor Schauberger through a crack in the door.'

'Then what?'

'What do you mean?'

'Then what did you do?'

'Went on holiday. It was finished as far as I was concerned.'

'You can take no for an answer?'

'I had no personal investment in this, Inspector. I was given a limited brief. I carried it out. That was the extent of my involvement.'

'Of course.' The inspector nodded as if satisfied. Oggle took a few sideways glances at Evelyn; it's almost impossible not to be impressed with Evelyn but Oggle gave a good imitation of it.

Evelyn said, 'There was someone caught in the blast, wasn't there Inspector?' Her voice was as cool as a reed flute.

'I didn't know that,' I said.

All the time she'd known this and said nothing.

'A woman is dead.' Wildheart was looking at me, not Evelyn. 'That's why we're here. This is a homicide investigation.'

Oggle nodded with satisfaction when he saw the look on my face.

Evelyn and I sat on the back deck to recover.

'She was in the room below, I read about it. She was a sex worker, I think they call them now.' Evelyn twisted the edge of her dressing gown.

'And you didn't tell me.'

Evelyn hesitated. 'I didn't know how fragile you were.'

'You were protecting me?'

'For as long as I could.'

'While I was protecting Tate and Rigold,' I said bitterly. 'Why did I do that? I should have dropped Jerry Tate as deep as I could in it.' But I knew why I'd done that. I wanted to stay here, love Evelyn and build a life. Or was it just that the instinct to protect the company ran too deep?

'Shit wouldn't stick to him.'

'You're right, he'll be up and gone by now. There'll be no record of him ever having been. A woman dead! What galls me is how expendable I am to Tate. Implicate me in murder, set me up as a suspect or open to an accessory charge, no sweat to Tate; not a second thought.'

I saw it as if I were seeing it for the first time.

'Just like you'd squash a bug,' she said shuddering. She looked small, huddling in the ragged night air. Like a little girl under a grey sky of brass.

'There's Rigold, out in the backroom busy washing his hands while Tate sets me up, no sweat to Rigold. I should have dropped his arse in it too.'

'Don't even think about it,' Evelyn said, getting up and leaning over the balcony until the earth swayed beneath her.

'But I am thinking about it,' I said.

'This is not the last we're going to see of Mutt and Jeff,' Evelyn said.

She looked for a moment like a slender wild animal, poised on the edge of the deck for sudden flight.

We went back to bed but there was no finishing the night's business. Evelyn kissed me tenderly and went directly to sleep. I might have done the same thing, and fooled myself, if I hadn't suddenly sensed *you* about somewhere.

Between halls, between windows, somewhere across the driveway to the garage, there lay a pathway between universes. If *you* could come and go, why couldn't I? Why, in every insomniac hour I had spent in this bed, did I go on suspecting that you had somehow engineered this whole thing, levered me here to take your rap, not giving a damn about Evelyn or anyone else, faking yourself as me and getting away with Evonne, my retirement fund, the carefully shored-up accounts, everything.

But you would need help. Switching universes isn't quite the same thing as jumping trains. You encountered something from far out of leftfield that gave you the opportunity. the opportunity to get one up on me.

Professor Kober.

He was the only piece in the jigsaw that remotely fitted. His device tapped into quantum maths, negative friction; what other side effects might it have apart from producing a trickle of electrons?

I got out of bed, tense with excitement, got dressed and wandered into the kitchen. The fruit juice was still sitting on the bench and I poured myself another glass.

Kober's hostility to me, not opening the door, his pretending not to know me when I now had evidence, from no lesser person than Inspector Wildheart, that *you* had visited him at least seven times, his evident ambivalence as to whether to trust me or throw me out, his lectures on Schauberger…could mean that he knew who I was, knew that I was not *you.*

Seeing me was the last thing he needed. Or expected.

Then Kober would know who I was, know I was your counterpart.

And he had been trying to warn me!

You , maybe working in cahoots with Kober, taking the designs for his machine with you into my universe with the mission of contacting Kober number two, who I had never met, and handing the plans over – if that Kober had not already invented it. Then at least, if he was thwarted by Tate here, his design would survive in another universe; a seed passed across that permeable membrane between worlds.

I was sure you'd be happy to pay that price to get out from under your disintegrating situation here- a situation I was only now just beginning to mend.

It was a beautiful theory, almost entirely self-consistent except for a couple of minor matters. Such as, how you did it. And why you were trying to kill me. Why not just deliver your blueprints to Kober II and stay undercover while I copped the flack here for you?

Why come gunning for me?

I should probably ring Inspector Wildheart and confide all this to him, I thought and slipped out the door across the windy passage to the garage.

I wanted to check out the .22, just to make sure. *You'd* tried to kill me in the museum today; even there you'd found a place where the fabric of time had worn thin. But you'd botched the job, that much was clear. You didn't have the control over this thing that you thought you had. That fitted in with everything I knew about you.

The rifle was still there, just as it had been last time I looked. The same gutted carcass of a fly on the cobweb over the window. Dust on the cartridge box.

I left the house with my collar turned up, confident that I would be alone. Not even Walsh would be out on a night like this, moaning and wind driven.

But he had almost certainly been waiting for me. He must have known I was home. He was standing under the red pine in its dark, silver shadows keeping his silent vigil. He was motionless enough to have become a part of the iconography of the street, its silent houses, its hoard of shadows. The wind died, leaving the air heavy and thick with a restless stillness.

I wasn't overjoyed to see him, but I couldn't avoid him, he'd made sure of that.

I'd had enough of Sam, I'd outgrown him. This reminded me of his wariness when I first met him, and his allusion to some difficulty between you both; perhaps you once reached the point with him that I was now approaching – the novelty had worn off and you wanted to be alone.

I expected the old soldier to make some pronouncement,

the way he usually did, but he said nothing as I approached and continued to stare moodily into the middle distance, as if my company were unwelcome.

'Looks like the flowers have survived the hurricane all right,' I said brightly, although some hadn't. A branch had fallen across the bed, stabbing a few pansies to death.

'Yes,' he said stoically, but not without a touch of pride. I bent down and gently lifted the fallen branch up. The pansies stayed wounded, shaking their fat little funeral crosses of purple.

We said nothing for a while, then, since we didn't know what to do with each other, decided to walk up to the top of the road to Simon's Point. We walked in mutual silence, like old soldiers.

By the time we got to Simon's Point the wind had dropped further, leaving a clogged moistness in the air, as if our own breath were following us. Houses were spread out below, decked in their fairy lights. To the north of the city lay the great belt of darkness that were the land; to the east, flashes of hard, brittle starlight gave the ocean a frosted look, like the top of a vast cake.

'Old insomniacs never sleep,' I said, as we sat down on the park bench provided and took in the view.

'Do you ever think about death, Harry?'

'Not until you mentioned it.'

'Death is the demise of sleep, maybe, not the beginning of it as people imagine.' He spoke with a certain precision that made me wonder if he hadn't had a tipple or two before leaving the house.

'The death of sleep,' I laughed. In the heavy atmosphere the laugh didn't go anywhere.

'Yes, and dying is staying awake forever.'

'Don't discourage me. I haven't slept since this whole thing began.'

'You're not going to tell me what it is, are you Harry? How you keep changing. God, I wish I was fifty again. At fifty changes are still possible.'

'I'm not fifty yet,' I said automatically. 'It has nothing to do with age.'

'It doesn't matter,' he said with pessimism. He had the martyred air of one who would not tell his story, not yet. 'You know Harry, you remind me of a crossover. Deserters who would cross enemy lines to join us. We expected them because we aimed propaganda at them, but we never quite trusted them. I mean, we never trusted them with any real secrets.'

'Why not?'

'Because you could never read a crossover. They gave out double signals. Their loyalty was always subject to their own judgement. That was dangerous.'

'Do me a favour, Sam.'

'What is it?'

'You're a trained observer, right?'

'Right! You never lose that kind of training.'

'Like a kind of spy.'

He looked uneasy. 'An insomniac becomes a spy by default, Harry,' he said apologetically, playing off the truth against himself – hard to tell who was the winner.

'It doesn't matter,' I said, echoing his words. 'You watched our house. We had a falling out. Tell me, did you see anything strange going on at our place? Did you notice anything?'

'What sort of thing?'

'Anything that might have caught your attention.'

He deliberated.

'Nothing.'

'Nothing?'

'Nothing at all.'

I don't know what I expected from him. Certainly no revelation. He was sitting bent over his shoulders like a bird whose wings have lost the air. He was embracing the faith of nothing-at-all, casting his crucified limbs at the feet of old age and stasis. His face had closed down. Even when he looked at the flowerbed it was the same; a fallen army, outflanked at every quarter, a windswept corner of nowhere.

'What of the flower planters?' Those symbols of Walsh's commando youth. 'Did you see them again?'

He shrugged. Just another hope that had come to nothing; a new twist to an old bitterness. He hunched deeper into his history.

'I stopped the cheque,' he said. 'I thought you knew.'

Come morning, Evelyn sloped into the kitchen where I was making coffee, still rubbing the sleep out of her eyes. She flicked back her rumpled hair and looked more gorgeous than ever, gold tints emerging in her hair, the freckles on her arm glowing like little amber specks against the creamy whiteness of her skin. In the morning sun it was easy to see how close she'd come to being red-headed.

We stood side by side, watching the jug boil.

'All night I dreamed of riding horses, isn't that so passe, so fucking Freudian?' Absently, she rubbed a lovebite on her shoulder.

I gambled a guess. 'You were a horsey girl in your teenage years.' I flicked on the coffee grinder and watched it whiz the grounds to dust. Today was going to be a long day.

'Oh all the way. Did I ever tell you what I called that horse?'

'You may not have.'

'Fat Boy.'

'Wow.' I poured the boiling water onto the coffee grounds

and watched the explosions of amber. I wanted to know more, more about her and Fat Boy and everything about her, everything I had to pretend I already knew.

We took a tray outside onto the deck. The air was thick and humid and the steam from our mugs rose sluggishly from the swirling surface. Evelyn yawned and stretched out her arms. Probably the best thing to do, I thought, was to go back to bed and make love all day.

'I'm not looking forward to the staff party tonight,' I said.

'I'm dreading the staff party.' She blew the steam sharply away from her cup.

'We were brave about it last night. And Canada.'

'Last night was last night.'

I didn't push it. She was sensitive this morning; there was some splinter in paradise. I said, 'I've decided to go and visit Professor Kober.'

'After yesterday's little visit from the police, do you think that's wise?'

'I have to clear it with him.' The coffee was still too hot and my shirt was already thick with sweat.

'Clear what?'

'Any implication that I had anything to do with that explosion...'

She put her cup down decisively. 'If you want my opinion you should stay well clear. Keep as far away from this Tate guy as you can.'

'This has nothing to do with Tate.'

'Spoken like a true cowboy. Christ, I wish this next hurricane would just come and get it over with.'

I went and sat beside her and kissed her and knocked over her coffee. She laughed and kissed me back. A spreading fragrance came up off her skin, rich and warm, amber and silk.

'Sorry Harry, I've got this foreboding. Something with big, heavy feet striding towards us out of the murk.'

'Let's just go back to bed and make love then.'

Her laughter rose, a little hesitant at first, then caught flight, rising up through the grey air with the flash of warmth and colour.

13

Professor Malcolm Kober stared at me from through the dirty Perspex window of the paint-peeled caravan. He'd joined a row of semipermanents that fronted a grassy street near the concrete convenience block of the caravan park.

He opened the door and stood looking at me. He had that same wild-eyed appearance I'd seen in the mirror on returning from Farewell Spit.

'Mr Backmann,' he said without enthusiasm, 'I didn't think I would see you again.'

Awkwardly clutching the laptop, I said, 'This is a personal visit, Professor Kober.' Suddenly, I found it hard to account for why I was there. The far-reaching understandings I had had the night before, after the visit of the police, now seemed more far-fetched than anything else.

Kober gave no sign of friendliness as he stood to one side to let me in. I might have been the police or the CIA; when he looked at me he saw nothing but defeat. The inside of the caravan was packed with computer gear. There wasn't much else but a mattress and some blankets.

'You saved it,' I said, gesturing to the computers.

'I saved nothing,' he said woodenly.

'I didn't do it,' I said.

'*Naturlich*' he snarled. 'You are the wrong tool for that job.

For that job, they use a different tool.' His speech was slower, more lugubrious, more German; his grip on English seemed less sure. 'For your job they need plausible bastards, like you. But perhaps in your case they make a mistake, *nicht wahr?*'

'Why do you say that?'

'Because the tool mustn't have any…how do you say it… consciousness.'

'You mean conscience.'

'Ah.'

'Who are they? These Specials. You have never explained.' I placed the laptop carefully in the mess.

'They are agents of the *Reich*!' he shouted suddenly. There was fire in his eyes. 'Mr Backmann, I feel like punching your bloody face.'

Evenly, I said, 'I can understand that, Professor, I…'

'Good, I am most happy.' Then he stood back a pace and hit me, hard, on the jaw. It was not the punch of a scholarly man, rather one who has done a lot of welding and steel fixing. Then he hit me a second time, just as hard, and got me in the stomach the third time as I went down. His floor was covered in dust, bits of copper wire and microchips. I'd never been beaten up before, not since school. This then, was what I'd really come here for.

'Now we shall have a cup of tea?' he said, in the same tone of voice he'd used to tell me he was going to hit me. He scrabbled among some circuit boards and pulled out an electric jug.

I watched while he found an extension lead and plugged in the jug. One of the computers turned out to be a fridge, from which he drew some milk. Two cups appeared from behind somewhere else. It was like a conjuring act. He moved the way he spoke, slowly and deliberately.

From the floor, I said, 'I take it without milk – black and weak.'

As he found some tea I pulled myself into a sitting position and rubbed the bruise on my leg where the whale had hit me. I said, 'Professor, can you tell me the difference between memory and the imagination? Can you tell me, scientifically, where to draw the line?'

He took a long time getting the tea ready and not answering. When he turned to me there was real surprise on his face which pleased me greatly. I don't like being taken for a mindless toady, someone else's tool; I have my own piece of the action.

'Memory is mother of the imagination,' he said ponderously. The jug began to shake.

'Did Schauberger say that?'

He poured the tea. 'No, no. Samuel Taylor Coleridge said that.'

And , not without a certain professorial malice, he grinned.

You are very foolish to come here,' Kober said, sipping his tea.

You may be right,' I said ruefully, rubbing my jaw where he'd hit me.

Kober waved that minor matter aside. 'They will wonder why you have come. You must make yourself a target, Mr Backmann.'

'They've already destroyed your machine, Professor.'

He waved that aside too. Another minor matter. 'It is me they wanted to kill. What if they destroy the machine? I build another one. So they must kill me.'

'These are the Specials you're talking about?'

'You don't believe me about these Specials, do you, Mr...'

'Call me Harry.'

'I don't want to. I told you that, we cannot be friends.' He drank his tea down decisively, as if I should do the same and get out of there.

'I think I've met one of your Specials.'

That got his interest. I told him about Tate, how Tate set me up, watching him carefully for a reaction. He nodded grimly.

'They are here,' he said to himself. 'Even here they follow me. To the other side of the moon.'

'What?'

It is a saying in German, it means very far away.'

'But surely, Professor, you already must have known something of this. After all, you have been in New Zealand for some time. I had visited you several times. You had already received some payments from…'

Kober slammed his cup down and got to his feet. 'I received nothing! And I told you the first time, I had never seen you before in my whole life.'

There was something here that didn't add up, but Kober was too touchy to take it any further. Besides, I was preparing myself for the big leap.

'Professor, before I go I want to know, could these Specials be hunting down your machine, not just in this world, but other parallel worlds, worlds like ours in other dimensions, I mean?'

'You know of these worlds?' he asked quickly.

'I come from one of them,' I replied calmly.

He gave an acute look, then examined the tea leaves in the bottom of his cup. My cup still sat beside me, untouched. 'You should get out of here now,' he said in a very low voice, more like a growl.

'Why?'

'You have seen the designs for the machine? They showed you?'

'Not me. In my world there was no Kober assignment.' In my world, I thought, Kober might be long dead, like Julie

Horton – the Specials might have caught up with him long ago. And *you* might have escaped to get away from Tate... but how?

Kober suddenly looked very frightened. It was as if he'd just seen something that wore the face of terror. 'You must leave here now, Mr Backmann,' he said, opening the door for me. 'You were foolish to come.'

I stood my ground, ready for another poke in the jaw if necessary. I was sure he believed me. 'You have to tell me, Professor, is it possible, with your machine, or some modification of it, to jump over worlds like...' I tried to think of a watery analogy for him, 'like salmon jumping up a waterfall?'

'Salmon can jump up waterfalls because they follow reciprocal currents of energy,' he said, his voice savage with anger and fear all mixed up. 'And there may be copies of my machine. Your friend Tate and his friends will already have constructed one, you can be sure. Steal it first and then destroy me!' He was pushing me towards the door. 'Get out now! Get out!'

I hung in the doorway. 'Could your machine be used...'

'I know nothing of other worlds, Mr Backmann. That is fantasy. I am an engineer. I look for free energy, that's all. My machine works on the principle of the vortex, and, as you must know...' he prized my fingers off the side of the doorway, 'inside the great vortex all worlds are born and die.'

He went to bundle me out the door. 'They will kill me, and they will kill you too, Mr Backmann,' he shouted through the wall. 'That is what they will do.'

Driving away from the dismal caravan park, I felt free of Kober. I had discharged my obligations to him, and it seemed that he had nothing more to tell me about my situation. I saw no reason to divert from my strategy, which was to consolidate my relationship with Evelyn and make a go of it in this screwy world.

With Evelyn by my side I could face my monsters – Rigold, Canada and Coveny. Tate, I decided, had already left the country. He'd have paid for a professional to bomb Kober's offices and was probably well out of the way when the explosion took place.

I doubted, despite Kober's grim prophesies, that he would be bothering me any more. I was a tool he might want to use again sometime, he had no motive to kill me. Kober of course was wrong to assume that Tate had been in possession of his designs for a long time; if that were the case, he would have known a lot more about them than his questions indicated. It was more likely, I thought, that he sent someone to break into Kober's offices to steal the designs before blowing the place.

From Tate's point of view that would be mission accomplished, and he would have even less cause to bother me.

Further, since I had had nothing to do with this latest explosion at Kober's office – I had been in Nelson, after all, the perfect alibi – sooner or later Inspector Wildheart and the stony-faced Oggle would leave me alone.

I could even face *you* down, given half a chance.

Evelyn prepared herself very carefully for the staff party. With scientific exactitude and attention to minute detail, her face became a subtle mask. There was no visible sign of any make-up, but a heightened sense of shape, line and plane.

'You're very beautiful,' I said. Watching her was like watching the ocean; I never tired of it.

Gravely, she turned her head away from the mirror and smiled faintly in acknowledgement of my worship. Her mirror image turned with her in perfect counterpoint.

'There'll be other beautiful women there,' she said calmly, dabbing at the corner of her eyes. 'Younger women.'

'Not like you.' In many respects, loving her in this hopeless manner was the very worst thing that could have happened to me. I didn't need the intoxication of shoulders or the ecstasy of armpits; I needed to look out for myself and stay on red alert. I needed objectivity and poise.

Especially tonight. I had goose bumps about tonight.

She kissed me, briefly, her lips brushing mine like a butterfly wing. 'And there's some sort of surprise in store. We're to rendezvous at Customs Street and get into minibuses. Then we will be taken to a secret destination.'

'I can't wait.'

'Some whiz kid in the PR department has thought up a special entertainment for us.' There was a final touch of something around the eyes.

I was sitting on the edge of the bed with my laptop, ostensibly working on the Canadian project, reading the profiles of the people I'd be dealing with, clicking back in with the memory of my previous visit. Monsieur Dumond, Quebec, wife owns racehorses. He'd be the chief back-room power broker for the Canadians. About every half hour or so he would stop whatever he was doing and take a few politically incorrect puffs from an obscenely large cigar.

'I'm going to have to do my job again, I suppose,' Evelyn said, half to herself. She didn't sound as if she relished the prospect.

'What's that?'

She was cheerful, trying out her face in the mirror in a number of expressions. 'Come on Harry, you know the game. I play up to the boss, charm him off his feet, convince him that I'm the classiest woman in town...'

'Which you are.' I got out my suitcase and began packing clothes for Canada; shirts, ties, underwear. Canada was a mere thirty-six hours away.

'Thank you. Convince him that I wouldn't be living with anyone less than the most dynamic executive around. You know, if I've got class you must have it too.' She raised one flirtatious, neatly arranged eyebrow at me. Pepsi would love it; he'd go for it, hook, line and sinker.

'It's all true of course.'

'Come off it! Aren't you just playing it out for retirement?'

'Am I?'

I left her to her facecraft and wandered across the lounge, trying to focus on the coming party; there would be a lot of people there. Too many people knowing too much about things of which I knew nothing.

The thought made me tense up inside and in need of a nervous piss. Standing there, striving for balance, I got the shakes. My body flashed on and off like a firefly in twilight, and quivered as if not properly attached to my bones; for a moment I thought I was having a heart seizure, so rapid and lumpy was the movement of muscles in my chest. I leaned my head against the door and the burst of colour in *Glad Day*. I didn't want to look at the Redeemed Man right then. I was undergoing something more than just panic.

Something was turning me inside out.

I went into the bedroom to read Timmy a story before Tess arrived to baby-sit. It was a picture book about a little boy who, having been chastised by his mother and sent to bed without his supper for being naughty, sailed away to a land of monsters whom he tamed and led into revel. Timmy enjoyed the story, though he'd all but grown out of it; he enjoyed the pictures; particularly the one of the little boy riding on a furry monster's shoulders. Most of all, he just enjoyed snuggling into me.

Teddy gave me a blind stare as I went out.

Afterwards, I wandered into the lounge and approached the vase which by now only dimly remembered the forget-me-nots.

I was going to make it. One way or another.

Evelyn wore a pale blue, low-cut dress that fitted her exactly, setting off her long fair hair swept back over her shoulders as if she'd just brushed it before bed. Her bare shoulders and arms shone sleekly.

I had a good look at my face before I left, as if I were in danger of forgetting it. I saw a pale, ordinary looking man with a wide, intelligent forehead and a small, sensual mouth. I saw too, the lines of shock around my eyes and hoped I was the only one to see them. If you looked hard enough there was something of the wild, staring man I saw in Vernon's bathroom mirror, and on the face of Professor Kober before he hit me.

Tess arrived and bustled us out the door but at the last minute we hesitated. Neither of us wanted to leave the house. Timmy gave me a big hug. I'd hardly got to know him again after Nelson and the way his little arms went around me I could tell that he knew it too.

Timmy idolises you, you know.' Evelyn said as we got into the car. 'He loved it when you read to him tonight. He makes all those Lego creations for you to look at.' She took a quick look at herself in a pocket mirror. 'And that Lego house, it's all for you.'

I slipped the keys into the ignition. 'Somehow, you know, Timmy is me.' I said it before I knew what I was saying.

'That's a very strange thing to say, Harry.'

I didn't start the car. I was no good at this psychological stuff – I'd never liked it. 'All the things children don't know about the world make me sad.'

Evelyn grinned, the kind of grin someone has when the joke is on them. 'I thought you might be planning to try to take Timmy with you if you left me. Cultivate him to isolate me.'

I started the car. 'I feel like I've been to hell and back,' I said, turning off the engine again.

She put her hand over mine, her palm and fingers resting lightly on the back of mine. Her voice was soft, inviting trust. 'Harry, remember when we first met, you bought a bottle of wine and took me down to the bay, remember what you said?'

'I think so.'

She dug me in the ribs, 'What do you mean you think so? Gone shy all of a sudden?'

'Maybe so.'

'Go on!' A trembled entered her voice. 'I want to close my eyes as I did then, and hear your voice saying that, just the way you said it then.'

I laughed lightly, 'That's a pretty tall order.

'Just say it, Harry. You used to say it all the time after that. It was our magic formula.'

'The ties that bind,' I murmured. I tried to remember if I'd done something like that with Evonne, something that would pass muster in this situation, but could find nothing. This magic formula must have been magic formula must have been *your* own invention.

Evelyn said nothing. I remained as I was, a living statue, one hand on the key, itself stillborn in the ignition. The silence lengthened. The sea roared in my ears. Her hand stayed on mine, fingers very still.

'I'm sorry,' I said, voice hoarse, as if I'd been talking for hours, 'I can't say it. I don't want to go back. I want to start again, from now. From last night. I'm frightened to utter those old words because, somehow, they failed us.' I shrugged helplessly, but not helplessly enough.

Her voice was even. 'All right Harry, but you can't just wipe out the past. The past happened. Some things were said I want to believe in.'

My hand turned and the motor started. 'I just can't try to build back up on memories.'

Sam Walsh stood at the top of the drive like an apparition, like a prophet of doom. His lined face was as bleak as the bitter, chemical light shed by the streetlamp above. There was a fixed look on his face and in his posture, as if he's gone to sleep at attention. He looked very old.

'Did you see what happened?' he said in a tight voice. I looked and saw that the flower plots had been destroyed, desecrated, the flowers ripped up and scattered, the imported soil thrown all over the footpath and the road.

Evelyn leaned over my shoulder to look. 'What happened?'

'Vandals, barbarians, horrible twisted people. I came out this morning and there it was.'

I said, 'You still wanted to help the planters, didn't you, even though you stopped the cheque?'

'It's a good thing I did stop it,' he said gloomily, 'if this is what it's going to come to.'

He turned back on the wrecked plots. 'How come there are such people in the world?'

Paterson wandered to the entrance of his drive and joined us. He seemed amused by the overturned plots.

'There's not a single one left,' Sam Walsh said, 'and it's the same down by Crocker's Store. They got that one too.'

Paterson shook his head. 'In Singapore,' he said, 'they whip slimeballs for doing stuff like this. With a cane.' His eyes lit up. 'It marks them for life and they never forget.'

'That's right,' Sam said with emotion. 'Nothing else gets

through to animals.'

'They'd get nothing more than a slap over the wrist for this here,' Paterson said. 'Like those taggers with their spray paint. Cops pick 'em up and give 'em a kiss on the cheek.'

'Not even that. I rang the constable on duty. He wasn't very happy because it was six o'clock in the morning...'

Paterson shook his head. 'Unbelievable. The force is asleep at six a.m.'

'Anyway, he told me there was not a lot they could do because the flowerbeds shouldn't have been there in the first place. In bylaw terms, the verge was already in a vandalised state. Now can you make any sense of that?'

Paterson said, 'I'd flog them.' He smiled at us through a thick moustache, leaning down so he could get an eyeful of Evelyn who pointedly looked the other way.

Sam Walsh looked grim. 'I won't put the flowers back in their weenie beds.' A broken lilt which had to be Scottish.

'Neither will I,' Paterson said, walking away. His shoulders were hunched up around his ears, his fingers flexed.

'Anyway, they'd just get destroyed again,' the old man said. 'The vandals always return. Barbarians at the gate.' He turned to me. 'Do you know why people do this sort of thing?'

'No,' I said.

'It's a good thing I didn't give them that money,' he said.

I waved to Sam as I pulled out. It must have looked like a salute for the old man mechanically raised his hand up to his forehead.

Evelyn looked back at him as we drove off. There was something unforgettable about him, something that made you want to look back.

'So that's how you spend your sleepless nights.'

'That, and walking.'

'Why walking?'

'It's better than sinking.'

For the first time that evening she was able to laugh.

I've decided I'm going to look for a job,' she said as we hit the motorway.

'What?'

'We need income. Besides, there's no reason for me to be economically dependent on you. That's just a pressure on you.'

'What about another baby?' I said without thinking, the idea surfacing as I spoke. I thought of the whale with her baby deep inside her, a heartbeat within a heartbeat. A child of our own would cement my relationship with Evelyn, cement me into this new universe.

'For God's sake, Harry, have you gone crazy? That's the last thing I thought I'd hear you say. Right now we need a baby like we need another mortgage.'

'Still, it would fit in with starting all over again, wouldn't it?' The idea was growing on me. All that love for Evelyn would find expression.

'Jesus, Harry. This is wild. This really is wild. I don't believe what I'm hearing.'

My voice was mild. 'OK. I'll withdraw the suggestion. It was just a passing idea.'

'Maybe, but you meant it didn't you?'

'I guess I did.'

'That's what amazes me. As soon as I mention getting a job, you want a baby. You want me helpless and dependent, is that it?'

I looked out at the passing traffic; this is my turf, I thought, this stretch of motorway, my circuit between stations, my overbridge, my world. A car swooped past and I caught a brief glimpse of a face at the back side window, staring out blank and uncomprehending.

'We used to talk of having a second child.' I hoped this was so; Evonne and I had talked of it.

'I want a job. I want to get out into the world and do things. I don't want another baby.' She looked alert and nervous. The fingers of her right hand were galloping on her knee. That beautiful calm she possessed in front of the mirror was gone.

'Is something bothering you?' I swung the Ghia onto the motorway into light traffic, choosing the medium speed middle lane.

'I'm getting all hyped up and I don't know why. Like we're going to sail on the *Titanic* or something. Maybe it's this talk of babies. I can't understand why you said that about having a baby. It's thrown me for six. It just doesn't fit in. I'm spooked.' In the rear view mirror I saw a car coming up fast behind us.

'I feel it too. Perhaps we shouldn't go to the party, like we said this morning. We'll go somewhere else. A meal and a bottle of wine. Candles and polite waiters.'

'Not if you want your job we won't.'

The car behind swerved into the left land and roared past on that side. There was a slower car sitting in the left lane in front of him, which I was steadily overtaking, and the mad bastard who'd just arrived gunned for the narrowing gap, refusing to get trapped behind the slowcoach.

'Christ!' I yelled, hitting the brake, giving the mad bastard room to shoot the gap. Suddenly I heard a horrible grinding noise, like metal scraping along concrete, and looked wildly around for the smash-up, wondering where I'd hear that same noise before, quite recently. There was nothing, just the mad bastard burning off into the distance and a few other cars proceeding as normal.

'What's wrong?' Evelyn said. 'What's happened?'

'I thought I heard a crash.' I said, bewildered. I could still hear it echoing down a long tunnel – the sustained screech of metal.

I kept driving.

At the rendezvous point, two minibuses were already full. There was a general milling around of company employees as the third bus loaded. I saw two mask-like faces at the window of the nearest bus looking out at us; their faces were dead white and their lips and eyes were black in the current gothic fashion.

Most of those on the bus I knew only vaguely, or by sight, except Sophie, whose polite, friendly manner did not change from office to party. It was a little like being in a lift. I did know Roy Jolly,a clerk in statistics, and we exchanged pleasantries while Evelyn talked with Sophie. Roy was looking forward to the party and had already had a couple in anticipation. He was grinning and rubbing his knees, looking at two girls from the typing pool with short skirts and shiny legs.

Roy started talking to the girls, making them laugh, making his own face go red above the collar. The passing streetlights flickered over his features.

Evelyn's strange tension did not go away. I could hear it in her voice as she spoke to Sophie.

'Tell me,' Roy said, 'where do aliens do their shopping?'

'I don't know,' one of the girls said.

'At a New World supermarket,' Roy said.

The girls tittered. Roy's neck bulged against his collar with pride.

'What the hell is that?' he said suddenly, jerking around. The minibus had slowed and I looked out to see that we were approaching the old red brick railway station. The road was lined with billboards advertising beer, and, walking along in front of the billboards were four Nazi soldiers herding a prisoner between them. I saw the prisoner was half-naked and staggering, the soldiers stopped and gave stiff-armed salutes to the passing minibus. I saw a shaven head and a red and black mohawk.

'Hey,' Roy Jolly said, grabbing one of the girls by the arm. 'Isn't that a riot?' He was staring out the back window, laughing. 'What a bunch of clowns.'

'Then have a squiz at this one,' a voice from up front said.

We slowed right down past the looped drive of the old railway station where, at the corner, more Nazi soldiers had crucified someone on a lamp post. The victim was a woman with a black bra, panties and black boots that came up over her knees. Head shaved smooth. The soldiers were jabbing her with spears. They paused to salute the minibus and other passing traffic with their spears.

'Whaddya know!' Roy whooped. A buzz of response ran through the bus.

The girls laughed nervously.

'I think I've heard about this outfit,' Roy said.

'I don't think it's funny, I think it's sick,' Evelyn said loudly. 'Sick and stupid.'

A quiet fell over the bus, and we passed a Nazi captain carrying a whip to the scene of the crucifixion in silence. He flourished the whip at the van. Roy was still grinning, but had sense enough to say no more.

'Good on you,' someone said to Evelyn. I recognised an older woman who had worked in the office for years. The ranks of these old faithfuls were growing thinner as the years wore on, their place being taken by smoother, blander temps like Sophie, standard models who can switch companies without blinking.

'Must have cost the company a packet,' Roy said.

I took Evelyn's hand and found it bunched and curled in

on itself, like the hand of an arthritic. She was looking rigidly out the window.

The company had taken over the floor of a restaurant, and the party was in full swing when we arrived. After half an hour or so, I relaxed somewhat. There seemed to be no anomalies, everybody's names fitted their faces, and their details were as I remembered. Everybody ate and drank and laughed and talked just the same, except Evelyn of course, who charmed whichever way she turned. Pepsi was genial and Evelyn thawed under the warmth of everybody's admiration. The Nazi incident was put behind us. A glass or two of wine went down and a sparkle entered Evelyn's eyes. I stayed with fruit juice, and concentrated on being as blandly plausible as possible. I realised that when I was with Evelyn in public, people tended to treat me with a certain deference; I didn't have to say a lot to keep up a front. It was turning into a pleasant evening.

It stayed that way until Cranner turned up, late, escorting a woman I had never seen before. The table greeted them and called their names as they sat down. The woman's eyes flickered around the table. It was a dark-eyed, lustrous glance. She had an unusual name and I had to hear it twice before I got it. Hera. Hera Cranner. Cranner's wife. And I remembered her, viewed through the window of a bus when following Evonne. It was the same, moody face. Exotic cheekbones.

Cranner's wife.

Except that Cranner didn't have a wife, at least in my old universe. Here he had an incredibly attractive wife who didn't fit with Cranner at all, or at least my image of Cranner. I'd always felt a certain pity for the worm because he couldn't get a girlfriend, or at least keep one, and the fact that he had a woman like this meant I had to re-evaluate the man, especially if she were as smart and ambitious as she was beautiful.

I took a sidelong look at her as they took their seats, trying to figure it out. She was dressed simply but stunningly in black, had long raven-black hair and a broad sensitive face with high eyebrows and large, shining brown eyes. Discreet as I was, she sensed my scrutiny and slid her eyes around in my direction, meeting my acknowledging nod with a polite but brilliant smile. I was suddenly glad they were seated at the far end of the table, giving me time to work out how I would handle a conversation with her if I had to, how I would keep her talking and mask my ignorance. If I could handle an unexpected sister, I could handle an anomaly like this.

A waiter paused by my shoulder and filled my glass with white wine. I looked at it, making no move to pick it up.

On one side, Mary Delany said *sotto voce*, 'Enter Cranner, with husband.'

Across the table Sophie picked it up but her face did not change. She looked at me but her glance was neutral, like that of a professional, a nurse or someone. She never gave anything away, Sophie, her face never cracked.

'The whole gang's here,' Pepsi said from his spot near the head of the table.

There was appreciative muttering and murmuring and raised glasses.

'We've got to raise a glass to Harry Blackman and Ken Cranner, who are going to Canada,' Pepsi said. 'They served us proud there before, and, weather permitting, I'm sure they'll do the same again in a few days.'

'Amen,' Mary Delany said, but I noticed she was watching Hera Cranner the whole time. I wondered to what extent Hera Cranner was the brains behind her husband, which would account for why Delany was treating her with such wary respect.

'And I'm happy to announce that Evelyn is going with

Harry again, to keep him on the straight and narrow I guess. Although it didn't work last time.'

There was a round of genial laughter at my expense. Expression of how difficult it would be to keep me on any straight and narrow. I joined in to show what a good sport I was. I grimaced and grimaced.

'Seriously, it's lonely there in a foreign country, in the war zone of the negotiating room. I'm more than happy that our chief negotiator will have both a friend and his wife to support him.'

There was a round of more substantial applause that I did not join in.

Dinner arrived and I ate, leaving the wine untouched, tuning in and out of the conversational banter. Evelyn ate quietly and thoughtfully, engaging in a little light conversation with her other neighbour, Mary Delany's husband Tom, a businessman in his own right with some knowledge of company affairs.

While waiting for dessert, Mary Delany told a joke. Telling jokes, she said was a symptom of her Irishness, because the Irish can't resist telling a joke. At least half the table tuned in. Mary was famous for her jokes, her Irish jokes particularly.

'A Scotsman, an Englishman, a Frenchman and an Irishman go into a restaurant. The Scotsman orders some haggis, the Englishman roast beef and the Frenchman bread and wine.'

She made a storyteller's pause, and looked around the table. Her accent grew noticeably broader. 'When it comes to the Irishman's turn to order he thinks for a long time and then says, "Oh, that's all right, I'll just have a little bit of everyone else's."'

There was a round of appreciative laughter.

There was an after-dinner speaker, a famous cricketer who made wisecracks all the time and got everybody laughing. I laughed along too, pushing my chair away from the table and cradling my fruit juice with all the appearance of relaxation.

After the famous cricketer had cracked his last joke to thunderous applause, the party entered a less formal phase as people moved around and chatted. I figured if I kept circulating I'd be OK, and found myself in a group with Mary, her husband, Tom, and a couple of men from the science section. Having always found Tom's manner somewhat hostile and insinuating, I had never spoken much to him and was surprised when he drew me to one side as if eager for my company.

'All in a bustle for the Canadian trip, eh?' he said, while Mary kept up a line of chatter with the science boys who were busy being vague about the extent of the Dairy Flat find.

I agreed and smiled. 'Mary's pretty well tied up all that.'

Tom rolled his eyes to heaven. 'It seems that everybody is going to be pleased when this one's over.'

I nodded, a little more distantly this time.

'You more than anyone else, I imagine.' He looked as if he had something stuck in his throat.

I laughed and turned side on to the man, as much to deflect him as anything else. Hera Cranner walked past looking the other way, her arm brushing mine. I caught the perfume of her hair, which was both musty and sweet.

'You'll have your work cut out for you, the international pricing situation being what it is,' Tom said, somewhat fatuously, but uneasily too, like a man with something else on this mind.

'It's a complex situation,' I said, renewing my dislike for him.

'Particularly with regard to shipping costs,' he said insistently. Suddenly he seemed to make up his mind, and drew me further aside. Tom was a thin man with grey, unhealthy-looking skin and an intense face. A good company wife knows how to evaluate as well as charm a client or a colleague. Mary Delany's husband was doing the same, only he didn't bother with the charm part. Who would he be reporting to after the party? Harry doesn't look too good...there's something on his mind.

I looked up and saw Evelyn in animated conversation with Pepsi, whose hand was resting on her arm and who was laughing generously. He was wonderfully open with his laughs. She was busy doing what she said she would do, and the old bastard was falling for it.

'These are delicate negotiations,' I said, puzzled by his drift – he'd know all this from Mary.

He smiled as if he were having a particularly pleasant interchange and his voice was soft. 'Particularly delicate for you, I imagine, if word of the Maritime deal were to get out.'

And with that little parting shot he whisked away into the crowd. I turned back to Mary and the scientists, pretending to tune into their data gubble conversation, wondering just what the hell Tom had been trying to tell me. 'But will the Dairy Flat field be worth developing? In view of these big finds in Aussie...' There were things I wanted to ask Mary, and I moved to one side to stand by the bar along for a moment, waiting for her to shake free. I placed all questions to one side to clear my mind. I thought of a rugby ball and the way it bounces. Because of its shape you can never quite predict the rebound; only when it's in the air does it become predictable. There were photographs of me somewhere, in the first fifteen at school looking steely and determined, ball in hand.

Suddenly Hera Cranner was standing beside me, holding a couple of glasses in her hand. Again, the smell, like damp roses. She flicked a quick, social smile at me and said very quietly, so quietly she seemed hardly to have spoken. 'You might at least have rung me.' She had a husky voice with a quiver in it.

A missing piece of the puzzle fell out of the sky and hit me with a hurt smile. I wished then that I hadn't gone through with all this pretending to be *you*, that I'd opted out far earlier, when the idea occurred and I could have got on a plane and got out. Right out. When the first signs started to show. Before the trap was this far sprung.

She offered me a cigarette and I took one, even though I'd never smoked in my life. Obviously you did, sometimes. Her hand trembled slightly. I'd heard her voice before, once, when I'd rung a number I'd found on the desk. Cranner's home number with two circles around it. While lighting up, I took the time to deal with what I now knew – Evelyn's suspicion, Peter Coveny's contempt, the motel card in your pocket. I also saw Cranner in new light; the cuckold may suspect but never finally know. I remembered the look I got when returning from following Evonne on the bus.

I glanced up to see Evelyn watching us. Her eyes flared briefly, like a rabbit's eyes in a spotlight.

'It's been a mad time,' I said. 'I had to go to Nelson.' Still covering up for *you*, who allowed your marriage to drift onto the rocks, who alienated your son and who took a flirtation with a colleague's wife to dangerous lengths. This was not Harry Blackman. I looked the other way and there was Sophie, watching me over the rim of her glass, the same neutral expression on her face. Roy Jolly was blabbing away but she was taking no notice. Somehow she knows, I thought. There's always someone who knows. Maybe Hera had rung you at the office. The whole place was full of eyes. Sophie was well placed to know what was going on.

Hera smiled briefly, the way we do with an acquaintance. Her face was a casual mask. She looked as if she were just pausing, having a quick word on the way somewhere else but her eyes riveted upon a lovebite on my neck. 'I figured that when you didn't turn up last week. You're going with Evelyn to Canada. That'll be nice.'

Busy falling in love with Evelyn as I was, I did not find it strange that you fell in love with Hera Cranner, across whose face there whiplashed a moment's jealousy.

'I'm sorry, Harry, I now we can't expect too much of each other.' She smiled for the benefit of someone approaching. She was still holding two glasses but leaned forward gently and touched her hand against mine. 'Keep in touch.'

I ordered a gin and tonic from the bar. Into the glass went the enormous, crushing unfairness of it all. Now the trap had been sprung it was too late.

Pepsi came up and sat down beside me, a glass of Pepsi in his hand. He looked like an imitation of himself, and I had to turn away for a moment, so that nothing of my feelings would show.

From this moment on, I was without protection. My strategy of pretending to be *you*, pass as you, quietly replaced you in your life, was in ruins. I was on my own. Finally, it was not Tate or Pepsi who had brought me down but you. This little timebomb had been ticking away ever since I'd arrived, waiting for the right opportunity to explode.

Thoughtfully he said, 'You know, Harry, sometimes I think we forget the important things of life.' He gestured to where Hera Cranner was talking to Evelyn, smiling and nodding at something Evelyn was saying. 'Like our womenfolk, for example. We forget the beautiful things. The blessings.' Coming out of his utterly pragmatic mouth, it sounded profoundly true.

'You're right,' I said.

His eyes never left the two women; the fair and the dark, beauty with beauty. 'Have we forgotten about beauty, Harry?

I mean as a culture?'

I wondered if someone had popped something into his Pepsi.

'We've almost certainly forgotten something,' I said, with more intensity than I intended.

'I'm old-fashioned, Harry. When I was a kid we used to go out on Sunday drives to admire nature. We'd go to rivers and beaches and pine forests. I was bored shitless at the time, but looking back I can see that what we were searching for was beauty.'

'Uh huh.' I could hear the violins, but what I could see was how easy it would be to dash my glass against the side of the bar, rip open his shirt to reveal his chest, already scarred by a double bypass operation he'd had five years ago, and plunge the broken end of the glass into his belly, spilling his guts all over the bar stool. A piece of nightmare sitting on a bar stool.

The white coats could have me then.

Evelyn said something and Hera laughed. Hers was a slow, sexy contralto. I wished I could hear what they were saying.

'We don't appreciate what we have until it's too late,' Pepsi said. The hearty edge had worn off his voice, which was tinted with melancholy.

I asked, 'Have you seen that slogan, "Practise random kindness and senseless acts of beauty"?'

'No I haven't but it sounds very positive.' Pepsi was recovering now from his momentary lapse. His eyes were sliding around the room, doubtless in search of his next conversation.

I laughed. 'A woman pulls up at a highway tollgate and says to the booth operator, "Here's some money, I'd like to pay for half a dozen cars behind me," and drives off. The next day a man pulls up at the booth and gives the operator five hundred dollars, saying, "Give this to the lady who paid my toll yesterday."'

Pepsi chuckled as if I had told a dirty joke. 'I never knew tollbooth operators made so much in tips,' he said, already turning as Evelyn and Hera Cranner approached. I wondered if his brief ode to natural beauty was not simply some nostalgia for the days when he could attract such women. 'We were just reminding ourselves of the important things in life,' he said, waving his glass in the air.

'And what's that?' Evelyn said, full of brittle gaiety.

'The company of beautiful women, of course.'

Evelyn tossed her head flirtatiously. 'I'm sure you enjoy plenty of that.'

'Not as much as I would like.' He clapped me on the shoulder. 'I'll leave that to young fellas, like Harry here.'

'Not as young as you would think,' Evelyn said.

Pepsi grinned. To Hera he said, 'And tennis. You've been winning more competitions?'

'I only play for fun now. My competition days are over.' She moved her head a little as she spoke and her hair slid around her shoulders; its darkness contained many colours. Her voice was deep and throaty.

I turned to catch Evelyn's eye but she was brightly involved in the conversation.

'I'd like to play tennis,' Evelyn said. 'Do you think I'd be good at it?'

Hera said, 'It takes a lot of practice.' Her smile flashed around to me.

'I'm sure you would be good at anything you took on,' Pepsi said to Evelyn, as if that were the end of it.

'You flatter me,' Evelyn said.

I slipped up to the bar for another gin. Anything, anything at all. I leaned intently over the bar and signalled the barman, suddenly wanting a drink more than anything else in the world. Evelyn followed me, leaving Hera talking to the boss.

'I want to go home,' Evelyn said in a calm voice. 'As soon as possible.'

'Of course,' I said, downing the glass and gesturing the barman for another.

'Before you get drunk.'

'I won't be getting drunk.'

Ken Cranner joined us. 'How was your Nelson trip?'

'It was good to see my father again, but he's not well.'

'I'm sorry to hear that.'

Evelyn let out an explosion of breath.

'Did you enjoy the cricket stories?' Ken asked her.

'More than I enjoyed the street theatre.'

Ken laughed. 'That was a bit of an embarrassment, wasn't it? All that Nazi stuff.'

'Very amusing.'

He turned to me. 'What's wrong with your father, Harry?'

'His heart. He gets that grey look on his face.'

Hera Cranner joined us. 'We must get together and have dinner sometime,' she said, smiling. Her eyes, full and dark, flickered briefly to me.

Ken Cranner signalled the barman. I emptied my glass.

Evelyn looked at us all from one to the other as if she were seeing everybody for the first time. I knew exactly how she felt. 'I'm going home,' she announced.

At that moment the lights went out, two broad spotlights focused on a clear area, and, as some jazz-infused rock music began, a woman in a plain black bodysuit entered the lit area and began to dance. I watched but I didn't see it, aware of the four of us, a little cluster at the bar, faces set towards the dancer. I saw a woman crossing and uncrossing her hands, as if she were trying to work out some secret, potent spell on herself.

She finished to long, sincere applause. When I stopped clapping Evelyn was gone.

14

The 'secret destination' had been very near the Customs Street car park, the minibus tour being pure diversion, and just as I hit the street I saw Evelyn's form vanishing towards the car-park building.

I paused. Even now I didn't have to live through these coming hours in which the truth would have to be told. I'd had my chance to speak, last night. The best of times, the worst of times – and now it was simply the worst of times. I turned my doomed feet in the direction Evelyn had taken.

Telling Kober was one thing, telling Evelyn quite another. A lot worse than trying to confess an affair.

'I'll drive if you're too drunk,' Evelyn said as I caught up with her on the ground floor of the car-park building. She gave the last word a very ugly inflection.

'I'm not drunk at all,' I said mildly.

'But it might put you over the Breathalyser limit.' She pulled some keys out of her bag and shook them, not saying anything about the wine she'd drunk. I hadn't realised she kept her own set of keys. Evonne never did. I'd unconsciously assumed, when she made her exit from the party, she'd have to wait for me.

I stood in the doorway of the car park for a moment, looking around at the inner cityscape. A light rain had fallen and the street was as black and shiny as an oilskin coat. There was a flicker of lightning running around the world followed by a quick spasm of thunder. Hurricane Luke on the horizon.

It was true I'd only had three gins but I felt as if I'd had fifteen; my feet kept having to accommodate themselves to the contingencies of the ground, streets and buildings wheeled around me with bright, garish movements, doing a seasick dance of their own. The advance guard of the hurricane had arrived but it was utterly silent. Lines of mist advanced through the air like murky seahorses, soundlessly smashing into the sides of buildings. The air was on the move but there was no wind; the earth beneath was shifting to meet it. There were patches of dry and damp space. I looked back at the line of cars stranded between floors of concrete and saw Evelyn unlocking the driver's side door of the Ghia. She made big shadows on the concrete walls, her head tossing proudly on her shoulders. The door opened and Evelyn, with shadows, vanished. Suddenly I could smell the sea, rich and mixed; city docks, oil, smoke and salt. I followed to the car, opened the door and closed it again without getting in; the closing door made a dull, solid sound.

'Let's take a walk to the wharf,' I said through the window. I wasn't sure about getting into the car. There was a constriction in my throat. I was afraid that if I got in and shut the door I wouldn't be able to breathe, or get out again. Instead we would go to the wharf and I would tell her everything within the sight and the sign of the ocean.

She hesitated, the key already in the ignition, her face set towards the windscreen. 'Why don't you just go on your own and throw yourself in?' Her voice wasn't nasty or bitter or anything, just very matter of fact.

'I need you to give me a push.'

She was too angry and betrayed to stop and think. In one

movement she got out of the car and slammed the door behind her. The noble old Ghia Serenissima rocked. We crossed the downtown square in silence and walked along the concrete waterfront, where I could look over at the wharves, lonely and deserted at this time of night under the lidless stare of public lighting.

'Fancy it being Hera Cranner,' Evelyn said. 'It stood out like a sore thumb. If that's the expression.'

I didn't say anything. I wasn't ready yet, I'd never be ready. The reason I hadn't told her my story yet was cowardice, simple and straightforward; I was afraid of the truth.

'Or are you going to try and deny it? That would be fun to watch in a gruesome sort of way. Harry in denial.'

We stood by a fast-food diner, now closed, and looked across to where a ferry rode peacefully by the dock. I heard ghostly noises, as if gulls were crying or whitecaps were breaking over rocks. Looking down at the oily swell, I thought how the surface of the water was like the rich texture of the skin of the whale. I walked to the edge of the wharf and heard the slap and gurgle of the water beneath.

I murmured, 'Things aren't always what they seem.'

'I'm sure they're not. They never had been. Is this a philosophical point you are making? About truth? A touch of Descartes, perhaps? The "evil genius" at work?'

She looked down into the water and watched it moving about. The water moved her face about. She'd gone beyond the truth now as far as her Harry Blackman was concerned; she didn't care what I said. Truth? I didn't know the meaning of the word. Beyond belief, she was. She stared into the viewless room where the final death throes of love take place. The final horrid clutch before the letting go. The last flickers of love dying on her face. It was not a pretty sight; the death of hope made her ugly.

'I'll tell you everything,' I said, sitting on a low seat facing the wharf and the harbour. Now that the moment had arrived, I didn't feel that confident.

'Wait!' she said, snapping her fingers, standing in front of me. 'Let me guess. You and Hera Cranner are secret agents combating an alien invasion of earth by means of Herr Kober's energy device. This necessitates numerous motel meetings.'

'Not quite.' I wiped tiny beads of moisture out of my hair. A car swung around behind us, its headlights making halos of everything. Would the truth be any less fanciful?

'I'm incredibly glad to hear it. Now get this, Harry, there is only one thing that will satisfy me. The truth. I want an account of it, blow by blow, no lies, no evasions, no half-lies, no digressions.'

'You'll get it.'

She laughed out loud, her voice as piercing as a seagull's. It wasn't a laugh at all except by some distant family relationship,. More like a derisive shriek. Or the sound of a doomed person falling over a cliff. I thought of old Sam Walsh, cancelling his cheque and finding his miracle had been cancelled too; like Sam, I had missed my moment. Last night there might have been half a chance.

The trap set for me at the beginning was now fully sprung. Or so I thought.

The water moved in under the wharf, making greedy, gulping sounds. I leaned down and felt the rough edge of the wood in my hands. A splinter slid, easefully, into my flesh.

'Do you know what gets me, Harry, what really gets me? It's not that you should be screwing that woman but the fast one you've tried to pull on me. The soft soap and deception, the bullshit and the cover-up. All those false trails you created. Lying to Timmy with Lego. Running around saving whales. Lying to me with kisses, and last night...last night...' She stared into her private horror. 'It wasn't me you were making love to last night, it was her...you were showing me...' She shuddered. 'Making the body lie. So your body would lie to mine. That's why you were so...different.'

'Evelyn...'

'Don't Evelyn me, Harry. You've Evelyned me for the last time. Never again.' She slammed her hands towards each other as if she were crushing something, and stood stock still, rocking slightly backwards on her heels, closing her eyes, her face a grim rictus. A horrible lucidity had caught up with her. Another car swung behind us and caught her like that in a shadowless, photographic illumination. Her eyelids flicked up, eyes wide and staring, voice deadly calm. 'I'll tell you what I'm going to do, Harry, so you'll know what's coming. So you'll have time to think it over, and appreciate it. I'm going to screw you for every cent you have or are ever likely to have. I don't want half, the way they do in divorce settlements, I want the lot; the house, Timmy, everything. I want to leave you with nothing. Nothing. But your job. Because you'll need your job,' she nodded grimly to herself, 'you'll need your job to pay me, and you won't have a job if I ring up Cranner and Pepsi. I don't want to shut up about this, I want to scream it from the rooftops. I want to watch you squirm on the end of a public hook. I want to see Ken Cranner's face. I want to see everybody running for cover.' She gave a huge snort of satisfaction at the thought. 'And I want to see the butcher arrive, in all his glory, to put an end to people like you forever, because you suck and you suck and you suck and there's no end to it, you're never satisfied.' She snapped her fingers. 'It's your time to pay. You can buy my silence and protect your Hera from all that shame and humiliation, but you'll have to pay. I mean *pay*. Do you understand?'

I nodded. There was no way I could abort or forestall this

great rush of grief and rage, and in no way should I have tried to do so.

Her grief passed into madness. I saw her walking towards me out of the streetlights with the drugged gait of a prostitute, a grotesque leer on her face, 'Why don't we have a baby, Harry? A nice sweet little baby. Christ Almighty! A baby! That would have kept me out of the way very nicely wouldn't it? Nicely strapped down to the fucking goddamned house! Nailed by a pregnancy to the floor while you go out fucking after hours.' It was all falling into place for her.

I got up off the seat needing to do something, and she stepped back, frightened, as if I were a dangerous animal. Car headlights caught us both again, as if we were on stage. As the glare swung past, black shadows buckled around us.

'Go on, assault me, Harry. Hit me as hard as you can.' She thrust out her face and bared her teeth at me, her face haggard in the cold illumination of the streetlamps. The water crushed up under the wharf beneath us. 'Lash out so I can put you inside for the night. For a week. With the deros and wife-beaters. Where you fucking belong. Hit me!'

I began to cry.

She flung herself at me, screaming and tearing at my face. I held her at length, fending off the worst of her assault, keeping my head bowed so I didn't have to look at her. For a moment I thought of killing her, here in this place of creaking shadows. The murderer, Harry Blackman, would put his hands around the victim's throat and she would gurgle and make all the appropriate noises. Into the water, weighed down by incredulity and grief. No open ocean for her. Distraught husband at police station. Woman drowned after staff party. Tragic accident.

'Let's go home,' I said, in the gentlest voice I could find. 'I have a long story to tell you.'

Evelyn shook her head from side to side. Her voice was a hoarse whisper in her throat, as if she had already been strangled.

I couldn't face it. I turned and walked the other way.

I strode off down the waterfront to the sound of a band playing mindless, happy music from a nearby bar, looking for all the world as if I were going somewhere, arriving at a bus shelter where a drunk was lying, covered by a tattered coat. He stared at me, blank and expressionless. Then he smiled in greeting, and raised his arm, puppet-like, in assumed comradeship. An unholy brotherhood. A three-quarters empty bottle was clutched in his other arm. Red and white neon moons lit him with alternate glows through the driving mist.

I didn't return his greeting. I just waited there, as if something else was going to happen. I could be someone just standing there, waiting for a bus or taxi. There was a burst of laughter from the bar across the road, and the band struck up the syrupy chords of *She Wears My Ring*.

I retraced my steps, walking near the edge of the water, putting one step in front of the other, carefully, water to one side, land to the other. There was a subdued flicker of lightning and a dull rumble to the north.

Evelyn was sitting on the bench facing the harbour. She wasn't waiting for me, she was just sitting there, like someone who had forgotten how to move.

'Here we go,' I said. 'The moment has arrived.' I said it aloud to the empty docks grown huge with night and mist. At the end of the wharf one bare lamp bent its head over in a lone halogen prayer.

'What moment?' She spoke mechanically, from out of an endless moment.

'The one I've been putting off for three weeks hoping I could get through.'

'Three weeks? That's a laugh…'

'Before tonight, I'd never met Hera Cranner. Never seen her in my life…'

'What…what?' An infinitely tired endless moment from which she could not escape. Suddenly I heard the staff party ringing in my ears as if it were still going on, and probably it was. The drunken, unselfconscious stage as the smiles on the faces of the caterers become more strained; those smiles have to last a long time. Evelyn sat on the wharf frozen in disbelief.

'And up until three weeks ago I'd never seen you either. I am not your husband. I've only been pretending, or trying to. In the world I come from, I have a wife called Evonne.'

My words pulled her from her time warp. She moved as far away from me as the bench allowed, then stood up, facing me, her eyes huge and staring.

'Think about it for a moment. That night I missed the meeting about Canada, you were surprised, remember? That was when it started. I walked into a strange house. I'd never seen you or Timmy before. I've been ad-libbing ever since, flying blind, making it up as I go along and papering over the cracks.'

'I remember that night,' she said slowly. 'The way you looked at me when I got into bed…'

'I'd never seen your body before.'

Her mouth opened to laugh but no sound came out. Yet I caught a flash of something, nothing as direct as a look, rather a hesitation of the body – the moment of impact when the truth hits, and is recognised by the body, if not the mind.

'Think about it, Evelyn. Last night you said yourself that I was different, remember? I looked different and talked different and everything, remember? I nearly told you then.

Fuck! I should have told you then. I didn't want to spoil the moment.'

It wasn't just her head that started to shake back and forward in negation, but her whole body. 'This is too fucking much, I'm going back to the car.' She turned and walked away. I got up and followed.

'And I made love differently. You sure as hell noticed that.'

We made a dive between multiple, zooming lights.

'Get fucked, Harry. Go to her. Go to Hera with your story. Tell her you've never met her.'

'That night,' I said, walking in tune with the little green biped in the pedestrian light. 'That first night. Think about it. That was when my behaviour began to change, wasn't it?' I ticked them off. 'I began to take an interest in Timmy, take an interest in you, get cold feet on the house deal. You see in my world there is no house deal and Peter Coveny...' It all sounded so thin.

'Shut up, Harry.'

Halfway across the downtown square, two drunks, their arms around each others' shoulders, wove in our direction. One broke away and fronted up to me. He was short and heavy with big shoulders that turned in upon themselves. His eyes were blank, like a zombie's and they fixed in the middle of my chest or somewhere over my left shoulder.

'Get fucked mate,' he said.

I nodded. 'Good-o.'

The other drunk, who was tall with a long, droopy face, appeared to focus on me, lock me in his sights. 'Look after your head, man,' he said, pulling the other drunk away. 'They don't give them away free.'

'What I think is happening now,' I said, as we walked beneath the heavy arches of the car-park building, 'is that you believe me, and that's impossible, so think of what it's like for me.'

'Why didn't you tell me straightaway then, Harry, why didn't you just walk up to me in the kitchen that first night and say "Who the hell are you, and where's what's her-name? – what did you say her name was?'

'Evonne. I nearly said her name a couple of times, I got it half out. It's so similar to yours.'

She stood with her hand on the driver's door, remembering my near slips. 'Did you love her?'

'Yes.'

'And why didn't you tell me, why go on with the farce?'

'It wasn't a farce for me. I thought you'd decide I was mad, you know, as in insane, and I'd lose everything. The other Harry, your husband, just left a great big fucking mess for me to clean up.'

'I think you *are* mad. I'm frightened of you. I'm frightened to get into the car with you.'

'There you have it. I was right; it's your best option in terms of trying to understand it. Take me to a syringe; I'm down to bedrock now. There's only the truth left. And as I said, I think that underneath you believe me.'

She snapped her fingers as she'd done before. 'I know, you were abducted by Jerry Tate who turns out to be an alien and got taken onto a UFO where strange things were done to your body and your mind.' Still she did not unlock the door. Her tone was flippant but her eyes were chips of jade. All round me nothing but flint and concrete.

'Sorry.' I started to cry again. It was Evonne, her name was out there now, in the open. I'd had no time to grieve, no time to breathe. I don't cry easily; it had taken Evonne fifteen years to teach me how to cry when crying was required, and even with her gentle coaching it was still not a natural thing for me to do. I don't know if *you* ever cried, but the way Evelyn stared at me made me think you never had. It was a new thing for her to see Harry Blackman broken down, leaning on the old Ghia, my head in my arms. She said nothing but flicked open the door locks, so I could get in.

'I just can't make any jokes,' I said through a haze of tears. I didn't know how to say it without sounding crazy. 'I've lost a world.'

I got into the car and waited. She stood by the door. 'You're wrong about one thing, Harry,' she said, bending down to talk but still not getting in. 'I don't believe it, but I am puzzled.'

'About what?'

'You couldn't think this fantastic thing up yourself. You're just not that smart. You're devious and you're double-dealing, but you are not imaginative.'

I agreed with her. Not about the devious part, but certainly the underlying idea. I'd never have thought something up like this in a thousand years and she knew it. If my assumed stupidity was to be my saviour in this situation, who was I to argue?

'And Hera Cranner puzzles me.'

'In what way?'

'She was not just angry with you, she seemed bewildered…'

She toyed with the door handle. Still she could not make up her mind.

'You're not half as frightened as I am, I said.

She looked at me and believed me and got into the car.

Evelyn drove. I sat and watched the city. It was composed of verticals and horizontals edged with synthetic light. Everything jarred up against everything else. I scratched the back of my hand and felt no sensation, it felt like the back of someone else's hand. From the approach, the bridge was an abstract of lights, an exercise in pointillist form. An arc slung across nothing. A line of lights going up into nowhere. We floated up one side into mist, and our beams carved shining paths in the dark. Around us, other shadowy, ovoid beasts did the same. Here we go, I thought, the final phase.

Herr Kober had predicted this.

'By the way,' Evelyn said, her voice cool and natural. 'The police have been sniffing around Lexon. There's some investigations going on into company fraud. Mason has been interviewed.' She was putting the whole thing on hold and doing what *you* and her always did in a crisis – talked about work.

'Mason! Shit, who told you this?'

'Hera Cranner. I think she was trying to warn you about something. Through me, that is.'

'And I don't know what it is. Your husband probably did. *Him.*' I thought furiously, trying to tie this in with Tom Delany's strange hint. Someone had got the word on Maritime, but who? There was no time to think about that.

'But what sort of fraud would Mason be involved in, other than the normal, everyday sort?' She looked genuinely puzzled; there were surely greater frauds in heaven and earth than were dreamed of in her philosophy.

'In this weasel world,' I said, 'Mason is obviously involved in some shady dealing. Cranner knows or is involved too. Hera Cranner must know her husband is involved. But why warn me? I mean *him.* Maybe *he* was involved too.' I knew the answer was staring me in the face, but I couldn't see it yet. Not the full shape of it. 'Cranner may know about your husband and Hera. It would give him a motive for revenge.' I tried to laugh. 'I call him my counterpart, the other Harry. I don't like him.'

'You're going to stick to this other world business?'

I studied her profile. Her face was totally composed, like

someone sitting for a painting. I wanted to take her hand before it vanished into varnish and texture.

'Be my ally, Evelyn,' I said, feeling horribly earnest. 'I'm alone in this. I'm alone *here*. I've fallen in love with you. This is it for me. If I don't have an ally, I have nobody.'

'You believe this stuff, don't you Harry?'

'I don't just believe it, I live it. I'm a one man *Titanic*, zooming between ice floes.'

'What if you are a multiple personality or something?'

'Then tell where I've been all my life. I've even got a sister I never had. She knew, even though she had to be drunk to see it.'

'Paula!'

'Ring her and ask her. But Vernon never noticed. He only saw what he feared to see. Timmy knows.'

'Harry, is Mason going to Canada for Lexon?'

'Probably.'

The lights cut temporary, angled shapes out of her face. She was thinking hard, she was trying to put it together; in that respect we were already allies.

I said, 'Whatever the police have got on Mason, Big Bill will be shitting his pants. The cartels are illegal, remember? How many shredding machines does it take to stay out of court? And when the cartel starts to break ranks, like we're doing with this Maritime deal, that's the right time for the law to strike.'

'I got the impression that the police weren't chasing cartels, rather some sort of accounting fraud within the company.'

'Makes no difference. When the cat is among the pigeons, all the pigeons panic.'

She had to laugh. I took it as a good sign. 'I'll say this for you, Harry. You're doing a bloody good imitation of being someone else.'

When she hit the motorway, Evelyn put her foot down. I watched the speedometer creep up towards a hundred and ten. 'There'll be speed cameras,' I said. The orange arc lights were flicking by like so many discarded matches.

'Good-o,' she said, as bright and breezy as Biggles setting out on a mission in an old propeller-driven fighter, and edged the speed up, heading towards a hundred and twenty, gripping the steering wheel with white knuckles and staring fiercely at the road markings as if they were a line of tracer bullets heading towards her.

'Chocks away,' I said.

The whizzing roadscape turned into an orange blur which was moving by quite lazily. In that blur, shapes came and went like virtual creatures. Then the orange deepened and the road was sheeted with blood, as gleaming and slippery as peeled back skin. We were driving up the arteries of an open heart surgery operation.

After nudging a hundred and fifty Evelyn dropped the speed in anticipation of our exit. The noble Ghia whined like a million slaves screaming. The flood faded and the blur turned into flicking orange arc lights. At eighty we seemed to be crawling along. Neither of us said anything until right at the end, when we sat in our driveway and she had turned the motor off.

It was a moonless night and the streetlights were enclosed by advancing haloes of mist, like an extra body. I could see down the driveway to the house. It was an ordinary looking, well-to-do house in an ordinary looking, well-to-do suburb, apparently comfortable with its mortgage.

'I want a divorce, Harry,' she said, slipping the keys out of the ignition and into her pocket.

I stared at the house. 'I can live in this world but I can't sleep here.'

'You poor bastard,'she said.

Tess was lying on the couch in front of the dead TV screen. Evelyn walked right past her into the bedroom. I went into the kitchen and had a drink of water.

'How was the party?' Tess said from the couch, voice dozy.

'A whiz,' I said. 'They had all sorts of entertainment, Nazis in jackboots and other sadomasochistic displays...'

'Who...what...?' Tess struggled into wakefulness. 'Aren't you home a bit early?'

Evelyn appeared in the lounge doorway. She'd taken off her coat but was otherwise still in party dress. She sparkled like a star in empty space. 'I'm sorry, Tess, I don't mean to push you out the door, but it's just not fair to drag you into this.'

Fully awake now, and sitting up, Tess said, 'Drag me into what?'

Evelyn didn't answer.

Tess summed up the situation in one swift, venomous glance my way. 'Do you want to come home with me?' she said to Evelyn.

'I am not going to be the one to walk out of this house, nor am I going to disturb my child peacefully asleep.' Evelyn replied tartly.

Tess jumped to her feet and grabbed her cardigan and coat. 'Keep in touch, love,' she said, kissing her sister on the cheek. 'Any time.'

She made a dive for the door without even looking my way. Only at the door did she pause and turn to me.

'Your best course,' she said, 'is to pack up and get out of here.'

She spoke with the power of an oracle.

I was lying on the single bed like a traveller in a strange motel, throwing out any thoughts as soon as they arrived, when I heard our bedroom door open and close quietly. The room shifted on its axis, as if we were moored at sea and the wind had changed. The door to my room began to alter, its outlines growing fuzzy. Then there were two doors, one superimposed on top of the other, but not perfectly. There was a blurry foot or two between. Something rested on me, like a perfume or an invisible intimacy. There was an expectant taste like a cool spoon on the tongue.

And there was a shadow across the doorway; a man strangely refracted at the waist, slipping between the doors, something in his hand. In the act of turning towards me. Carrying a small, slim rifle.

I didn't have to taste the air to know.

This was *you*.

Only for a second.

Like ritual lightning.

Long enough for you to see me and to know who I was. Long enough to begin to swing the rifle towards me. I could see the barrel turning, the bore seeking me out like a single black nostril. I rolled out of the bed onto the floor and you didn't have time to bring the barrel around; your window of opportunity was so brief you were dissolving in the fuzzy air before the barrel found its mark. Oddly, the rifle went first and your hands were left, finger hooked around a trigger of air.

The finger tightened on nothing.

15

I got up early in the morning to leave for work before Evelyn woke.

I was going to work because I had nothing else to do. Whatever else was going on in my life, I always went to work. It didn't matter how exhausted I was or in what world I was in.

As I poured milk into my cup, I thought of you and last night's murder attempt. Kober had warned me as much. But why you? Why not Tate, or one of his operatives? No, this was nothing to do with Tate – this was *you*. You had your reasons, and I didn't know what they were.

Out of habit, I cleared the answerphone. I had one new message.

Kober's voice came abruptly on the line.

'Mr Backmann. I have been a fool. I didn't know. I was blind. You see, for me nothing changed. Just the tobacconist turned into a fruit shop. I didn't think about it until after you'd told me your story.' The sound of ragged, deeply drawn breath. 'This *other* Kober, he is a genius. I was making mud pies, he was studying the vortex. Which is the physics of the black hole.' Another ragged breath. 'This is from the horse's mouth. For nearly three weeks now I have been trying to break a code that protects one of my files. I thought I must have set the code before the first accident, and forgotten it. Last night I broke the code. I found plans, Mr Backmann, designs for an… understanding. They are not the plans for my generator. They are *his* plans, the *other* Kober, for *his* device, not a generator, but something I don't understand, something which plays with fields generated by the mind. This other Kober, he treats the mind as a vortex. Opens up channels, understand? Decodes frequencies. He escapes from the Specials into your world; I come here.'

I cut the message off and ran it through again to the same point. Yes, I did understand. Kober was from *my* world. That's why he didn't know me. But he didn't realise it himself! Would I have realised, I wondered, if Evelyn had not appeared? How long would it have taken me? And Kober had no family. Auckland was not his familiar habitat anyway; he was already an alien in an alien land. So some shopfront changes overnight – what's that to him? Easy enough to ignore if nothing else apparently alters. The bakery that sells hot bread is still at the bottom of the street. His suppliers still have the same telephone numbers, the whores at the corner wear the same perfume.

We could be walking through different worlds each day and not know it.

Kober's voice went on. 'He, this *other* Kober, has already gone over, that was the first accident, but it was not an accident. He destroyed his machine so the Specials couldn't get it. Destroyed all the evidence. Left them nothing, I understand him there.

'He crossed over and that's why I'm here. My simple machine came with me. What you call the egg. My little mud pie. The Specials, your Mr Tate, sent the other Backmann, your *counterpart*, over after him. That's why you're here…but listen…look on your computer, your laptop, Mr Backmann, the plans your counterpart stole are there…the designs of this mind enhancer. This other Kober, *he* knew your counterpart had stolen them. He knew the Specials were closing in. He had to escape…but you must understand, this *other* Kober was mad. He was dissolved in his own genius. The process, this Kober effect,' his voice could not hide a momentary surge of pride, 'is dangerous. It involved the heart, the mind, and the effect is unpredictable. Every time somebody goes over, a new configuration…'

At that point the answerphone cut him off at the knees. I imagined him raving on into a dead machine. But it didn't matter, I'd heard enough. Enough to fill in a few gaps.

Poor Kober. He'd only discovered free energy!

While the other Kober, he'd opened up something else, discovered a whole new property of vortexes hardly dreamed of in Schauberger's philosophy.

Pepsi, Delany, Cranner, they knew nothing of this, nor did Coveny. You had been playing a much bigger game – a gateway to another realm. Who wouldn't play for stakes like that? And you needed money, five or ten million dollars, splitting your odds between the house deal, the McBride kickback and the share speculation. If they all came in you might have had half a chance of building one of these mind machines for yourself, engineering your own getaway.

But you crossed over, I guessed, before you were ready, probably on Tate's orders. Kober was right. Tate would have a machine, his backroom boys would have been working parallel to the other Kober. Tate would have sent you over to kill this other Kober who'd escaped him by switching worlds. Tate would want sole control of the other Kober's invention. *You* were Tate's hired killer.

Now I had the chance to play for the same stakes.

I'd just put the phone down when Evelyn appeared in her dressing gown looking wide awake in a bug-eyed way. She used the last of the boiling water, which I was just going to use to top up my coffee, to pour a coffee for herself.

Her mouth screwed up as the bitter brew hit her taste buds. 'I'm not going to Canada. I couldn't take it. I want a divorce immediately.'

'Perhaps I won't go myself.'

'That's your job on the line,' she said, retreating to the bedroom, coffee in hand.

Hurricane Luke hit full on as I was driving to work. The sky turned first grey and dirty, then dark as evening, and the wind punched at the line of cars all with their headlights on flowing slowly up the Harbour Bridge. It seemed as if, with mechanical obedience, they were following one another up into nowhere, vanishing into the dark, slanting rain.

On the bridge itself, I felt a trembling deep in the massive steel body; the wind bent itself around the girders that held our flimsy lanes in place and whacked against the cars, screaming. The clouds kneaded the sky; they rolled and boiled like a speeded-up movie scene.

Heading at a snail's pace down the bridge to the deeper murk beneath, I pulled out my cellphone and punched out Coveny's number.

'Sell Southern Oil. Now.'

'Now? Why?'

'I've just got the word. The Dairy Flat field's a dud. Initial expectations not met is the word, and the word moves fast. New Aussie fields are breaking.'

His voice was terse. 'Have you told the others?' His voice shook as if the wind was blowing through it.

I was ready for this one. I even knew who the others were. I'd almost figured it in the car last night, talking to Evelyn. The little cartel of criminals the police were trying to track down. Coveny's unholy coven. This was the missing piece. The share speculators. Cranner, in it up to his neck. And Mason, sharp-eyed for a quick buck on the side, fiddling the books at Lexon to raise investment money. The big share scam. This little criminal band stretched across the management levels of two companies. Coveny was in it of course, and probably Coleman. And *you*. You were in the thick of it, fully committed, everything hanging on the line.

'I want out before them, that's why you've got to move. I've got maybe half an hour on Cranner. Put all those stocks up now and the guts will drop out of them. Just put mine up…'

'You're telling me?'

'Yes, I am. I'm instructing my lawyer. And I want the money to go to account number…' I reeled off the number of an account that had no overdraft facility and therefore no debt.

'For God's sake Harry, why? Why not pull it back to our investment account and go from there?' He was yelping at the prospect of the money heading south, away from his trust account. I was ready for that too.

'So I can get my hands on it, buddy,' I said slowly and very distinctly, braking gently as red lights appeared in front of me.

He was silent after that and I took the opportunity to hang up. I would get that money. It was not enough to pull me out of the hole you'd dug for me, but I'd draw it out and get it into a new account, at another bank, before the shit hit, even at this late stage; get some control into my life.

I tucked my laptop hard in beside me.

Damage control.

Sophie was in her place, not a hair out of place. For the sky people, there was no hurricane except at morning tea as an object of conversation. Cranner was in his office, head bent over his desk; the weasel already at work. I wondered how much he'd found out about Hera and *you*. How much he suspected. How much he'd been told. Relationships are like cartels – when you break ranks you stay out of sight – but someone always sees you.

Sophie said good morning in exactly the same tone of voice she used every morning; if anyone were going to mention our hasty departure from the party last night, it would not be Sophie.

I looked around the strategic mess of the offices with what was almost affection. After the strangeness at home, the office was homely and familiar; a carrion comfort, I knew, but I luxuriated in it for the moment.

My own room too had that feel of a refuge, a home away from home. I sat for a time pretending to be reviewing my options and watched the hurricane from the luxury of my sky tower. Except I didn't have any options. A deep-seated shudder of concrete. A spasm of steel. These structures moved, I knew, swayed gently back and forth under stress.

On the desk, the familiar tight clutter of papers and files. Last minute Canada stuff. Loose ends. Tight deadlines. The squeeze.

The first thing was to check out the laptop to find these designs Kober had been raving about. I was half-ready to discount the professor's phone message by this time. The two bombings had unhinged his mind. He'd listened to my story and adopted it for himself, taken it over, turned himself into the crossover.

After all, I'd already checked the laptop and found nothing. I watched, mesmerised, as it went through its motions, stacking up functions in readiness for use just like I should have been doing in readiness for Canada.

Everything looked just as I remembered it. Yet it was *your* laptop, not mine. That very first night I didn't have it with me in the car. I'd left it at the office, which meant it had entered the realm of things that lay in your world.

But it didn't take me long to notice something anomalous – there was far less memory available than the files and programs could account for. I rechecked my results three times, adding up the memory space required by each document and programme, and comparing the total with what the machine was using.

I was about to delve further when the phone rang. It was Sophie. Would I go to Pepsi's office? Yes, of course.

I stared at the laptop. Somewhere, hidden away, there was an invisible file.

Mary Delany sat in Rigold's chair, swivelling it to and fro. She had dark rings under her eyes.

'Where's the boss today?'

'Away, he's probably got a hangover from all that soft drink.' She gestured to a chair. 'I'm in the saddle for the day and my eyes are still popping from the bubbly.' She popped them at me to demonstrate.

I sat down. 'Tom said a strange thing to me last night,' I said, hoping to be spared a more detailed tour of her hangover.

'I know,' she said, rubbing her eyes as if polishing them. 'He shouldn't have said it.'

'What? You mean you didn't put him up to it?' I wanted to keep on the offensive with Mary; I had a funny feeling about what might happen if she got on top.

'That's right. He was talking way out of turn.'

'Then there's been no leak on the Maritime deal?'

There was a long pause as she thought. Her fingers moved lightly on the polished desk as if she were tracing something in Braille. Her eyes followed the movement of her fingers.

Perhaps she was hungover; perhaps she'd never thought I'd ask such a question outright. Perhaps *you* would never had handled the conversation this way, and somehow she was picking up on it, desperately trying to adapt to the new Harry. I didn't know if she was really thinking or just power playing. Then she leaned back and put her hands behind her head just as Pepsi would.

'I didn't exactly say that, Harry.'

'Then you'd better spell it out for me.'

'I can do that in one word. Lexon. Big Bill.'

'And who slipped them the word?'

She didn't answer but waited for me to figure it out. She must have thought I was awfully slow coming up with the answer. Suddenly I thought of something I'd seen days ago and had forgotten – Cranner walking past Vulcan Lane with somebody in tow. A tall man bending towards him. Mason! Cranner had been talking to Mason of Lexon.

'Cranner,' I said aloud. 'But why? Why should Cranner tip off a competitor?'

'It's a good question,' she said, her face impassive.

'It's Canada,' I said, reaching forward into the scenario. Big bill would blow it open in Canada. He'd wait until then. And blast me out of the water. 'I'll be dead meat,' I said. The lie exposed to the whole cartel. Very pretty. Harry Blackman served up on a platter.

She stirred the surface of the desk with her finger. The way she did it, slow and deliberate, let me know I'd not reached the end of it yet. Like the entrails of some slaughtered animal, it kept unravelling.

'It'll make Cranner look like a staunch defender of the cartel within the company.' But how would that actually help Cranner? I wondered.

Mary Delany was smiling faintly. She looked up from the

desk which had proved so fascinating and met my eye, looking like one of her Irish ancestors, a poacher caught out with the bloodied game still dangling from one hand.

'Of course,' I said slowly, seeing it as I said it, 'I'm not going to be the only dead meat.'

She nodded again. 'Keep thinking, Harry,' she murmured.

It's Pepsi, I thought, suddenly seeing it all, chilled by the realisation. Pepsi's head would roll with mine if he couldn't hide behind me. His own northern bosses would distance themselves from this shabby side deal with Maritime, if it broke.

They'd drop Pepsi like a hot potato as soon as the law moved on them.

And who stood to gain the most from that?

Mary Delany of course, she whose hands were completely clean, who was Pepsi's natural successor with me out of the picture, Cranner in my place. I was just a pawn. The meat in the sandwich. Someone to be taken out in the course of getting at the real target, the wily Pepsi Rigold.

And there she was, already sitting in his chair, facing me with the quiet smile growing. Perhaps she was enjoying watching the dawning of understanding on my face.

'Does the boss know about the leak, yet?'

She hesitated, about to lie to me, then changed her mind. Her voice was as gentle as the summer breeze through the heather. 'No one's told him yet, Harry.'

So when the shaft came, it would come out of the blue. Finally, after all these years, Big Bill had Pepsi by the balls. Big Bill would choose his moment for maximum embarrassment – my public beheading.

'Do you believe in free trade, Harry?' she asked casually, looking out at the silent tempest beyond the double glass. It was so dense with moving air that nothing of the city could be seen but the dim outlines of the nearest towers, remote and mythical.

'I suppose I do. Why ask?' I wasn't in the mood for free-wheeling discussions.

'Have you ever heard of the potato famine in Ireland in the 1840s?'

'Vaguely. I don't see the point.'

'The point is that while the Irish starved when the potato crop failed, wheat was being exported out of Ireland and into England by the shipload.'

'Why?'

'Because the Irish had no money to pay for wheat. No tariff protection. The people couldn't afford to eat the wheat they grew. All in the name of free trade. The English believed in free trade because it suited their pockets. They ate toast for breakfast made from Irish wheat while discussing the advisability of sending troops to Ireland to put down the food riots. It's a bloody good thing nobody wants to study history any more.' She held onto her delicate head.

'What are you telling me this?'

'Open competition, Harry.' She tried her poacher's grin. 'Some of that wheat was smuggled back into Ireland. And sometimes the smugglers got caught. Guess who sold them out?'

'The Irish. Their fellow man. Or woman.'

'Always their own worst enemies, the Irish.' She sounded very sad. Betrayal, the Irish way.

'We're talking about sawing off the limb I'm standing on, Mary.'

She shrugged. 'You'll take redundancy, afterwards.'

There was silence as the word redundancy went on repeating itself in the empty air.

She looked somewhere over my left shoulder. 'You'll take

it, you'll get a good settlement. You'll be one of the lucky ones.'
The darkness around her eyes deepened.

'One of the lucky ones,' I repeated.

'I'm only looking at where you'll be after Canada, Harry. Being realistic.' She tapped on Pepsi's desk, summoning his ebullient presence. 'You can't tell me that you haven't made some plans.'

The way she said that made me wonder if she knew about the secret Southern Oil investment group. Which included Cranner of course. I wonder if she knew that.

I unglued my tongue, which was sticky in the dehydrated air. 'Of course, I could refuse to be your lamb for the slaughter. Give Pepsi a little ring. Let him know Cranner's a Lexon spy for starters.' And tell him the plot, I thought. He can ring Big Bill and head off the ambush with a deal.

'We don't think you'll do that.' Her voice was as flat as an Irish gangster's.

'Why not?'

'Cranner is the last person you'd want to antagonise, Harry.' Her voice was soft and touched with an Irish lilt that made it sound full of charm. Again that funny, indirect look over my shoulder.

She was pausing to let that one sink in. It sank in a long way. Rigold might be deeply displeased to hear of *your* affair with Hera Cranner, but he'd put me against the wall for the Southern Oil share scam. And Cranner would be just the person to drop me in that little pile of shit.

'It's not a pretty picture, Harry,' she said, rubbing her cheek as if she were growing stubble. 'You must have looked at it yourself.'

Of course she knew about the fucking shares. She was probably putting up the money for Cranner. Thinking along these lines, I wasn't prepared for what she said next.

'And if you looked at it, you must have noticed an account in the name of Orf.'

So she knew about your kickback too. She had me every which way.

I got up. 'So Tom really did blow the gaff? I tried to picture that unpleasant man having the guts to tip me off. Why? He had no love for me. Maybe he hated her enough.

She didn't bother to answer me, but I knew it was true. She pressed her fingers against her temples. 'Harry…' She looked around the room. 'My turn will come too. You know that.'

But I didn't know that. I turned and confronted Cranner standing in the open doorway, leaning against the upright. Mary would have seen him over my left shoulder. He looked through me as if at Mary. If I were waiting for him to smile I was wasting my time. I glanced back at Pepsi's desk.

Behind Mary, the chaos of cloud was like a silent, moving abstract.

Approaching my office, I passed Sophie who looked up from her work. 'You had a call,' she said in a clear, sweet voice.

'Who?' I said distractedly.

'The woman said she'd call back.' If there was the faintest emphasis on the word woman, it was because I noticed it.

'Thank you, Sophie,' I said, using her name to indicate I'd noticed.

She lowered her eyes demurely to her computer screen and I knew, by the prickling at the back of my neck, that Cranner was approaching.

Without turning around I went into my office. I badly wanted to call Evelyn; I badly needed to think. There was an idea percolating at the back of my mind that might save me yet, at least from this Maritime tangle.

I stared down at the waiting computer screen.

I'd just lost my job.

As I sat down the phone rang. Cranner passed like a grey ghost across my doorway.

His wife was on the phone. 'Harry, is it a good time to talk?'

'No.'

'Evelyn knows about us, doesn't she?'

'Yes.'

'God, Harry. We knew this would happen sooner or later. You predicted it yourself, remember?'

'What did I say?'

'You said, "Evelyn's going to find out. She already subconsciously knows." That's what you said.'

'I was right.'

'I thought she was going to murder me at the staff party. How did she find out?'

'I don't know exactly. She just said it stood out like a sore thumb.'

Her voice went lower, quieter. 'This is the finish, isn't it Harry? I'm not crossing Evelyn, not unless you leave her.'

'Is that what you want?'

'I don't know now, I honestly don't. I'm frightened. If Ken found out…I'm frightened of what he might do. He's capable of some horrible revenge. You don't know how ruthless he is.'

'I think I do.'

'He's already working against you, Harry. Trying to set you up. He's capable of tremendous jealousy.'

'How's he setting me up?'

'Over the McBride deal. He doesn't know I know. He thinks I'm stupid. He thinks I just sit there at the dinner table with a blank mind.'

'The tennis,' I said. 'I think he knows Evelyn doesn't play tennis.'

'Christ. I only used that excuse once.' The urgency in her

voice turned to muffled panic. 'I have to stop seeing you, Harry, you know that. We went into this with our eyes open.'

'It's true.'

'Goodbye, Harry.' It was perfect, right down to the tremble in her voice. The painful end of the painful affair.

'There's just one thing,' I said, having resolved to ring Pepsi. 'What is it?'

I thought I owed Hera this, at least, on *your* behalf. 'He already knows.'

There was a horrified gasp at the other end and the line went dead.

I swept all the Canadian stuff off the desk onto the floor. Everything. All the tight piles. I noticed my passport shuffle to the top. Then the laptop followed, but more gently. Finally the desk was cleaned smooth without even a layer of dust on top. Having an utterly clean desk is like being born again. Your mind becomes a *tabula rasa* ready for a whole new set of instructions, a new and bold cursive script.

The laptop and the hidden files should have been my first priority, but it was Rigold I was thinking about. The job loss and Delany's machinations pushed thoughts of Kober and Tate to one side. Rigold! It all hinged on a Pepsi freak. If I did phone him, it would be regardless of the Hera affair or the share deal or even the McBride bribe. Who cared when arses were at stake? Pepsi could step right in. He could send Mary Delany to Canada instead of me, or put Cranner's neck on the block. He could crack another Pepsi! He could fight! The last thing he'd want to do is go down with me.

I picked up the telephone, confident that he would fight, that he would brush away all the trivial matters such as who was screwing whose wife and whose money was green; I knew I could rely on him to be a realist. Both our jobs were at stake. He and I could close ranks; e was an old street fighter when it came to this sort of stuff. Delany and Cranner had made a big mistake.

I tapped straight through to his cellphone line and listened to the connection tone throbbing into the cybervoid. At the same time, and to save time, I opened the utilities folder on the laptop and had a look around.

Pepsi answered, sounding grumpy.

'We've got a lot to talk about,' I said.

'You choose your moment,' he said tersely.

'Is it not convenient?' I pitched a formal tone, to let him know I wasn't ringing him about his headache.

'I don't want to hear. I don't know what you're tied up in, and I don't want to know.'

'What?' Was this closing ranks?

'Its up to you to sort this out, Harry, and to do it in such a way that the heat doesn't come on anybody.' Rigold was afraid. Had he already guessed what was coming?

'The heat's already on me.'

'Don't come whining to me about it.'

What the hell was going on? Some kind of slippage was occurring; my control over this conversation for a start.

'Your head could roll with mine on this,' I said, wondering how far I needed to spell it out.

'Come to your senses, Harry. Personally, I'll give you as much help as I can, but this is a strictly hands-off-affair.'

'It's a bit late for that. The whistle's already blown. The bell tolls.'

A certain authentic grimness came into his voice; he was taking off his gloves. 'Look, Harry, I only have so much patience. I spent an hour with two rather unpleasant detectives telling them over and over again that I know nothing. And I suggest you do the same. Did you hear that, Harry? I told you I hate this undercover stuff.'

I had heard it but I'd stopped listening. Through the front glass panelling of my office I saw Inspector Wildheart and Detective Sergeant Joe Oggle. They were conferring with Sophie.

'You better add a couple of noughts to my golden handshake,' I said to Pepsi.

'Mr Blackman, yesterday you visited a caravan park and saw Professor Kober. Is that correct?'

'Certainly.' I offered them a chair, which they refused, wondering how the hell they always knew when I visited Kober. Oggle, the kind of man who looks more comfortable on his feet than sitting down, looked right through me, his usual apparently indifferent self, but Wildheart seemed grim and out of sorts. No longer the friendly schoolmaster. His voice was like dry sherry, and there was steeliness in it.

'Why?' He looked curiously at the pile of stuff I'd swept onto the floor. It looked as if someone had ransacked the office.

'To assure him of my goodwill, see if I could help him.' I glanced down at the screen of the laptop and noticed that you'd installed a new Norton utilities program. I flicked on the screensaver, which was a beach ball that kept changing shape and colour. Oggle watched my every movement, eyes riveted on the laptop as if it were a bomb.

'And what happened?'

'He knocked me down, he's got quite a punch for a professor.'

'And then?'

'Then he made me a cup of tea.'

Wildheart paused and looked at me, blandly, as if he were thinking of something else. He raised an eyebrow at his partner. The other half of the Mutt and Jeff pair went into his routine.

Oggle came in punching. 'How much money did you offer him?'

'Money? I didn't offer him money.'

Oggle looked impatient. 'But you told us the other day that you offered him money, and a lot of money you said.'

'That was before,' I said, realising at once that Oggle knew this and was enjoying fucking me up. It looked like the more he fucked me up, the more he would enjoy it.

'How much was it?'

'The figure went as high as fifteen million dollars. Nothing was settled.'

'He didn't even take any money?'

'Not a cent. He's too proud. Now tell me what's going on.'

Joe Oggle said, as if trying to get my story straight in his mind, 'Tell us, what was it you negotiated yesterday.'

'I didn't negotiate. It was a social visit.'

'A punch on the nose and a cup of tea.'

'That's right.'

'So you parted the best of friends?'

'Not exactly, no, but I'm glad I went.'

'Professor Kober is dead,' Wildheart cut in as if interrupting a social chat. 'He was shot and his caravan soused with accelerant and burned. I think we should have a really long talk.'

'What a good idea.' I would drop Tate in it with the greatest of pleasure, and Pepsi too if I could manage it.

I picked up the phone. 'Sophie, screen out all calls for an hour will you. Divert any Canada inquiries to Cranner.' Also with the greatest of pleasure.

'Yes, Mr Blackman,' Sophie said. 'Your wife is on the line right now – will you take her call?

To the waiting police, I said, 'Excuse me, please, I have one private call to clear, then I'll be with you.' Behind them, coming from his office, I saw Cranner.

Inspector Wildheart nodded pleasantly but made no move to leave the room. Suddenly he looked like he had all the time in the world. Cranner saw the police and stopped, turned and walked back in the other direction.

'Harry?' Evelyn's voice sounded small, not because of the telephone but because she had somehow compacted it into one tight ball, one determined core. 'Harry?'

'Yes, it's me.' I wished I had somewhere to take the phone, to get away from police ears.

'When did you get to the office?'

'Why?'

'Just tell me.'

'About two hours ago.'

'That's not possible.'

'Why not?'

'Because I saw you…' her voice broke out of its tight container, 'ten minutes ago, hanging around the garage.'

'But hold it a minute, just hold it right there.'

I picked up the cordless phone and walked out of the room. The only place I could go, where I wasn't broadcasting to the rest of the floor, was the toilet.

Sophie watched me take the telephone into the toilet.

'If you saw me ten minutes ago, then who are you talking to?' I said into the phone. 'Ten minutes is hardly time for me to get to work.'

She was frightened now. 'What's going on Harry? Are you trying to play funny games with me? Men can do all kinds of weird, desperate things when their wives want to leave them.'

'Like at being in two places at once?'

'Then what's going on? I saw you coming out of the garage.'

'Was *he* holding anything?'

'No, I don't think so. Harry, what is this?

I told you last night. My counterpart. Your Harry. Somehow he's managed to find a way of appearing here, back in his own universe. The man you saw is really your husband. And he wants to kill me. He wants to kill me because there's something on my laptop he doesn't want me to discover. Something he wants himself...'

I was putting it together as I spoke. At first you hadn't wanted to kill me, just torment me a bit and get hold of the laptop. I'd seen you on that second night, trying to pick it up. When that failed you grew more desperate. You were stuck in my world without the *other* Kober's designs. Stuck with my laptop. Then, when you couldn't get your laptop, you aimed to unhinge me, kill me if all else failed, because if I found out how to follow you over, you would probably be returned here, reciprocal motion, as Schauberger would call it, to face all your music.

'Not this crackpot stuff again.'

'You've seen him yourself. I don't have time. Mutt and Jeff are in the office waiting for me. Kober has been murdered.'

'Harry! What's happening to us? You could be arrested?'

'Look, I want you to do something. Go to the garage and find the .22 and the ammunition. That's what he's after. Take it down to the garden and put it underneath the garden shed.'

'This is too weird, Harry.'

'Just do it. And remember what I told you last night. Every word was true.'

'I'll do it, Harry,' she said.

'I love you,' I said.

Oggle had found my passport on the floor and was quietly leafing through it, when I got back to my office.

They listened politely to my story of Jerry Tate, his sudden appearance, the meeting in Pepsi's office, his open-ended money offers, the Kober visits, the cellphone calls. It was not so much that they didn't believe me, they just looked at me. If I had told them that I'd crossed over from another universe and that I was just pretending to be the Harry Blackman they thought I was, their faces would not have changed.

They simply went off to check my story. Oggle was on his cellphone as soon as he was through the door. They would soon discover that there was no record of any Jerry Tate that fitted my description. Pepsi would deny everything. No one else would have seen Tate come in or go out. There would be no airline tickets. The cellphone number would be disconnected. There would be nothing. Not so much as a motel stub.

And then they would be back to see me.

How long did I have? Three or four hours?

I looked up in time to see Cranner hurrying somewhere. He'd be wondering very hard about the police, thinking about his pal Mason, no doubt – let him wonder. There were a few surprises coming his way too.

I might even get Pepsi to change his mind and back me up on the Jerry Tate story, because my next call would have to be to Pepsi's bosses in New York and I didn't think he would want that. Wouldn't want them hearing about Maritime from my mouth. Very unpleasant having me run amok with a double murder charge hanging over my head.

Pepsi would talk to me again, but it would have to wait until I could get to the car. There was no hanging around the office passing pleasantries with my boss while *you* were hanging around the house.

Except for the unresolved matter of the invisible file on the laptop.

It took me a frustrating hour to crack it. An hour I could ill afford. You had hidden the file away under a cloak of invisibility made possible by your fancy Norton program. You'd further camouflaged it by giving it the title of some obscure computer function, a number of which you'd also made invisible.

I was checking a list of these files, impatient to the point of screaming, when, finally, I had it.

And there it was, page after page of schematics, diagrams, graphs, instructions; everything from hand drawings with scribbled notes in the margins to computer generated graphics. I noted that the document had not been altered for eight months.

You'd had it for eight months. Long enough to do some serious plotting. But that meant that Tate had had it for that long too, because you'd have had to deliver the goods. And Tate, with the resources behind him, would have had time to master the Kober effect.

It didn't look like a design for a machine to me, nothing hard and fast, steel and brass - it was more like an explanatory text. There were plenty of vortexes and maths everywhere, scribbled around the margins like some spidery border design. There was one full colour, full depth representation of the human brain with vortexes shot through it like hurricanes off the coats of continents. Mathematical notation followed them down into infinity.

That this was the work of the other Kober, there could be no doubt. All the commentaries and notes were written in German.

I had to move and think at the same time. This proof that Kober, also, was a crossover, and that *you* had the key to how it was done, gave a whole new depth to the situation. You risked double-crossing Tate by keeping a copy of the other Kober's designs. You kept it for your own purposes. Here was the key to the house, the share speculations, the McBride kickback and a lot of obsessive behaviour that had puzzled me.

You'd been secretly planning to use the Kober designs, get yourself into the technology, be master of the universe rather than Tate's bum boy. But something went wrong – you went over without the laptop.

I was on my feet and looking around the office. I scooped up all my papers, airline tickets and the passport I'd abandoned. The ingredients of a getaway, and I'd swept them onto the floor! No wonder Inspector Wildheart had stared.

There was nothing that I needed to take except my briefcase, my cellphone, and of course the laptop. The Canada stuff could stay where it was, on the floor in a big heap. The closer Canada came, the further away it seemed.

At the door I was struck by a sudden thought. Tate had been acting as if he knew nothing about my Kober's energy device, his 'mud pie.' Tate had cross-questioned me on the most basic aspects as if they were new to him.

Because they were. Tate had not predicted a counterpart Kober arriving here with yet another device. The final pieces of the puzzle were maddeningly close, but one thing I did know; possession of the Kober plans gave me considerably more leverage in the whole situation that I'd had so far.

I looked back at my room with the uncanny chill that I was leaving it forever. This might have been your office, but it was mine too, virtually the same, and there was so little of me in it to take away.

I got as far as the front desk. 'Mary wants to see you,' Sophie murmured as I approached.

'I'm sure she does.'

'Have a nice day.' She gave me her corporate-ready smile.

'Sorry, I've made other arrangements.'

Sophie didn't look up to laugh, all I saw was the machine-precision parting of her hair as she bent to answer the phone.

I was two steps past the desk when Sophie called me back.

It was Inspector Wildheart. They had located Jerry Tate.

I drove out of the cement innards of the car park, straight into the teeth of the maelstrom. Hurricane Luke was doing its worst to downtown, emptying the streets of pedestrians and throwing anything around not bolted down. A dustbin lid rolled in front of me, bowled along by invisible hands, and I stopped at the entrance, wondering how wise it was to venture out.

A car cruised slowly past. A hideous, grinning face looked out at me from the side window. Someone had added vampire fangs in red ink. A hand waved a bottle of beer. Another masked face thrust out, shouting something. A bat mask, like a black bat clinging to someone's face.

They were not the only hurricane party goers. At the bottom of the street I saw a group of revellers hooning towards the park, waving cans of beer. Some were in fancy dress, with masks, others content with outlandish pants or antique jackets, and all were daring the wind. They came swarming out of a side road just as a white stretch limo pulled up at a pedestrian crossing. The mob surrounded the car, hooting and cavorting, their costumes flying madly in the wind. A clown tried to ride through them on a monocycle handing out advertisements, but kept falling off. He had a wide, red grin painted on his face. As the lights changed and the limo pulled slowly away, a window was wound down and a slim, elegant arm emerged, a white porcelain hand negligently giving the revellers the fingers.

16

The Central Police Station has very little to recommend it to the eye. Built in the sixties, it hardly aspired to skyscraper status, more that faceless, nondescript look; more concrete than windows, it was a mid-century exercise in bureaucratic architecture.

I arrived with what amounted to a police escort, because there wasn't much else on the roads. I twice tried to ring Evelyn on my cellphone and got nothing but hurricane static.

The driver in the car behind me turned out to be Sergeant Oggle. Surprise!

We both dashed inside the building to escape the lashing wind.

He sat me down at a chair and table inside an otherwise empty room and asked me everything I could remember about Jerry Tate.

A stenographer crept quietly into the room.

I didn't ask for a lawyer, and made that obvious, then I gave it to him. Tate as I knew him, right down the undrunk coffee.

I had to make a lot up too. About my first meeting with him. At every point I drew in Pepsi. He had set up the first meeting, a year ago. Tate had given me a cover story, to be an agent for a special branch of the energy industry. I created a fiction for Oggle that probably more or less equated to *your* life. Of course nothing in my fiction included the secret file on the laptop, which I kept firmly gripped in my hand.

No, I'd never done this kind of work before.

Then it was back to Tate. What was his accent? His clothes? Physical characteristics, his manners?

I did my best. I had observed Tate closely and Oggle knew I was cooperating, he wasn't silly and didn't come on with his 'bad cop' act.

All the time I clung onto the laptop with unyielding fingers. Oggle glanced at it a couple of times but said nothing.

The interrogation came to an end and Oggle got to his feet and led me into another room. He invited me to leave my laptop with some attendant, an older, pensioned-off cop in charge of a rack of shelving, but I declined.

Politely. Oggle lead me through the series of boring corridors filled with hurricane-panicked cops dealing with crazy bastards trying to drive on exposed highways.

We arrived at another room where Inspector Wildheart was sitting with a stranger. A hippy-looking guy with long, unkept hair turned into dreadlocks and a scrappy beard. He was dressed in big, baggy cotton pants, wore a long white kurta, Indian style, with a handwoven, brightly coloured waistcoat.

He jumped up when I came into the room and turned towards me.

It was Jerry Tate.

Sergeant Oggle took up a post by the door.

'Hey man, who the fuck are you? They told me there was someone who knew me. You're not a cop are you? What in the fuck is going down here?'

The hippy Tate looked scared. Hair fell in sweaty rat tails across his forehead and clung to his cheeks.

I glanced across at Wildheart, who raised an eyebrow. Here

was my witness. This was my show.

'Hello Jerry,' I said, sitting down on the seat opposite him. 'Jerry Tate.'

'Come on, man,' he said, a whine entering his voice, 'don't pull any shit. Are you a lawyer or something? Christ!' He smashed his fist down into his palm. 'So you know my name. I've never seen you before.'

'You know me.'

'Listen man, I was in Kathmandu, just grooving. I'd done a spliff and got the munchies, right? Then I went on down Freak Street to find some takeaways and suddenly I'm here. Fuck! This goddamn wind blowing. Everything dark. Where am I, somewhere in Australia?'

I tried to keep the interest out of my voice. 'How long ago was this?'

'I told these guys. Just a few hours.' He held up his watch. 'That's Kathmandu time.'

I turned to Wildheart. 'I've got to get home,' I said.

As Wildheart and Oggle escorted me out, the hippy Tate yelled, 'This is a bad trip man, a hell of a bad trip.'

I had to agree with him.

I was taken to another room with another table and chairs. Wildheart wandered restlessly about the room while Oggle took up his post by the door.

'Is this your Jerry Tate?'

'It looks like him but it can't be the guy.'

'Why not?'

I had no answer. What would Wildheart say if I told him this Jerry Tate was a crossover. The Tate we were after had slipped down a vortex. Probably chasing *you*, and the other Kober.

I decided to answer Wildheart with a question. 'Why would

a senior operative,' and I stressed the word senior, 'use a dumb cover like this?'

'You thought you knew him?'

'So I did, at first.'

'And then?'

'I started to doubt. He doesn't talk or act like Tate.'

Oggle sucked in his breath. Wildheart looked very unhappy. His tone was sombre, like a prosecution lawyer reading out the accusations. 'I don't like this at all. Today you give us the name Jerry Tate and a good description of him. We get back to the station to find that this guy calling himself Jerry Tate has come in, distraught, no money except a few Nepalese rupees, no passport, no airline tickets, no nothing – just a watch showing Kathmandu time. Which our time makes just four hours after Kober's murder. And you can't make a positive identification. Your boss denies all knowledge of him. What the hell is going on here, Harry?'

'I told you before…'

'I know what you've told us. You put us on to this Tate guy. We admit, he's interesting.'

'I know as much as you do. I'm out of my depth in this too.' He could see as much of the truth as I was telling.

Wildheart made me wait while he read the deposition I'd just given to Oggle. His puzzlement deepened. This guy's had his head raddled,' he said, half to himself.

I didn't disagree. The hippy Tate has said it himself – this was a bad trip. Tate had set me up as major suspect for Kober's murder before he crossed over. Get rid of two birds with one stone. This proved that Tate had had access to the Kober technology. And he'd used it.

The hippy Tate was his counterpart.

And that's why *you* were trying to kill me. Because I had the plans. You knew that sooner or later I'd discover them. Want to use them for myself. You'd made a grab for the laptop first, that night I'd seen you by the couch bending over, then moved onto killing me instead. Somehow using the Kober effect.

'It doesn't make any sense as a cover story,' I said, thinking along with Wildheart the way I used to do with Pepsi, and Wildheart agreed.

Finally, Wildheart came to the conclusion I was waiting for – he didn't have enough evidence to hold me. The hippy Tate was useless as a witness, and was really just a headache for him. Somehow I got the feeling that he blamed me for the hippy Tate's appearance, that it was my fault for somehow conjuring him into existence.

'We are not happy, Harry,' he said by way of conclusion. 'We have two dead bodies and you are the link between them. We'll be watching your every move.'

I nodded. I was getting out of there.

'Oh, by the way,' he said, as I turned towards the door. He had a charred piece of paper in his hand. 'We found this at the caravan site. It was rolled up into a little ball in his palm. Translated, it says, *One day mankind will be able to walk through these worlds at will.*'

He paused to make his confusion more profound. 'Do you know what that means?'

'It means,' I said, 'that Kober knew he was going to die. He thought Tate was one of the Specials. Their eyelids blink every thirty seconds, he said. He told me that they would try to kill me too. I am happy to have police protection.'

Wildheart looked at me long and hard. 'You are withholding evidence,' he said at last. 'That's what you are doing.' He gave me his card. 'Call me. Call me when you're ready to tell the whole story. But don't leave it too long.'

A telephone call interrupted him. Wildheart listened for some time as he received a report. The Nepalese authorities had no record of any Jerry Tate. He had never been in Nepal. The hotel name given had no record or memory of him. This confirmed for Wildheart what he already suspected. The hippy Tate was lying. Therefore I was probably lying. He'd hold Tate and let me go. That was his strategy. He'd give me a bit more rope.

Oggle escorted me to my car. He watched me put the laptop on the floor of the passenger's side.

'Watch out for the winds,' Oggle said. 'They're a real bitch.'

Police were stopping traffic at the base of the Harbour Bridge. A wet, official face peered in at my window.

'Closing the bridge in fifteen minutes sir, you won't be able to return today. We're advising everybody to get off the roads as soon as possible.'

'Have a nice day,' I said as I pulled away and he laughed.

I was one of the last in a trickle of vehicles going over the bridge. I had this sensation that we were swinging in mid-air, that the hurricane was whirling us up and far away from land, when my cellphone rang. I risked taking a hand off the wheel to answer it; the sky couldn't come any closer than it already was but the harbour below could.

'I sold the shares, Harry, just like you told me, but no one else has moved. I hate this breaking ranks. You've got to have balls of steel for this sort of work. Why not wait eight hours...'

'Have you transferred the money?'

'That's what I was talking about, for Christ's sake. What are you doing, where are you, you're not driving around in this weather are you?'

'I'm driving through a cloud. Now stick the money into that account.' I had a card for that account in my briefcase. Once that went through I'd have some ready cash.

'I'll have to take my fee,' he whined.

'Do it right now,' I said. 'And thanks for everything.'

'Don't try anything funny, Harry,' he said as I hung up.

Ahead of me lay the North Shore, looking as empty as the day before Maui fished it up from the bottom of the ocean with his ancestor's jawbone.

A couple of miles from my exit, the traffic thickened up, a bitsy traffic made up of people racing for cover, to get their precious vehicles home and into their garages.

I was on the phone to Pepsi when I saw something I'd forgotten about – the other Ghia. I couldn't see how you could be lurking around the house and driving on the motorway at the same time.

'I have to talk to you,' I said to Pepsi, 'before the police get to you again.' I braked as the traffic slowed.

'They're already on their way,' Pepsi said.

'I've told them about Tate and the meetings in your office.'

'You silly bastard.' He sounded almost sad about it.

The Ghia was right beside me, close, too close; racing to pass in the outer, right-hand lane. I was in the middle lane, out of the slow traffic to the left often lining up for exits, and the speedsters on the right who were always in a hurry, and I was able to watch the Ghia as it pulled ahead, noting further dents and signs of neglect. My car was starting to look like *yours*.

'You have to back me on this, Rigold. You have to tell the police the truth about Tate.'

'I wouldn't back you if you were the only horse in the race, Harry.'

'Then I can't go to Canada to carry the can for the Maritime deal. The cat's out of the bag already, did you know that? Cranner is spying for Lexon.'

I wanted to grab hold of him, shake him out of his stupidity.

Suddenly the right lane slowed down and I shot past the Ghia, catching the briefest glimpse of a lone figure behind the wheel. The right lane freed up again and the Ghia slid by once more, this time swerving deliberately close, attempting to push me across into the left lane. Behind me there was a truck, a big rig with 'Fat Boy' in letters of flame over the grill. To my left there was an old green Bedford clattering along.

I needed to get in behind the Bedford to catch my exit.

'Who gives a shit about Canada, or the Maritime deal…' his voice dissolved in a burst of static,'…petty schemes and grubby little kickbacks…what goes on around my own office…'

'You have to tell the truth to the police,' I shouted.

My lane slowed and the Bedford on the left pulled ahead. I could see people in the back and suddenly realised who they were. Here were Sam Walsh's Guerrillas of Goodness, doing me a random kindness by opening a bit of a gap on my left. I gunned into it, getting out from beside the maniac in the Ghia.

Pepsi's voice suddenly cut in, loud and clear and full of steel. 'You can't pull the company into these murders, Harry. That's the rule the Specials operate by. You know that. You've always known that. You can't try…'

The other Ghia tried to cut into the space that I had left in the middle lane, looking as if he were chasing me. The rig coming up behind gave a trumpeting, primeval blast on its horn. The Ghia swung dangerously between the two lanes. My exit was coming up on the left and I dampened speed further, allowing a gap to open up between me and the Bedford.

The rest happened very quickly, or very slowly. Fat Boy ploughed into the back of the Ghia which rose into the air as if it had been kicked like a football.

The Bedford went next, swerving to avoid the flying Ghia, it lurched in front of the rig. Then the Bedford too was flying through the air. What happened next was impossible. The Bedford landed again, front first, miraculously saved; it went down on its ancient steel knees but it didn't crack. Against all the laws of gravity and steel it lifted and kept rolling along on a wing and a prayer.

I'd already gone, lifting into clear spaces on steady wings, cruising up above it all.

The exit ramp had arrived exactly on time.

It was a peculiar sensation, being picked up and raised above the screech and tear of metal. I was suddenly soaring above the action as if I were lifting off a runway. Quickly I pulled over. When I got to the railing the accident was still going on. Fat Boy lay skewered across the three lanes, with cars piling in behind, shrieking and sliding. Six or seven cars had crashed, with crunches still going on down the line, blocking the exit I'd just swung up.

One car had been driven against the median barrier where it lay, upside down, crushed. It was the other Ghia Serenissima. I stood there watching it while everything went silent around me; the air was pushing in and pulling out as if it were breathing. Normal sound was restored, then cut off again. Slowly all the bits of metal below settled into place, and when the sound came up I could hear the frenetic cry of a siren.

I closed by eyes and when I opened them, more than a few moments seemed to have passed. Already red light was spilling over the road, swelling and collapsing, as the police arrived from the other direction. The wind-shredded motorway took on the lurid colouring of a holocaust.

I toyed with the idea of going down but the scene was a melee of people and shadows, and cordons were being thrown up. Red and orange flashing lights were shaken by the wind. Shrieks and cries phased in and out like a wavering radio drama. Stick figures ran between the mangled forms of cars, waving their arms.

I watched while some of them lifted a body, head and shoulders first, from the Ghia Serenissima, wrapped it in a blanket from head to foot and laid it out on the tarmac. Was this really you?

I turned back to my own Ghia.

I'd always looked on the other car as a clue, a message that I would eventually unravel, but now I saw that this was not so. Before it could reveal itself, this clue had shattered in a bloody death; whatever it may have signified, if anything at all, was lost to me forever.

What I had to do now was to get home.

I didn't think my car had started because I couldn't hear the engine, but when I put it into gear and lifted the clutch it pulled away quite happily and floated forward.

The houses of the familiar streets slid by, looking silent and deserted under the hammer of the wind. I drove with exaggerated care, as if a negligent moment could flick me back to the motorway. The big rig, its wheels locked, cruising almost gracefully into the Ghia. The Ghia rising up in front of me like a fish on the end of a hook.

I stopped at the nearest shopping centre and used my card at a cash machine. I was relieved to find that Coveny had done what he'd been told to do. I took the time to stand there and take the maximum allowed amount, fighting a growing impatience.

Everything was narrowing down now. The clues collapsing behind me with every passing moment, avenues of retreat being cut off. But surely now Evelyn would believe me? Now that she had seen both of us, she would know.

There was a swing of wild hope inside me as I pulled the last of the money out of the machine and stuffed it into my briefcase. I had no clear idea of what I would use it for, I just knew we'd need it, somehow, Evelyn and I. It represented a tangible asset in this crisis, the one small victory I'd managed to wrest from this world.

I drove slowly, and parked a good hundred yards from the house. The day had now grown into a uniform, murky twilight; the whirling clouds overhead had grown so thick that colour had drained out of everything, leaving a scratchy looking black and white world.

I slipped the briefcase under the seat and activated the locks. Then I slipped out into that black and white world, the laptop firmly gripped in both my hands; I wasn't going to leave that anywhere. It wasn't cold, or even ferociously wet, but everything gave way before the wind, the fury of Luke. It felt as if the rain was still on its way, still gathering across the far acres of the Pacific ocean.

I got halfway to the house and stopped. Sam Walsh was there, standing at the top of the drive. He may have simply been gazing out over the valley, or staring down at our place more likely, but there was something in his stillness that froze me. In the shadows of the wind-torn red pine, he looked as if he were weeping. There was something monumental, Herculean, about him as he turned away from the house. I stayed frozen, hoping he wouldn't see me, but I was too late.

He stood there peering at me for a moment, probably assuring himself that it was me. Then he beckoned. It was an odd mechanical gesture, as if he had to fight some powerful inertia just to raise his arm, lever his wrist, pull me towards him with the crook of his arm. There was something about the way he stood, as if he were signalling in semaphore, not merely down a drive but across a world. The second time the gesture was unmistakable; he looked like an explorer, beckoning his weary team on into the face of the storm, a dead general urging on a phantom army. I wondered if he'd really seen me, so deep was he in his time.

I took a step forward. He seemed to have some special message for me, some information he wanted to impart. All along he's known something, I thought, something he's never talked about, at least not directly

I took another step forward and, as soon as he saw me coming, the old man turned abruptly and walked off vigorously down the hill. When I reached the top of the drive, I slipped into the meagre protection of the same red pine in time to catch him in the distance, heading downhill with a determined, soldierly walk, one arm still marching, not looking back. Leaves and debris scooted down the street as if he were drawing them along with him.

Instinctively, I glanced at the wrecked flower plot. The already uprooted plants lay passive in the face of this new battering.

Then I looked down at the house. The lights were on, there was nothing to be seen. No police car in the drive. No skulking doubles of Harry Blackman. I should go down there, now, talk to Evelyn. Make sure she is OK.

Thinking of Evelyn, I realised that I was operating on the absurd faith that once I saw Evelyn everything would be all right. She would believe me and together we would bluff our way through it. After all, what did the police really have on me? Nothing. I'd find a new job. Those were the slender hopes I was riding on.

'Harry!' It was Sam's voice, sounding further away than he was, phasing in and out with the wind. There was an urgency in his voice. 'This way!'

He had paused before the corner opposite Crockers store, half looking back, half waiting. His hair stood up as if it were being pulled.

He knew something, I was sure of it now; something I needed to know before I got to the house.

After a final look down the drive, I made up my mind and set out. As soon as I started walking he turned and set off again. The wind was behind me now, tipping me down the street after him.

I was quite a bit closer by the time he reached Crocker's corner, and I was just about to call out when he turned and faced me. He was standing under a willow, which in turn was under a streetlamp, and the shadows were shredding his face. Then, with one military stride, he went on around the corner.

Where the hell was he leading me?

I reached Crocker's corner, noticed the wrecked flower plot there too, and without pausing, turned the corner in pursuit.

There was a jarring sensation, as if there'd been a slight earthquake, and the air around me shifted. There was no Sam Walsh, just an empty street. Not empty, it was filled with pale afternoon light. I could hear a noise in the air, like wind in power lines, but there was no wind.

No wind.

High, motionless cloud.

The clear-throated call of a tui.

I paused and drew air into my lungs. It tasted of magnolia and rhododendron. I turned very slowly, examining the terrain. Nothing had changed; everything was in its right place just as I remembered it.

I looked up at Crocker's corner a few yards behind and saw the smooth, well-established verge grass which had never been tampered with. There had never been a rogue plot of flowers here. Here Hurricane Luke was never a threat; Sam Walsh was an ordinary old neighbour who did not suffer the anguish of destroyed flowerbeds, or haunt the streets at night like some ghostly guide. And a hundred yards or so up the road Evonne and Timmy were at home. A few steps away. In this world Peter Coveny was a benign friend, Pepsi an amiable, bluff, straight-shooting boss. Mary Delany was a trusted workmate, Cranner an up-and-coming young rival, nothing more. In this world there was no Hera Cranner, and more importantly, no Evelyn Blackman – at least in my life. Evelyn would be out there somewhere, in the jazz of the city lights, living another life, just as Evonne was doing in *your* world. I wanted to make the least disturbance I possibly could, to create not a wrinkle on the surface of the night. Not a crackle through time. I hugged the laptop, which had come through with me.

After all, my existence itself was a provisional matter, but if I were back in my world then all I had to do was turn around and walk quietly back to the house. Once I got inside, I would be safe. Evonne would greet me, I would settle down beside her in bed, my knees drawn up to my chin, blanket over my head.

Eventually the memory of Evelyn would go away, dwindle to a sharp, clear point and vanish.

I was too afraid to try that. A step back, around Crocker's corner, could all too easily hurl me into the hurricane again. Before me lay the calm vista of my own world; a quiet bay, an ancient pohutukawa tree.

I took a step deeper into that world. Nothing happened. The sky didn't fall in. I took more steps, feeling like a baby learning to walk. My feet were tiny compared to my body. I was going downhill, a gentle slope. I kept moving; my feet worked fine if I didn't think about them. I didn't have to think about anything. Nothing else seemed to matter except a niggling question: had Walsh led me here, knowingly?

Had he guided me home?

My feet carried me on down the zigzag road to the stony beach below. The wrought-iron bench will be there, I thought, beneath the pohutukawa, rooted deep enough in this world, surely, to hold my frail weight.

I could wait there until hell froze over.

Every step seemed to carry me deeper into the enchantment of this world. The stillness of the afternoon was poignant and delicate to an exaggerated degree in comparison with the tumult that had gone before. The light whipped up patterns on the ocean, as easy and as shifting as the colours in the marbling woman's tray.

I might have been the only living, breathing human here – a necessary solitude.

The Pohutukawa, looking ancient and bent, hung out over the quietly lapping tide. I could see the wrought-iron bench sitting empty beneath it. Here was a place to wait out time. I could sit on that bench and remember – hold tight to everything familiar.

There was a whispery hush that stretched for miles. As I approached the bench beneath the branches, scales of light fell on my face. When I breathed, it was as if I'd sucked through a chilled glass tube, the air was so fresh and crisp. Had the air of my own world ever tasted as sweet?

In the late, slanting sun, the ground in front of me was a surging mass of fractal shadows. I took a step, and then another. I tested the ground. The ground held. I took my seat. The rusted iron held; the bay spread out before me.

Paradise. I'd never known I'd lived in paradise.

I sat back and contemplated it.

Across a short stone and sand beach, the ocean seethed with unfiltered Brownian motion, pulling the world apart into points of light and putting it together again as waves. It made up colour as it went along, flipping from blue to green and green to silver and silver to blue to black. The points of light played pins and needles over my skin like a trillion nano-blades; there was nothing here which stood between me and the world but my shivering skin. It was a marvellous light, igniting everything it touched as a glow from within. It had a gentle way of cupping small things, and an outright blaze on the rocks and peninsulas. It diffused itself in the pale yellow of the sand and surfed along the curl of a breaker.

If there were paradise then time did not exist and I could be here forever, giving praise for having escaped from your crummy world.

I remembered a story I had read as a schoolboy in which the devil offers a man a watch with very special properties. At any moment the man may stop the watch and stop time, trigger eternity. Whatever he is doing and feeling at that moment would go on forever. But if he fails to do so before he dies, he must pay the price – his soul on the usual terms. The man takes the watch, convinced that when the moment arrives he will stop the clock and trick the devil of his bargain. The time, however, as the devil well knows, is never quite right; the moment never ripe enough, full enough, complete enough. Expectation never dies. Even in the throes of sexual ecstasy there is a reservation, the awareness that there must be something greater, something more pleasurable, something more orgasmic. Paradise is always still around the corner. Finally, of course, having put off the moment too many times, death claims his soul. The joke of that story was that the man does, in the end, trick the devil, for he kept the watch which the devil forgot to reclaim, and he was able to stop it while sitting at a gambling table on the hell-bound train. The train which would, now he'd chosen his moment, never arrive at that ghastly station.

That man had obviously never had a moment like this, sitting under a tree on an old park bench watching the bay on a mild afternoon, currents of light passing over his skin and the taste of sunshine on the tongue; never sat and listened to the swift creature sounds the waves make in the rocks and caverns, nor felt the world settle on an even keel around him, naturally, upon its own miraculous fulcrum, the sun balanced against the horizon, the horizon balanced against the earth, the earth leaning on its own centre. Between the before and the after. No before, no after.

I wasn't aware of time; there was no time. I didn't exist at all, at least not in the manner Descartes would have insisted upon, but there was existence – pure, formless. I was dissolved in paradise, spread and smeared thin through its glitter.

I got up from the park bench, took a few steps forward and lay on my back on the sand and the stones, spread my arms and legs their maximum distance from the pearl of heat I could feel in my navel. The sand crept into my skin. An ant tickled the hair along my arm. I wanted to feel the world right along my body; the same world that touched the back of my head, also touched my heels.

I looked up.

Viewed from upside-down, the pohutukawa didn't just grow, but rather, heavy with creation, it soared out into the world, balanced titanically against the rock from which it sprang. It didn't look as if it could possibly hold there but would have to fall into the sky, ripping out the rock as it went. It didn't feel all that weight, that enormous weight of trunk and branch, because it was balancing against the earth, leaning against the sky; it stood at its own fulcrum, passive, weightless, balanced.

I closed my eyes so I didn't have to consider the outright miracle of it.

The tree had posture, damn it, while I had none. No sky held me up. No certain earth held me down. No metaphysic of rock rooted me. I was balanced against nothing but myself, and was spinning through life like a Catherine wheel, limbs outstretched, floating from world to world.

I was not Harry Blackman, the name was strange to me – strange that it ever had been my name. I had devolved from whale to starfish, from starfish to pebbles. I crossed the boundary between life and death because there was no boundary. Even death did not stand out from the chorus of sand and ocean and history and love with any final voice.

When I opened my eyes there were stars. One by one and in filaments. A whole universe of stars.

While I had been lying in paradise, the world had turned, hours has gone by without me noticing. There was a hot, sharp feeling all the way through my body, like a comet passing through my flesh. That was me, Harry Blackman, abandoning eternity and re-entering time, taking up his role. There were stones sticking into my shoulders, an ache deep in my skeleton and a cool breeze upon my face.

What I really wanted to do was to huddle up on the park bench and wait for dawn in paradise, hold up and hold out there for as long as I could until hunger or something else drove me to move. That was impossible, of course. If my whole experience in this world had been about anything at all, it had been about taking responsibility, facing up to the new, emergent Harry, who was neither the old Harry who had lived with Evonne nor the man who betrayed Evelyn. Events would never have unfolded the way they did if I had told the truth on the first day. Had it out with Evelyn there and then, with my coat in my hand, dinner sizzling on the oven and the word *honey* hanging on my heart like a caress. I burned with shame remembering those first few days, how frivolous and cowardly I had been – treating it all as a big joke.

It was a painful birth, lying there on the stones under the

twilight; Harry Blackman giving birth to himself, stepping back into his frail bones; me facing the fact that I would have to return, go back up the hill, back home and face whatever I might find there, take my chances with a new turn of the wheel. Re-enter life. The sharp, hot feeling didn't go away. It was like compassion in the pain it caused, the ache of beauty; it was like terror for there was no escaping it. I felt like I was being embraced by an angel. I looked up and followed the starry arc of sky down to the seam it made with the ocean.

It is time to move, the angel said. It is time to walk back out of this world, which is like the eye of the hurricane, back to Evelyn's world.

It was time for *you* to meet *your* counterpart.

I got up and sat on the beach a short distance from the ocean's edge. I could feel the damp from the last high tide on my buttocks and thighs. The silence was deep and well established, with a comfortable feel to it. It was a quiet night with little traffic around. A few domestic lights peppering the valleys and hillsides. A moon hidden, yet still giving a gentle wash of light to the landscape.

As I started back, the moon came out from behind high, serrated clouds and lit the street with a frail silver lace. Up the road I could see the flat-roofed, pink house that looked purple at night. There were no gnomes holding court on its lawn.

It was time to abandon paradise.

The journey looked infinite. Back up the zigzag to the top of the hill. But I didn't intend to go that way.

A short walk along the waterfront took me to the bottom of our property. Making a clumsy effort of it, I jumped the fence and began to work my way up towards the house. It was slow going, one hand only available, the other protecting the laptop.

If you were about, you would certainly not be expecting me from this direction. If Wildheart and Oggle were about, I'd have some advantage.

I crept from shadow to shadow, revisiting the lower garden that Evonne and I had spent so much time on. The remains of a rock-terrace herb garden, abandoned by Evonne because of the steep walk back when she was pregnant, and never revived, were still dominated by some hardy rosemary plants. An overgrown stone circle which, Evonne had told me, was a primitive calendar, marking out the four directions and the major solstices, had also survived but was swamped by herbs and grasses.

The sense of Evonne was so powerful I couldn't shake the feeling that she was close by, very close, giving me all the help she could. Always, too, I was tempted by the illusion that all was well, I was back on my own home territory, a long and strange nightmare over. I had died maybe, back there on the motorway, and had come home here, to my old world. Evonne would be in bed. Timmy would be asleep…

But as I drew closer to the house, I could feel the resistance building up. It built up in the body, registered in the bloodstream, crystallised around the muscles, agonised at the joints. Sam's awkward, beckoning gesture had been like that. It was more than just a garden I was traversing, more than just a hill I was climbing, more than just a house holding its distance, I was bringing a whole world with me. A sister dimension.

But the resistance was building up in the world too; the light cool breeze from the ocean had died and everything was hushed and stilled. The leaves of a tree fern quivered. The fern creature I thought I'd seen was everywhere, imprinted in every shadow, a multiplicity of fern creatures rustling and all holding tight to their world.

I was approaching some vaster ring-pass-not.

I had arrived at a small flat piece we'd sculpted out to make a vegetable garden. In sight of the house and not too far from the small dark hulk of the garden shed where, in the other world, I'd asked Evelyn to leave the .22. From here I could turn and look down the valley, tickled by wisps of mist, at the invisible route I'd followed, and across the sweep of the northern coast opening up ahead, dark and bulky in the moonlight, glittering here and there with clusters of lights like sparklers. Delicately, the peninsulas merged their limbs with the dark-blooded ocean.

There was no time for the view, for it was the house itself that caught my attention. Every light was on, the door was thrown open to the front deck. As I watched, Evonne came onto the deck. I knew it was Evonne by the quick, light way she moved. She came to the railing and stared down in my direction.

She knew I was out there. Evonne would know. Her body went still. She was waiting there, waiting for me to take the last steps.

In this quivering silence the worlds stood counterpoised. Beyond the house, the driveway lay as still as the rest of the world. The red pine hovered.

I lifted my right leg to take a step and the balance shifted, the scales tipped; when I lifted my left leg, the world creaked to the other side. I took two steps like this and stopped again.

Evonne was still there, as silent as a tree fern herself. I went to call out to her but no sound would form in my throat. Anything as final as a cry could tip the balance of the worlds.

So near yet so far.

Slammed sideways, dropped through the air and landed with

a crash of wind and hard driven rain, the frenzied threshing of everything around me.

I clung to the earth while Hurricane Luke did its work.

The house above me was closed up and battened down. There was something final in the darkness in which it crouched.

After an eternity of wind I was able to move. I crawled toward the garden shed, bringing more of the driveway and the road above into view. The red pine was whipping about in a convoluted dance. Behind it, the night was a turbulent cave. A sky that had closed in upon itself, made of itself a tight tunnel, a tunnel perhaps, a funnel for wind. Lit from below by the city, rags of low cloud scudded above like foam over the surface of rough seas. Branches were tossed about within their own shadows; trees kicked against the sky. There were no stars but points of brightness came and went like fairy lights, like eyes blinking on and off. Everything glistened and shone. The sky contracted with a sudden burst of lightning.

My visit to my home world had been nothing more than that. Merely to show me, to remind me. The eye of the hurricane.

Then I saw *you*.

You were coming down the driveway towards the house with a briefcase in your hand, a .22 swinging in the other. There was no mistaking you. The way you hesitated, moved; you were on red alert too, ready for murder.

The briefcase was mine, of course. You'd been waiting for me all afternoon, waiting for the kill, waiting for the laptop to fall into your hands; Sam Walsh had almost certainly saved my life by leading me down to the beach and back, briefly, into my world. My not showing up had unnerved you. Maybe you were holding Evelyn as hostage. Whatever, finally, despite the storm, you'd gone in search of me and found the Ghia.

It would be easy for you to figure out where I'd hidden the money.

'You'd managed to soak up all the money now, from both the worlds. Everything was riding your way. Except of course you didn't find the one thing you most wanted to find, that which you would murder for – the laptop. Your laptop with the other Kober's plans.

I scrabbled a few yards further and found what my grasping fingers were searching for – the weapon was there, at my fingertips. It put itself right in front of my hands. And the bullets too, little snub-nosed hunks of lead sitting on tiny canisters full of explosives, which snuck into my fingers like hard-backed insects, eager for the grooved rigour of the bore.

Good for Evelyn. She had trusted me this far, I could trust myself the rest of the way. We would see who was the killer around here.

You hadn't noticed me. I was in the shadow of the garden shed and you were looking towards the house. Your body hung in mid-air in the shape of a question mark, poised between worlds.

I could have killed you then, when I had a chance, but I didn't believe in death enough, maybe, or didn't love enough, maybe, otherwise you'd never have had the chance you had.

You were still looking at the house when a light came on in the back bedroom window. The back-porch light flickered on too. Evelyn pulled aside the bedroom curtain and peered out. It was only a moment, just long enough for me to catch the terror on her face.

You saw it too, because you didn't know which way to jump. There was a new pressure building up. I wanted to giggle, fire off lots of .22 shells in your direction and tell you that you couldn't be in two places at once. The universe wouldn't stand for it. You were warping the fabric of creation itself to satisfy your greed.

Evelyn appeared at the back door, which she slammed behind her as if putting an end to all kinds of coming and going. She stood on the porch, tall and strong, peering towards the garage. Thank God you had never managed to defeat this woman.

There wasn't much light, and what there was tossed and threshed about, but she saw *you*, nevertheless, saw the gun in your hand. She screamed something, the wind clawing at her voice.

You turned towards her, keeping the gun loose in your hands. It wasn't her you were after, but you were desperate. Maybe you knew that Tate was already on your trail, probably believing that you had the Kober files.

Evelyn cupped her hand to her mouth. 'Harry!' she screamed. Her arms turned like frantic windmills while the wind hammered at her pale nightdress, ballooning it with sudden shapes or flattening it against her body. Making herself a perfect target.

'Get inside…you'll get hurt,' I heard *you* shout. You were playing cowboy, riding shotgun for your own ghostly stage.

Evelyn stepped out onto the narrow back deck, and held her arms up high in the air, letting the wind have its way with her hair and her body, and screamed out a curse. It came from far inside, deep at the base of her backbone. As the curse was brought forth and uttered, the wind changed direction and funnelled it your way. It rolled over you like a cement angel with a powdered hand. It entered into your body with cemetery claws.

Then she lowered her arms as if she were pulling down the sky on you. You cursed back at her and began to fumble with the rifle. I could see by the way you moved that you hated her; that's what the affair with Hera Cranner had done, no doubt.

Don't we come to hate those we have to deceive? You were capable of killing her now, out of sheer, desperate rage. She'd stood in your way too long, was that it? A hatred deep enough for you to ride its vortex back to this world.

I put down the laptop and took the rifle in both hands. There was no way I was going to let you kill Evelyn.

I stepped out from the shadows of the woodshed to get a clear shot at you. You saw me, the moment I appeared. Your head fell sideways across your shoulders as you started to pull the .22 up in my direction. You were moving slowly as if fighting some huge gravitational effect. This corridor between the worlds was unstable, all the powers of order conspired against it. Time warped around it. Pieces of the world were whipped away.

You kept on dragging the .22 around. It was taking you ages. I was able to get there first because I had my rifle already raised. I could pull the trigger at any moment.

What delayed me was the sight of Evelyn, behind you and slightly to one side, sunk to her knees and staring at me; her eyes were huge and dark in her head. Now she knew. Now she had proof. She knew I had to pull that trigger, the knowledge was on her face.

I gave you a moment to change your mind, to realise that this time I was one step ahead of you. But you didn't stop. You were halfway through trying to kill me and couldn't stop; fear and hatred had taken over. However you were doing this, working the Kober effect, but imperfectly, was a tremendous strain on you. The veins were standing out on your neck, your jaw tearing sideways at your lower face in the enormous effort of holding the two worlds alongside each other. The house was shimmering as if not made of the same material as the earth around it. It had become detached from its surroundings, unbolted from the air, the hillside and valley, the bright beads of houses strung out along the coast. It appeared to float, just out of sync with everything else, about to switch sides, fade from this universe back into my own maybe. You were playing with the Kober effect before you had understood it.

I pulled the trigger.

At the moment of impact, *your* eyes flew wide open and I flew into them. There was no moment of transition.

I saw myself through your eyes as I fired. There I was, waist-deep in shadow, standing by the garden shed, the rifle raised, pointing at me.

One of the shots passed through my ribcage, smashing ribs and muscle, the other severed the aorta. I bled inside my own body; my ribcage filled up with blood, my lungs began to drown.

Behind the killer with the rifle, I saw a shadowy figure that quickly materialised into Sergeant Oggle. Like a rugby player in slow motion, he was making a dive. But it was not for my murderer, standing with his back to him, gun still raised, but for the laptop lying on the ground behind him. My laptop. Of course Tate would have wanted a detail like that taken care of before he crossed over, and what better man to choose for the job than Sergeant Oggle.

My killer turned and snatched the laptop from Oggle's grasp. Oggle yelled something, but the wind ate the words out of his mouth. He sounded like a dog with a single-syllable bark.

I clutched at my side, where the bullet had entered, but it was too late. My life was drowning me. Suddenly I was lying on the ground, watching the house slip away. It dipped beneath the lawn like a ship sinking or something going behind a screen.

Then the world followed it. A great weight of agony.

When I looked up from where I was lying, by the garden shed, the driveway was empty. There was no sign of your corpse. The laptop was fused to my fingers.

You had gone; there was no Oggle, no Evelyn. The house was where it should have been. There were stars behind the red pine. There was a restless, wet feeling to the night, but no hurricane.

A woman was standing on the back deck, in the darkness, staring out towards me.

I had never seen her before.

There were worlds behind the red pine, worlds behind worlds.

'Is that you, Harry?' the strange woman said. 'What are you doing out there? You're late.' There was a touch of anxiety in her voice.

Suddenly, irrelevantly almost, I thought of the wrecked Ghia lying upside down on the highway. That Ghia had not belonged to *you*. Or *me* I heard Kober's voice, as it was being cut off, 'The effect is unpredictable…' I saw old Sam Walsh waving me through, the colonel of the spirit guides. He'd known.

One day mankind will walk through these worlds at will.

The door opened behind her and the woman was joined by a child who clutched at her nightdress.

'What is it?' the child asked. It was a little girl. Tammy, maybe.

'It's nothing,' the woman said, and looked down the hill towards me. 'Daddy's home at last.'

Again I thought of the wrecked Ghia.

The little girl clapped her hands. 'Daddy!' she cried out, her voice ringing through the tingling air.

No, I thought. Daddy may be lying dead on the highway.

Or murdered by his own hand. Or the hand of an assassin.

'Is that you, Harry?' she said again. For all the fear in her voice, she sounded like a brave person.

I could be brave too.

Leaving the.22 lying on the moist grass by the garden shed, and holding the laptop steady, I stepped out of the shadows.

'I'm here,' I said.

Also by Mike Johnson

Novels
Stench
Driftdead
Lethal Dose
Zombie in a Spacesuit
Hold My Teeth While I Teach You to Dance
Travesty
Counterpart
Dumbshow
Antibody Positive
Lear: The Shakespeare Company Plays Lear at Babylon

Shorter Fiction
Confessions of a Cockroach/Headstone
Back in the Day: Tales of NZ's Own Paradise Island
Foreigners

Poetry
The Raising Light Trilogy
Ladder With No Rungs, Illustrated by Leila Lees
Two Lines and a Garden, Illustrated by Leila Lees
To Beatrice: Where We Crossed the Line
Vertical Harp: The Selected Poems of Li He
Treasure Hunt
Standing Wave
From a Woman in Mt Eden Prison & Drawing Lessons
The Palanquin Ropes
Sketches
Selected Poems

Non-Fiction
Angel of Compassion

Children's Books

Flippity Fluppity Flop, Illustrated by Daniela Gast

A House With No Windows, Illustrated by Ingrid Berzins

Kenni and the Roof Slide, Illustrated by Jennifer Rackham

Taniwha. Illustrated by Jennifer Rackham